Praise for *Point of No Return*:

'An unnerving conspiracy that is another indictment of the war in Iraq and the imcompetence and corruption of the so-called "nation building" going on there. Exhilarating stuff' *Guardian*

'Lovers of action novels will find in Delillo a hero well-suited to gunplay, tense chases, doomed bravery and anguish' *Morning Star*

'Edge-of-the-seat reading and not to be missed' *West Australian*

Praise for *Never Fear*:

'Tight, tricky and wickedly complicated, with sharp, swiftly drawn characters' *Kirkus Reviews*

'Edgy and enthralling' *Belfast Telegraph*

'Fear is the one thing that definitely runs through this crime thriller like an electric current never releasing its grip' *Northern Echo*

'A thrilling introduction to a new cop heroine' *Birmingham Post*

'A snappy and assured thriller' *Sydney Morning Herald*

Praise for *Run the Risk*:

'Shows Scott Frost's blend of action and psychological intrigue is here to stay' *Daily Mirror*

'Cracking outing for Frost's LA cop heroine Lt. Alex Delillo' *Peterborough Evening News*

'Fast paced, plenty of action and a great plot. Excellent read' *Nottingham Evening Post*

Scott Frost is a screenwriter whose credits include *Twin Peaks* and *The X-Files*. He lives in Montana.

By Scott Frost and available from Headline

Run the Risk
Never Fear
Point of No Return
Don't Look Back
Wait For Dark

wait for dark

scott frost

headline

First published in 2010 by
HEADLINE PUBLISHING GROUP

First published in paperback in 2010 by
HEADLINE PUBLISHING GROUP

1

Cataloguing in Publication Data is available from the British Library

ISBN 978 0 7553 4652 3 (B-format)
ISBN 978 0 7553 7792 3 (A-format)

Typeset in Plantin by Avon DataSet Ltd,
Bidford-on-Avon, Warwickshire

Printed in the UK by CPI Mackays, Chatham, ME5 8TD

Headline's policy is to use papers that are natural, renewable and recyclable products and made from wood grown in sustainable forests. The logging and manufacturing processes are expected to conform to the environmental regulations of the country of origin.

HEADLINE PUBLISHING GROUP
An Hachette UK Company
338 Euston Road
London NW1 3BH

www.headline.co.uk
www.hachette.co.uk

For Valerie, whose fierce heart is always there

one

'We found a small mass in your right breast,' said the doctor. 'Now I understand that this may sound bad but, at this stage I don't want you to overly worry about it. We need to run some more tests before we come to any conclusions,' the doctor added.

For some reason, at that moment I noticed that the doctor giving me the bad news had very thick hair in his ears. I'm not sure why I noticed it then, but being told not to worry by a man with thick dark hair in his ears didn't sit quite right with me. Maybe it's the cop in me, but it's like listening to a suspect profess his innocence while sweat streams down his forehead and blood glistens on his shoes. Or maybe it's that I'm on the verge of panic. Since I had turned forty six years ago, I had gotten a yearly mammogram, and for six years there was never anything to be found. I had no history of it in my family. I never found anything when I self-examined. Why did number seven turn up so different?

'You mean I shouldn't be worried as in the scenario where the man pointing the gun at me probably forgot to load it?' I asked. 'Or I shouldn't be worried because the suspect just put the gun to his own head and pulled the trigger?'

He smiled, which wasn't exactly the response I was hoping for.

'I forgot you're a policeman.'

'Woman, policewoman,' I said, feeling a strong sense of gender pride.

He smiled again and I was fairly certain I saw the hair in his ears grow.

'Why didn't I find it when I self-examined?' I asked.

'It's small, easy to miss. I'll show you,' he said and stepped over, taking hold of my hand and placing my fingers on my breast.

'Can you feel that?' he asked, slowly moving my fingers over the area.

It's one thing to look at a mammogram and see something that is little more than a small shadow. But it wasn't a shadow now; I felt the mass, touched it. It was there, inside me, a tiny bomb waiting to go off.

I tried to say yes but for a moment words eluded me.

'From its appearance, in all likelihood it's a small cyst that poses no danger, though I would like to do a biopsy just to be certain.'

I nodded. 'So it's the first scenario.'

'It's a very simple procedure that we can do on an outpatient basis.'

'When you say mass, that sounds a lot like a lump.'

He smiled again and I tried very hard not to look at his ears.

'I don't think it would be productive for you to overthink this,' he said.

'Is there some part of being a detective that you don't understand?' I replied.

'Trust me,' he said, sounding like a triple homicide suspect who had just left a trail of bloody footprints back to his victims' bodies.

'Trust really isn't a part of my job description,' I said. 'When would you want to do it?'

'We'll schedule you for next week, there's no rush.'

I had made this appointment six weeks in advance and only got in that early because of a cancellation. One week sounded tantamount to being rushed into surgery to repair a severed artery.

It was three o'clock when I walked out to my car. The thermometer read a hundred and thirteen degrees in Pasadena. It's the kind of temperature that makes scientists certain that every piece of ice on the planet is going to melt into a puddle. And it's the kind of heat that makes cops sure it's only a matter of time before people begin killing each other.

I slipped the key into the ignition but then reached over with my left hand and felt my breast. How one part of the body can be such a source of terror throughout someone's lifetime I have never understood. When I was a teen I worried they would not grow as desired. And as you get older, well, that goes without saying. I have always thought of them as relatives that had come for Thanksgiving dinner. No matter how well they behave, you're always waiting for that one thing to go wrong. And just when you finally think you're safe and have gotten through another holiday, out of the blue something flies out of their mouth and all hell breaks loose.

And now it had happened. The thing you always thought happened to someone else had happened to me. As a cop I should have known there was no such thing as that mythical other person who always took the fall.

Listening to the words people choose is half of what I do. The difference between an arrest and a suspect walking free is often little more than the way a sentence is structured. Walking out of the doctor's office I had replayed his words at least a dozen times in my head. The doctor hadn't said the word cancer, but it was there, underlying every word he spoke, and by not saying it, its presence seemed all the stronger.

So here I was, going on forty-seven, professionally in my prime, sleeping with my almost ten years younger partner, and scared to death by a shadow in a picture. The perfect postmodern woman.

As I drove across town I decided that there would be no point in telling anyone what I had just found out except, perhaps, my daughter Lacy. If, as the doctor was saying, it was nothing, or at least nothing that a little outpatient surgery couldn't correct, there would be no point in spreading that kind of news. And if he were wrong, there would be plenty of time for panic later.

The outside heat meant call levels into dispatch were already at a rate that stretched the limits of the department's ability to cope when I walked into headquarters.

As the temperature rose, minor traffic disputes were escalating into games of high-speed chicken as otherwise normal tax-paying residents tried to drive their fellow commuters into trees so that they could get home to their air conditioning. In places, the blacktop on road surfaces was beginning to melt. The members of a city council nearly came to blows and the meeting was adjourned when it couldn't reach consensus on a motion to add the word 'if' to a resolution supporting Tibetan independence. A young married couple in their non air-conditioned apartment arguing over the placement of an Einstein refrigerator magnet began testing the limits of energy and mass by throwing knives at each other.

When I arrived back at headquarters I quickly scanned the list of calls that were now piling up from across the city, then closed my office door and called my daughter across town at UCLA.

Lacy was silent for a moment after I told her.

'There's no history in our family,' she finally said. 'Is the doctor certain?'

'I felt it,' I said.

'It's probably a cyst,' she said.

'That's what the doctor said,' I answered.

'Have you been feeling OK?'

'Until today, yes.'

'Then you have nothing to worry about,' she said.

If I could be as fearless as my daughter, I would be a happy woman. Barely in her twenties, she's survived a divorce, the death of her father and being kidnapped by a homicidal lunatic, and still nothing seems to faze her.

'Have you told anyone else?' she asked.

'No,' I answered.

'You think you might?'

'I don't see the point, not yet,' I said.

'What about Harrison?' she asked.

'Why would I do that?' I said.

'He's your partner and you're sleeping with him.'

I had been under the impression that my relationship with my younger partner was a closely held secret. The notion that I would be looked on as the cougar of Pasadena PD was not one I relished.

'I thought that was a secret,' I said.

'Fucking is never a secret for long,' she said. 'Nothing wrong with getting support from someone, it's natural,' she said.

'It's not that kind of a relationship,' I said, not entirely sure what I meant by it except I had never been able to shake the lingering fear that Dylan was going to find himself attracted to a younger woman. Adding breast cancer into it certainly wasn't going to make me any more alluring to him, or maybe that's me prejudging in a very unfair way.

'Well, what kind of a relationship is it?' Lacy asked.

'For whom, him or me?' I said.

'You're afraid to commit to it, you're always afraid of that. You think it will help you avoid pain.'

There was no bullshitting my daughter; her ability to know me better than I understood myself was always a little disconcerting.

'Divorce will do that,' I said.

'You might give yourself a little credit, him too,' Lacy said.

'Nothing is that simple.'

'Of course it is.'

'Is there any other part of my fragile psyche you want to dissect?' I said.

'You might try to remember that a woman packing a gun is pretty hot.'

'I'll try to think of that next time I draw my weapon.'

Lacy was silent for a moment.

'Do you want me to come and stay at home?'

'We're not there yet,' I said.

My office door opened and Detective Dylan Harrison leaned in against the frame.

'Is this a good time?' he said softly.

'You have no idea,' I said to him.

'About what?' Lacy asked.

'I have to go, Dylan . . . Detective Harrison just walked in,' I said. 'I'll let you know about the other thing.'

'Tell him, take a chance, you might be surprised,' she said.

'I've had all the surprises I can handle at the moment,' I said.

I glanced over to Dylan. He had abandoned his tie and jacket. His blond hair was ruffled and his shirt clung to the broad lines of his shoulders in the heat. Just below his green eyes a small crescent-shaped scar marked his cheek from the explosion as we rescued my daughter from the kidnapper.

'It'll be all right,' Lacy said. 'And try to remember that you're hot. Love you.'

She hung up and I held on to the phone as if it were a rope I was clinging to over the edge of a cliff.

'Lacy?' Harrison asked.

I hung up and nodded.

'Everything all right?' he said.

I took a breath and looked at him, trying to decide whether to follow my daughter's advice.

'Yes,' I said, ignoring it. 'Do you have something?'

'You know when it was last this hot?' he said.

'The late Jurassic period?'

'July seventeenth, nineteen seventeen,' he said.

'The world was trying to destroy itself. World War One,' I said.

Dylan nodded. 'Preview of coming attractions?'

How a single day could so completely spin off the rails from where it began I was having trouble imagining.

'What possible reason is there to think that the social fabric of the world, other than my own, is on the edge of a precipice?' I said.

We looked at each other for a moment in silence and then Chief Chavez stepped in. A big bear of a man, his once jet-black hair was now streaked with grey. The dark skin on his face was creased with age and the burdens that came with the responsibility of leadership. He had recovered from the physical injuries suffered when he was taken hostage by a maniac at the Rose Bowl, though one look into his big, kind, sad, grandfatherly eyes and I knew that a piece of him would never be the same. His eyes didn't have the sparkle that I had associated with him ever since I had known him, didn't have the humour that Lacy, his goddaughter, loved about him. I had killed the man who had held him. And even though I was untroubled by my actions, my desire to save him my only thought, I knew the Chief had shouldered the burden that I had taken a life more heavily than I had.

'All the utility agencies have issued stage-three alerts for the entire southern third of the state,' he said. 'Rolling blackouts could begin anytime. There's even talk of the entire power grid collapsing for an extended period. LAPD just put their department, all jurisdictional divisions, on tactical alert in anticipation of looting once it's dark. Every other department from San Diego north is doing the same thing.'

'Including us,' I asked.

The Chief nodded. 'I just gave the orders.'

I glanced at Harrison then walked over to the window. Outside, a bee was bouncing off the glass again and again as if it was trying to escape from the heat. I reached out and touched the window. It felt like the surface of a stove burner.

'You think the bee knows something we don't?' I said and then looked back at the Chief. 'You have any other good news?'

'You're the last two in the squad available, everyone else is out helping the black and whites which are an hour behind in response time.'

'You want us out on the street?' I asked.

Chavez shook his head. 'No, I want you here for when the first call comes in.'

'You mean the first homicide call.'

The Chief nodded. 'Dispatch is overloaded, they're going to begin routing calls up here, so you'll also have to start answering phones. Only the most serious calls will receive immediate response, the rest will be logged and responded to when units become available.'

'That could be hours, if at all,' I said.

The Chief nodded.

'How do we define the most serious?' Harrison said.

'You'll know,' he said.

'And what do we tell the rest?' I asked.

Chavez took a breath and shrugged. 'Anything but the truth. We have enough problems out there.'

Chief Chavez turned and walked out. The bee began tapping against the glass faster. I imagined at any moment it was going to burst into flames. As if Chavez's words had unleashed something, my phone began to ring and then an instant later stopped as the lights started to flicker and we heard the distinct sound of every computer in the squad room click off as we lost power. I looked back out the window and the bee was gone.

'Perhaps it does know something we don't,' I said.

The silence in the building was unsettling.

'I wouldn't make any plans on going home for a while,' I said.

'The emergency generators should start in a minute or so.'

Another sound became audible from outside. It seemed far away at first, like a distant scream, then it began to grow in intensity as if it was moving toward us.

'Do you hear that?'

Harrison nodded.

'What is it?' I said.

Harrison stepped over to the window and listened.

'Car horns.'

'The beginning of chaos,' I said.

The lights began to flicker and the hum of electricity returned as the emergency power kicked in and the phones started ringing. We lingered for a moment listening to the sound outside then Harrison walked back to his desk and I stepped to mine and picked up the first call.

For the next two hours the phones rang off the hook. Fifteen calls reporting stolen air conditioners. Countless calls reporting people stuck in elevators. Six domestic disputes, two bar fights, one call citing evidence in the Bible that the world was going to end in fire, thirty-five calls asking that I restore electricity. And one call demanding that the secret government files about Tesla and direct current be released or he would spill the beans himself.

As dusk approached, the number of calls began to fall. During a lull, I stepped over to the window and looked out across the city. The pale orange light of the setting sun appeared as if the color had been burned away. The office buildings of downtown had emptied hours ago. In the street below, there was no pedestrian traffic and only the occasional car passed. Even the sound of car horns had subsided.

Harrison stepped in.

'Anything?' I asked.

He shook his head and I looked back out on to the street.

'It's as if the city is holding its breath, waiting to see what will happen once darkness falls,' I said.

My phone began to ring, ending the brief drought in the action. I glanced at the San Gabriels in the distance, lit in the bright orange of the setting sun, before resignedly turning around.

'You want me to get it?' Harrison said.

I shook my head. 'Not unless you have information that it's my mother on the other end.'

I walked over and picked it up.

'Pasadena Police.'

I heard what sounded like a shudder run through the person as they tried to take a breath.

'Can I help you?'

'No,' said the voice, barely above a whisper.

'We're very busy,' I said and started to hang up.

'Is this the Homicide Department?'

I stopped and brought the phone back to my ear.

'Yes. Can I help you?' I said.

'I'm afraid you're the ones who will need help,' the voice said.

It was a male voice, slight traces of an accent, upper-crust blue blood from the east coast but possibly English. I motioned to Harrison and he picked up the other phone to listen.

'And why is that?' I asked.

'Because once night falls, I can't stop him.'

'Stop who from what?'

He said nothing.

'What is it you can't stop?' I asked.

'The darkness.'

'It's called a power outage.'

'What's your name, officer?' he asked.

'It's Lieutenant, what's yours?'

He took what sounded like a deep breath and when he spoke again, his voice sounded slightly higher in pitch.

'You're the female detective in charge, aren't you? You've been in the papers.'

'And you need to find some air conditioning,' I said. 'Why don't you come down here, we have lots of it.'

'Yes, you both look very comfortable.'

Harrison and I immediately turned and looked out at the hundreds of windows in the opposite building, searching for a flash of movement or something to give away a presence, but with the glare of the setting sun it was hopeless.

'I see you,' he whispered and the line went dead.

I looked again out of the window for a moment and then glanced back at Harrison.

'What do you make of that?' I asked.

'You mean discounting the possibility of heatstroke?'

'What did he say? Once night falls, I can't stop him.'

'Stop who?' Harrison said.

'And from doing what?' I stared at the window across the street. 'He knew this was Homicide.'

'And he knows who you are.'

I nodded. 'I'm the only Lieutenant, it's not that much of a guess. "The female" – curious choice of words.'

'Or carefully chosen.'

'What did you make of the voice?'

'I thought maybe east coast, but he sounds English, though the accent's worn off a bit. I'd say he was educated, spent a lot of time in America. Thirties maybe, but that's a guess. You think he was talking about a physical darkness or an interior one?'

I thought about it for a moment.

'Maybe both.'

'You think we need to be worried?'

'See if you can get a location on the call,' I said.

Outside, the sun dipped below the horizon and a line of shadow began moving across the city. Harrison called dispatch, spoke briefly and then hung up and stepped back to the window.

'The call came from the office tower across the street. It's a brokerage firm on the sixth floor. Beckwith, Myers and Dunne.' Harrison looked over to me. 'Maybe another of our financial wizards just cracked in the heat.'

I stared at the bank of windows as a siren became audible. It grew in intensity and then stopped as a fire truck pulled up outside the entrance to the building where the call had come from.

'Could be a coincidence,' Harrison said with little conviction.

A fireman walked around to the side of the truck, removed an axe and started toward the entrance of the building.

'You really think so?' I said.

Harrison shook his head and we started for the door.

Stepping outside into the heat I understood why the call level had dropped as the afternoon went on. Violence requires many things to be effective, energy being one of the primary ones, and it's difficult to work up a rage if your only care in life is finding a piece of shade and clinging to it.

The few people going from buildings to cars moved determinedly across the pavement as if fearing their shoes might burst into flame if they paused or hesitated. With each step we took I could feel the moisture being sucked from my body. From my lips, my skin, even my hair, which by the time we reached the fire truck felt like dried grass about to go up in a brush fire.

The fire engine company captain was standing by the truck when we reached it. I recognized him from several emergency response planning meetings the city holds each year in the event of fire, flood and God knows what.

'Captain Jensen,' I said.

'Lieutenant,' he said, looking at the both of us with a certain curiosity. 'They usually have Homicide responding to elevator calls too?'

I shook my head. 'We were tired of air conditioning, felt like getting some heat.'

He looked at me and smiled. 'I joined the wrong union.'

'What's happened, Captain?' I asked.

'We got a call thirty minutes ago that someone's trapped in an elevator,' he said. 'We've been going from one building to another doing these calls since the power was lost.'

'Has anyone exited the building since you arrived?' I asked.

'Not that I noticed.' He gazed at me for a moment. 'What's going on, Lieutenant?'

'Is the elevator stuck on the sixth floor?' I asked.

He looked at me in surprise. 'How the hell did you know that?'

I glanced over to Harrison.

'Beckwith, Myers and Dunne,' he said.

'Have your people reached the elevator yet?' I asked.

He nodded. 'They just got there. Is there a problem?'

'It's probably nothing, we're just following up on something.'

His radio crackled with a call from inside the building.

'Captain.'

'What do you got?' he responded.

There was a pause on the other end.

'Lopez?' the captain said into the radio.

'You better see this, Captain.'

The captain looked over to me, his eyes asking the question, what the hell is going on?

'Don't open that elevator,' I said.

two

Using a large flashlight, the captain led us up the darkened stairwell. With each floor we gained, the temperature seemed to rise another ten degrees. In places the air still contained the faint scent of aftershave and perfume from the last employees to find their way down to the exits hours before.

We stepped out on to the sixth floor and the captain motioned down the empty hallway. A beam from one of the other firemen's flashlights moved across the far wall like a tracer round.

'Around that corner in the center of the building,' the captain said.

We walked to the end and turned the corner. The glow of lights and the silhouettes of several firemen were visible halfway down the corridor. We reached them and stopped. They were standing ten feet from the elevator, their lights trained on the doors.

'What's up?' the captain asked.

One of the firemen glanced at the elevator. 'You tell me, Cap.'

I stepped past them and looked at the doors, Harrison following right behind me.

'What the hell,' the captain said. 'This what you were expecting, Lieutenant?'

I shook my head. 'I don't know what I was expecting,' I said and glanced at Harrison.

'That looks like blood,' the captain said.

'It is blood,' I said.

Sticking to the shiny surface of the doors was a blood-soaked hundred-dollar bill.

'What the hell's going on here, Lieutenant?' asked the captain.

Several long streaks of blood had slid down the surface of the doors from the still wet bill.

'Metaphor,' I said.

'Excuse me?' the captain said.

I looked over to Harrison.

'He's left a message,' Dylan said.

I nodded in agreement.

'What message?' asked Captain Jensen.

I turned to him. 'Blood money. Can you open the doors enough for me to look inside?'

'We open it, we'll have to break the interlocks,' one of the firemen said. 'We got no response from anyone inside.'

'That's what I'm afraid of,' I said. 'Break 'em.'

The captain nodded and two of his men went to work. One wedged a crowbar into the crack at the top of the doors and they opened several inches without any effort on the firemen's part.

'This door's already been forced.'

Harrison quietly slipped his revolver out of its holster and held the gun at his side.

'I think you better step back,' I said to the firemen.

They moved away from the door.

'Can I use your light, Captain?' I asked.

He handed me the flashlight and I moved over to the opening in the doors and carefully shone the light inside. I stared for a moment and then shone the light around the rest of the interior, hitting something on the back wall. There was no one inside and the rest of the elevator appeared untouched. I turned to Harrison and held out the light to him.

'What do you make of that?' I said.

Dylan slipped his pistol back in place and shined the torch inside.

'Are you seeing the same thing I am?' I asked.

Dylan nodded. 'He's drawn a set of eyes on the wall, like they're looking through the open door.'

'What was it he said on the phone? "I see you." ' I turned to the captain. 'Did this call come from the emergency phone inside the elevator or somewhere else?'

'It was probably a landline from in the building. Most of the cell circuits are jammed right now, you can't get through.'

I looked at Dylan. 'Beckwith, Myers and Dunne.'

He motioned toward the darkness down the hallway. 'It should be at that end.'

'Captain, I need to borrow another of your lights,' I said.

One of the other firemen handed Harrison a flashlight.

'You get yourself and your people outside,' I said. 'If we need anything, we'll come and get you.'

Jensen hesitated. 'And if you don't come and get us?'

'Call a cop,' I said.

They picked up their equipment and headed back toward the stairs. I watched them disappear around the corner and then the glow of their lights vanished and I heard the sound of the stairwell door close.

I turned and looked toward the other end of the hallway and the offices of Beckwith, Myers and Dunne. My hand slipped down to my Glock and I raised the flashlight into the darkness.

'You know, so far the only thing that he could be charged with is vandalism and defacing currency. Maybe he's had his fun and it's over.'

I stared at the shadows on the edge of the flashlight's beam.

'Were you ever afraid of the dark as a kid?' I said to Dylan.

He shook his head. 'No. It was the monsters hiding in the dark that frightened me,' he said with a smile.

'I'll watch the doors on the left,' I said. 'You watch the right.'

We moved down the hallway, checking each door as we went. They all appeared to be locked, nothing out of the ordinary. Ten feet from the end of the hallway we stopped and pointed our lights on a set of double doors. Raised gold letters read Beckwith, Myers and Dunne.

'You don't think it's over, do you?' Harrison said.

'No, I don't.' I stepped forward, reached out and

touched the door on the right. It slowly swung open a few inches and stopped. 'He brought us over here. The eyes in the elevator could be as much about us seeing something as him watching us.'

I pushed the door all the way open and raised my light into the interior. A large sleek desk covered the length of the far wall; couches and club chairs filled the rest of the room. Doors led out on either side of the desk into the interior offices.

'Reception,' Harrison said.

I stepped up to the desk and moved the light across its surface. There was nothing out of place or that didn't seem to belong.

'Nothing here,' Harrison said.

I looked over to one of the doors leading to the offices. 'If he's left more messages, it wouldn't be here.' I glanced back and forth at the two doors. 'Which side would be facing our building?'

Harrison thought for a moment and then nodded to the door on the right. We moved over and opened it. It was a large open room with row after row of workstation cubicles. Glassed-in offices lined the exterior walls along the windows. The light of dusk lit the room with a soft warm glow. I turned off the flashlight and set it on a desk.

'This could take a while,' Dylan said.

'I don't think we have much time.'

'What do you mean?'

'What he said. "Once night falls, I can't stop him." '

I looked out the windows into the fading light.

'How long before it gets dark?' I asked.

'Forty-five minutes, an hour at most.'

'He's gone to a lot of trouble to get us in here, he wouldn't want to make it too difficult. Short of hanging a great big sign, where would you leave something for us to find?'

Harrison looked over to the glass-walled offices against the windows.

'The office he was watching us from,' Harrison said.

'You start at that end, I'll start at this one.'

We moved to the offices and began to search them one by one. They were all identical in size and furnishing, and the more the individual tried to make the office their own, the more it seemed to be exactly like all the others. Computer terminals, spreadsheets, performance reports, a picture of a child, a vacation, dogs, gold plaques with sales awards, good luck charms, softball trophies, baseballs signed by Dodgers past and present.

As I stepped in to look over the next office, the faint sound of a phone ringing became audible from somewhere else in the building. I quickly stepped back out of the office and Harrison did the same. We started walking toward each other, looking for the source. Four offices down I stopped and opened the door. In the fading light, the blinking of the phone line stood out.

Harrison rushed over as I looked into the interior of the room. I started to step in and Dylan reached out and touched my arm.

'He could have rigged something,' he said. 'Let me take a look.'

With the trained eyes of a bomb technician, Harrison knelt down and looked across the floor.

'The floor looks clear,' he said and stood up.

'He didn't bring us here to blow us up,' I said as the phone rang again and again.

'I want to check the phone,' Harrison said.

I looked at the blinking light and then out the window at the quickly fading light.

'We don't have time,' I said and rushed over to the desk, reaching for the handset.

'Alex, let me be sure about it,' Dylan said.

The phone was an inch from my hand.

'When was the last time you were sure about anything?' I said and looked at Harrison for a moment, then closed my hand around the phone, hesitated as it rang again, took a breath and picked it up.

'Yes,' I said.

There was breathing on the other end. Dylan stepped over to another phone, wrote down the number on the display and then picked up the table extension to listen.

'You brought us here,' I said into the silence. 'Maybe you should explain yourself.'

'You please me, Lieutenant,' said the same voice I had heard earlier. 'An average cop would have stayed in the air conditioning, taken more annoying calls from overheated residents and poured a nice cold Fresca.'

'Blood money, very clever,' I said.

'I didn't want it to be too complicated for you in case, like most police officers, you lacked creativity.'

'So what happened? Did Beckwith, Myers and Dunne

lose money in your pension plan or are you saying they're guilty of murder and have to pay for it?'

'It's all there for you to see, Lieutenant. All you have to do is look.'

I looked around the room for some hint of what he meant. On the wall to my right he had drawn another set of eyes.

'What is it you want me to see?' I said.

'You better hurry, Lieutenant, it's almost dark.'

I stared at the eyes for a moment then turned and looked in the direction they were gazing. Nothing stood out, he had drawn nothing, altered nothing.

'Tell me what you want me—'

I fell silent as my eyes landed on a photograph hanging on the opposite wall. It was a picture of a couple who appeared to be in their early thirties, their arms around each other, standing on a white sand beach in front of a sailboat floating in emerald water. The woman had long blonde hair and the man short, neatly cut dark hair. They looked in shape, happy, and successful – a poster for the American dream. Around it were half a dozen smaller snapshots of the same couple in various places.

'What have you done?' I said.

He said nothing.

'What have—'

The line went dead. I set the phone down, walked over to the picture and removed it from the wall.

'Check the speed dial on the phone, see if it's programmed for home,' I said to Dylan. 'I'll see if I can find an address.'

I started going through the desk, trying to find anything that would point to where this couple lived.

'It's here, a six two six area code,' said Harrison.

He hit the speed dial and handed me the phone, and took over going through the desk. On the fourth ring a machine picked up. 'You've reached the O'Briens, neither Jim nor Cathy are available, leave a message at the annoying beep.'

'There's nothing here,' said Harrison.

In a bookshelf behind the desk I saw a stack of phone books.

'There,' I said. 'Jim and Cathy O'Brien.'

Outside, the light was quickly fading, there were no shadows from the setting sun any longer, just a dull grey light. Harrison flipped through one book and then started on another until he found what we were looking for.

'James and Cathy,' he said.

'That's it.'

'It's a Pasadena address, 1213 Sequoia.'

We started for the doors.

'See if there are any squads in the vicinity.'

We rushed out into the dark corridor toward the stairs. As we passed the elevator, I stopped and looked back at the bloody hundred-dollar bill stuck to the door.

'I can't get through, the circuits are all jammed,' said Harrison, slipping his phone back in his pocket.

I stepped over to the bill and held the light up close to it.

'What is it?' Dylan asked.

'It's all there for you to see, all you have to do is look,' I said. 'Do you have your knife with you?'

Harrison removed a small knife from his pocket and handed it to me.

'Am I missing something?' he asked.

I shined the light on to the eyes inside the elevator.

'Those eyes are looking at something, just like the ones in the office.'

Harrison looked at the drawing and then followed its sightline.

'It's looking at the back of the bill,' he said.

'Exactly.'

I opened the blade, slipped it in behind the bill and began to peel it away. An image had been drawn on the back. It was a black circle surrounded by streaks or a halo of light.

'It looks like another eye,' I said, holding the light up.

Harrison studied it for a moment and then shook his head. 'That's not an eye in the sense you're thinking of.'

'What do you mean?' I asked.

'I think that's a drawing of a solar eclipse.'

'An eclipse?'

Dylan nodded. 'A number of ancient cultures referred to the moment of totality as the "Eye of God". It was considered a harbinger of great events, both good and evil.'

I looked at it for a moment. 'A twenty-first-century version of an eclipse.'

Harrison nodded. 'A blackout.'

I stuck the bill back on to the elevator door for crime scene technicians to retrieve, and then we started for the stairs.

three

Intersections were still jammed with cars trying to work out whose turn it was to drive through, but the rest of the streets were nearly empty. Stores were closed; every bus we saw was packed to capacity. No one wanted to be on the streets once darkness fell.

Nearly a half hour had passed by the time we made it across town and reached 1213 Sequoia. The house was in the hills to the west of the arroyo. It was one of those homes built on stilts that hung over the edge of a steep ravine. From the street the view stretched across what must have been the entire basin. Here and there tiny specks of light from home generators shimmered in the darkness, or a ribbon of headlights cut a narrow path in the darkness, but otherwise it was as if the entire city had simply vanished into a black hole.

With darkness, the temperature had dropped, but the air still felt as if a struck match would ignite it. I took a few steps, then stopped and looked up toward the sky.

'Stars,' I said.

There were thousands of them. It was as if the clock had

been turned back a hundred or more years. In a lifetime in LA I had only witnessed a scene like this once before when the Northridge earthquake struck in the middle of a January night, crippling the power grid. I remember hearing that kids in the inner city rushing out of their shaking buildings were confronted with a scene above them in the night sky that was as unreal to them as the shaking ground.

I glanced around. We were on top of a thin ridge. Across the street there were no houses for half a block. The home to the left of 1213 had a 'For Sale' sign in the tiny front yard. The lot to the right was empty of any dwelling.

I walked over to the edge of the ravine and shined my light down toward the back of 1213. From what I could see the house hung thirty or more feet above the side of the hill. Harrison stared at the house, his eyes moving across all the visible windows.

'Not even a candle flicker inside,' he said. 'There's either no one here, or they don't need light any more.'

We walked up toward the front. Harrison checked the garage, and I walked over to the front landing and stopped. There were no handbills, no newspapers drying in the heat.

'The garage is locked, I can't tell if there's a car inside,' Harrison said.

I stepped up and knocked on the door. There was no response. I tried again with the same result.

'What do you want to do?' Harrison asked.

I pointed the light on the mail slot next to the door. There seemed to be something under the lid.

'Could just be mail,' Harrison said.

I reached over and lifted the lid to the mail slot. A dollar bill fell out and landed at our feet, backside up. The light hit the note.

'You think so?' I said.

Harrison shook his head. 'If it's a message like the others, he lost me.'

I stared at it for a moment.

'It's not right, he's altered something,' I said.

'I don't see it.'

I reached down and carefully lifted it by a corner and held it up to the light. There was a tiny triangular hole in it.

'Son of a bitch,' Dylan said.

'The all-seeing eye.'

'He cut it out.'

'I think he just invited us inside.' I looked at the Latin above the hole in the bill. 'Annuit Coeptis.'

'He favors our undertakings.'

'You mean God favors,' I said.

Dylan nodded. 'That's the general idea.'

'More good news.'

I slipped the bill back into the mail slot then reached out and took hold of the door handle. It turned and I pushed the door open as Dylan removed his weapon and held it at his side. We took position on either side of the open door.

'Police,' I yelled into the dark interior. 'Mr O'Brien, Cathy, this is the police.'

Not a sound came from the dark interior. I slipped my

Glock out, raised the light and stepped around the door into the house, with Harrison following right behind me. It was a large open space. Parquet floors spread out to the far wall of windows. To our right a stairway descended into darkness.

'Let's clear this floor before we do the bedrooms,' I said and began moving into the living room. The furniture was contemporary and expensive, the walls covered with old movie posters from the golden age of Hollywood.

Harrison stepped into a bathroom off of the entry and then out.

'Nothing,' he said.

I moved through the living room and into the dining and kitchen area to the left. Two plates and cutlery sat on the dining table. In the middle of each plate some uneaten fried eggs had been left to dry in the heat, a thin film covering the dull yellow yolk.

'Looks like they were interrupted during breakfast,' Harrison said.

I turned to the kitchen, moving the light across the countertops until the beam found the refrigerator. It was a large subzero, stainless steel. Half a dozen snapshots covered the right door. Most of the pictures were like the ones we found in the office, the happy couple on vacation at the beach or the ski slopes.

'No kids,' I said.

I reached to open the door and then abruptly stopped. My heart began to beat faster.

'Look at the eyes,' I said.

Harrison stepped over and looked at the pictures.

'They're gone,' he said. 'He poked them all out.'

We stared for a moment, silenced by the ability of a simple gesture to create such a visceral sense of violence.

'He wants us to see something again,' I said.

We both stared at the refrigerator doors, thinking the same thing but neither particularly wanting to act on it.

'I should have become a forest ranger,' Harrison said.

'Too late.'

I took hold of the refrigerator by the edge, pulled it open and shined the light inside. There was nothing out of place. It was the most orderly refrigerator I had ever seen. Meals had been labeled for the next five days in advance. I closed it and then opened the freezer.

We both stared at what it revealed.

'Money,' Harrison said.

There were several stacks of it, all neatly bundled inside freezer bags. A handwritten note was placed in front of it.

Harrison read the words silently to himself. 'F. Scott Fitzgerald, with a few of the words changed,' he said.

I read them aloud. '*The rich are different from us, they never get caught.*'

Dylan read it again to himself and then turned to me.

'There must be thousands of dollars here,' he said. 'I'm guessing that's not part of his pension plan.'

I nodded. 'No, it's probably part of everyone else's.'

I reached out and took one of the pictures from the refrigerator. 'We need to find out everything we can about O'Brien, his clients, friends, partners . . . enemies.'

'We don't have a body yet,' Harrison said.

I looked at the stacks of money again. 'The man we're after isn't a thief.'

'Which makes him what?' Harrison said.

I looked back into the living room.

'I think we're about to find that out. The bedrooms would be downstairs,' I said.

I closed the freezer door and moved toward the front of the house. We reached the top of the stairs and started down. At the bottom, the hallway turned to the left. There were three doors on the right and one at the end. I ran the light across them.

'The doors are all closed. I don't imagine that's an accident,' Harrison said.

'He's set a stage for us.'

'Why?'

'To scare the crap out of us,' I said and looked at Dylan.

'It's working,' he said.

'Fuck him,' I said softly.

I walked up to the first door and stopped, then took hold of the handle, pushed it open and raised the light and my weapon. It appeared to be a guest bedroom. I stepped inside and swung the light across the room.

'Do you see anything?' Harrison asked.

I stepped back out and shook my head. 'Nothing. On to door number two.'

I moved to the next door and opened it. It was a home office with two separate workstations and all the usual things that go along with a plugged-in life.

'An office,' I said to Harrison, moving my light across the two desks, looking for the smallest hint of something out of place. In front of one of the computers was a yellow legal pad. Halfway down the pad the writing on it stopped in mid-sentence. Other than that there was nothing obviously out of place.

'Nothing here. Open the next door,' I said.

I lingered for another moment, trying to find whatever it was our man wanted us to see, but it eluded me. I stepped back out into the hallway as Harrison pushed open the next door. He stood in the doorway for a moment then turned to me and shook his head.

'Bathroom. I don't see anything here either.'

'He's playing with us, just like the phone call.' I looked at the last door. 'Whatever he brought us here to find is behind that door.'

'It should be the master bedroom,' Harrison said.

I started toward the door but abruptly stopped and focused the light on the center of the door at eye level.

'He's put holes in it.'

'Eye holes,' Harrison said.

'To look out, or in?' I said.

I stared at them, not able to shake the feeling that behind the two dark holes in the wood was a presence, watching our every move.

'I think they're there for us,' I said.

I moved cautiously up to the door, reached out and tested the handle and then stepped back.

'It's locked. He wants us to do it his way.'

'I'm not sure that's a good idea,' Harrison said.

I stared at the holes for a moment and then turned off my light.

'What are you doing?' Harrison asked.

'There's something there,' I said. 'Turn your light out.'

Harrison hesitated. 'Voluntarily plunging ourselves into darkness doesn't sound like a good idea.'

'Go on,' I said.

He switched his light out and then we both saw it.

'I'll be damned,' Harrison said.

The two holes faintly glowed in the darkness like the eyes of an animal reflecting in the night.

'There's a light inside,' he added.

I flipped my light back on and shined it directly on the two holes. I could see nothing of what was waiting on the other side.

'A peep show,' Harrison said.

'I'll take a look.'

'It's still empirically a bad idea.'

'Looking in places you shouldn't always is,' I said. 'And it's the one rule we can't stop ourselves from breaking.'

I stepped cautiously forward and then leaned in toward the doors to place my eyes against the holes. The closer I came to them, the faster my heart began to beat. As my eyelashes touched the edges of the holes, I saw into the room and immediately jerked my head back as if a jolt of electricity had traveled through me. My breath caught for a moment, my hand tightened around the handle of the Glock.

'Alex?' Harrison said.

I took a couple of deep breaths to slow my breathing.

'It's not a peep show, it's a house of horrors.' I looked over to Dylan. 'Eyes,' I said. 'Wide open, staring at me.'

'Are they real?' Harrison asked.

'I don't know. If they are, they're not like any I have seen before.'

Harrison stepped over to the door, put his face up to the holes, looked in and then stepped back and shook his head.

I pounded on the door and called out. 'Mr O'Brien, this is the police, open the door.'

Not a sound came from the other side. I turned to Dylan.

'Can you break this in?'

He nodded and moved over.

'Carefully,' I said. 'He must be right on the other side.'

Harrison placed his hand against the wall and then executed a kick just below the door handle. The wood around the bolt cracked. He then leaned into the door until his weight completely snapped the frame and the door opened a few inches.

I stepped up and gently pushed the door; it moved without any resistance at all.

'Mr O'Brien?'

'Alex,' Harrison said, reaching out and grabbing my arm.

He shined the light down on to the floor under the door. The carpeting was covered with bloodstained money. I pushed the door open wide enough to step through then raised the light. There was money spread across the entire room; bloody handprints were visible on the walls.

Like any place that violence has touched, the room felt unnatural. It was no longer a bedroom; it had been transformed into something else, something not even a part of this world.

'Where did he go?' Harrison said softly.

I took another step in, and motioned to Harrison to pull the door back toward us to see what was behind it.

'Now,' I mouthed silently and as Harrison pulled the door back I raised the light and my Glock.

The door swung past me and I saw a blur of movement as the head rolled across the door and stopped, its open empty eyes staring at us.

'I think we found Mr O'Brien,' I said.

We stepped back, our lights illuminating the severed head suspended by a thin nylon line nailed into the top of the door. A small flashlight hung from the same cord, pointing down at the head. The white tip of a vertebra shone brightly against the dark flesh of the wound.

'Jesus,' Harrison said and then looked away.

I forced myself to continue to look and to understand what I was seeing before revulsion made it impossible to function properly.

'No cutting marks, no tears on the skin, this was done in one clean cut,' I said.

'I should have read my job description more carefully,' Harrison said.

'Try to focus,' I said and Dylan nodded.

I swung the light around the room and stopped on the bed. A bloodstained pillow lay at the top of the bed, a sheet covered the rest of the body, except for the arms lying above the sheets, the hands neatly clasped at the waist.

'That would be the rest of him,' I said.

I looked at the handprints on the wall and then back at the blood on the bed.

'The blood on the walls is drier than what's on the bed,' I said. 'What happened in this room had been going on for some time.'

'Where's his wife?' Dylan said.

We swept the room with our lights. To the left of the bed was a large walk-in closet, to the right the master bath.

'I'll check the bath, you take the closet,' I said.

I walked over to the bathroom, being sure not to step on any of the bloodstained bills spread across the floor. The door was half open. I pushed it the rest of the way. The large mirror above the countertop had been smashed. There were more bloody handprints on the glass.

The shower curtain had been pulled across the tub. It was streaked with blood. The steady drip, drip, drip of water from the showerhead came from behind the closed curtain.

I moved the light across the curtain. There seemed to be a shape behind it, but I couldn't tell. I reached out and took hold of the curtain and swiftly pulled it back. The water in the bottom was darkened with blood but there was no body.

'Dylan,' I said.

Harrison walked over to the door of the bathroom.

'Anything?' I asked.

'I think some clothing is gone, there're some empty drawers.'

'His or hers?'

'Hers, from the look of it.'

I raised my light on to the wall of the shower where a message had been written.

'Look at this,' I said.

Harrison read the words aloud. '*One for the money*.' He turned to me. 'You think we have a class warrior on our hands?'

'Does this look like war to you?' I asked.

He shook his head. 'No, this looks like something else altogether.'

I nodded in agreement. 'He enjoyed this.'

I looked back out toward the hallway. 'We're going to need to go through the other rooms very carefully.'

'You think there may be more messages we missed?' Harrison said.

I looked back at the writing on the wall, and then around the rest of the bathroom.

'Is there anything you see here that suggests he's finished?' I said.

Harrison shook his head. 'No, this looks more like a beginning.'

I walked over to the bed and looked down at the headless corpse.

'This isn't a beginning,' I said.

'What do you mean?'

'Look at that wound. One clean cut. That takes either surgical training or practise.'

'You think he may have done this before?'

'Let's talk to the FBI, see if anything here matches something in the serial killer data bases. Could be wound types, something about the victim, someone in the financial world, could be the use of words by the killer, or the way he contacted us.'

'And if it doesn't?'

'He has an English voice, we'll try Scotland Yard.'

I heard the creak of a door swing shut upstairs and the latch fall into place.

'Turn your light out,' I said softly.

We moved quickly back to the hallway, using the light hanging on the door to guide us and stopped at the foot of the stairs. There was no sound of movement above us, no light. I raised my weapon and moved cautiously up until my head cleared the first-floor level and I could see into the rest of the house, then I raised my weapon and turned on my light.

I looked at Harrison on the step below me and shook my head. He motioned toward the front door. It was closed.

'Could have been the wind,' he said.

I moved up to the door, pulled it open and stepped outside. Somewhere in the darkness I heard the sound of a car engine, but there were no headlights visible.

'Do you feel enough wind to close that door?' I said.

Harrison shook his head. 'I don't feel any wind at all.'

I looked up and down the street.

'I see you,' I whispered.

'You think he was here?' Harrison said.

I nodded. 'He watched us enter the house. He stood here as we moved through the house.'

'Why would he risk that?' Harrison said.

I looked over to our squad car and the hair on the back of my neck rose.

'That's why,' I whispered.

In the back seat of the squad was the dark shape of a figure. My hand tightened around the Glock and we moved toward the car with our weapons raised. The figure didn't move. I stepped off the curb and walked around the front of the squad and stopped a few feet from the passenger door, my weapon trained on the figure.

'Get out of the vehicle,' I said.

The figure didn't move. I motioned to Harrison and he stepped up next to the door and took hold of the handle.

'Get out of the—'

I stopped and my heart began to pound against my chest.

'Open it,' I said to Harrison, lowering my weapon.

I turned on my light as Harrison opened the door.

'Mrs O'Brien?' I said.

She wore only a bloodstained slip. Her hands were bound at the wrist with duct tape. Her vacant eyes stared straight ahead.

'Cathy O'Brien,' I said again.

Her eyes flashed to the left and right as if looking for something creeping up behind her.

'You're going to be all right,' I said. 'You're safe now.'

She began to tremble then slowly turned, her eyes looking blankly through me.

'I'm a policewoman.'

'She didn't hear you,' Harrison said.

I reached out and as my fingers touched her hand, she began to scream.

four

Within an hour the full apparatus of law enforcement had descended on the O'Brien household. Crime scene technicians were combing the house. The coroner investigators were carefully documenting everything about the body and the head before removing it for autopsy.

Chief Chavez took one walk though the house then retreated to the street. He was staring out across the blacked-out basin when I walked up to him. In the distance the orange glow of two fires was visible.

'There have been reports of looting at a music store and a grocery store in Hollywood,' he said. 'Half a dozen building fires have broken out across the city. Just south of downtown a squad car had a running gun battle with a stolen Range Rover that lasted for ten blocks.' He glanced down at his watch. It was just past nine o'clock. 'And it's still early.'

In the distance the sound of another fire engine hitting the streets became audible. Chavez took a breath and shook his head.

'Is this what the end looks like?' he said.

'The last I checked,' I said, 'the sun is still planning a comeback in the morning.'

He looked over to me. Even in the darkness I could see the weariness in his eyes. He had spent his adult life trying to stop crime and then he was repaid for his efforts by becoming a victim of it. The illusion that we were somehow keeping a lid on society by our work no longer held much water for him.

'This too shall pass,' I said.

He smiled. 'Quoting Solomon, are we?'

'My old Jewish aunt,' I said.

He turned and looked over to the house, then took out a pack of cigarettes from his jacket pocket and lit one up.

'Why didn't he kill her?' asked Chief Chavez. 'Why did he leave the wife alive?'

I shook my head. 'She's in shock, we may have a better idea when she's able to speak. Harrison's at the hospital in case she says anything. What does seem certain is that he isn't concerned with keeping his identity secret. In fact, it's probably just the opposite.'

'He wants to stake his claim of responsibility.'

'That would seem to follow,' I said.

'Is that good or bad?'

'Both. We might get lucky because he's not afraid of being caught. If he makes a mistake, we get an ID.'

'If,' Chavez said.

I nodded. 'The dark side is that he wants credit for his deeds. That makes him very dangerous. Unless I'm wrong, I'd say he's killed before.'

'You're certain there are going to be more?' he asked.

'It seems inevitable.'

'Because of the words he wrote.'

I ran through the details of what I had seen, trying to make sense of it.

'Because of everything. The phone calls, the messages, even the way he killed O'Brien. Something's going on here that doesn't feel right.'

'I'm not sure I follow,' Chavez said.

'Everything he's done suggests the work of a serial killer.'

'I agree,' Chavez said. 'So what's your point?'

'I'm not certain, but it's like watching a badly written play, it doesn't quite ring true.'

Chavez took a deep drag on the cigarette and then flipped the glowing ash into the street.

'That doesn't tell us much about what he's going to do next,' he said.

'If his victims are somehow linked, then maybe we'll find something in O'Brien's life that will mean something, or possibly in the wife's story when she's able to communicate.'

'And all the stuff about darkness and the all-seeing eye?' Chavez asked.

'His way of saying we're no match for him.'

'He's belittling us.'

I nodded. 'If this is what it appears to be, there's basically two different kinds of serial killers. One that kills out of rage, and the kind that kills out of contempt.'

'He thinks he's superior to us,' Chavez said.

'Yeah,' I said.

'And if this is something else?'

'Then he's probably even more dangerous.'

The Chief turned to me. 'He called you.'

'Yes.'

'Coincidence?'

'It would be unlikely.'

'Which means he knows who you are,' Chavez said.

'My face was on TV, that's all it means,' I said.

After the events at the Rose Bowl the year before where I killed a man attempting to assassinate the Pope, saving Chavez's and a few other thousand people's lives at the same time, I was for a very brief time a reluctant victim of the twenty-four/seven news cycle.

'Is that something we need to worry about?' Chavez asked.

I shook my head. 'I think we have enough to worry about without that.'

I wasn't sure whether Chavez believed that, or even if I believed it entirely, but either way the killer had chosen me and there was little I could do about it, short of handing in my badge and walking away.

'Was there anything in the other three rooms downstairs?' Chavez asked.

'No, they seem untouched but CSU is going through them now.'

'What do we know about the victim?'

'The blackout is slowing down everything. What I can say for sure is that he was thirty-two, married, a broker at Beckwith, Myers and Dunne, and he had thousands of dollars in crisp bills inside his freezer in the kitchen.

We'll have an accurate count on the money by morning.'

Chavez looked at me.

'O'Brien wasn't a random victim,' I said. 'He was chosen precisely because of that money. We find out where it came from, we might be on to something that could point to who did this, or who the next victim might be.'

Chavez looked at the houses down the street. 'What about the neighbors?'

'The nearest occupied house is several lots away. The home next door is vacant. Canvassing of the occupied houses has produced nothing; no one saw or heard anything that was out of the ordinary.'

'And what do we know about what happened inside?' Chavez asked.

'Marks on the bed and his wrists indicate he had been bound there for a period of time, several days at least. His death was much more recent, a matter of hours at most. Once we're able to talk with people at the brokerage firm we should be able to establish exactly how long he was out of the office and possibly held.'

'Do we know anything from the method of death itself?'

'Decapitation is the ultimate display of power and degradation, with a long and prominent place in history and myth. What we know from the wound itself is that given the amount of blood loss, he was alive and probably conscious as the blade was used to sever his head. Given the precision of the wound, the knife would have been a minimum of a foot long.'

A fuse appeared to have been lit behind the Chief's eyes and anger rose in his face. He tossed his cigarette into the gutter and stamped it out.

'Son of a bitch,' he said and turned to me. 'The wife saw all this?'

'Yes.'

He shook his head and the muscles in his jaw flexed as he clenched his teeth.

'It gets worse. There are two sets of marks on the bed where the cords were wrapped around.'

'She was tied down too,' Chavez said.

I nodded. 'From her state, my guess is that she was lying next to him when he was killed. The blood on her slip should match his. Same with the walls.'

'My God,' he said softly and then looked out at the blacked-out city. 'This too shall pass,' he said and then turned to me. 'You don't have a Jewish aunt.'

I forced a smile. 'Everyone has a Jewish aunt. They just don't know it.'

He looked again into the distance, his eyes focusing on the glow of the fires.

'Solomon passed his kingdom on to his son and it dissolved into chaos and went to pieces. So much for Old Testament wisdom. Catch this bastard, Alex.' Chavez started to walk away then stopped and looked back. 'When do you expect the next victim to appear?'

'Sooner rather than later,' I said. 'If he's planned all this out, as what took place here suggests, it could be happening now. The backdrop of the blackout clearly appeals to him although I think that it's safe to assume he couldn't have orchestrated that as well. It seems likely that he just took his opportunity.'

'People are afraid of the dark.'

I nodded.

Chavez looked down the darkened street. 'They may have reason to be tonight,' he said and walked toward his squad.

It was nearing ten o'clock by the time I managed to leave the crime scene. I drove toward downtown and the hospital where Cathy O'Brien rested in intensive care. The streets were mostly empty. A few cars full of gang bangers had been stopped and booked on charges of endangering public safety by ignoring calls to stay off the streets except in case of emergency, but so far the large-scale violence that had erupted in spots in Los Angeles had not happened in Pasadena. In residential neighborhoods people sat on their front steps and porches trying to escape the heat inside. In front of apartment buildings the sidewalks were filled with people sitting in lawn chairs around lanterns or small barbecues, chatting with neighbors they barely knew as if there was a collective sense of safety in numbers – like tribes gathered around camp fires awaiting the arrival of dawn.

Harrison was waiting at the entrance of the trauma unit when I arrived. Unlike the rest of the city, there was nothing quiet about the scene unfolding in front of me. Ambulances were parked two deep outside the entrance. Through the glass doors I could see patients on gurneys and sitting in wheelchairs, all lined up against the wall as they waited their turn.

'What's happening here?' I said to Harrison.

'Heat-related mostly. A few assaults, some car wrecks, but mostly just the heat.'

We stepped through the automatic doors and the sound of the sick and injured assaulted my senses. Though the air conditioning was running, the collective heat of so many bodies in a confined space had pushed the temperature to nearly that of outside.

'It's apparently like this in every hospital all over the city,' he said.

An old woman with the dark skin and features of a Mayan Indian, wearing a faded yellow dress, lay motionless on a gurney, a rosary intertwined in her fingers. It didn't take a doctor to know that she had already succumbed to the heat.

'Paramedics are so overwhelmed they're telling the public to transport themselves if they can,' Harrison said, looking at the old woman. 'People have been brought in who are already gone. They have no place to put them at the moment.'

'Where's O'Brien?' I asked.

Harrison motioned down a hallway to the left of the admissions desk. We worked our way through the crush of sick and injured and took the stairs to the second-floor intensive care unit.

The nursing station was a picture of calm compared to the emergency room. There were no moans of pain or cries for help. Just the occasional peep of monitors going off and pages over the PA system.

Intensive care was set up in the shape of a large octagon,

with the nursing station in the center surrounded by the rooms, which had large windows to enable observation of the patients. Harrison led me over to a room on the south side and we stepped up to the glass.

Cathy O'Brien lay motionless, an IV attached to her left arm, bandages on her wrists where the skin had been abraded by the cords tying her to the bed. Tubes fed oxygen into her nose. There were bruises on her neck that I hadn't noticed when we found her.

'They have her sedated. She would lie silently for a while then open her eyes and begin to scream. It went on like that for the better part of an hour before they got her quiet.'

I noticed large padded restraints just below her elbows, securing her arms to the bed.

'Are those necessary?' I said.

'Every time the paramedics in the ambulance tried to put an oxygen mask on her, she would fight back. It continued here. Even after sedation, when she was unconscious she'd begin struggling as if trying to get away from him in her dreams.'

'The bruises on the neck?' I said.

'Finger marks,' Harrison said. 'From the varying shades of hemorrhaging they appear to be multiple sets.'

'She was choked at different times on different occasions, hours if not days apart,' I said.

Dylan nodded. 'From the deepness of the bruising and the placement on the neck, the doctors guess she was probably brought to unconsciousness each time.'

I played the thought out.

'Which to her would have been no different than dying,' I said.

The muscle in Harrison's jaw tensed as he looked in through the glass.

'And then she would wake up and find she was still alive and go through it all again,' I added.

'Yeah.'

'Anything else?' I asked.

'There are what appear to be teeth marks on her lips.'

'Bites?'

'Could be. There are also several marks on her forehead right at the hairline, as if she was nicked or scraped by a fingernail as he held her down.'

I placed my hand up on the glass and stared through the window at the machines monitoring her respiration.

'Does that mean something to you?' Harrison asked.

'No wonder she was fighting the mask, she was afraid of suffocating. I don't think those are bite marks on her lips,' I said.

Dylan looked at me. 'You lost me.'

'They were made by teeth, but they're not bites.'

'Which makes them what?'

'She didn't just experience a simulated death,' I said.

Harrison shook his head. 'I still don't follow.'

'He would have been bending over her, one hand on her forehead tilting it back, his fingernails digging into her as he held her in place. The other hand was lifting her neck.'

I saw the flash of recognition in Harrison's eyes and he looked toward the still figure in the room.

'He went too far with one of the chokings and she stopped breathing,' Dylan said.

'He giveth and taketh away,' I said.

'Mouth to mouth.'

I nodded.

'He brought her back,' he said.

'In a manner of speaking.'

Harrison shook his head. 'The depth of her nightmare keeps getting worse.'

'Was she sexually assaulted?' I asked.

Dylan shook his head. 'No indication of it.'

'Has she said anything?'

'She screamed something a couple of times when she was struggling against the restraints.'

'What was it?'

Harrison slipped a notepad out of his pocket and looked at the words.

'The first time she said, *him not me*. The second time she screamed, *take him, take him*.'

'Nothing else?'

'No.'

One of her arms violently twitched and she shook her head and then her body stilled again.

'You understand what she was saying?' I asked Harrison.

He took a slow breath, his eyes fixed on her.

'I wish I didn't,' he said.

I nodded in agreement.

'She was screaming for him to take her husband, not her,' said Dylan.

We both fell into silence for a moment.

'When do the doctors think she'll be able to communicate?' I asked.

'Physically, twelve to twenty-four hours. When she'll be emotionally able, they had no estimate.'

My pager buzzed and I slipped it from the waistband of my slacks. It was from Detective Dave Traver, my old partner. All it said was, 'Call immediately.' I picked up my cell but the circuits were still overloaded. I walked over to the nursing station and showed them my badge.

'Do you have an outside line I can use?' I asked.

The nurse motioned to a phone at the end of the desk. Traver answered on the third ring.

'An envelope was left on your desk,' he said.

'Left?'

'Yeah. No one saw anyone, the squad room was empty when I walked in. I'm checking the surveillance cameras to see if they picked up anything. I think you better see it right away,' he said.

'Have you opened it?'

'No.'

'Then how do you—'

'I didn't, the Chief looked at it and said to call you. There's some writing on the outside of it.'

I looked over toward the windows of Cathy O'Brien's room.

'What does it say?' I asked.

'The woman policeman.'

I looked at Dylan. One of the monitors began beeping

and the nurse behind the desk got up and rushed into one of the rooms.

'What?' Harrison asked.

I looked back over to Cathy O'Brien's room.

'We had a visitor,' I said.

five

Traver and Chavez were standing at the door to my office as if reluctant to cross the threshold when Harrison and I walked up.

'Have you looked around the rest of the office or the squad room?' I asked.

Traver nodded and ran his hand over his flat-top haircut. Big Dave was a throwback. The kind of flat-foot detective wearing cheap suits you'd see in a 1950s movie. In every way he was a cliché except for the size of his considerable heart.

'Nothing seems wrong anywhere,' he said.

'He must have watched us walk out of the building and over to Beckwith, Myers and Dunne,' I said. 'Then came in and dropped it.'

'Did you check the surveillance tapes yet?' Harrison asked.

'They're doing it now,' Traver said.

I stepped past Traver and the Chief and walked up to my desk. The brown manila legal-size envelope lay on my desk front and center. 'The woman policeman' was written in what appeared to be red magic marker. The flap of the envelope was tacked shut in one spot. I opened a desk drawer where I kept a box of latex gloves, removed two and slipped them on.

'Can I use your knife?' I said to Dylan.

Harrison opened the knife and handed it to me. I slipped the blade under the flap and twisted it until the seal broke.

'I don't imagine there will be anything but have forensics checked this for prints and saliva?' I asked.

Traver nodded.

I opened the flap and then spread the envelope open and slid the contents on to the desk. We stared in silence for a moment. It was an eight by ten photograph. There was a figure in the picture, but the quality was grainy and it was difficult to make out clear details. I flipped it over and looked on the back. There was more writing.

'*They know who they are and must be punished,*' I said, reading the words.

'Punished? For what?' Chavez said.

'We figure that out we may be on to something,' I said.

I turned the picture over and we looked at the image again.

'Does this mean anything to anyone?' Chavez said.

'It looks like a picture taken of a television screen,' Traver said.

'Or a computer,' I said.

Harrison stared at it for a moment.

'He takes a picture, puts it on the computer and takes another picture of the screen that's out of focus,' he said.

I stared at the blurry face of the figure but there was too little detail for an ID.

'Why send you a picture of someone you can't possibly identify?' Chavez said.

'He's teasing us, he doesn't want us to know who it is, not yet. He's giving us only as much information as he wants us to have.'

'So what does he want us to know?' Chavez asked.

'Or not know,' I said.

'It could be his next victim,' Chavez said.

Harrison leaned in, looking at the image. 'Or he wants us to see something else.'

'Else?' Chavez said.

'The rest of the picture. Look, he's standing in front of a car,' Harrison said. 'Or he just stepped out of it.'

'That looks like the sign of a restaurant behind him,' Chavez said. 'El something Tacos, I can't make out the middle word, the last one looks like Asada.'

Traver looked closely and shook his head.

'You see something, Dave?' I asked.

He straightened. 'Maybe it's the car he wants us to notice.'

'What about the car?' I said.

'That's not just any car. Look at the sweep of the hood and the shape of the grille. That's an Aston Martin DB5, I'd bet on it.'

Harrison looked more closely. 'You're right.'

'I drive a Volvo. What does that mean?' I said.

All three of them looked at me as if I had just insulted the entire genetic make-up of the male species.

'It's a classic,' Harrison said.

'It's *the* frickin' classic,' said Traver.

'What is it?' I asked.

'James Bond's car,' Chavez said.

'*The* James Bond, Sean Connery's Bond,' Traver added.

'A car like this would be valuable?' I asked.

'If you have to ask the price, you can't afford it,' said Traver.

I looked at Harrison. 'The rich are different from us, they get away with it,' I said.

Harrison nodded. 'We get a name, maybe there's a connection to O'Brien.'

'Would there be many of these driving around the streets of LA?' I asked.

'No. That model was only made in sixty-four and -five. A little over a thousand of them were produced,' Traver said.

'One thousand and twenty-one, to be exact,' Harrison said.

I looked at them as if I had just stepped into another reality.

'You really are from Mars, aren't you?' I said.

'Second crater from the right,' Harrison said.

I picked up the photograph. 'We need a name.'

'I'll check with the Department of Motor Vehicles for a registration,' Traver said.

'Let me look at that again,' Chavez said.

I held the picture up for him to examine. He slipped his reading glasses on and stared into the image.

'I think I know this place,' he said.

'The restaurant?' I asked and he nodded.

'I don't remember the name, but I'm sure I've eaten there. The shape and color of the building are the same.'

'You're positive?' I asked.

He smiled. 'Would this face lie to you about a taco? Yeah, I'm sure. It's on Ventura in the valley near Laurel Canyon. It's one of those places that have pictures on the walls of celebrities who've eaten there. The tacos are all named after famous Latino stars. It's very popular. The building's bright red, you can't miss it.'

'He wants us to see this place,' I said to Harrison.

A uniformed officer stepped to the door.

'You got something?' Traver asked him.

The officer shook his head. 'When the power went out, the security system crashed and nobody noticed that it didn't come back on with the emergency generators.'

'So we got no pictures at all?' Chavez asked.

'No. They're trying to reboot it now.' He turned and walked out.

'How the hell would he know that?' Chavez asked.

'He wouldn't,' said Harrison.

'So he got lucky,' Chavez said.

I thought about it for a moment.

'Maybe not,' I said.

'What do you mean?' Chavez asked.

'Anyone walking through those doors would know the camera was there. So either he has intimate knowledge of our system, or . . .'

'Or he wanted his picture taken,' Harrison said.

I nodded.

'Why would he do that?' Chavez said.

'To let us know he's not afraid of us,' I said.

The lack of cars on the road and the empty dark streets seemed unnatural to LA. There was nothing peaceful or nostalgic about it. There was no turning the clock back to some earlier moment in time when Los Angeles briefly shone as a paradise. That line had been crossed so long ago that the kind of stillness surrounding us now became ominous. The crowds, the traffic, the sig alerts, the bad air, the noise had become the security blanket we wrapped ourselves in even as we complained about the endless irritations that accompany the simplest of tasks. Taking it away revealed the truth lying just under the surface that everyone knows is there but doesn't want to think about – that with something as simple as the flip of a circuit breaker, the whole house of cards that is life in LA could come tumbling down.

There was no escaping the illogical feeling that the blackout wasn't just the perfect storm of circumstances come together to plunge us into darkness, but as much a part of our killer's plan to terrorize as was the knife that severed his first victim's head, and that with every step we took, every mile we drove pursuing him, he was watching us.

The flashing lights of squad cars and the glow of red flares lit the darkness where the 134 freeway passed over the 5. A truck had taken the corner too fast and lost control. Its load of milk had spilled across the roadway, giving the upturned truck the appearance that it was floating on a white lake. As we slowly passed, our headlights reflected off a coyote's eyes where it stood on the perimeter of the emergency lights, sipping on milk.

We pulled off at Laurel Canyon and drove south to Ventura. An LAPD cruiser sat in the middle of the intersection, the two officers watching the few vehicles that passed, measuring its occupants for any potential threat and waving them past.

Half a mile east we saw what we were looking for and stopped.

'It could be the one in the picture,' Harrison said. 'The lines of the building look similar.'

The tacoria was across the street, a free-standing stucco building with a small parking lot next to it. Its bright red paintwork was unmistakable even in the darkness. I looked up and down the street for anything that gave the impression that it didn't belong. There were no empty cars parked within several blocks, nothing moved on Ventura.

'Do you see anything?' I asked.

Harrison shook his head. 'So why did he want us here?'

I stared at the building for a moment and then swung the squad around to the other side of the street and stopped in front of the restaurant.

'To see that,' I said, staring at the sign.

I opened the door and stepped out as Harrison did the same.

'That's why the building's red,' Harrison said. 'El Diablo Tacos.'

Below the lettering on the sign, a small red figure with a forked tail, holding a taco, had been painted. Dylan looked at it for a moment.

'You think he's saying he's the devil, or he's doing the devil's work?'

'He didn't get us here to see this because he likes carne asada,' I said.

We walked up to the front of the restaurant. Another devil was painted on the glass door.

'Images of an eclipse, the Eye of God, the coming of darkness, the beheading, the riddles,' I said.

Harrison nodded. 'It all works, even the money in the O'Briens' freezer. He takes victims that have given in to temptation.'

'Doesn't exactly narrow the field very much in Los Angeles,' I said.

I turned and looked up Ventura again.

'You think this was all he wanted us to see?' Harrison said.

I walked over to the door and shined my flashlight on the lock. It was untouched. I then directed my light into the interior. A hallway behind the cash register led back into darkness.

'Let's check out back,' I said.

As we walked around to the side of the building, the thump of an LAPD helicopter broke the silence. In the distance I could see its spotlight cutting a path of light toward the ground as it began to circle in a tight pattern, searching for something trying to hide from its spot. I reached the back, stepped around the corner and raised my light. There was a large trash dumpster against the back of the building. The smell of rotting food rose from its interior in the hot, still air.

I stepped around the dumpster and stopped.

'He's been a busy boy tonight,' I said.

Dylan stepped up beside me. The back door to the building was ajar.

'He wants us to look inside,' I said.

Something moved inside the dumpster and we spun around, drawing our weapons. I motioned to Dylan and he went over and took hold of the lid of the dumpster as I stepped up, with my Glock and light trained on the top edge of the container.

'Now,' I said, and Harrison flipped it open.

The stench poured out like a gust of wind, the buzz of flies filled the air. I held my breath and pointed the light into the interior. The tail of a rat disappeared down into the soiled wrappers and rotting food.

'Pigeons with paws,' Harrison said, and closed the lid.

I stepped away, cleared my lungs of the stench and looked over to the back door.

'Why would he want us inside, Alex?' Harrison asked.

I glanced back to the east where the helicopter had been circling. The sky was black and empty – the helicopter had vanished. I walked over to the door and took a position next to it. I leaned in and looked down the dark hallway, then stepped back.

'What are you thinking?' I said to Harrison.

'I'm not sure,' Dylan said. 'If that sign is what he wanted us to see, we saw it.'

I pushed the door with my foot and it swung open. Nothing moved inside, there was no sound. I looked back to Harrison and started to speak when the deafening shudder of the helicopter passing over the top of the restaurant shook the ground. The darkness turned to day as the white light of the helicopter's night sun encircled us.

'Empty your hands and hold them in the air,' came over the copter's loudspeaker. 'Empty your hands now,' they repeated.

We both knelt down to place our weapons on the pavement as a squad car came around the back of the restaurant and skidded to a stop. The doors were flung open and two officers stepped out and trained their weapons on us.

'On the ground now!' one of them yelled.

I held my hands out wide so they could see they were empty and lay face down on the pavement.

'Do not move!'

One of the officers approached from the front as the other walked around behind us and kicked our weapons away.

'We're police officers,' I said, but my words were lost in the whirl of the helicopter's rotors.

'Arms behind your back,' said the one in front of us and then the other quickly knelt down on Harrison's back and cuffed his wrists.

He then moved over to me, repeating the process, driving his knee into the small of my back with all his weight.

'We're the pol—'

'I didn't tell you to speak,' said the one on top of me as the cuffs closed around my wrists. He kept his weight on me for another moment and then stood up.

'We're clear here,' one of them said into his radio.

I was pulled up by my arms and walked over to the squad

car as the other cop did the same with Harrison. The helicopter pulled out of its tight circle and headed off to the west, its night sun slowly moving back and forth across the ground like a ray from a bad B movie. One of the officers walked over and picked up our weapons; the other one came up to us and shined his flashlight in our faces.

'Congratulations, you've just busted two homicide cops,' I said.

I couldn't see his face in the dark for the light in my face, but I would have liked to.

'Can you take the light out of our eyes?'

'You have ID?' he asked.

'Even a badge,' I said. 'Look down on my belt and you'll see it.'

He pointed the light down on my badge.

'My partner has one just like it,' I added as the other officer walked up with our weapons.

The first cop slipped the wallet holding my badge and ID out of my belt and checked it. He looked at it for a moment then handed it to his partner.

'Pasadena?' said the cop holding our weapons. 'Lieutenant Delillo,' he added, barely concealing his annoyance with our presence. Even on a good day most LAPD officers thought of officers from smaller jurisdictions as little more than glorified mall cops, and this was far from a good day.

'That's right. His name's Harrison. Would you uncuff us now?'

He hesitated and glanced at his partner but made no move to undo the cuffs.

'What are you doing over here, Lieutenant?' asked the second one, who clearly was the senior of the two.

'Investigating a homicide,' I said. 'And what are you doing, investigating taco theft?'

They unlocked the cuffs and handed us our weapons. In the darkness their faces were little more than dull outlines.

'We received a call that a burglary was in progress,' said the first cop.

I glanced at Harrison and then looked around. Directly to the east of us was a flood control channel; beyond that was a dark neighborhood.

'When did this call come in?' I asked.

'We got it two minutes ago.'

'You thinking what I'm thinking?' I said to Harrison.

'He's watching,' he said.

'Could be,' I said.

'Anyone either out front or back of here could have seen our lights.'

'Who's watching?' asked the second cop.

'The bogey man,' I said. 'It's possible we're all being messed with.'

'What brought you here, Lieutenant?'

'We got an invitation,' I said.

'Was that door open when you arrived?' asked the first cop.

I nodded. 'We were just about to check it out when you arrived.'

'We'll take a look,' said the senior cop.

'It would be better if we did that,' I said.

'Don't worry, Lieutenant, we won't mess up your crime scene.' He turned and started for the back door.

'I didn't catch your name, officer,' I said.

'Baski,' he said, without turning. 'You can call me Sergeant.'

'If you see anything unusual, Sergeant, don't touch it,' I said.

He stopped and looked back. 'Don't touch anything?' he said. 'They teach you that in lieutenant school? I would never have thought of that.'

They walked away over to the door of the restaurant and then both entered. Harrison stepped over, watching the glow of the officers' flashlights filtering out of the dark interior of the building.

'He's laughing at us,' Harrison said.

I nodded. The two cops reappeared out the door and walked back over.

'It's all yours, Lieutenant,' said the sergeant. 'Lock up when you leave.'

We stepped away from their squad as they got in and drove off.

'Shall we see if Sherlock missed anything?' Harrison said.

I nodded and we walked over and entered the back of the building. The hallway led past two bathrooms and into the small dining area next to the kitchen. As Chief Chavez remembered, the walls were covered with celebrity photographs. There were a few faces I recognized, some of whom had been dead for at least twenty years. Most of the pictures were probably members of Screen Actors Guild who had a few guest shots on a soap or a sitcom then began handing out their eight by tens at every restaurant they ate at in hopes of landing another gig. In the center of one of the walls of pictures was an empty space.

'One's missing,' I said.

'I'll check tomorrow and see if they know which one is gone,' Harrison said. 'You see anything else?'

I nodded and moved the light across the room; at the far end a small eye had been drawn on the wall.

'His game continues,' I said.

six

The rest of the night passed like a slow-moving fever dream that never quite reaches a climax. At 3 a.m. it was eighty-two degrees. The violence that had erupted earlier in the night across Los Angeles began to ebb as the heat finally subdued even those most intent on havoc. At four thirty-eight the hum of electricity began to spread across the basin as one grid after another came back online. The stars that had for a few hours lit up the night sky began to slip away one after another until all that was left were a few dull points of light.

I drove home to Mariposa with Harrison and stopped in the middle of the street before pulling into the driveway.

'What is it?' Harrison asked, his eyes holding on me.

'I need a time out,' I said.

'From the case?' Dylan asked.

'From everything,' I said and then pulled into the driveway.

As we walked through the front door, Dylan slipped his hand under my blouse and pulled me against him, then he undid the buttons and my shirt fell away as if taken by a breeze. His hand moved up across my stomach to my right breast – I hadn't thought about it since we had begun picking up the dead and I sure as hell didn't want to think about it now. He slid my pants down to my ankles then guided each foot carefully out, slipping my socks off with the same motion.

'How do you manage it?' I said, trying to remember to breathe.

Dylan's hand moved across the small of my back and slipped my underwear down to the floor.

'Manage what?' he said, moving his hands slowly back up the length of my legs.

'To not make me feel self-conscious.'

His right hand moved around to the inside of my thigh, spread my legs and kissed me.

'I don't. You do that all by yourself.'

As we walked into the living room, I undressed him, trying to move slowly but gaining speed with every item I removed. We made love on the couch and floor and then again until we were both exhausted. When we had finished we stood together under a cool shower until not even the other's body could keep us standing and we retreated to the bed.

The few times I managed to fall asleep I bolted awake as the image of a single motionless eye watching me returned. As the dawn began to break, I sat up and looked out the window facing the rising sun coming up over the San Gabriels.

A thin ribbon of orange light began to outline the mountains against the dark purple of the sky above. I heard the soft rustle of sheets and then the warmth of Harrison's breath on my shoulder. He slipped one arm around my waist and then the other over my breasts.

'Lacy knows about us,' I said.

'Is that a problem?' he asked.

'You know what she said to me?'

'No.'

'Fucking is never a secret, not for long.'

'Did you think it should remain one?'

I nodded. 'That we are sleeping together may not exactly be good news for either of us inside the department.'

'Lacy is not the department.'

'Does it ever occur to you that we only make love after someone has been violently murdered?' I said. 'What class of dysfunctional behavior do you suppose we fit into?'

'To believe that dysfunctional behavior in personal relationships exists, one would have to accept the premise that there is such a thing as normal behavior.'

'The first time we made love I was holding a gun in my hand,' I said.

He shook his head and his hand slipped from my breast and stroked my neck.

'Sometimes you think too much,' he said. 'Not everything is supposed to have meaning beyond what it is.'

'Everything has meaning beyond what it is,' I said. 'As a homicide detective, you should know this.'

His hand slipped down over my breast again.

'Every gesture, every word, silence . . . every touch.'

'What's wrong?' he asked.

'Normality,' I said. 'I was just wondering what that would be like.'

'I'll be normal for you, I'll even marry you if that's what you want.'

He reached up and placed my hand on his over my breast with the lump deep inside. I let his hand gently caress me, trying for just a moment to pretend nothing had changed. Then I slipped his hand away.

'I've tried normal, it didn't work out,' I said.

'So we won't be normal.'

I reached up and covered my breast with my hand. Without even being aware of it my fingers began to search for the tiny lump and then I stopped myself.

'I'm ten years older than you, what if I can't give you the things you want?' I said.

'And what is it you can't give me?'

'You may want a family someday.'

'Is this your way of trying to let me down, of telling me that you've had enough?'

I took a breath, my heart pounded against my chest and I shook my head.

Dylan slipped his hand round my waist.

'I've never known you to be afraid of anything. What are you afraid of?'

'Time,' I whispered.

The next time I was aware of anything the alarm clock radio was going off, a DJ's voice playing over the radio.

'*It's going to be another scorcher in the southland today, a hundred and ten in the valleys, near one hundred at the beaches. Los Angeles Police report that overnight there were seventeen arson fires, over two hundred burglaries, thirty reports of shots fired, five murders, and fifty-eight reports of looting. No figures in yet on the number of warm beers consumed. The forecast for today is more of the same, not a cloud in the sky, more blackouts, more cracks in the fabric of society . . . can't you people just get along . . .'*

My phone began to ring. I leaned back into Dylan's body, took a deep breath, turned the radio off then got out of bed, walked to the dresser, and answered. It was Traver.

'Tell me you have some good news,' I said.

'When was the last time you got good news at six in the morning?'

'It was worth a try. What have you got?'

'We just got a call that Caltech security found the body of a student on campus,' said Traver. 'I think you better see it.'

'Is it connected to the O'Brien case? Or another one? How do they know it's a student?' I asked.

Traver paused, clearly not having any answers.

'All right,' I said. 'We'll figure it out when I get there.'

I didn't bother asking for any more details and Traver knew me well enough not to offer any. That he thought I would want to take a look for myself told me all I needed to know – something wasn't right about it.

'Where on campus?'

'South end, near the library. You want me to call Harrison?'

I looked over at Dylan's stirring body silhouetted against the coming light of dawn.

'I'll pick him up,' I said. 'Have you traced the cars yet?'

'The DMV's system crashed when power was restored, they're still working on it. I have an interview set up with one of the partners at Beckwith, Myers and Dunne at nine.'

'Make sure they know we want no trouble accessing O'Brien's records. If you have to, get a search warrant to wave in their faces.'

I hung up as Dylan sat up and swung his legs over the edge of the bed.

'You better get dressed, I have to pick you up.'

He looked at me for a moment without moving.

'Last night,' he said.

'What about it?'

'You made love like someone rushing to get out of a burning building.'

'Did I?' I asked even though I knew he was right.

'You have doubts.'

'I have doubts about most things,' I said.

Dylan got up and slipped on his pants and shirt in silence and then stopped.

'Do you want to step away from this?' he asked.

'This?'

'Us.'

I looked at him for a moment.

'Do you?' I asked.

He took a breath and shook his head. 'I also don't want to be here unless I'm what you want.'

'You're what any woman with half a brain and two eyes would want,' I said.

'I'm not interested in any woman.'

'Thank you,' I said.

I looked at him for a moment, my head filling with thoughts and questions. If I lose my breast, will you stay? Harrison had already lost a young wife. At times his eyes appear to be searching for her. Would my struggle be one he wouldn't be able to shoulder?

'I just need to work some things out,' I said.

'Things?'

I nodded.

'That you can't talk about with me.'

'Not just yet,' I said.

'So we should take a break from this.'

I tried to speak but my voice faltered.

'I don't know,' I finally managed to say.

Dylan looked at me for a moment and then buttoned his shirt.

'Well, when you do know, let me know.'

We drove in silence down from the foothills toward town. A thin brown band of smoke from the fires the night before hung in the sky to the west. There wasn't a breath of wind. It was just past seven in the morning but already the sun was asserting its authority on the day. Pedestrians waiting for buses clung to whatever shade they could find around trees or street signs while others held newspapers or brightly colored umbrellas over their heads.

We drove down Lake and turned east on California until we reached the campus. As we drove in, the library tower was visible through the trees. There were few students about. Little sign of any activity at all except for the black and whites parked ahead and the yellow crime scene tape strung up marking the scene.

'It's summer break,' Harrison said. 'The only students around would be ones working on research projects.'

Traver was waiting at the perimeter when we stopped and got out. The library was the tallest building on campus at ten stories high. On the sidewalk along the side of the building a large yellow tarp had been spread out over the body. In places the blood had flowed from underneath the tarp and collected in a pool next to the grass where a dry surface film had already formed.

'He came off the top of the building,' I said.

Traver nodded. 'As far as we can tell. He's a real mess.'

A security guard sat in his three-wheeled scooter next to one of the squad cars.

'He the one who found him?' I asked.

Traver nodded. 'About five thirty a.m. He doesn't have much to add. He says he took one look, turned away and called us.'

'Anyone from the school been notified?'

'The Dean of Students is apparently on the way.'

I looked up at the tower rising ten stories above us.

'He picked the right building,' I said and walked over to the security guard. He was Filipino, I guessed, early thirties at most.

'Was the library unlocked last night for any reason?' I asked.

He shook his head. 'No,' he said with a slight accent. 'But some students have keys.'

'When was the last time you came by the library before the time you found him?'

'Maybe three or three thirty.'

'And you saw or heard nothing then?'

He shook his head and I walked with Harrison and Traver over to the tarp covering the body and slipped on a pair of latex gloves.

'Let's take a look,' I said and pulled the tarp away from the corpse. An arm was twisted underneath the torso; one of the legs was bent ninety degrees out from the knee. The bones in the other leg appeared to have been crushed. He was face down; massive fractures had deformed the head.

'What do you see?' I said to Harrison.

Dylan studied the broken twisted body and then looked back up at the top of the building.

'He hit a good fifteen feet from the base of the building.'

I nodded in agreement.

Harrison walked around the body, looking down at the blood splatter pattern on the concrete and grass.

'The pattern's all away from the body,' he said. 'He was moving in this direction almost as quickly as he was falling.' Dylan turned to me. 'He didn't just step off. He came off the top of the building at a full run.'

I stepped over and knelt next to the corpse. 'The question is, was he running away from something, or to this.'

'You don't run away from anything on top of a building,' Traver said. 'You got nowhere to go but down.'

'You think it's a suicide?'

'What else could it be?' he said.

I looked up at the top of the building. 'What if down was a better option than staying on top?'

Traver shrugged. 'What could be worse up there than falling ten stories on to concrete?'

'That's what we need to figure out.'

I reached over and slipped the dead man's wallet out of the back pocket of his pants and opened it.

'Driver's license and student ID,' I said, handing it to Harrison.

'Terry Pullian,' he said. 'Twenty-four years old. That probably makes him a grad student.'

I looked at the body and its position.

'This school's full of the smartest people in the country,' I said.

'The world,' Harrison added. 'They're not just brainiacs, they're *the* brainiacs.'

I stepped around the body. He had landed about three feet short of the grass.

'Dave's probably right,' I said.

'But?' Harrison said.

'But what if he's not?'

'You got me,' Traver said.

'What are you thinking?' Dylan asked.

'Someone like this probably doesn't do anything in this world without calculating every possibility down to the fraction of fractions.'

Harrison looked at me and then back toward the top of the building.

'You think he ran the numbers in his head and figured the distance that was needed to reach the grass, and then the speed with which he would hit the ground and the probability of survival if he made it?'

'It's possible,' I said.

'The odds of living through this still would have been virtually non-existent,' Harrison said.

I looked up at the top of the building. 'But what if they were preferable to what was up there?'

'These are big ifs,' Traver said.

'Possibly,' I said.

'I don't see it,' Traver said. 'The power was out, the only reason to come here would have been to go up to the top and do this.'

I knelt back down next to the body and patted down each of his pants pockets.

'I don't feel any keys,' I said and stood up.

A car pulled up to the perimeter tape and a woman in her early thirties rushed out of the car and over to one of the uniformed officers.

'Is the Dean of Students a woman?' I asked.

Traver nodded and I glanced down at the body.

'Cover him up,' I said.

Traver pulled the tarp back over him and Harrison and I walked over to the woman waiting at the tape.

'I'm the Dean of Students,' she said.

She was in her early thirties; short cropped blond hair with the ends tinted red. She wore jeans, flip-flops and a T-shirt with an image of a chromosome printed on it.

I introduced us.

'Jamie Greer,' she said. 'Is it a student?'

I nodded. 'He has an ID. Do you know a Terry Pullian?'

She began to react before I had even finished speaking. Her hand covered her mouth as she let out an audible gasp as if I had struck a blow.

'Would you like to sit down?' I asked.

She shook her head and crossed her arms over her chest and held herself.

'Do you . . . know what . . . Jesus,' she said, shaking her head.

'We don't really have any answers yet,' I said. 'All we know at this point is that he came off the top of the building.'

Her eyes fixed on the tarp covering the body as she tried to grasp what I had just told her.

'Came off?' she said. 'You're saying he jumped off the building?'

'I'm saying he appears to have died as a result of a fall, but that determination won't be complete until an autopsy.'

She shook her head as if refusing to believe it.

'Did you know him?' I asked.

She shivered as if she was cold in the ninety-degree heat and then haltingly nodded.

'It's my job,' she said softly.

'How well?' I asked.

She stared past me for a moment as if she hadn't heard me.

'You didn't really know Terry,' she said.

'What do you mean?'

'He was more like a comet that occasionally passed through your orbit.'

'And that means what?' I said.

She took a deep breath to calm herself. 'In a place full

of really brilliant people, I've seen Terry make Nobel Laureates feel inadequate.'

'Had he been having any troubles of any kind that you know of?'

She looked at me in astonishment. 'Terry didn't have trouble. He wasn't of this world.'

'We're all of this world, Miss Greer.'

She shook her head. 'Not on this campus. I don't think he's ever had a moment of struggle in his life.'

'What was he studying?'

'He was on a research grant at the Jackson Center.'

'And that's what?'

'It's part of the Bioengineering Department. The Jackson Center for Neuromorphic Systems Engineering. He was getting his doctorate – his second, if I remember. He got his first one from MIT when he was twenty.'

'We'll need all his personal information for notification of next of kin,' I said.

She nodded. 'I'll have to get that from my office.'

'Did he live on campus?'

'No, he lived off.'

'We'll need that address.'

'I'll go get it for you.'

I stepped away with Dylan and looked back at the building.

'Let's take a look.'

We walked over to the entrance of the library and stepped inside.

'If he had come in before power came back on, he would have taken the stairs,' I said, motioning toward the emergency stairwell at the south end of the lobby.

We walked over. A sign next to the door read 'Roof access'. I opened the door and looked inside. Nothing seemed out of order so I stepped back out.

'We'll check the stairs when we come down,' I said and walked over to the elevator.

We rode the elevator to the top floor. It was devoted to administrative offices. Two short flights led up to the roof. The door was ajar. The emergency alarm on it had been heavily damaged and loosely hung by one screw; the wires inside had been pulled loose.

'This is hard-wired into the building's system,' I said.

Dylan nodded.

'So he came in after the power was back on, sometime after four. And he didn't want anyone else to know he was up here,' I said.

'Not surprising if he was intent on suicide.'

'Or if he didn't want someone to know where he was.'

I pushed the door open and stepped out on to the roof. The surface was covered with small pea gravel. A series of vents and a large air-conditioning unit appeared to be the only structures present. I scanned the expanse of gravel, looking for anything that was out of place.

'Do you see anything?' I asked.

Harrison shook his head. 'He would have gone off over there,' he said, motioning to the south.

We walked over to the south side and peered over the edge to where the body lay under the tarp.

'Look at the gravel, you're right about him running,' I said.

A series of deep impressions had been made in the pea gravel leading to the edge. I turned and looked back across the roof. Nothing appeared to have been left behind, nothing was out of place. No sign that a struggle of any kind had taken place, just a series of footprints marking where a life had come to an end. 'There's nothing here,' I said.

'You want to take this any further?' Harrison asked.

I knelt down and looked at the last footprint in the gravel before he took flight.

'What's bothering you?' Harrison asked.

I shook my head. 'Details that don't make sense.'

'That's not unique.'

'As the reigning brainiac of the Pasadena PD, what do you know about neuromorphic engineering?'

'Funny. Not much. It's relatively new,' Harrison said. 'I think its basic framework is one of trying to mimic neurobiological systems with technology.'

'In what applications?'

'Endless, take your pick. You think of anything in nature controlled by a nervous system, even a primitive one, and it probably has an application. Vision, motion, you name it.'

I looked over the edge of the building.

'Flight,' I said.

Harrison nodded. I stood up and glanced at my watch. We were due at Beckwith, Myers and Dunne within the hour to meet the partners.

'Let's get Traver on the details here. It's going to be another long, hot day,' I said.

seven

Crime scene technicians had gone over both the elevator and O'Brien's office in the brokerage firm and had come up with the series of random prints you'd expect from a public space.

We walked over to O'Brien's office and stood for a moment looking through the glass walls. Evidence tape sealed the door. Print dust was visible over nearly every surface in the office that might result in a print.

'You looking for anything in particular?' Harrison asked.

'If I knew the answer to that, we might be approaching an understanding of what's happening,' I said. 'And we're a long way from that.'

A receptionist walked over and led us into a dark wood-paneled conference room where two of the partners were waiting. Charles Beckwith was a man of about sixty who looked like he spent more time on the tennis court than on the phone with clients. He wore an expensively tailored pinstripe suit and shoes that appeared to be alligator. Allen Dunne was younger by at least ten years. The warm tones of Beckwith's skin were a sharp contrast to the paleness of Dunne. He wore a steel-grey suit, not as flashy as Beckwith's, was wiry thin, and from the look in his eyes I suspected he worked endless hours and slept little.

'We're here to help you in any way we can,' Dunne said. 'Losing a friend in this horrific way is unimaginable.'

'Our other partner Derrick Myers died last fall while on holiday in France,' Beckwith added.

'On holiday?' I asked.

'A boating accident,' Dunne said.

'We miss him a great deal,' Beckwith said.

'For reasons of continuity within the firm,' Dunne said, 'we've kept Derrick's name.'

'We understand Cathy O'Brien survived,' Beckwith said.

'Yes, she's in intensive care,' I replied.

'Do you have a suspect?' Dunne asked.

'We have no ID, but we do have a suspect.'

'So this wasn't random?' Dunne said.

I shook my head. 'No, it was very specific.'

'And you have reason to believe that this suspect was inside our offices during the blackout?'

'No, we know he was inside,' I said. 'We're going to need access to all of O'Brien's records, including client information. We can get search warrants, but I would rather not have to waste time.'

'You think this is connected to the firm?' Beckwith asked.

'Everything is connected until we eliminate it,' I said. 'Tell me about him.'

They glanced at each other, not sure what I meant.

'Do you mean professionally or personally?' Beckwith asked.

'Both.'

'He was a senior associate specializing in institutional clients,' Dunne said. 'Both public and private institutions.'

'So he didn't work with individual investors?'

'No,' Dunne said.

'What institutions?' I asked.

'He handled a number of municipality investments, small to medium size cities and their pension plans. He did the same with various institutional endowments, and then a number of private company pension plans.'

'He was very talented,' Beckwith added.

'And very good at what he did.' Dunne added.

'Had his clients lost money in the last year?' I asked.

'Everyone has lost money,' Dunne said. 'The funds under his management are like every other in the world. But in general terms they outperformed the industry average.'

'What can you tell us about his personal life?' Harrison asked.

Each looked to the other for an answer.

'Working as intensely as we do, when people leave the office, there isn't a lot of social interaction once you reach the senior level Jim had,' Dunne said.

'We have box seats at Dodger Stadium, I know Jim went two or three times a year to games.'

'He was happily married,' Dunne added.

'How do you know that?'

He thought for a moment. 'I guess that was more of

an assumption on my part, he never said anything otherwise.'

'Did he ever say he was happy?' I asked.

Dunne was silent for a moment.

'We never talked about that,' he finally said.

'Are there any employees you can think of who might have been close to him that we could talk to?' I asked.

Neither had an answer.

'How about outside the company? Did he ever talk about that part of his life?'

'I think he went down the Colorado River on a raft once,' Beckwith said.

'Like I said, Lieutenant, people here tend to live two lives, and they don't mix much,' Dunne said.

'His killer left a series of messages,' I said.

'What kind of messages?' Beckwith asked.

'A blood-soaked hundred-dollar bill, images of the all-seeing eye like you find on the dollar.'

The meaning wasn't lost on Dunne.

'Are you suggesting that the killer believes he has providence on his side?'

'That's a possibility,' I said. 'He also left a written message.'

'What?' Dunne asked.

'The rich are different from us, they get away with it,' Harrison said.

'What the hell does that mean?' Beckwith said.

Dunne silently replayed the words and shook his head. 'I'll explain it to you sometime, Charley,' he said to his partner, then turned to me. 'Are you suggesting this killer is conducting some kind of a private class war?'

'We don't know enough yet to answer that,' I said. 'Did you trust Jim O'Brien?'

'In what sense?' Beckwith asked.

'Was his work ethical?'

Dunne leaned back and smiled. 'You mean was he one of the people working in the markets that have driven the world to the edge of the abyss through greed?'

'I wasn't thinking on a global scale, but now that you mention it,' I said.

'We trust all of our employees,' Dunne said.

'He never gave you any reason to think he had acted inappropriately with his clients' money?'

'No,' Dunne said. 'If he had, he would no longer be here.'

'Your client list is only as good as your reputation,' Beckwith added.

'When was the last time you saw him?' Harrison asked.

'A week ago,' Dunne said. 'He was on vacation.'

'And you hadn't talked to him in that time?' I asked.

'Once,' Dunne said. 'Three days ago.'

'What was the nature of the conversation?'

'He had a question regarding one of his clients and research money the government was offering.'

'What sort of question?'

'I have contacts within government and he wanted me to look into the kind of restrictions that came with the funds in terms of how they could be invested.'

'And did you find out?'

Dunne shook his head. 'The wheels of government turn slowly.'

'What institution was this for?' I asked.

'Caltech.'

Dylan glanced at me.

'He handled investments for Caltech?' I asked.

Dunne nodded. 'Along with half a dozen other schools.'

'Do you know anything about the grant he asked you about?'

'Just the name. Something called the Medusa Program.'

'What branch of government does it come through?'

'The Defense Department,' Dunne said.

'Lieutenant, can you give us some idea when we'll have access to Jim's office?' Beckwith asked. 'There is information we'll need to service his clients.'

I shook my head as I stood up. 'No, but we'll let you know as soon as we can. We may also have to remove his computer and any files that may be of use.'

'Is that necessary?' Beckwith asked.

'We'll see. We'll be in touch,' I said.

I took a step toward the door and then stopped and turned around.

'There was one other thing,' I said.

'All you have to do is ask, Lieutenant, we'll help you in any way we can,' Dunne said.

'That's good to know,' I said. 'Can you think of any reason Jim O'Brien would have nearly seventy thousand dollars inside his freezer at home?' I asked.

They sat in silence for a moment, though I could see in their eyes that they were silently running through every possible explanation and what implications it could have for the firm.

'His freezer?' Dunne finally asked.

I nodded. 'Right next to the chocolate chip ice-cream.'

'And the killer didn't take the money?' Beckwith asked.

I shook my head. 'And he knew it was there,' I added.

They glanced at each other and then back to us.

'I can't imagine,' Dunne said.

'Perhaps his wife can answer that question,' Beckwith said.

'Let's hope so,' I said.

As they walked us out, the lights flickered for a brief second and everyone in the room instantly stopped what they were doing and held their collective breaths, waiting for the power to go out, and then went right back to work when it didn't.

When we stepped outside, the temperature had risen another ten degrees. Waves of heat rose up from the road. The tires of a passing truck made a sound as if the rubber was melting as it passed over the street's surface. We walked to the squad and stopped.

'That wasn't what you would call warm and fuzzy,' Harrison said. 'They're nervous about something.'

'If you were part of an industry that had lost a few trillion dollars and one of your employees just had his head cut off, you might be a tad nervous yourself.'

'What do you want to do?' Dylan asked.

'See if there's any connection between the dead student and this Defense Department funding program,' I said.

'Medusa,' Harrison said.

'That name mean anything to you?' I asked.

Dylan shook his head. 'Are we going somewhere with this or are we grasping at straws?' he asked.

'You think it's a stretch?' I said.

Dylan nodded. 'Even really bright people kill themselves. The photograph is what we should be concentrating on.'

'I agree, but check it anyway.'

My phone rang and I picked up.

'Alex.' It was Chavez. 'Cathy O'Brien woke up from her sedation, ripped her IVs out and ran out of ICU.'

'They lost her?' I asked.

'No, they found her wandering around the morgue.'

'Is she talking?' I asked.

'In a fashion. I think you better get over there.'

eight

Harrison headed over to Caltech and I made the short drive to the hospital. The crush of patients had slowed with the return of power and air conditioning, but there was still a five-hour wait and it was showing on the patients' faces.

Cathy O'Brien had been moved to the third floor. I showed my badge at the nursing station and asked for her doctor to meet me upstairs. Through the window into her room I could see that her eyes were open, but she was staring motionless at the ceiling. Her forearms were bound to the bed rails with heavy cotton restraints just above the wrists. A few minutes later a resident showed up. His name was Shaboud, and from his accent I guessed he was Iranian.

'You're the policewoman who found her?' he asked.

'Yes. Is she capable of talking?'

'She can talk, but she isn't making any sense. We put her on a low dose of Loxapine to quiet the hallucinations. It seems to have helped.'

'What kind of hallucinations?' I asked.

'She was under the impression that her husband's head had been taken by someone and was hidden in the morgue.'

'Are the restraints really necessary?'

'We can't have patients wandering around the hospital.'

'That wasn't a hallucination, Doctor.'

He looked at me and smiled. 'Lieutenant, I think you should leave the medical judgements to us.'

'Did you talk with any of the staff who were on duty when she was admitted?' I asked.

'No,' he said unapologetically.

'Did you look at the marks on her wrists before using the restraints?'

'Yes, that was why we used the forearm restraints instead of wrist ones.'

'What year are you in, Doctor?'

'Second year.'

'Second year. You didn't think to ask how she got those marks before you tied her down again?'

'Lieutenant, is there a point to this? We have a very full hospital.'

'Those marks were where she was bound to a bed and forced to watch as her husband's head was cut off and hung from a door. She wasn't hallucinating in the morgue, Doctor, she was trying to find her way out of the nightmare her life has just become.'

He stood silently for a moment, looking like a student who has been caught cheating and wants to find a way out of the room.

'Next time read her chart completely,' I said. 'Now you need to get an attending psychiatrist down here with experience in violent trauma and you need to do it now.'

'She should never have been moved up to this ward, it's not my fault.'

He must have seen my reaction to that statement in my face; he looked at me for a moment then turned and walked quickly away. I opened the door and stepped into Cathy's room. She didn't turn her head as I walked in, but I could see her eyes track me as they followed me across the room to the bed.

'Cathy,' I said.

Her eyes glanced in my direction then turned back to the ceiling.

'I'm Lieutenant Delillo, I found you last night.'

She continued to focus on the ceiling.

'I need your help to find the man who did this,' I said.

If she heard me there was no indication.

'I know you've been through a terrible ordeal. I want to help you.'

Her eyes seemed to be trying to struggle to focus through the fog of the drugs.

'It's all right,' I said. 'Take your time.'

She closed her eyes and took a deep breath, but still said nothing.

'Your parents are on a plane, they'll be here in a few hours.'

Cathy's hands tightened into fists.

'We'll talk later, you just rest now. Another doctor will be here soon and they'll take care of you.'

I started to turn away when she closed her hand around the bed rail and began to shake it. I turned back, reached out and placed my hand on hers. She shook the rail a few more seconds and then stopped. She glanced at me, focused on me, her eyes wide with what looked like the rush of adrenalin.

'What is it, Cathy?' I said.

The door opened and a new doctor walked in carrying her chart. Cathy flinched at the sound of the door shutting and I squeezed her hand.

'It's all right,' I said.

She closed her eyes as if waiting for something to happen. The doctor was a black woman, tall and slender, early thirties, her long hair in tight cornrows with beads. She walked to the other side of the bed.

'Cathy, I'm Doctor Moikenah,' she said with a soft African accent.

O'Brien's eyes began to move across the room as if searching for a hiding place.

'It's OK,' I said. 'She's going to help you.'

The doctor reached over and placed her hand on the restraint and undid it.

'You're going to be all right,' she said. 'You don't need these.'

She undid the restraint and looked at me. 'You're with the police?'

I nodded and identified myself. 'I found her last night.'

'Would you undo that?' she said, nodding to the restraint.

I undid it, slipping it carefully from Cathy's arm. Cathy seemed to take no notice.

'Has she talked to you?' Moikenah asked.

'No. I think she wants to, though.'

The doctor reached out and placed the palm of her hand on Cathy's forehead. The frantic sense of fear in her eyes seemed to settle.

'You're going to be just fine,' Moikenah said in a soft, soothing tone. 'The strange way you feel is because of the drugs they gave you. We're going to take care of that.'

Cathy's eyes looked over to me.

'Is there something you want to say?' the doctor asked her.

She looked back at Moikenah as if searching for something.

'You must not worry about anything now. We'll go one step at a time, there's no rush.' Moikenah looked over to me. 'Perhaps you can come back later.'

I nodded.

'You can help me later,' I said to Cathy. 'I'll come back.'

I started to step away and she took hold of the bed rails again and shook them. I turned back to her.

'Do you want to talk, Cathy?' the doctor asked.

She closed her hands into fists.

'What is it?' I asked.

She appeared to try and speak but didn't manage to form any words.

'It's OK, there will be time to talk later.'

She shook her head.

I reached out and placed my hand on her fist. Her hand flinched from the contact and began to shake.

'It's all right, you're safe, he can't hurt you here,' I said. 'You're not alone.'

The tremors in her hand slowed and her fingers began to relax, then slipped around mine and held on to my hand.

'Where's my husband?' she asked, her voice hoarse.

I looked over to the doctor, not sure how to answer the question.

'He's not in this building,' Moikenah said.

'He wouldn't want people to see him like that,' Cathy said.

'No one will.'

She took another deep breath then her body seemed to relax and she sank back into the pillow.

'If you can, I need you to answer some questions,' I said. 'Do you understand?' She closed her eyes and nodded.

'Can you tell me what the man who did this to you and your husband looked like?'

She thought for a moment then shook her head. She opened her eyes and looked around the room as if she wasn't sure of her surroundings.

'I can't remember anything.'

'You don't have to now, in time you will, it's OK.'

'It was dark, the whole time, so dark.'

'Like the lights were out, or you had something over your eyes?' I asked.

She nodded.

'Something over your eyes?'

She nodded again.

'Did he say anything?'

She looked at me for the first time and then moved her lips but made no sound.

'Is there something you're trying to remember?' I asked.

She seemed to nod, but when she tried to speak, the words failed her.

'Perhaps that's enough for now,' the doctor said.

'When I come back, you can tell me then.'

Her eyes locked on to me.

'You let the doctor take care of you.' I said and started to walk away.

'Nothing can help you,' she said softly. 'There'll be another tonight and then another and another until he's finished.'

I started to walk toward her but she held up her hands as if trying to push me away.

'OK,' I said, and stood still.

Cathy took several shallow breaths as if she had just finished running up a set of stairs, and then nodded.

'What else did he tell you?' I asked.

She fought the effect of the drugs or fear or both, closed her eyes for a moment and then looked at me.

'He's doing this for you,' she said.

I shook my head. 'I don't understand.'

'He admires you,' she said, her voice rising in pitch. 'He said you inspire him.'

She reached out as if to grab me and her eyes filled with rage.

'Who are you?' she screamed.

The doctor reached out, trying to calm her.

'Why . . . What kind of a person are you . . . *why?*'

Cathy sank back on her pillows in tears.

'I think you better step out,' the doctor said.

I started to say something but the doctor just shook her head.

'Could you wait outside?' she said. 'I would like to talk to you.'

I looked down at the figure in the bed, then turned and went out into the corridor. The door closed behind me and I tried to take a step but was frozen in place, in shock at the words Cathy had just spoken. My breath caught short, my hands were trembling. He's doing this for me? I inspire him? My heart was pounding against my chest and I felt as if I was falling down a steep slope.

My phone rang and I slipped it from my pocket. It was Harrison's number. I let it ring half a dozen times before I answered.

'Yes,' I said, barely managing even the one word.

'Alex, are you all right?'

I forced some air into my lungs and then took another breath. The downward slide began to slow.

'I'm not sure . . . What is it?'

'Wait, did she talk to you?' Harrison asked.

From inside the room, I could hear Cathy's heartbroken sobbing.

'In a fashion. I'll tell you when I see you,' I said. 'You find something?' I changed the subject.

'Yeah, and you're not going to believe it,' Dylan said.

My heart rate began to settle.

'I think there's little I wouldn't believe right at this moment,' I said.

'Pullian's research was funded by the Medusa Program,' Harrison said.

I heard his words, but it took a few seconds to step completely out of the moment I had just walked away from.

'Say again?' I asked.

'The dead student, he was working on that grant O'Brien had asked Dunne to talk to Washington about,' Harrison said.

'You're certain?'

'I just got off the phone with the Dean of Students.'

'Do you still want to consider his death a suicide?' I asked.

The door to Cathy's room opened and Dr Moikenah stepped out.

'We need to see his apartment. Where did he live?' I said to Harrison.

'Just north of campus, one sixty-two Chester.'

'I'll meet you there in twenty minutes,' I said and hung up. I turned to the doctor. 'Sorry. Is she all right?'

'She's quiet again,' Moikenah said.

I reached into my pocket and took out a card and handed it to her.

'If she says anything else, I would appreciate a call,' I said.

As she slipped the card from my hand, she noticed the trembling in my fingers.

'Are you all right, Lieutenant?' she asked.

I nodded unconvincingly.

'What did she mean he was doing it for you?' she asked. 'Who was she talking about?'

'The man who murdered her husband . . . I apparently

inspire him,' I said and shook my head. 'It's nothing, it's a game he's playing.'

She studied me for a moment. 'And he's included you in his game?'

I nodded. 'It would appear so.'

'Do you believe in the presence of evil, Lieutenant?'

'As what?' I asked.

'A physically present force,' she said.

'That inhabits or takes over people?' I asked.

She nodded.

'No,' I answered. 'When all is said and done, people do terrible things, and sometimes there's a reason and other times there's none at all.'

Her soft brown eyes looked at me.

'You believe it, though, don't you?' I said.

'I grew up in Rwanda, Lieutenant. I'm alive because I hid under the bodies of my family for three days after they had been murdered by neighbors with whom they had shared food and memories their entire lives. Every day of my life I've tried to come up with an understanding of those days. And the answer is always the same.' She paused. 'Evil does exist, Lieutenant, and one look into your eyes and Cathy's eyes tells me it's after you.'

'Is that a clinical diagnosis?' I asked.

She shook her head. 'A survivor's,' she said.

'I'll keep that in mind,' I said.

She started to turn then stopped as if there was something else she needed to say.

'What is it, Doctor?' I asked.

'Perhaps it is not my place to say but I have some experience of this kind of evil.'

'I'm listening.'

'If what she said is true and the man who killed her husband believes you to be an inspiration, be careful.'

'How so?' I said.

'The line separating adoration and hatred is easily crossed, particularly with violence,' Moikenah said.

'You're saying I could become a target.'

She shook her head. 'I'm saying you *will* become a target. It's inevitable.'

'Thank you, Doctor.' I reached out and shook her hand. As she held mine, she looked at me for a moment longer.

'But then I'm not a detective, perhaps I'm mistaken. I hope for your sake, that I am.'

'No, I don't think you are,' I said.

The lights in the corridor flickered on and off several times, then settled and for a moment the unnatural hum of fluorescent lights filled the air. She looked up at the lights then back to me.

'Will we be losing power again today?'

'Very likely,' I said.

'This man she talked about, he will wait for the darkness before he kills again?'

'Yes. He seems to think the darkness is a metaphor for his work.'

She shook her head. 'No, it's no metaphor, not to him.'

'What do you mean?' I asked.

'A person who kills in the darkness does it for two very specific reasons.'

'Go on.'

'Either there's shame attached to the act, and they don't want their face to be seen – their violence often contains a sexual component. They don't want to be caught, so they act in secret.'

'And the second?'

'They derive a sense of power from it, almost as if it is another presence helping them commit the violence. It makes them stronger, they don't fear capture because they don't believe an inferior being is capable of stopping them.'

'He's left images of the all-seeing eye behind,' I said.

She pictured the image for a moment.

'So he's the second kind,' she said.

'How can he see me as an inspiration if I'm inferior?' I asked.

'You're not, at least not yet,' she said.

'I don't follow.'

'Has he communicated directly with you beyond leaving behind the image of the eye?'

'Yes, he called me on the phone.'

'To truly feel his power, he must have someone or something of equal power to defeat. Do you have a history with serial killers that he would know about?'

I nodded.

'That's why he picked you,' she said.

'Yes, but how does this help me?'

'Every brilliant student feels they must surpass their teacher to prove themselves. Think of yourself as his teacher.'

'I've had better images in my head,' I said.

'When that time comes, he could become careless and step out of his normal pattern.'

'How will I know when that moment occurs?'

Dr Moikenah shook her head. 'I don't know, it could be almost anything – a different weapon, choice of victim, he could kill in the daylight. Anything.' Her pager went off and she checked it. 'I must go.'

'Thank you,' I said.

'When it does happen, Lieutenant, that is when he will come after you. You must remember that.'

She looked at me for a moment longer.

'Good luck,' she said, then turned and walked away.

nine

Terry Pullian, the dead student, lived on a tree-lined street of older apartment buildings just north of the Caltech campus. Harrison was waiting outside when I pulled up and stepped out.

'He's on the second floor, the window on the right,' Dylan said.

It was a Spanish-style building with a terracotta tile roof. The white stucco was dirty with the soot of LA's air.

'Did he live alone?' I asked.

'No one seemed to know at school,' Harrison said.

We walked to the front door inside a covered arched entryway. There were six mailboxes inside. Pullian's name was the only one on number four. I lifted the lid on the box and looked through the slot. There was mail jammed inside.

'Looks like he hadn't picked his mail up for a few days,' I said.

The lobby held the odor of carpet cleaner and years of foot traffic and dust that no amount of cleaner could mask. A center stairway led to the second floor. We walked up to the landing. The sound of a television drifted out from the apartment to the left. Pullian's was to the right. Dylan stepped to the door with Pullian's keys and started to slide the key into the lock, but stopped.

'The door's not locked,' he said, reaching down and turning the handle.

The bolt cleared and Dylan pushed the door open. Hot stuffy air rushed out into the hallway, carrying the scent of fast food chicken. There were no lights on and the blinds were drawn over the windows.

'It must be a hundred degrees inside,' Harrison said.

I stepped in and reached around the door to a light switch and flipped it on. A single bare bulb on a ceiling fixture illuminated the room. We both looked around in silence for a moment without speaking.

'What do you make of this?' Harrison finally said.

'I don't know,' I said.

A large living room spread out in front of us. Two computers sat in the middle of the bare floor with a large notebook between them. There was no furniture. The floor was covered with sheets of paper, some crumpled, some untouched. I reached down and picked up a sheet. Both sides were covered with minute handwriting done with a fine-tipped pen.

'Look at the walls,' Dylan said.

In places it was covered with writing just as fine and delicate as on the sheet of paper I was holding in my hand.

'I guess he didn't entertain a lot,' I said.

'At least not as we understand it,' Harrison said.

I looked down at the sheet of paper and began to read.

The words were familiar, yet at the same time unrecognizable.

'This isn't English, I'm not sure what it is,' I said. 'Do you recognize it?' I handed the page to Dylan.

His eyes moved intently across several lines of writing and then he shook his head in amazement and reached down, picked up another sheet from the floor and looked it over.

'I'll be damned,' said Dylan.

'What?'

'This isn't any language,' he said.

'There are hundreds of pages of writing in here, it must be something.'

Dylan nodded. 'Yes.'

'So what is it?' I asked.

'Unless I'm mistaken, I think it's a new language,' Harrison said.

'What do you mean, a new language?'

'I think he's created his own, even down to the letters. Look at them. These might be based on our alphabet, but I don't recognize it from history or any other language.'

'Is that possible?' I said. 'It's one thing to write a few pages, but this is more than that.'

Harrison nodded and walked over and picked up the notebook sitting between the computers. He opened it and began to page through it.

'This is amazing,' he said.

'What?' I asked.

'It's the same as what's on the loose sheets, only this is highly organized.'

I walked over and looked at it; there was something familiar about it that I couldn't put a word to.

'Does this remind you of something?' I said.

Harrison nodded. 'Unless I'm way off, I think he's created a dictionary.'

'Does Caltech offer linguistics?'

Dylan shook his head. 'No, he must have done this in his spare time.'

I looked around for a moment in wonder. 'What was it the Dean of Students said? He wasn't of this world? She got that right.'

'I'll open a window and get some air in here.' He started across the room and stopped. 'What's that sound?'

I started to shake my head because I didn't hear it, then it was there.

'The high-pitched buzz?' I said and Harrison nodded.

'It's not electrical,' he said.

A small dining room off to the right led into the kitchen. A hallway to the left led to the bedrooms. I stepped over to the dining room. Like the living room, there was no furniture and the floor was covered with more papers. I walked through to the swinging door into the kitchen and pushed it open.

The odor of fried chicken was nearly overpowering.

'He didn't have much of a diet,' I said as Harrison stepped up behind me and looked in.

Like the other rooms, there was no furniture. Every inch of counter space was covered with empty boxes and buckets of fried chicken. A plastic garbage bag sat in the sink, nearly overflowing with discarded bones.

'I think I just gave up eating chicken,' Harrison said.

I walked over to the refrigerator and opened it. The shelves were filled with cartons of mashed potatoes and coleslaw, all unopened. The door held half a dozen cartons of orange juice. I closed the refrigerator and stepped back to the door to the dining room.

'Do you suppose there's a word for what's gone on inside here in his new language?' I said.

'I think it would take more than one word to describe this,' Harrison said.

I walked back through the dining and living rooms to the hallway leading toward the bedrooms.

'The buzz is coming from down here,' I said.

The hallway was dark. There was a door at the far end and two on the right, all closed. I flipped the light switch but nothing came on. I walked up to the first door, stopped and listened.

'The sound's not from in here,' I said, and then turned the handle and pulled the door open.

It was an empty closet.

'At least there's no chicken,' Harrison said and stepped up to the next door. 'The sound's coming from in here.'

He pulled the door open and we looked into the dark room. The sound was instantly recognizable.

'Flies,' I said.

Harrison nodded. 'A lot of flies.'

'Why aren't they flying out the door?' I said.

Dylan stepped in, found a light switch and turned it on. Several large glass aquariums and two smaller ones sat in the middle of the room, but instead of being filled with water and fish, the only occupants were flies. In front of one of the small aquariums an elaborate light system had been set up and a small video camera.

'You want to take a guess at what's going on here?' I said.

Dylan walked over and looked at the camera and lights.

'It's a high-definition camera,' he said, kneeling down and examining the glass container. 'He was recording flies.'

'Could this have something to do with neuromorphic systems engineering?' I asked.

Harrison nodded. 'That would be my guess, but beyond that I wouldn't know where to start.'

I stepped back into the hallway. The next door was a bathroom. The medicine cabinet held nothing out of the ordinary. Two towels hung on a rack, a washcloth over the shower curtain bar. The only thing that suggested the occupant was a little unusual was the presence of eight toothbrushes, laid out on the counter next to the sink.

'They're all different colors,' Harrison said. 'One for each day of the week.'

I nodded. 'But why the eighth one?'

'You think he had a regular visitor?'

There were two drawers in the vanity. The first one was empty, the second held several combs, nail clippers, Band-Aids and a hairbrush. I reached down and pulled a long strand of hair from the bristles of the brush.

'Someone spent some time here,' I said. 'And she was a redhead.'

'Could be old,' Harrison said.

I picked the brush up by the end of the handle and sniffed it.

'You can still smell the shampoo,' I said.

I set the brush down, walked to the bedroom at the end of the hallway and opened it. Unlike the rest of the apartment, the light had been left on. A bed frame with a mattress sat in the middle of the room. The sheets had been slept in and left unmade. There was a dresser against the foot of the bed, a chair in front of that.

Harrison stepped in beside me and looked it over.

'It's nearly suburban compared to the rest of the apartment,' he said.

'There's nothing against the walls,' I said. 'He's put everything in the center. Why would he do that?'

'So he could see the walls, Harrison said, stepping around the bed.

'But there's nothing on them,' I said.

'Maybe he was going to write on them like in the living room and never got to it.'

I went over to the wall and began walking around the perimeter of the room, running my hand over the surface of the paint. Behind the bed, I stopped.

'This has been painted recently. You can feel it, the texture changes in places, but it's not uniform, not even close.'

Harrison walked over and ran his hand over the surface.

'You're right, the newer paint is smoother.'

'What do you make of it?' I asked.

Dylan stepped back from the wall a few feet and stared at it. 'Perhaps he used the wall like a blackboard and just painted over old writing the way you would use an eraser.'

I ran my hands over the paint again.

'This feels more precise than that,' I said.

Harrison studied it for another moment.

'I think I get it,' he said.

'Get what?'

He walked back around the bed to the door and reached out to the light switch.

'Watch,' he said and then turned off the light.

The room went black except for the wall I was standing in front of.

'Glow-in-the-dark paint,' I said.

We stared for a moment in silence.

'Do you suppose Pullian is actually a killer?' Harrison said.

I shook my head. 'We'll need Crime Scene to go over every inch of this apartment.'

'I'll make the calls,' he said and then came and stood next to me.

'I see you,' Harrison said, reading what had been written on the wall. 'The same thing he said to you on the phone.'

I nodded.

'If Pullian didn't kill O'Brien, then what is all this?' Harrison said.

'A victim,' I said. 'The lights go out during the first blackout and he sees this on his wall.'

Between the lingering smell of the chicken and the buzz of the flies, the air in the room began to feel as if it was unbreathable, even dangerous if you stayed too long.

'I need some air,' I said. 'See what else you can find, I'm going to step outside.'

I took another look at the words on the wall then walked back out to the living room and then out the door and down the stairs to the front walk. A breeze had begun to blow outside, but it offered little reprieve from the air in the apartment, and the sun on my skin felt as if I was standing next to an open flame. I stepped back into the shade of the entryway.

In the distance the sound of a car horn became audible and then another and another until the sound merged into a single constant tone. A moment later the front door opened and Harrison stepped out.

'We just lost power,' Harrison said.

I nodded.

'I made the call to Crime Scene, they're on the way,' he said and then his light-green eyes focused on me in the way only a lover's can when he knows a secret is being kept.

'What's going on, Alex?'

'What do you mean?'

'I mean it's not like you to walk out of a scene like that.'

'I once had a bad experience with fried chicken,' I said, trying to smile.

'But that's not why you walked out,' he said.

'It's those words,' I said.

'What happened at the hospital?' he asked.

'You should be a detective,' I said.

'That's not an answer.'

'He left a message with Cathy O'Brien,' I said. 'It's probably why she's alive.'

'What kind of a message?'

'A fan letter,' I said.

Dylan shook his head. 'To whom?'

'Me,' I said.

'You?'

'Yes. He says he's doing this for me, that I inspire him in his work,' I said.

'His work?'

I nodded. 'Murder.'

'That's crazy.'

'I think the clinical term is completely goddamn crazy,' I said.

'Where do we go with this?' Dylan asked.

I shook my head. 'A man was tied to a bed and decapitated, and an odd genius who watched flies in glass cases and only ate fried chicken threw himself off a building because I inspire a twisted monster.' I looked at Dylan. 'I don't know. Where do you go with that?'

I stared into the lobby of the building.

'What kind of a life is this to live? Why would a rational person choose to live this way? Can you answer that?'

'No, but you can.'

'Can I?' I said and shook my head. 'Right now I'm not so sure.'

'Maybe you need to walk away from this one,' Dylan said.

'To where?'

'When I worked in the bomb squad, it was easy to measure success. Things either went bang or they didn't. If you've taught me anything since I joined Homicide, it's that every case we walk into begins with failure because no matter how good we are at what we do, we can't bring the dead back any more than we can change the qualities in human nature that make us such a damn mess. You know as well as I do that he hasn't done what he's done because of you.'

I looked at Harrison and smiled. 'It doesn't really matter what I believe, it's what he does.'

'So where do we go with this?' Harrison asked.

'If the doctor treating Cathy O'Brien is right, in the end this can only go in one direction.'

'Where is that?'

'Right at me.'

'You?' Harrison said.

'If he truly sees me as some kind of a foil or inspiration, at some point he's going to have to prove that he has surpassed me.'

'And to prove that, he'll need to kill you.'

I nodded. 'If the doctor's right, that would seem to be the logical progression.'

Dylan studied me for a moment. 'And you think she is right.'

'Yeah. It makes a kind of sense that's difficult to ignore, and if she is right, we might be able to use this to our advantage.'

'By setting you up as a target?'

'I think I'd prefer a different word than target, but that's the general idea. The real question is how many people is he going after before then?'

'I'm not sure I like where this is going,' Dylan said.

'If we can get him to focus on me sooner rather than later, we might be able to save some lives.'

'And it might get you killed.'

'So the question is how do we draw his attention away from the other victims he's focused on,' I said.

Dylan shook his head. 'No, the question is should we put you on a plane to somewhere.'

'We have ten hours before it gets dark and he takes another victim. You really think I should just walk away? Wait for dark and see someone else's dead body?'

'Of course not, but I'm not prepared to risk your life to save theirs. So what do we do?'

I looked up at the window to the apartment on the second floor.

'We work the connections between the two victims.'

'The Medusa Program.'

I nodded. 'We find out what it is and then every possible link between the victims. If we're lucky we get a connection to the photograph of the car Traver's tracking down.'

'And if we don't?' Harrison said.

'Then the answer's here.'

'Pullian?'

'There's no way you just walk into a life as odd and as private as this one out of the blue,' I said.

'You think he knew his killer?'

I nodded. 'Like the dean said, he could make Nobel Laureates feel inadequate, and one look inside here, you know he didn't let just anyone into his life. And you don't climb to the top of a building to hide unless you're certain of the danger following you. As soon as he saw those words on the wall inside, he must have known what it meant for him. And he chose to run off the top of the library rather than face it.'

'But why didn't he come to us?' Harrison said.

'Well, it certainly wasn't because he didn't think it out.'

I worked through the pieces of the puzzle, trying to see how they fitted, or more precisely what didn't fit.

'Who doesn't go to the police when they're in trouble?' I said.

'The guilty,' Harrison said.

We looked at each other for a moment.

'Are we thinking what I think we are?' Dylan said.

'Pullian was a part of this plan, or was at the beginning, and got cold feet, or maybe he believed our killer's plan was something else and when he realized what it was exactly, it was too late.'

'There is a kind of twisted logic to it, but I still have trouble with why?'

'Can you explain what we saw in that apartment?'

Harrison shook his head.

'Stupid people don't commit brilliant crimes,' I said.

'So who are we looking for?' he said.

'A partner Pullian would have considered his intellectual equal, and that's got to be a short list.'

'Another student?' Harrison said.

'The Leopold and Loeb of Caltech,' I said.

'That's not exactly a comforting thought.'

'Someone must have noticed something or someone new or different in his life, even a life as peculiar as his.'

'Maybe that someone kept a toothbrush upstairs,' Harrison said.

'And has red hair.'

Harrison nodded. 'I don't think it's natural.'

'What?'

Harrison reached into his pocket and removed a small photograph of Pullian sitting at a table staring at something just to the left of whoever had taken the picture. He had no expression on his face, or at least not one that was readable. Sitting next to him was a young woman with shoulder-length brown hair, smiling brightly at the camera, her arm around Pullian's shoulder.

'It was in his sock drawer,' Harrison said.

I looked at the picture for a moment.

'A romantic to the end.'

ten

A small memorial had already sprung up outside the library on the college campus. Some flowers, votive candles, and then the kind of things you would only expect from a college like this – pictures of nebulas, a calculator, mathematical equations, a specimen jar with a fly inside buzzing around, and some bird feathers, a reference, I suppose, to his brief flight.

The heat was already beginning to build inside the administration building when we walked into the Dean of Students' office and sat across from her desk. The open windows offered no relief.

'I just got off the phone with Terry's parents,' Greer said, her voice still containing the emotion of the conversation. 'They're in Vermont, it took me several hours to get in touch with them. Apparently they live off the grid. As you might guess, he came from an interesting family. They're on their way here now, though.'

'I'll need that number,' I said.

She nodded and handed me a small notepad with all Pullian's information on it.

'The coroner's office talked with them earlier and they called me asking if I had any more information.'

'What did you tell them?' I asked.

'Just that the police were treating it as a suicide.'

'Did they say when they last saw him?'

'Two years ago,' she said. 'I got the impression that they had lost touch with him when he came to Caltech, but I didn't press them for any information, they were understandably quite upset. Was there anything in his apartment that gave any indication why he did what he did?' she asked.

I glanced at Harrison and he handed her the photograph.

'Can you identify this woman?' he asked.

She took the picture in her hand and stared at it and started to shake her head, but then stopped.

'Her hair is different.'

'You know her?'

She nodded. 'She used to be a student here. She left in the spring for personal reasons, which usually means either academic or emotional trouble or both. In her case I think it was emotional, but that's just a guess, as she left rather quickly.'

'You remember her name?'

'Zara King, she was one of our humanities students. I remember her because in a school full of technical minds, the humanities students are often more . . . I'm not quite sure how to say this.'

'Normal?' I said.

She nodded. 'Something like that.'

'Would your records have contact information?'

'They would, if I could get into them. All our files are electronic and with the power outage . . . Whether the information would be current or not, I couldn't say. Is this important?'

'Yes. Who might know how to find her?'

'Her faculty advisor Professor Jean Little might have stayed in contact, you could try her.' She wrote down the number and handed it to me. 'That's her home number, she doesn't have courses this summer.'

'Who can tell us about the Medusa Program?' I asked.

'Terry's research?' Greer asked.

'Yes.'

'Professor Burnett runs the Jackson Center where Terry was based, he would be the one to talk to.'

'Is Burnett on campus this summer?'

She nodded. 'I spoke to him an hour ago about Terry. He's in his office now. Would you like me to call him and tell him you're on the way?'

'Thank you,' I said and got up from the chair. 'Do you have any students from England?'

'Yes, quite a few. We have students from virtually every major industrial country.'

'Do you think you could get me their names?'

'I'm a little confused, Lieutenant,' she said. 'Is there something about Terry's death that I don't understand?'

'There's always something about a death that we never understand, Miss Greer,' I said. 'If you could just get us those records, I'd really appreciate it.'

*

We left a message on Professor Little's answering machine and then met Elliot Burnett on the steps to the building where his office was. He was in his late fifties with deeply tanned skin and had the thin build of a runner. The only part of him that gave away his age was the long gray hair that fell nearly to his shoulders.

'It's dark and hot inside, I thought it would be better to talk out here,' he said as we walked up.

We introduced ourselves and we sat down in the shade on the steps of the building.

'You want to know about the Medusa Program?' he asked. 'In particular, Terry's work?'

'Yes.'

He looked up at the pale sky washed of color by the heat and haze.

'If climate models are correct and our energy use continues at its present growth rate, days like this are going to be the norm,' he said, wiping a bead of sweat from his temple, then turning to me. 'I'm curious as to why two homicide detectives are here investigating a suicide while the city is heating up like a pressure cooker.'

'It's what we do, Professor, we ask questions.'

'About brilliant young men who jump off buildings for no apparent reason?'

'There are always reasons people die, Professor, we just may not understand them.'

'Indeed,' he said.

'Something about his death beyond the obvious troubles you?' I asked.

He looked us both over for a moment.

'As it must you, given your presence here,' he said.

'What is it?' I asked.

He considered for a moment. 'The intellectual inelegance of it?'

'The list of brilliant people who have killed themselves is a long one, Professor.'

He shook his head. 'It's not just that Terry was one of the most brilliant minds I have ever encountered teaching, he did nothing without first engaging in very serious internal debate. I can't imagine him taking his own life because I don't believe he wouldn't have been able to come up with a better solution.'

'Perhaps the problem he faced was unlike any other,' I said.

'I don't see it. It's a poorly thought out equation.'

'How well did you know him?'

'I knew him, but I wouldn't say well,' he answered.

'Tell me about Medusa.'

'It's a program from the Defense Department. In general we don't seek out money with strings attached to the military, but within certain parameters we will go after funding, and that was the case with Medusa.'

'And those parameters would be?'

'The ability to apply the results in fields beyond the source of the funding, in this case the military, or on another level.'

'How did Terry's work fit into this model?'

'A bit of both.'

'And what was it?'

'He was studying the common house fly,' Burnett said.

'More specifically, its nervous system, eye, and motor controls. It was potentially ground-breaking work.'

'I must have missed that quarter in science class, but what was he trying to do?'

'Have you ever tried to swat a fly out of the air?'

I nodded.

'The capacity of the fly's very simple nervous system doesn't fully explain its ability to avoid objects in flight. To put it simply, it can change direction before its system has fully recognized a threat. Terry called it the "trigger". He was trying to understand it in hopes of finding applications for its use.'

I looked at Harrison who smiled.

'I can see how this would be interesting to the military. A plane or a missile that had that capability would be very useful,' Dylan said.

Burnett nodded. 'Terry hoped he would find applications even for individuals.'

'Reacting to a threat even before you become cognizant of it?' Harrison said.

Burnett nodded. 'Exactly. Its possible uses go far beyond just military designs. He talked about the potential for it to work even at the cellular level, giving the body the ability to detect a threat such as cancer before the immune system is capable of identifying it. You can imagine the uses.'

'Yes,' I said, inwardly resisting the urge to move my hand to my breast. 'Had you noticed any changes in Terry lately?' I asked.

'Changes?'

'His mood, his focus. Something you had never seen in him before.'

'To notice something like that you would have to accept that such a thing as a normal state existed in Terry,' he said then paused and reflected on something. 'One time a few months ago he said something that didn't seem like the Terry I knew.'

'What was that?'

'He talked about a movie. It was the only time he had ever mentioned seeing one. I think he found them trivial, like a lot of modern popular culture. Do you remember the film *The Third Man*?'

I nodded.

'Joseph Cotton and Orson Welles,' Harrison said.

'Yes, that's it.'

'Post-war Vienna, wasn't it?' I said.

'Exactly. There's a scene in a Ferris wheel.'

'The cuckoo clock scene,' said Dylan.

'You remember it,' Burnett said.

'What did he say about it?' I asked.

'He said Orson Welles was right about all the little dots that were moving down below them – what would it matter if a few of them suddenly stopped moving?'

'Dots?' I asked, trying to remember the scene.

'People,' said Dylan. 'Welles was talking about how unimportant other lives were and that it wouldn't matter if a few of them weren't there.'

Burnett nodded. 'That was it, just that one comment.'

'But you remember it,' I said.

'Yes.'

'Why?'

'It was the only time I had ever heard Terry say something that so clearly marked him out as different from the rest of us mere mortals. The only time I ever thought he could be cruel.'

'But it never came up again?'

'No.'

'Did Terry keep an office on campus?'

'He had one but never used it.'

Harrison's phone rang and he excused himself and stepped away. I handed Burnett the picture of the girl.

'Did you ever see him with her?' I asked.

He looked at it for a long moment then handed it back to me. 'I don't think so, but I didn't see him much outside the lab.'

'Did he ever mention another student who he may have shared his unique world view with?'

'Not that I recall. Terry and most of those who reach this level of success are very driven and independent. It's a very competitive world.'

'So he had no friends?'

'Not that I knew of.' He handed back the picture of the girl. 'Maybe you should talk to her.'

'Are any of the other students doing research in the Jackson Center British?'

'No,' he said.

'Would Terry ever have had contact with the people who managed the research money funding his work?'

'I can't think of any reason he would.'

'In particular a man named Jim O'Brien?'

It took him a moment to place the name.

'Of Beckwith, Myers and Dunne?'

'Yes.'

'No,' he said. 'The students working on grants are only a part of the application process to obtain funding. Once it's secured, the administration takes over.'

'But you know O'Brien's name.'

'I believe I met him at a party given by one of the school's trustees. Why do you ask?'

'He was murdered last night,' I said.

He silently mouthed the word murder and immediately understood why I was here.

'You believe there's a connection to Terry?' he asked.

'Yes,' I said.

'In what way?' he asked.

'That's what we're trying to understand.'

Harrison walked back over, slipping his phone into his pocket. I handed Burnett one of my cards.

'If you remember anything about Terry or things he may have said or people he mentioned, please call me.'

Burnett nodded. 'Lieutenant, if the Medusa Program or anything else here in the Jackson Center is connected to this, and students are at risk, I need to know.'

'Of course. One other thing, Professor. Do you know if Terry was interested in languages?'

'Languages? I'm afraid I don't understand.'

'We found a notebook in his apartment that contained what appeared to be a dictionary for a language that he had created.'

He thought about what I had just told him and then smiled.

'Fascinating,' he said.

'What makes you smile?' I asked.

'Terry was the singularly least verbal person I have ever known. A casual observer might think he was nearly mute.'

We started back across campus to our squad, mulling over the irony.

'What was the call?' I asked Harrison.

'Zara King's humanities professor,' Harrison said. 'According to her, the reason she left had everything to do with another student she was in a relationship with.'

'Did she know Terry Pullian's name?'

'No.'

'Was there a break-up?'

'All she knew was that something had happened that deeply troubled Zara,' Dylan said.

'Troubled in what way?'

'According to Professor Little, Zara left school out of fear.'

'Of what?'

'It wasn't her academic work, according to Little, she was an enormously talented student. She was planning on doing postgraduate work in how language contributes to breakdown in failed social orders or states.'

'Language?' I asked.

Dylan nodded. 'There's that word again.'

'Why am I thinking of the dictionary we found in Pullian's?'

'For the same reason I am, even if I don't know what it

is. Little gave me King's address. It's in south Pas, although she wasn't sure if it was current.'

We walked around the corner of the library tower and I stopped.

'I don't think we're going to need it,' I said.

At the small memorial where Terry Pullian had died, a young woman was crouched on her knees, her hands tightly held in her lap. I reached into my pocket and slipped out the snapshot of Pullian and the girl.

'She's dyed her hair again,' I said.

eleven

Harrison hung back as I walked up to the small memorial and stopped a few feet from the girl. Zara glanced sideways without seeing then started to get to her feet. She was slight in build. Her nails were covered with purple polish that appeared to have been nervously chewed. Under the pale skin on her arms, I could see the faint blue lines of veins.

'Did you know him very well?' I said.

She turned in surprise toward me. Her long red hair had been cut short and dyed black. On the bottom rim of her sunglasses a tear hung. She quickly shook her head and started to walk away.

'Miss King?' I said.

She stopped in mid-stride and her left hand moved across her midsection as if she was trying to shield herself from a blow. Under the cover of her glasses I could just see her eyes darting left and right, looking for an escape route. She reminded me of a nervous deer about to take flight.

'You are Zara King, aren't you?' I asked.

She started to shake her head.

'I'm with the police, my name is Lieutenant Delillo. I need to talk to you.'

'I think you have the wrong person,' she said.

'No, I don't think I do,' I said.

Her hand wound into a tight fist.

'I have to go,' she said.

'Zara, I wasn't asking to talk to you,' I said. 'I need your help.'

She glanced nervously around, her eyes stopping on Harrison.

'He's with me,' I said.

Her eyes found the badge on my waistband and then she looked back down at the burning candles.

'Not here,' she said.

'Where?' I asked.

She looked nervously around at the other buildings and the people walking by.

'Anywhere but here.'

I nodded. 'Somewhere safe,' I said.

Another tear slipped from the frame of her glasses and slid down her cheek, and then she looked up at the top of the library tower.

'Where would that be?' she asked.

We walked Zara to our squad and then drove away from campus until she stopped looking over her shoulder to make sure that we weren't being followed. On a side street a few miles from campus we parked in the shade of a large magnolia tree. Zara stepped out and removed a cigarette from her purse, lit it and took several quick drags.

Harrison and I got out and I leaned back against the door of the squad.

'Is it true that Terry jumped?' she asked.

'Yes,' I said.

Zara shook her head then took another drag on the smoke.

'Bullshit,' she said softly.

'Why do you say that?' I asked.

'Because he just wouldn't.'

'What I know is that Terry took the stairs all the way to the top of the building during a blackout, broke on to the roof and then ran full speed across the top of the building and off into the air. Why do you think he would do something like that?'

She shook her head. 'I don't know. You're the cop.'

'But I didn't know him, you did.'

She smiled sarcastically. 'Know him? Boy, you aren't even close.'

'You did have a relationship with him?' I asked.

'That would depend on how you define relationship.'

'You keep a toothbrush at his apartment,' Harrison said.

She nodded. 'Right next to number seven.'

'And you were in love with him,' I said.

She took a deep breath then tossed the cigarette on to the ground and snuffed it out with her sneaker.

'I don't know. Doesn't matter now, does it?'

'The relationship ended and you quit school,' I said.

She reached into her bag and took out another cigarette.

'What were you afraid of, Zara?'

She put the cigarette up to her lips. Her fingers were trembling.

'The dark,' she said.

Dylan glanced at me.

'Why do you say that?' I asked.

'Terry changed.'

'What do you mean? How?'

'He thought he could literally change the world. Other people talk about it, but he actually believed it.'

'But something altered that belief?'

She nodded.

'What?'

Zara took a deep breath, took off her sunglasses and rubbed her light blue eyes. They were red from tears, and the circles under them suggested she hadn't had a full night's sleep for a long time.

'What changed him?' I asked again.

'He met someone smarter than him.'

'And that changed him?' I said.

She nodded. 'You have to understand, Terry literally believed he was the smartest person on the planet. Adjusting that premise rocked everything about his world.'

'Do you know who it was?' I asked.

'No.'

'He never mentioned a name?' said Dylan.

She shook her head.

'He never talked about this other person in any context?' he asked.

'He talked about this voice that was unlike any he had

ever heard. That it had brought a clarity to the world that he had been missing.'

'How did it change him?' I asked.

'He began to see people differently.'

'How so?'

'I think he began to see them . . . us, with contempt,' Zara said.

'For what reason? Anything in particular?'

'Everything.'

'We found a notebook in his apartment. It looks like a dictionary but it's a language we had never seen.'

My knowledge of the dictionary clearly surprised her.

'You found that?'

I nodded. 'Was that part of this change in him?'

'No, that was just part of his life when he still believed that there was something good about the world.'

'Tell me about the dictionary,' I said.

'I had what I thought was a really brilliant premise for my senior thesis, that the societies that have survived unchanged through the world's development, those that haven't destroyed themselves, have done so because they don't have in their language the words that could tear the social fabric apart. I was thinking primarily of aboriginal groups. The rationale being how can you have hate, or conflict, if there are no words for it.'

'How did the dictionary fit into it?'

'Terry said rather than study something like that, why not just create a new language and save the world. I said it was impossible. So he did it in less than a week – an entirely new language with not one word for violence or anger. I always knew Terry was brilliant but it was then I realized that I would never be on the same level as him. It was right after that, that things began to change.'

'And that frightened you?'

'Not at first, but as time moved on it did,' Zara said.

'How?'

'It began by his dismissing my ideas about language and violence. He began to take on this view that violence was necessary.'

'Necessary?'

'As a means of change. It was all conceptual at that point. A kind of Übermensch worldview, though it wasn't about race, it was about intelligence. He once told me my premise about violence was all wrong. That the only reason those societies that didn't use these words as part of their language was because they were less evolved, stagnant and stupid.'

She reached into her bag to retrieve a cigarette, but the pack was empty when she pulled it out. She crumpled it in frustration and stuffed it back in her bag.

'I had never heard him use the word stupid. I got the impression he was talking about . . . the rest of us.'

'Did he ever act violently towards you?' I asked.

She took a breath as if to calm herself. 'No, I don't think he knew how to be violent, he hadn't figured that part of it out yet. But he could be violent with his words, he could dissect your thoughts, your feelings, he could reduce everything you believed in or held in your heart to nothing. It was as if he was beginning to despise the rest of the world.'

'And you think this change was because of this other person?'

'I don't think it was because of him, I know it,' she said. 'Terry's heart was good, I think he just got confused.'

'Did he ever talk about a movie?' I asked.

'Orson Welles,' she said.

I nodded.

'It was probably the only movie he ever saw,' she said. 'I think this other person turned him on to it.'

'You said you're afraid of the dark. What did you mean by that?'

'In one of the last conversations I had with him before I left school he called the world a place full of primitives who were afraid of the dark, corrupt and of no use to anyone. He told me to hide.'

'No use?'

'I might be wrong about this, but I think they were planning on killing someone,' she said. 'They may have already done it, I'm not sure. His discussions were never specific, they were always in the abstract like he was talking about an equation.'

'When was this?' I asked.

'April, that's when I left school.'

'Tell me what you know of this other person. Anything might be helpful.'

'I think he followed me once when I left Terry's apartment and was walking across campus.'

'Did you see him?'

She shook her head. 'Not in the way I think you mean,

I couldn't identify him. He was just a figure in the darkness watching me walk. It was creepy.'

'Did he follow you again?'

'I moved after that and I haven't told anyone my new address.' She thought for a moment and then found a memory she had forgotten. 'Terry once referred to someone he called the B. I don't know for certain, but I think it was him.'

'The B, like they went together? I asked.

She nodded.

'Could he have been a student?'

'Maybe, I don't know where else Terry could have met him. It's a pretty insular world on campus,' she said.

'Did he ever mention the name Jim O'Brien?'

She thought for a moment and shook her head.

'When was the last time you talked to Terry?'

'Yesterday.'

She reached up and took off her sunglasses again, as her eyes grew moist with tears.

'What did he say?'

'He said he was wrong and he was sorry and hung up.'

'Just that, nothing more?' I asked.

She shook her head.

'Did his voice sound different?'

Zara nodded. 'He sounded like the Terry I fell in love with.' She looked off in the direction of honking car horns. 'Terry wasn't alone on that roof, was he?' she said.

'No, I don't think he was.'

'So he was killed.'

'I don't believe he went off the roof voluntarily,' I said.

She took a short breath.

'Do you feel safe where you are now?' I asked.

'I think I know what happened to Terry.'

'What do you mean?' I asked.

'My apartment's on the fourth floor,' said Zara. 'Last night sitting in the dark, I thought he was coming for me.'

'The person Terry called B?' I asked and she nodded.

'I stayed awake, staring at the door, waiting for the sound of footsteps. I had it all planned. I was going to jump out the window if that door opened. I think Terry must have made a similar decision when he jumped.' She shivered as if she were cold and shook her head. 'There's no place to hide when it's dark everywhere.'

Overhead a police helicopter went cruising past, the thump of its rotors startling Zara.

'I packed up my car this morning. I can't stay here one more goddamn second.'

'I want to know where you will be,' I said.

She wrote down her cell phone number and promised to call me when she got wherever she was going and then we watched her walk quickly away, her head constantly turning from side to side like a frightened deer looking for cover.

'Übermensch,' Dylan said. 'It seems Pullian began to have doubts about the nature of his superiority.'

'His killer didn't,' I said. 'He murdered Jim O'Brien out of sport. He gave no more thought to killing him than a fox would a rabbit and then he chased Pullian off a ten-story building, watched him disappear over the edge into the darkness.'

'And when he was done, there was no one left who could identify him.'

'He's not done.'

'You think there'll be more?' Harrison said.

'Yes,' I answered.

'Because he can't stop himself?'

I shook my head. 'There's a meaning to these deaths, this isn't about homicidal lust. There's something going on here that we don't understand yet.'

'Something that connects a stockbroker with a genius?'

I nodded. 'Check with other agencies for any open homicides they have from April,' I said. 'We'll see if Zara's right that they killed before.'

'The B,' Harrison said. 'If the accent on the phone is real, he could have been calling him a Brit.'

'It could also mean a couple hundred other things. Check with Greer; see if the letter matches names of students from the UK. Past and present.'

My phone rang and I slipped it out. I recognized the number as the doctor's office. I resisted the urge to throw the phone under the wheels of a passing car and picked up. It was one of the nurses from the clinic.

'The full team took a look at your test results from yesterday and they thought it would be good to move up your biopsy if the time became available.'

'Team?' I asked.

'Every test is screened by the full team of physicians, not just your own,' she said. 'It's the standard procedure, nothing to be alarmed at.'

The sound of her voice reminded me of a gym teacher

named Miss Munson I had in high school who spent most of her time trying to sell her students on the one thing they were desperate to lose, virginity.

'Does this mean they've decided the suspect's gun pointed at me is loaded?' I asked.

There was a long silence on the other end as I imagined she tried to understand what I had just said.

'I'm sorry, I think I misheard you.'

'No you didn't,' I said.

'We have an open appointment at two o'clock tomorrow if you want to take advantage of it.'

'When do you need to know?' I asked.

'Now,' she answered. 'Would you like the appointment?' she repeated.

'Well, I'm expecting another dead body tonight so that may complicate my schedule,' I said, which only lengthened the silence on the other end.

'It's a simple procedure called a CNB. A needle will be used to extract a sample which can be tissue or fluid or both. There's no incision, won't leave so much as a pinprick.'

I looked down the street to where Zara had been walking – she was gone.

'Simple?' I said.

'Yes.'

'Well, I guess you would be a better judge of that than I would,' I said.

'With the paperwork, plan on being in the office for about forty-five minutes.'

'Fine,' I said and hung up.

I glanced at Dylan and then walked over to the squad

and got inside. He moved around to the driver's side and slipped in behind the wheel, but made no move to turn on the engine.

'I have a doctor's appointment from two to three tomorrow,' I said. 'It's nothing,' I added for no other reason than to cement in Dylan's mind that I was being less than candid.

'Something simple?' he said.

'Yes,' I said.

'Would this have something to do with what you're trying to work out?'

I looked at Dylan and heard the words roaring in my head that I couldn't say. I might have cancer, biopsy, I could lose a breast. I'm frightened.

'Stop being a detective,' I said.

'You're making it very difficult.'

'We know Terry Pullian was murdered but we can't prove it,' I said, changing the subject. 'We know his killer must have a face and a name, and that come nightfall he'll very likely kill again and we may be powerless to stop him. And we know that when we finally walk away from this life, we'll be no closer to understanding a mind like his than we were the first day on the job.' I looked at Dylan. 'When was the last time anything was simple?' I asked.

'I can't remember,' he said, his eyes lingering on me for a moment and then looking away. 'But that isn't really up to me, is it?' he said, then turned over the engine and started back towards headquarters.

twelve

Chief Chavez and Agent Utley of the FBI's behavioral analysis unit were waiting in the conference room when we walked back in. I had worked with Utley before on other cases, he had helped us track down the man who tried to kill Chavez. His rail-thin appearance and dark penetrating eyes always gave me the impression that he could slip in and out of the troubled minds he pursued with the same ease that a nighthawk sweeps up insects as it dips and dives at dusk. If what we were looking at was a serial killer at work then Utley gave us insight and access to information that only the FBI could produce.

The files on the O'Brien and Pullian deaths, along with crime scene photos, were open on the table in front of him and since I had not called him in, I could only assume he had information that I didn't.

'Do you have anything new to add to what's here?' Utley asked.

I took a seat across from him and picked up the photograph of Terry Pullian's broken body.

'There's little doubt that Pullian was chased off that

rooftop by the same man who killed Jim O'Brien. It's also clear that prior to becoming a target, Pullian may have become a partner in the planning of O'Brien's death and possibly took part in another killing sometime within the last few months.'

'Why?' Chavez asked.

'It was an intellectual exercise,' I answered.

'Intellectual?' Chavez said, barely concealing his disgust.

I nodded. 'The man we're looking for isn't your standard serial killer, if indeed that's what he is. What he's doing has more in common with a science experiment than anything else. Pullian found in the experiment a thread that had run through his entire life.'

'What thread?'

'That he was so much smarter than virtually everyone else around him that he began to see himself as different.'

'Smarter?' Chavez said. 'So naturally you start whacking people because we bore them.'

'Then Pullian met someone who thought the same. They weren't going after just anyone.'

'Of course that would be too easy,' Chavez said.

'If this is a serial killing, then at its foundation is a kind of moral superiority over those they choose to kill. My guess is that the victims somehow offended their sense of decency, whatever that would be for two killers. O'Brien was apparently a thief. He may have been chosen because of that or because he wasn't a big enough thief.'

'You said "if" this is a serial killing. What's the other possibility?'

'It could be exactly as it appears, but it could also be kind of a stage play at work to mask what is really behind the killing.'

Chavez turned to Utley. 'Do you agree with that?'

'I don't know enough to answer that yet,' he said.

'What happened with Pullian?' Chavez asked.

'Pullian wasn't a murderer at heart. As smart as he was, he had little emotional maturity. For the first time in his life he met someone who was more brilliant than he was. He followed along out of intellectual curiosity; perhaps he was a part of the plan to kill O'Neil, perhaps he wasn't. What does seem clear is that when the killing began, he became scared, and was murdered.'

'And his killer, who is he?' Chavez asked.

'It's possible he's a student at Caltech or a former student. He certainly is highly educated, possibly British. Beyond that, I'm no closer than when we began. I don't even have as much as a description.'

'You may be a little closer than that,' Utley said.

I looked at him. 'You have something?' I asked.

Utley leaned back into his chair and then reached down into a briefcase open on the floor, withdrew a manila file and placed it on the table in front of him.

'When I received your files on the case I ran all the information through the system.'

'You got a hit?'

'Not exactly. None of what I'm going to show you officially exists. The case file from which this comes is sealed. If, and I stress the word "if", an arrest is made, none of this information can be used to build a case.'

I nodded in agreement. 'What do you have?'

Utley opened the file and slid a crime scene photograph across the table.

'That's the body of an eight-year-old boy named Steven Miller who was murdered in a London suburb eighteen years ago. He was strangled and then stabbed a hundred times.'

'Exactly a hundred?' I asked and Utley nodded.

'His body was then put inside a plastic garbage bag and left on the side of the road to be picked up by garbage collectors.'

Utley removed another picture and handed it across.

'This was drawn on the kid's locker at school a week before he was killed.'

I looked at the picture for a moment then handed it to Harrison.

'Son of a bitch, an eye,' he said.

'It's about six inches across,' Utley said.

'It's not exact, but it's similar to the one we found in the taco restaurant,' I said.

Utley nodded. 'A week later the boy was dead and a week after that an arrest was made.'

He slipped another picture out and gave it to me.

'He lived one block from his victim, his name was Richard Shelton, he was nine years old.'

I looked at the photograph of the boy. It looked more like the kind of class picture you would get from school instead of a mugshot. He was looking directly into the camera with a wry smile on his face as if he had just aced a test instead of butchered another boy with a knife.

'When asked why he murdered his neighbor, he replied, 'Because he bored me." Being under the age limit of ten when he could have been prosecuted for murder, he was remanded to juvenile authorities until he turned eighteen, at which time he was declared fully rehabilitated and released, given a new identity, his records sealed, and set free into the world. While in custody he completed his high school studies when he was thirteen and a college equivalent by fifteen. They had no mechanism for him to do postgraduate work within the juvenile justice system.'

'In other words he's a genius?' I asked.

'Certifiable,' said Utley.

I held up the photograph of the eye.

'What did he say about this?' I asked.

'He said he had done it so Steven Miller would know he was watching him.'

'It wouldn't be the first time a killer uses the image of an eye. It's full of metaphors,' I said.

'I agree,' Utley said.

'So what else drew your attention?' I asked.

'Scotland Yard had been quietly keeping track of him. About a year ago Shelton vanished. It's their guess that he may have obtained another identity and left the country, though they have no proof.'

'What did he do for the seven or eight years he was out and about in England?' I asked.

'He went to Oxford University for two years, abruptly left, then drifted from one job to another. A teacher, a night clerk at a hotel, he even applied to become a policeman and got several weeks into training before his identity became known and he was forced out.'

Chavez walked over behind me and picked up the mugshot of Shelton. 'A nine-year-old killer.'

Utley nodded. 'Who never once expressed remorse for the murder.'

'What of his parents?' Chavez asked.

'Good middle-class members of the community, they ran a small store. No record of abuse in the family, no problems with alcohol or drugs. They're both deceased now.'

'There's more to this, isn't there?' I said.

Utley reached into the file and removed one more photograph.

'When I didn't get any more of a connection than the eye you found at the taco place, I expanded the search to include any outstanding homicides.'

'You got a hit on something?' I said and Utley nodded.

'Two months ago the body of a homeless man was found in the LA River channel by Long Beach Police. The victim was twenty-three and had a history of drug abuse and had lived on the streets for many years. He had been strangled and stabbed a hundred times, not ninety-nine, not a hundred and one. The cause of death was exactly the same as Steven Miller.'

I picked up the picture of the Long Beach victim. His dull half-open eyes stared up. It was not hard to imagine that the last thing he saw in this world was horrifying even to someone who had lived such a troubled life.

'It's possible that Shelton has once again become bored,' Utley said.

'I don't understand,' Chavez said. 'A homeless man in Long Beach. What's the connection to either of our victims?'

In the corner of the photograph something lying near the body caught my eye. It was a piece of paper or cardboard that was white with a red stripe or band across it. I handed it over to Harrison.

'What does that look like to you?'

Harrison studied it for a moment.

'A box of fried chicken. It could be the trial run killing that Zara talked about,' he said.

'Trial run?' Chavez asked.

I nodded. 'Terry Pullian's girlfriend had concerns that something like this was being planned. Call it a test our killer was putting Pullian through.'

'Jesus,' Chavez said.

'Do you have the autopsy report with you?' I asked Utley.

'No, but I have a pretty clear recollection of it,' he replied.

'Did his stomach contain barely digested fried chicken?'

He thought for a moment and then nodded. 'How did you know that?'

'A wild guess,' Harrison said.

'You have no name or photographs of him as an adult?' I asked Utley.

He shook his head. 'The sealing of his records is absolute. In the court's view the person he became when he was released is unrelated to who he was as a child. To reveal that information would be a prosecutable crime.'

'Even with evidence that suggests it's possible he has committed another crime?'

'I presented the evidence to Scotland Yard and they said there was nothing they could do, even if it was conclusive, which they didn't feel this was. It's out of their hands.'

Chavez walked around the table and then leaned on the back of a chair and looked at the photographs on the table.

'How the hell do you create child psychopaths? Where do they come from? What have we so broken in society that this is what happens to our children?'

Utley shook his head. 'It would be nice to blame something within contemporary society, but it doesn't hold. In eighteen seventy-four a fourteen-year-old boy in Massachusetts was convicted of mutilating a four year old and a ten year old. He hid one body in a marsh, the other in a trash heap. And you can just imagine what kind of horrors the Dark Ages must have produced.'

'That's a pleasant thought,' Chavez said and then sat down. 'So who's the next victim?'

'I can't help you there,' Utley said. 'I'm having some images generated of Shelton, ageing his childhood photographs to show what he may look like as an adult. They may prove helpful, but they're just as likely not to. Beyond that I have nothing constructive.'

The Chief looked over to me.

'The next victim is related in some way to the car in the photograph,' I said. 'Traver's working on tracking down owners of Aston Martin DB5s, but the power outages are making it difficult to access DMV records.'

'There's nothing else?' Chavez asked.

I started to shake my head.

'There is something,' Harrison said and looked over to me. 'Do you want to tell them or should I?'

'Tell what?' the Chief asked.

I hesitated.

'What is it, Alex?' he asked.

'I'm not sure this is anything to really be concerned about.'

'Then there's no reason to not tell me.'

'According to Jim O'Brien's wife, when she was tied to the bed, her husband's killer told her that I inspired him.'

'Inspire?' Chavez said and I nodded.

'It's not entirely clear what that means,' I said.

Utley looked at me for a moment and then shook his head. 'I'm not sure I agree with that assessment.'

'I thought you might not.'

'Someone want to fill me in here?' Chavez said.

I looked at Utley. 'I'd like to hear what you think.'

'If this is actually true, at some point Shelton, if that's who we're looking for, is going to want to test himself against you.'

'Test?' Chavez asked. 'What do you mean test?'

'He's saying that when Shelton has tired of his list of victims, he's going to come after me.'

Chavez looked at me for a moment then over to Utley who nodded in agreement.

'That may be our best chance of catching him,' I said. 'All his other victims will be unaware of the danger they're in. We're in a position of advantage when that time comes.'

'Advantage? By dangling you over the side like a piece

of bait on a hook?' Chavez said.

'I hadn't visualized the metaphor quite like that, but yeah, that sums it up.'

'This is crazy.'

I nodded. 'Life does have a way of throwing unexpected things in your path.'

Chavez sat back in the chair, trying to get his mind around what I had just told him.

'What do we do about this?' he said softly.

'Nothing,' I said.

He stared at me. 'Perhaps someone else would like to venture an opinion?' He looked around the room.

'I have to agree,' Utley said.

Chavez turned to Harrison. 'Would you like to be the voice of reason here?'

Harrison looked at me and shook his head. Chavez quickly stood up from the table.

'I'm pulling you off the case,' he said.

'You do that, you're just putting someone else in danger. Who are you going to pick? Harrison, Traver, some uniform one year on the job whose only experience is writing tickets and putting up yellow tape around a crime scene? This isn't our choice, it's his.'

His gaze moved beyond the walls of the room, his eyes lost in concentration as he tried to find an argument against it.

'We're not at that point yet,' I said. 'He has more victims before he gets to me. We have time.'

'How will you know when that point comes?' Chavez said.

I looked over to Utley.

'You want to answer that?' I said.

'My guess is he'll tell you,' Utley said.

'Your guess?' said Chavez. 'And what if you're wrong about it?' He turned to me. 'What if he surprises you? What happens then?'

'The same thing that happens every time we've ever gone out on a call,' I said.

Chavez drew a deep breath and then looked at Harrison. 'You don't leave her side, not for one second until this is over.'

Harrison nodded.

'Well, just make sure he doesn't surprise you,' Chavez said and walked over to the door. 'I have a meeting with the Mayor about contingency plans for when night falls.' He opened the door and then looked at me. 'Could I have a word with you?'

I got up from the table and went to the door. The Chief stepped out of the conference room and I followed. We walked toward his office down the hallway. As he reached the door to his office, he stopped.

'The money you found in O'Brien's freezer, is that of any help?'

I shook my head. 'Beckwith, Myers and Dunne are doing their best to make sure we don't connect it to the firm. We're going through O'Brien's computers, trying to find any connection we can to Pullian, the car, Caltech or the money, but so far we've come up with nothing.'

'But you think there is a connection.'

'There's a common thread running through this, we just haven't found it yet.'

He took hold of the handle to his office door but hesitated.

'Are you all right?' he asked. His big dark eyes held on me and for a moment I wondered if somehow they saw the lump concealed inside me.

'I'm fine,' I said.

'And my goddaughter?' he asked.

'Lacy's fine. She takes after her godfather,' I said. 'She likes to tell me what I'm doing wrong with my life.'

He smiled and his big brown eyes locked on to mine and then looked out into the squad room.

'You think there's something to this connection of Utley's – the boy in England?'

'He's not a boy any more.'

'No.'

'The use of the eye, the death of the transient. The fact that he is among a relatively few people on the planet who are actually smarter than Terry Pullian. Yes, I think it's possible.'

He was silent for a moment as he digested the information.

'You expect there to be another victim tonight, don't you?' he said.

I nodded and he held on to the thought for a second as if trying to find another answer.

'Then it will be a long night,' he said, and turned and walked into his office.

thirteen

The blackouts rolled across southern California through the afternoon from one city to another. As the clock approached rush hour, Pasadena had been in and out of power half a dozen times, each one a little longer than the outage preceding it, each one raising the level of calls coming into dispatch.

I attempted to sleep for a few hours on the couch in my office but found little rest. In the half twilight of semi-consciousness, I tried working the facts, looking for the thread of information that would connect events, but instead of finding any clarity, all that stood out were the terrible images that Shelton, if he was our killer, had left behind like a fever dream.

'Alex,' said a voice and then a hand softly gripped my arm.

Harrison was kneeling next to the couch. I sat up, shaking off the haze of half sleep, and then looked out the window. The sky was the color of a pale cantaloupe, the setting sun reflected off the slopes of the San Gabriels. I glanced at my watch. It was nearly seven thirty; the sun would be down in twenty minutes.

'Do you have something?' I asked.

Harrison nodded. 'Traver found three cars. One's in a museum collection, another's owned by a real estate developer.'

'And the third?' I asked.

'A professor at Caltech.'

I wasn't certain I had heard him correctly.

'Caltech? You sure?'

Harrison nodded. 'He lives in Sierra Madre above Hillcrest. Traver's checking out the real estate developer.'

I got up from the couch and started for the door.

'What do you know about him?'

'His name's Lawrence Simms. He runs something called the Laboratory of Experimental Finance. Very cutting-edge economics theory, from what I've been able to gather.'

'Is there any connection to Pullian?'

Harrison shook his head. 'Not that I've been able to find, at least not direct.'

We started down the steps toward the parking lot.

'Not direct. What does that mean?' I asked.

We stepped through the doors and outside into the parking lot. The heat felt like a pair of warm hands closing around you and gently pressing against your face.

'There is a connection to O'Brien,' Harrison said.

'And that is?'

'Up until six months ago Simms was on the board of Beckwith, Myers and Dunne.'

'What happened six months ago?' I asked as we reached the squad.

'Neither Beckwith nor Dunne have returned my calls. But it gets more interesting than that.'

I began to open the door but stopped.

'How?'

'According to his bio, before coming to Caltech two years ago, Simms taught at Oxford.'

'You're suggesting a possible connection to Shelton?' I said.

'Well, I know how you hate coincidence.'

I looked at him in surprise, then over toward the mountains. The line of shadow from the setting sun was beginning to creep up the slopes.

'Do you know if Simms is on campus this summer?'

'According to Dean of Students Greer he's not teaching any classes but is working with some graduate students on a research project.'

'Did you call him?' I asked.

'Yeah. I got the machine, the same with his office at Caltech. I put a call into Monrovia PD to get a squad at his house. They said they would try if one became available but they made no promises. Where d'you want to go first?'

On a good day it was a twenty-minute drive to Monrovia, though what passes for a good day in southern California now seemed difficult to remember and that was with working traffic lights.

'He won't be at campus with no power, let's try his house.'

*

Drivers trying to avoid the chaos of no traffic lights on city streets had turned the 210 freeway into a parking lot. Working our way across town on side streets with the flashers lit up and cycling the siren now and then, it was nearly an hour before we reached Monrovia.

A dark column of smoke from a fire rose into the still air of twilight as we turned up into the foothills where Simms lived.

'No lights here either,' Harrison said, looking up toward the dark neighborhoods that stretched to the base of the San Gabriels.

Four blocks into the foothills we passed the burning house; it had been reduced to little more than a collection of blackened sticks with ribbons of flame dancing across the surfaces. Gawkers lined the sidewalk across the street. A stream of water, covered in light grey ash, snaked its way downhill past the lengths of hose strung across the side-walk and street. On the brown lawn of the destroyed house a fireman stood next to a yellow tarp with the distinct outline of a body underneath. Even with the air conditioning going in the car, the sharp bite of smoke could be tasted with each breath.

'You forget sometimes,' Harrison said as we drove by.

I looked at the crowd watching from the other side of the street and nodded. A man in his thirties had his arm around a woman with short black hair who held a Kleenex up to her face.

'You forget that real life continues?' I said.

'That people go to work and get sick and fall in and out of love and laugh and cry, and die for the smallest of reasons, or none at all, while we chase something that is just as oblivious of them.'

The young woman holding the Kleenex looked in my direction and followed us for a moment until we moved away from the house.

'It even happens to us,' I said.

The smell of fire began to drift away. By the time we stopped outside Simms's address the sun had been down for nearly twenty minutes and the light was failing rapidly. We sat for a moment sizing up the house. Nothing was visible through the windows.

'No candlelight or lanterns, no car in the driveway,' Harrison said. A young girl walking a Dalmatian was the only thing in sight. 'How does a college professor own a car worth a couple hundred grand?'

'Experimental economics,' I said. I stepped out of the squad. 'Let's find out.'

Monrovia with its large lawns and front porches was built in an era when people still had time to take strolls after dinner and visit with neighbors. A concept so lost now that the street we were on almost had the make-believe feel of a set on a movie lot. Simms's house was a large craftsman-style building that sat on a rise a few steps up from street level. We crossed over and up to the front porch. The morning paper sat untouched at the base of the steps.

I stepped up on to the porch and knocked on the front door. There was no response from inside. Harrison went over to the front window to look in.

'Blinds are drawn.'

I knocked again and the result was the same. We stepped down off of the porch and over to the driveway that ran along the right side of the house. A large two-car garage sat behind the house next to the back yard. The overhead door was closed.

'Should be a side door,' Harrison said and walked around to find it.

I turned and looked at the back yard and the house. There was a small lap pool in the yard and patio next to a set of French doors that led into the house. I started to turn back toward the garage when I noticed an object in the water in the pool.

'There's a Toyota in there but no Aston Martin,' Harrison said, walking back from the side of the garage. 'A car cover's hanging on a hook next to the empty space. He must be driving it.'

'Or someone else is,' I said and stepped over to the edge of the pool. 'Can you tell what that is on the bottom of the pool?' I said.

Harrison walked over and peered into the dark water.

'Looks like it's stuck in the drain.'

A pool net lay on the grass on the other side. Harrison walked around, picked it up and slid it into the water and slipped the object on the bottom into the net and brought it up. As it cleared the surface I saw the dull eyes staring blankly into space.

'A cat,' said Harrison.

He lifted it over to the side of the pool and ran his hands over it.

'Don't appear to be any wounds on it,' he said.

I walked over to the set of French doors and looked into the darkened interior.

'There's something inside here,' I said, reaching down and taking hold of the handle. The door was unlocked and I pushed it open. I took a few steps inside and stopped. The hot, still air seemed to resist my movement as if it had weight and mass. Harrison walked over and slipped out a small mag-light from the back of his belt and shined it across the room. It was a living room, expensively furnished in what looked like original mission-style furniture.

'Short of a body, what are we looking for?' Harrison said.

I shook my head. 'I don't know.'

I walked across the room to a coffee table. A large digital weighing scale sat on it. A fine dark dust covered the surface. I reached down and ran my fingers across the stainless steel of the scale's surface and then sniffed my fingers.

'What's that smell like to you?' I said, holding my hand out for Harrison to sniff.

'College,' he said.

'Dope,' I said.

'Like I said. High quality,' Harrison added.

'I think you had more fun in school than I did,' I said.

'Maybe we found out how he affords an Aston Martin.'

'Let's take a look around.'

The kitchen and dining room were off to the left. A hallway led off to the right. A center stairway led up to the bedrooms. We moved down the hallway past a bathroom and stopped at the first door and pushed it open.

'A study,' said Dylan.

He stepped in and shone the light around.

'Look,' he said, holding the light on a photograph hanging on the wall. 'Oxford.'

One wall of the room was lined with books. The desk was neatly arranged with several notebooks, loose papers and a laptop.

'No sign of violence, nothing out of place,' I said.

'No spray painting,' Harrison said.

I walked back out to the hallway and the adjacent door and pushed it open.

'I need your light.'

Dylan stepped over and raised the light into the room.

'Laboratory of experimental finance indeed,' I said.

The walls and floor of the room were lined with thick plastic. A stainless steel table sat in the middle of the room. Against the wall to the left was a plastic-wrapped bale of dope. Dylan walked over and examined it.

'Fifty pounds, give or take,' he said. 'If this is high-quality stuff, you're looking at a street value of four hundred grand.'

'I guess that answers the question of how a college professor buys James Bond's car,' I said.

'I don't imagine this is listed in any class syllabus.'

I walked over to the table. It was neatly arranged with plastic bags and ties and rubber bands for the packaging process.

'Bring your light over here,' I said.

Dylan stepped over and shined the light on the table. A fine layer of dust covered it.

'He was here,' I said.

'Shelton?'

I nodded.

'Why do you say that?'

'I don't know.' I moved toward the door. 'We need to check upstairs.'

We hurried down the hallway into the living room and then up the stairs. The air on the second floor was another ten degrees hotter. A bead of sweat slid down my neck on to the collar of my shirt. A bathroom was to the right of the landing; in the hallway to the left were three doors. I moved to the first one, pushed it open and Dylan raised his light into the room.

There were a dozen or more boxes on the floor against the far wall but no furniture. The second door was a linen closet containing a few sheets and towels. We stepped back out and Harrison raised the light toward the last door.

'If something happened, it happened in there,' Harrison said.

We moved to the door and I took hold of the handle and pushed it open. Dylan stepped past me and raised the light, moving it across the room. A bed was against the far wall between two windows. A closet was off to the left, a bathroom to the right. Dylan walked over to the bathroom, pushed the door open and moved the light across the interior.

'Nothing,' he said.

I walked over to the closet and opened the door. Something came moving out of the dark and I caught a glimpse of eyes reflecting the light of Harrison's flashlight as I jumped back. As I turned, it glanced off my shoulder and landed at my feet. The cat darted left through my legs and then ran out the door and was gone.

'That's why I'm a dog person,' I said, catching my breath. 'Or I would be if I had a life where you could have one.'

I stepped back to the closet and looked inside. 'Bring your light over here,' I said.

Harrison stepped over and pointed the light into the closet. Simms's clothes were neatly hung, all in specific groups, shirts, pants, jackets, etc., nothing out of place, just as you would expect of an economist, even a drug-dealing one.

'There's nothing here,' Harrison said.

'There's a dead cat in the pool.'

I turned and looked around the room.

'Something's not right here,' I said.

'You mean other than Simms having a second career?'

'If you had four hundred thousand dollars' worth of pot sitting in your house, would you leave the back door open?'

'Point taken.'

'Look at the bed,' I said.

Harrison shined the light on the bed.

'What about it?'

'Everything else in this room is in perfect order, except that.'

'It's been made,' Dylan said.

'Yes, but badly.'

'A guy making a bed badly is not unusual.'

'It would be for this man,' I said.

I walked over to the side of the bed, took hold of the bedspread and pulled it back.

'What do you make of that?' I said.

Dylan looked for a moment and shook his head.

'Those are knife cuts. Looks like rage,' Dylan said.

The fitted sheet was in tatters, repeatedly torn and cut with what must have been a large knife. I ran my hand across the surface of the sheet and shook my head.

'I'm not so sure.'

'You lost me.'

I reached down and pulled the fitted sheet back to reveal the mattress.

'Look at the wounds in the mattress,' I said.

Dylan took a step closer and then moved the light across the bed.

'They're all the same size,' Dylan said.

'If this was rage, then it was a controlled version of it. How many holes would you say there are?'

His eyes moved across the bed, doing a quick calculation.

'Son of a bitch.'

'There are a hundred, aren't there?' I said.

Dylan nodded.

'The images of the eyes, a hundred wounds, it's like a signature.'

'Shelton?'

'I'm not ready to say it's him, but no one else is stepping into the light.'

'You think he wants us to know it's him?'

I shook my head. 'If it's Shelton, I imagine he assumes

his ID is safe. But he still wants credit for his work. He can't help himself.'

'If we're right and Shelton is responsible, why didn't he murder O'Brien the same way as the others?'

'I don't know, but like everything this killer has done, it's done for a reason.' I looked back down at the bed. 'What don't you see here?'

Dylan studied the bed for a moment. 'There's no blood, no evidence of a struggle. So where's Simms?'

'Whatever is happening here, it's all connected with Caltech, Beckwith, Myers and Dunne, and perhaps even Oxford,' I said.

'His office on campus,' said Dylan.

'I think we better take a look,' I said and we started for the door.

fourteen

Traffic moving back into the city was lighter than that trying to get out. In the darkness of the blackout, the only lights were those of cars and a police helicopter's night sun moving through the empty sky, its beam searching the ground like a predator.

As Harrison drove us back to Pasadena, I called Utley.

'Delillo,' he said.

'How much do you know about Shelton's time at Oxford?' I asked.

'Just what I told you before. He spent almost three years there, then left.'

'Can you find out more?' I asked.

'You found something else that points the finger at him?'

'If not at him, at least in his general direction.'

'I can talk to my contact at the Yard, but whether he has more information or is able to share it I can't make any guarantees. What do you need to know?' Utley asked.

'Did anything happen at the school that prompted his leaving? Did he go of his own accord or was he asked to leave? I also need to know if there's any connection to a professor of economics named Lawrence Simms who taught there at the time. It would also be useful to know what was behind Simms's departure from the university.'

'It's six in the morning there now, this may take a few hours. I gather this is important,' he said.

'Wake your contact up,' I said.

'I'll call you as soon as I get something,' Utley said and hung up.

It took another half hour to reach the west side of the Caltech campus off Wilson. No students walked the commons. The sound of a radio drifted from some unseen source, but beyond that the campus was empty. Rumors surrounding the death of Pullian had no doubt spread amongst the few students present and kept them inside behind locked doors or else they had abandoned the campus entirely.

A few cars sat in the lot adjacent to Simms's building but there was no Aston Martin present. A security guard met us and walked us to the building that housed Simms's office. The guard looked to be about nineteen, his uniform a size too big for his thin frame. He wore the heavy utility belt of a cop, with a can of mace and a nightstick that from the sheen on its surface had never been slipped out of its ring on the belt.

As we rounded the corner to the entrance, the dark shape of the library tower rose up in front of us. On the grass, the candles for Pullian still flickered.

'Which side of the building is his office on?' I asked the guard.

He looked up and pointed. 'Right there, on the third floor. I'm not sure exactly which window is his.'

'Professor Simms would have a key to the building, wouldn't he?' I asked and the guard nodded.

'Yeah, but without lights, nobody has been inside—' He stopped and looked up toward the windows. 'I guess I'm wrong,' he said.

I looked up as the beam of a flashlight swept across the inside of one of the windows.

'Is that his office?' I asked.

He shrugged. 'Could be.'

'Open the door now,' I said.

The guard opened the entrance to the building and then started to walk inside.

'Give me the key to the office. I want you to wait here,' I said.

'I'm not sure I'm supposed to do that,' he said.

'For ten bucks an hour, trust me, that's exactly what you're supposed to do,' I said.

He reluctantly handed over the key. 'Actually I make nine bucks.'

'How many other entrances are there?' Harrison asked.

'There's one on each side of the building.'

'That's it?'

He started to nod then stopped. 'There's the tunnels, I suppose you could count those.'

I had heard that there was an extensive system of old steam tunnels that ran under the campus but had never been sure they were more than an urban legend.

'There's an entrance to them inside this building?' I asked.

'Yeah, there's one in all the older buildings. It's at the far end in a utility closet. There's a danger sign on the door.'

'How many stairways are there?'

'One at each end.'

'We should go,' Dylan said.

I looked back up at the windows to the office – they were dark. We turned and started inside.

'Where's his office in relation to the stairs?'

'It will be a few doors to the right . . . I don't remember exactly, but his name's on it. You want me to do something if someone comes out who's not supposed to be in there?' the guard asked.

I stopped and nodded. 'See what direction they go in, and then do nothing until you get a raise to ten dollars.'

Harrison and I stepped inside and quietly closed the door behind us. The floors of the building were polished marble or granite. The ceiling appeared to be twelve feet high or more. I took another step and the sound bounced down the length of the building.

'It's like an echo chamber in here,' Harrison said. 'No one is going to sneak out.'

The stairway at this end of the building was twenty feet ahead on the right. We walked over to it, stopped and listened for any movement above us and started up. As we rounded the first landing I heard the muffled click of a door shutting from somewhere above. We froze and waited for the sound of footsteps, but they didn't come.

Harrison reached down and slipped his pistol out of his speed holster and we moved up to the second floor and stopped. No sound came from down the dark length of the corridor so we continued up to the third-floor landing.

'Over there,' Harrison whispered, motioning toward the doors to the right. 'It would be one of those.'

There were no lights visible under any of the doors. I shined my light down the length of the corridor to the other end of the building.

'Nothing,' Dylan said.

We moved down the corridor to the offices and began checking the names on the doors. On the third door, Simms's name was stenciled in gold letters on the dark wood. I moved my light on to the handle. There were deep gouges in the door next to the jamb.

I slipped my weapon out, held it at my side and listened for movement on the other side of the door. Nothing.

I nodded to Harrison and he reached out, took hold of the handle and tested it.

'It's open,' he said softly.

I stepped back and then nodded, my grip tightening around the handle of my Glock. Dylan eased the door handle until the bolt cleared the jamb and then pushed it open. We raised our weapons and lights and swept the interior of the office.

'Do you see what I'm seeing?' Harrison said.

I nodded and stepped into the room, cleared the space behind the door and then holstered my weapon.

'Is this making sense to you?' Dylan asked.

'Not entirely,' I said.

I stepped over toward the desk. The room had been ransacked. Files were open, papers spread across the desk and floor, a connection to a computer had been unhooked.

'This isn't like Pullian's or O'Brien's,' Harrison said.

I moved the light around the room.

'No messages left behind, no eyes, nothing,' I said. 'Someone was looking for something here.'

'It doesn't feel like it would have been Shelton,' Dylan said. 'And why would Simms ransack his own office?'

I stepped around the desk.

'So who was it?' Harrison said.

'And what were they looking for?' I added.

I picked up some papers on the desk. 'These seem to be mostly class notes and student papers.'

Harrison looked around the floor under the desk.

'There's no hard drive. If there was a computer, it might have been a laptop. Maybe they were after that,' he said.

'Which still doesn't answer why,' I said.

The sound of a door closing followed by footsteps echoed out in the corridor. We rushed over to the door and I pointed my light down the hallway, just catching the blur of movement around the corner on to the stairway at the far end of the building.

'You take these stairs and block this entrance, I'll go to the other end,' I said as I started moving.

Harrison hesitated. 'I'm not leaving you on your own.'

'I have one mother already and she's more than enough for anyone,' I said. 'And you said it yourself, this isn't Shelton. Now shall we go or discuss it some more?'

Dylan nodded and I took off running down the hallway to the far end as Dylan headed down the other stairway. At the top of the stairs I stopped and listened for movement below. The footsteps abruptly halted as if they were listening for my movements, then they began descending again.

I rushed down the stairs, hesitating just long enough to be sure that the movement had continued down. I took the steps two at a time until I reached the ground floor and then I stepped out into the hallway. There was no movement anywhere, no sounds. I looked for Dylan at the far end of the building but there was no sign of his light. I turned and started moving along the wall toward the entrance at this end of the building. Past a restroom I stopped and shined my light on a door on the other side of the hallway. It had been opened and not fully closed.

I raised my weapon on the opening and crossed the hallway until I was close enough to take hold of the handle and then I yanked it open. A metal set of steps led down into the darkness. I glanced back down the hallway but there was still no sign of Dylan and then I angled the light down the stairs. On the landing at the bottom of the steps were a series of electrical circuit boxes but I couldn't see anything else.

I stepped in and started down. The metal of the stairs reverberated with each step I took. The air was cooler as I descended, the concrete walls almost felt cold in comparison to the heat of the rest of the building. At the bottom I swung around. The door into the tunnels, marked 'Danger', was there just as the guard had said.

I raised my weapon and approached it, the light searching for the smallest movement of the handle.

'Breathe,' I said silently to myself as I moved closer. I

took a slow deep breath but it was as if the air had been sucked out of the room.

I stopped a foot from the door. It was made of heavy metal with reinforced hinges. I leaned in and listened for movement on the other side but nothing penetrated its thickness. I slipped the light under my arm and then took hold of the handle and turned it until the latch cleared, then I pulled it open and raised my pistol into the darkness.

There was no reaction. I slipped the light from under my arm with my other hand and pointed it down the tunnel. At the limit of the beam's light the darkness seemed to go on into infinity.

I took a step inside. Bundles of wires were strung along the top of the wall where it met the ceiling. Derelict steam pipes still ran along the opposite wall. On the wall someone had drawn an arrow pointing into the tunnel, with the word 'Hades' written underneath it. I listened for a moment then started to turn back to the door when the sound of footsteps came out of the darkness. Someone was running away from me into the darkness, their footfalls echoing through the tunnel until it sounded like there were a dozen sets of feet.

I started after the sound, moving cautiously at first and then running as fast as I could, my light cutting a shaky hole into the darkness which seemed to have no end. A hundred feet, two hundred, I wasn't certain. With each step I took, the louder the voice in my head grew, telling me to stop and turn back.

I ran until I saw a junction where another tunnel

crossed. I slowed to a brisk walk. A few feet from the crossing, I stopped to catch my breath, then moved the light left and then right into the tunnels.

By the time I heard the movement coming out of the darkness from the right, it was too late to react. I tried raising my weapon but the blow caught me in the chest and knocked me backward. My face hit the side of the tunnel and then a blow struck me in the stomach. The air rushed out of my lungs, my knees buckled and I fell to the floor. I tried to raise the Glock but I had no control over my hand as I gasped for breath.

'I'm just doing my job,' said a voice and then I heard the sound of footsteps moving away.

I lay for a moment with my face on the cool cement, listening to the sound of the footsteps. I pressed myself up on to my knees and tried to force air into my lungs, but it was as if a hand was trying to smother me. I managed a small breath and then another and with each one, it was as if the fingers closed around my mouth began to loosen their grip.

My face throbbed from where I had struck the wall of the tunnel, my right breast felt like a match had been held to it. I took as deep a breath as the pain would allow then looked around to gather myself. The flashlight lay a few feet away, flickering on and off. My gun somehow had stayed in my hand. I crawled over to the light, picked it up and then slowly got back to my feet. The sound of the footsteps moving away into the distance abruptly stopped.

I took a few shaky steps over to the junction of the tunnels and listened, but the sound of the footsteps didn't return. They hadn't faded away into the distance; they had stopped as if in mid-stride.

My breath began to return, though the pain in my face and breast remained. I pointed the flickering light down the tunnel where my attacker had fled.

He had said something, the words were there, but they didn't make sense. *I'm doing my job*. What job? What the hell did that mean? Who was down here and if it wasn't Shelton, who was it? Simms? That made no more sense than it being Shelton. Think, what are you missing?

I took one look back down the tunnel, then slipped my cell phone out of its holder on my waistband and dialed Harrison.

'Alex, where are . . .'

The signal began to break up.

'I'm in the tunnels,' I said.

'Did . . . say . . .'

'I'm in the tunnels,' I repeated and then lost the signal altogether. I put the phone away and started down the second tunnel. The beam of the flashlight would flicker for a moment, go out and then come on again. The tunnel took on the feel of an amusement park sideshow, walls and darkness coming and going, leading me further into a house of mirrors.

In the flickering light I saw the junction of another tunnel ahead. As I reached it, the light gave out, plunging me into darkness. I pressed myself against the wall of the tunnel and raised my weapon toward the junction a few feet away.

Where had the footsteps gone? No door had opened

and closed. Why did he stop? I looked back in the direction I had come, resisting the instinct inside me that wanted to retreat back toward the safety of the building. I hesitated for another moment then started forward again.

In the darkness I heard what sounded like a breath, barely there, more like a memory of what a breath was. There was another and then nothing. They seemed close, in front of me rather than behind. I shook the flashlight and the beam flickered on and then off, but it was long enough for me to see the opposite wall. There was something there – or was there? I hit the light with the palm of my hand and it flickered back to life. I hadn't imagined it. A bloody handprint was smeared against the wall.

I moved the light on to the floor of the tunnel. Blood arched across the cement as if a bottle had been shaken and its contents sprayed about. I started to move and then the light flickered again and failed.

I hit it with my free hand, trying to retrieve the light, but it refused to work. Slowly I moved forward until my hand reached the opposite wall and I followed it into the junction with the other tunnel until my fingers slipped on the surface of the wall where more blood must have covered it.

I stopped, listened for a moment then took another step and felt the fingers of a hand press against my ankle. I jumped back and my foot slipped on more blood and I fell backward, hitting the floor hard on my left side. The flashlight slipped from my hand, bounced across the floor, came to rest against the opposite wall and came back on, the beam illuminating the figure spread out in front of me. I raised my weapon.

'Police, don't move,' I said.

There was no response. Not a breath, no movement, nothing. The hand that had touched my ankle lay motionless, twisted at an awkward angle over the head of the figure lying face up.

I got back to my feet and stepped over the pool of blood that had collected on the floor and retrieved the light. I went over to the body and started to reach down to check for a pulse, but stopped. A gaping wound had opened up the right side of his throat. The bright silver cords of tendons and the white edge of a vertebra were visible against the dark muscle tissue. His heart had pumped out blood at an enormous rate. From the blood pattern on the tunnel walls and floor I figured he had taken no more than a dozen steps before collapsing. He would have been dead within sixty seconds, if not less.

How long I had been on the floor after being knocked down I wasn't sure. Three, perhaps four minutes. It took another minute or two to reach the junction of the tunnels, which meant the man in front of me had been dead no more than five or six minutes. I pointed the light up and down both directions of the tunnel, listening for the sound of movement, but there was nothing. If his killer was still here, he was watching silently just beyond the limit of light.

My heart pounded against my chest. My head began to repeat *run, get out.*

'Work it,' I whispered silently, trying to focus.

I thought I heard movement and spun around, but there was nothing there.

'There's nothing to fear but everything,' I whispered. 'Now work it.'

I trained the light on the victim's face. He appeared to be in his forties, slightly overweight, dark brown hair, a thick mustache, and brown eyes that stared lifelessly into space. He was dressed in a long-sleeved black T-shirt and black pants.

If this was Simms, he wasn't what I expected, though what I expected I wasn't sure. But why had he said the words he did when he attacked me back up the tunnel? I knelt and carefully rolled his body just enough so I could slip his billfold out of his back pocket.

'Earl Moon,' said the name on his driver's license.

I looked back down at him. There was no wedding band on his finger.

'What the hell were you doing in Simms's office, Earl?'

In the opposite flap of the wallet were the usual credit cards, and another ID that wasn't usual, a private investigator's license. In the cash flap of the wallet were twenty-six dollars in bills and a number of his business cards. I removed one of the cards and read it.

'Moon and Wong Investigations, confidential, discreet.' I looked down at his body. 'What the hell were you up to?'

The throbbing pain in my face returned and I reached out to the wall and steadied myself. Footsteps became audible, moving fast down one of the tunnels. I stepped back to the junction, trying to determine where the sound was coming from, but the echoes made it confusing. The sound then stopped and the last footstep rolled down the tunnel from my left.

I raised the light and the Glock, but if I was right about the direction of the sound, it was beyond the limit of my light. The footsteps started again and I began following them, moving as fast as I could down the tunnel. At a hundred paces I came to a junction with another tunnel and stopped. The footsteps I had been chasing had vanished. The only sound I now heard was coming from the direction I had just come from. A light visible back at the junction began moving fast toward me. I pressed myself against the wall and raised my weapon and held on the coming light for a moment, then lowered it when the light stopped twenty feet from me.

'Alex?' Harrison said.

He stepped up and looked me over, then reached out and gently touched the side of my face.

'Are you all right?'

I nodded, though it seemed there wasn't a part of my body that didn't ache.

'I think maybe a paramedic should look at that.'

I shook my head and a sharp jolt of pain pierced my breast where I had been hit.

'An ice pack or two, a little make-up and I'll be a model of feminine mystique again,' I said.

'Is that Simms back there?' he asked.

'No,' I said. 'His name's Earl Moon.'

I slipped his business card out of my pocket and handed it to Harrison.

'Moon and Wong. A private investigator,' he said. 'Confidential and discreet.'

'I think the discreet claim may have been overstated,' I said.

'He was the one in Simms's office?' Dylan asked.

'Yeah.'

'What is a private dick doing here?'

'According to a very brief conversation I had with him, he was just doing his job.'

'You talked with him?' Harrison asked.

'It was a one-sided conversation,' I said, reaching up and touching the side of my face. 'Shortly after our all too short chat I found him like that. Whoever did it ran down one of these tunnels, I'm not sure which.'

'His throat was cut,' Dylan said.

I nodded. 'Which seems to point to our man Shelton's fondness for knives, if in fact he did get a new identity and did leave England.'

'This is not exactly what we were expecting,' Harrison said.

'No, it isn't.'

'So we're back to the same question. Where's Simms?' Dylan said.

I looked back down the tunnel.

'Maybe Earl knew,' Harrison said.

'And that's why he was killed?'

'He must have known something that someone thought was worth killing him for,' Dylan said.

'I wonder,' I said, shining my light down the tunnel where I thought I had heard the sound of footsteps heading away.

'What?' Harrison asked.

'If he was hired by someone to go find something in a college professor's office, then my guess is Earl was probably more surprised than we were by what happened. Death has a way of doing that, particularly when it's violent.'

I looked back down the tunnel to where he lay dead.

'I didn't feel a cell phone anywhere on him, but he must have car keys in his pocket. He would have parked close to here, let's see if we can find it.'

I reached out and took Earl's business card back from Dylan.

'Moon and Wong Investigations. This is a Chinatown address.'

'He must have a partner.'

'If they work as confidentially as he did discreetly, maybe we'll find some answers.'

fifteen

As we waited for Crime Scene to arrive, we searched the tunnels where I thought Moon's killer had escaped from. All we found was an unlocked door that led into a geology building across the commons from where we had first stepped into Simms's office. Whoever murdered Earl Moon had then eased open a window in an empty classroom and disappeared into the blackout.

Using the remote lock and alarm on the keys we found in Moon's pocket we located a car half a block from Simms's building. A ten-year-old Toyota Camry with a dented fender and a dash dried and split by the sun. There was nothing inside that explained his presence in a college professor's office. Several empty bags of fast food from Burrito King, a Laker banner, a cheap digital camera in the glove compartment with dead batteries, and a set of golf clubs in the trunk.

Near midnight we left CSU processing Moon's murder site and headed toward downtown LA and the Chinatown address on Earl Moon's business card. As we rounded the last bend of the 110 freeway the glow of several fires became visible south of downtown where sporadic looting had once again begun. In the streets adjacent to the freeway I could see the fleeting shapes of figures standing in the occasional doorway or darting across a street as if trying to avoid detection.

'When was the last time you met anyone in LA who didn't have a cell phone on them or in their car?' Harrison asked as we made the bend toward the dark hills of Chavez Ravine.

I was holding a cold pack to the side of my face, trying to still the throbbing from where I had hit the wall.

'You think whoever killed him took it?' I said.

'A private investigator without a cell phone? It's the only explanation that makes sense.'

'Which means they wanted to know the calls he had made, and who he was working for,' I said.

'Which could put them in danger,' Harrison said.

We turned off the freeway and descended into the streets of Chinatown. Unlike the rest of the city where people had retreated to someplace safe, life in Chinatown seemed simply to have adapted to the changing situation. Grocers trying to save meat and produce from spoilage had set up tables on the sidewalk and were doing a brisk business. Lanterns were lit up and down the street, providing islands of light. A few restaurants had moved grills outside where cooks in white T-shirts stirred large woks over open flames, sending the smells of garlic, coriander and chili pepper into the hot night air.

In front of entrances to buildings, entire families had moved on to the sidewalk. Car stereos played a strange combination of rap and traditional Chinese music. Children lay on mattresses, old men sat in chairs chain-smoking, a woman walked down the sidewalk carrying two live chickens in each hand.

At Alpine we turned right, drove a block and a half and stopped in front of a two-story stucco building. On the ground-floor window a sign read Wang and Sons Noodles. A second door, which appeared to lead into a stairway, simply had Moon written above the number.

We stepped out of the squad and I glanced up and down the street. There was none of the activity that we had seen two blocks away on Broadway. No one sat out in front of the buildings, no scent of cooking drifted over the pavement. The only activity was the sound of rats rustling through the garbage of a dumpster across the street.

'His driver's license had this address,' Harrison said.

'A private eye living above a noodle factory in Chinatown.'

'Maybe he's seen too many movies.'

'Or just one,' I said.

I took out my cell phone and dialed the number on the business card. Through an open window on the second floor I could hear the sound of the phone ringing. On the fourth ring a machine picked up. 'You've reached Moon and Wong Investigations. Please leave a number and we'll return the call as quickly as possible. All inquiries are confidential.' I hung up and slipped the phone away.

'A woman's voice on the machine,' I said.

'Perhaps Wong's a woman,' Harrison said.

I walked over to the door and knocked on the glass and

got no response. As Harrison reached into his pocket and started to take out Moon's keys, a figure came walking around the corner toward us.

'Hold on a second,' I said to Harrison as he started to slip the key into the lock.

We waited as the figure continued to approach in the darkness and then stopped twenty paces from us.

'If you're looking for Moon Investigations, we're closed,' she said. 'If you're thinking of breaking in, there's nothing worth stealing, and if you're thinking of anything else, the gun in my hand says you should just turn around and get the fuck out of here.'

'We're with the police,' I said. 'If you have a gun, I'd prefer you keep it out of your hand.'

'I'd like to see an ID,' she said.

I slipped my badge off my waistband and turned on my flashlight, illuminating it.

'And your friend next to you?'

I shined the light on Harrison and he held up his badge.

'Yeah, you look like cops,' she said and started walking toward us.

I raised the light on her as she approached. She was Chinese, perhaps late twenties, slightly built and pretty. In her hands she carried two bags of what smelled like food from one of the restaurants on Broadway.

'Do you have a weapon on you?' I asked and she shook her head, stopping a few feet from us.

'Pepper spray,' she said. 'Would you mind telling me why you're here?'

'And you are?' I asked.

'Jean Wong,' she said.

'Of Moon and Wong?' Harrison said.

She nodded.

'You're a private detective?' I asked.

She shook her head. 'Me? No, Earl thought my face would help attract Chinese business. In return I don't pay any rent for the apartment upstairs.'

'You don't work with Earl at all?' I said.

'I do some translating for him when he gets a Chinese client, and I help him occasionally when he thinks it would look good if there was a secretary in the office.' She looked at us for a moment. 'Why are you here?'

'Does Earl also live here?' I asked.

'No,' she said.

'His driver's license lists this as his address.'

She started to shake her head then stopped. 'I'm not involved with him, if that's what you're asking. He has a little house in the north valley. Most of his work is following cheating spouses so he has his address listed as here because he's afraid some jealous husband or boyfriend might come after him.' She paused. 'Did Earl get himself arrested?'

'No,' I said. 'He got himself killed.'

She looked at me with the same unbelieving look I had seen on people staring at the Grand Canyon for the first time.

'Dead?' She tried to understand what I had told her but couldn't quite get her mind around it, or didn't want to. 'He's really dead?'

'Yes,' I said.

'Oh my God,' she said barely above a whisper. 'What happened?'

'Can you tell me anything about the job he was on tonight?'

'He was working?'

I nodded. 'You didn't know he had a job?'

She shook her head. 'I haven't seen him for a couple of days, I was staying with a friend from school. I'm in grad school at USC. Clients aren't exactly breaking down his doors. He works part-time at a Home Depot, in the paint department.'

'Would there be records in the office that could tell us about what he was doing, who he was working for?' Harrison asked.

'There might be, but he wasn't the most organized person you ever met.'

She took a deep, shaky breath and a light seemed to go off in her eyes.

'What kind of policemen are you?' she asked.

'We're homicide detectives.'

The full implications of our visit became clear to her.

'This wasn't an accident or something?' she asked.

'He was murdered,' I said.

She looked at me and then at the windows upstairs.

'Oh my God, did it happen here?' she asked.

'No, he was somewhere else,' I said.

'Was it somebody's husband?'

'I'd be very surprised,' I said.

She stood for a moment in silence.

'Someone killed Earl?' she said, as if trying to convince

herself that what I had said was true. 'Why would some-one do that?'

'That's what we're trying to find out,' I said.

'I think I need to sit down.' She stepped toward the door with her keys.

She started to slip the key in the lock and then pushed the door open without turning the key.

'Did you unlock this?' she asked.

I reached out my arm and guided her away from the door.

'Did Earl ever leave the door unlocked?' I asked.

'Never,' she said.

'What is the layout upstairs?'

She looked at me, not understanding my words.

'Jean, tell me the layout upstairs,' I repeated.

She thought about it for a moment and then nodded.

'My apartment is the first door, Earl's office is on the left. It's a couple of rooms and a bathroom.'

'Is there another entrance?' I asked.

'No.'

'Why don't you go sit in our squad car for a moment while we look upstairs,' I said.

Harrison slipped his gun out of his holster. Jean Wong stared at it for a moment, and then her hands began to tremble.

'I'll wait in the car,' she said and ran over to the squad, dropping one of her bags of food, which she just left where it lay.

I moved the light up the steps to the landing on the second floor.

'You don't really expect to find anyone up there, do you?' Harrison asked.

I shook my head. 'No, but then I'm not really sure what to expect any more,' I said and we started up.

With each step we took the scent of egg noodles became stronger until it seemed we were standing in a bowl of soup. At the top we hesitated and I peered around the corner and raised the light. The door on the left was open a few inches; the wood of the frame by the lock had been splintered.

Harrison stepped around me and kicked the door open and raised his weapon into the interior. I moved past him into the office. It was done up to appear like a waiting room. There was a couch and chairs against one wall and the secretary's desk in the center. Beyond the desk was a door into the second office.

'Nothing appears to have been touched,' Dylan said.

I moved around the desk to the second door, pushed it open and raised my light.

'It's the same in here,' I said.

I stepped inside and looked around the room. There was a telephone, a Rolodex, a calendar and some papers on the desk. On one of the walls was a photograph of Earl Moon standing next to a TV actor from *Fantasy Island* I recognized but couldn't name and a picture of the White House, which I guess was supposed to instill some sort of confidence in Earl's abilities as a detective.

The phone was a landline. I stepped around the desk and shined the light on the papers spread across its surface, looking for anything that might connect to the events from earlier.

'The desk in the other room appears mostly for show, and storing pens and rubber bands,' Harrison said as he joined me. 'Anything in here?'

I thumbed through the Rolodex – there didn't appear to be a single number inside.

'Nothing. It's like the office came in a kit from the Acme school of detectives.' I pulled open the top drawer of the desk. It was filled with takeout menus from Chinese restaurants.

A lower drawer was labeled as contracts. Inside was a row of files neatly alphabetized. About a third of the files contained paperwork. I pulled one out and looked it over. It was a one-page contract that obligated the client to pay Earl a sum of three hundred and fifty dollars a day plus expenses.

'From the look of this, Earl had maybe two dozen jobs in the last six months,' I said.

I picked up the phone and checked the numbers of the last few calls he had made. The first one was an LA number. I dialed it and got the answering machine to a Chinese restaurant. The second one was a Pasadena number.

'Does this look familiar?' I asked Harrison.

Dylan stepped over and looked at the number and shook his head. I hit redial and the phone made the call. Before the first ring, the line was answered and a voice came over the speaker.

'The offices of Beckwith, Myers and Dunne are now

closed. Regular business hours are seven a.m. to four p.m., Monday through Friday. If you know your extension and wish to leave a message, press it now. Please leave no messages regarding trades or transactions as they will not be honored.'

We both stared at the phone for a moment, not entirely believing what we had just heard.

'You think Earl was calling about his retirement funds?' I said.

We were both silent for a moment.

'Simms was on the board, wasn't he? Or was until a short time ago,' I said.

'They hired him to investigate him,' Dylan said.

I nodded.

'But why?' Harrison said.

'Simms must be connected to O'Brien, or they're afraid he is.'

Harrison nodded. 'The money in the freezer. Perhaps Simms had a silent partner in experimental finance.'

'It's possible,' I said, thinking out loud, 'that we've been gullible.'

'How?'

I shook my head and tried to work back through what we knew trying to see it a different way.

'Ten minutes ago you couldn't have convinced me that what we're investigating was about anything other than the homicidal rage of a sick man. The eye, the cryptic symbols, the darkness and messages, the manner in which he killed his victims.'

'And now?' Harrison asked.

'Now I'm not so sure.'

'Why?'

'Let's play a little game of "what if?" ' I said.

Harrison nodded.

'What do we know or think we know?' I said. 'Simms and Shelton meet at Oxford. Two years later Simms comes to Caltech, joins the board of Beckwith, Myers and Dunne.'

'Where he meets O'Brien.'

'Yes.'

'Which gets us where?' Harrison asked.

'What if Simms's experimental economics began at Oxford where he meets a brilliant young student whose past included years in a justice system where he learned the finer points of the business of drugs.'

Dylan nodded.

'Both Shelton and Simms leave Oxford. Simms then resurfaces at Caltech with his experimental take on economics refined to an even greater degree. He also joins the board of Beckwith, Myers and Dunne.'

So what happens next?

'And meets O'Brien and they go into business,' Harrison said.

'And then Shelton vanishes and appears here.'

'Looking for Simms?'

I nodded.

'Why?' Harrison asked.

Trying to rethink a problem you had thought was already understood was like having a word on the tip of your tongue.

'What was it Shelton wrote in O'Brien's house? The rich are different from us, they never get caught.'

'And?' Harrison said.

I raised my light to the picture of Earl and the actor from *Fantasy Island* on the wall.

'What if Shelton's playing a role to hide his real motivation?' I said.

'Which is?'

'Greed,' I said.

'Keep going,' Harrison said.

'For the sake of argument, let's say Simms and Shelton's enterprises at Oxford went bad, and Simms left for America without paying off his partner.'

'Shelton wants his slice of the pie?'

I nodded.

'So why didn't he take the money in the freezer?' Harrison said.

'Maybe he did,' I said.

'What do you mean?'

'We're assuming that the money we found was all there was. What if there was more, a lot more.'

'And Shelton left enough behind to support his cover story.'

'Yes.'

'How do Pullian and the dead transient fit into it?' Dylan asked.

I stepped over to the window and looked down on the street.

'That's not quite as clear,' I said.

'No,' said Harrison.

I took a breath and worked through the images of Pullian's strange apartment.

'If any of this is right, I think it's safe to assume that Shelton wants to get away with it.'

'Which gets us where?' Harrison said.

'To a patsy.'

'Pullian?'

I nodded. 'Let's say Shelton creates this persona of a monster, he still needs another warm body when the shit hits the fan.'

'So . . .'

'So he convinces an emotional cripple of a genius to take part in a Nietzschean Übermensch act of ridding the world of inferior and corrupt beings, and in the process creating the patsy that takes the fall and allows him to disappear back into the night.'

'Only Pullian had second thoughts, or sees through it.'

'And had to be eliminated,' I said.

Dylan stepped over to the window and looked toward the dark shapes of the downtown towers.

'None of which we have a shred of evidence for or changes the fact that Shelton's one brutal son of a bitch who killed his first victim when he was nine years old.'

'No,' I said.

'So assuming Shelton was the one who broke in here, what was he looking for?' Dylan said.

'Who Earl was working for and how much he knew.'

'If he thinks Beckwith, Myers and Dunne are involved, or know something that could lead to him, they could be in danger.'

I nodded. 'We need to have a talk with them.'

'Which still leaves Simms unaccounted for.'

'For his sake, I hope so,' I said.

'I'll start making some calls,' said Harrison, taking out his phone.

I crossed back over to the desk and began opening the rest of the drawers. My phone rang and I picked up.

'Lieutenant.' It was Agent Utley. 'When you have a moment I would like to know how you suspected any of this.'

'Any of what?' I asked.

'According to my source at the Yard, Shelton took one class from Simms nearly a year before both of them left Oxford.'

'Interesting. Only the one?' I asked.

'As far as I know.'

'Then something happened just before they both left?' I asked.

'Right again. Just prior to both their departures from Oxford, Simms was assaulted by a student.'

'Do you have any more details?'

'A few. The unnamed student claimed it was a result of improper sexual advances by Simms.'

'And Simms didn't deny it?' I said.

'No.'

'And he didn't file a police report of the assault either.'

'Exactly. Now how did you know that?' Utley asked.

'Old-fashioned police work. How soon after this did Shelton leave Oxford?'

'I don't have a date but it appears to have been a few weeks at most.'

'And shortly after that Simms resigned,' I said.

'He was supposed to stand in front of a peer review board but he resigned instead.'

'How soon after that did Simms leave England?' I asked.

'Days.'

'Would you keep working on Scotland Yard to get an updated ID on Shelton?' I said.

'Is there something I need to know, Lieutenant?' Utley asked.

'Shelton killed a private investigator named Earl Moon tonight. Cut his throat.'

'A private investigator? Why?'

'He took the wrong job and walked into the wrong office.'

'Which means?'

'Things may not be exactly as we had assumed,' I said.

'That doesn't exactly clarify things, Lieutenant,' Utley said.

'It's possible that Simms and Shelton were partners in a drug business,' I said. 'Though that idea rests firmly in the realm of conjecture.'

'A college professor?'

'Yeah. He's running another one here out of his house in Monrovia, or was. It's possible Shelton showed up to get a piece of the action, or all of it.'

'Can you connect Shelton to this?' he asked.

'I can't even prove Shelton exists,' I said. 'Unless you

want to count the dead. Can you keep working on London to get an updated ID on Shelton?'

'If you can prove any of this, that would help,' Utley said.

'When I have more, I'll get it to you.'

'OK, I'll see what I can do,' he said and hung up.

'Were we right about Oxford?' Harrison asked.

I nodded. 'It seems to fit,' I said. 'Any luck finding Beckwith or Dunne?'

'Beckwith's address is here in Pasadena above the arroyo off Linda Vista. I called but couldn't get through; he must not have a landline. Dunne lives in the Hollywood Hills. No luck getting through there either. You want to pay them a visit?'

'Yes,' I said.

'What about Moon's house?'

'That can wait.'

As we exited the building, Jean Wong opened the door to the squad and stepped out, her left hand remaining on the handle as if clinging to an escape rope.

'Did you find something?' she asked.

'Yes,' I answered.

'Is it safe, Lieutenant? Can I go in?' she asked.

I looked down the street where the limit of my night vision met the darkness.

'Not just yet,' I said. 'You'll need to find somewhere else to stay until the morning.'

sixteen

On a good night Hollywood Boulevard at 2 a.m. was at best a sideshow for the most adventurous tourists seeking a thrill ride through the underbelly of Los Angeles. This was not a good night. There was no one having their pictures taken next to Grace Kelly's star on the walk of fame. No groups of drunken college students carrying a friend out of the Frolic Room. No runaways willing to trade anything, including their bodies, for twenty dollars and some onion rings at Carl Junior's.

Los Angeles had declared a curfew for all but essential travel, though what constituted essential in a city built on make-believe was difficult to define. On the corner of Vine, a man lay face down on the cement, a black transvestite hooker in red hot pants rifling his pockets. On a rooftop at Citrus someone played a drum set, furiously beating out a cadence as two men swung bottles at each other on the street six stories below.

At Cherokee a trashcan had been set on fire and was rolling down the middle of the empty street. At the Chinese theater, armed security guards brandishing shotguns and forty-fives had built their own version of the Maginot Line to keep the footprints of John Wayne and Clark Gable from being pried up and carried off.

LAPD was too busy trying to plug holes in a leaking dam to stop for anything short of exchanges of gunfire. As we moved down the boulevard, groups of young men in baggy clothes would step out of the shadows of buildings to challenge any vehicle foolish enough to be traveling the streets. We were cops so we were allowed to pass but not before gang signs were flashed and shirts raised enough so we would see the chrome-plated nine millimeter tucked in the waistband.

At La Brea we left Hollywood Boulevard and turned up toward the hills. In places residents had put barricades across their streets in the hope that two sawhorses and a two-by-four would keep the violence erupting down below from spreading to their homes.

There was no real danger unless you went looking for it. This was not a breakdown of the tattered fabric that held Los Angeles together the way the riots had been. The only thing that unified those on the streets was the complete unlikelihood of getting caught. This was just old-fashioned fun, like Halloween for those with rap sheets. None of which mattered at all to those staying behind locked doors. Halloween wasn't for everyone.

We wound our way up Outpost until we reached Mulholland and turned west. In the darkness a few specks of light from Catalina Island where they produced their own power were visible, flickering like fireflies.

Dunne lived a block above Mulholland in a sleek

structure that in the darkness appeared to rise from the small front yard like a group of tumbling blocks and glass held together by thick steel cables. As we stepped out of the squad and approached the front door, a light shone on us from a window on the second floor of the house.

'I have a gun,' said a voice.

'I'd prefer you put it down,' I said.

There was a moment of silence.

'Lieutenant?'

'Yes,' I answered.

'I'll come down,' he said.

Through the glass of the house I could see the beam of the flashlight moving as Dunne came downstairs.

'I don't think he's gotten much sleep tonight,' Harrison said.

'Along with nine million other people,' I said.

We heard the sound of locks disengaging and then the door opened. Dunne stood in front of us in a T-shirt and shorts, the torch in one hand and a revolver in the other.

'I promise I won't pull my weapon if you put that away,' I said, motioning toward the weapon in his hand.

He set the gun down on a table next to the door.

'Sorry, there were rumors that looting was spreading to the hills.'

I shook my head. 'I think there's plenty enough to occupy them down in Hollywood.'

'Has something happened?' he asked.

'We have a few questions,' I said.

'At two a.m.?'

'Yes.'

'Why don't we talk out back, it's a little hot inside.'

He walked us through the house out into the back yard. The dark water of a lap pool reflected the shimmering light of the stars. The entire LA basin spread out below us like a dark hole cut open in the earth. We sat at a table alongside the water, and Dunne lit several candles. The faint scent of chlorine mixed with that of a lemon tree out of sight in the darkness.

'What's happened to bring you out here at this time of night?' he asked.

'Tell me about Lawrence Simms,' I said.

He looked at me and then at Harrison as if he had not heard the question.

'I'm sorry? I don't understand. Professor Simms of Caltech?'

'That's right,' I answered.

'What can I tell you?'

'He was on your board until a few months ago,' I said.

'Yes.'

'Why did he resign?' Harrison asked.

'As I understand it, to devote more time to his duties at school.'

'Can you tell me about his relationship with Jim O'Brien?' I asked.

He thought for a moment and then shook his head.

'I don't know,' he answered. 'I wasn't aware that there was one.'

'Has your company ever contracted work with a detective agency?' Harrison asked.

'A what?'

'A private investigator,' I said.

'No,' Dunne replied.

'You're sure?' I asked.

'I think so, yes.'

'Does the name Earl Moon mean anything to you?'

He shook his head. 'No, is there a reason it should?'

'I believe he was working for your firm, or someone in your firm,' I said.

He took a moment to consider his response.

'We employ over sixty people, Lieutenant. Now, is it possible one of those people hired someone like him? I suppose the answer is yes. Is there a reason in particular you're asking me?'

'He broke into Lawrence Simms's office tonight. I think he was looking for information that connected Simms's drug-dealing business to Jim O'Brien.'

'Did you say drugs?'

I nodded.

Dunne looked at us both for a moment and shook his head. 'I don't know what to say.'

'Try something,' I said.

'Lieutenant, you're saying a respected college professor and economist is a drug pusher?'

'I think entrepreneur would be a better description.'

'This is crazy.'

'The world is full of surprises,' I said.

'I'm still not clear why you're asking me these questions,' Dunne said.

'Think about it,' I said.

'Lieutenant, if you're implying that I or someone at my

firm is somehow connected to illegal activities, I think this conversation is over.'

'I'm not implying anything, Mr Dunne. I'm trying to stop a killer.'

'We are a respected brokerage firm.'

'Well, that must be a very unique feeling these days,' I said.

Dunne pushed back from the table. 'I think you should leave.'

Harrison and I stood.

'Can you think of any reason why one of the private investigator's last calls was to your firm?' I asked.

'No. Perhaps he invests with us,' he said.

'Does your operator keep logs of telephone calls?' I asked.

'I couldn't say.'

'When you can, I will want to see them,' I said.

He nodded. 'I will cooperate in any way as long as proper warrants are issued for anything dealing with the internal matters of the firm.'

'I'll have the warrants by morning,' I said.

We started to walk away then I stopped.

'There is one other thing I should mention before I go,' I said.

'Yes.'

'After breaking into Simms's office, someone cut the detective's throat. The blade went all the way to the vertebrae of the neck. He lived about another forty-five seconds holding his hands to the wound, trying to stop the bleeding as he gasped for one last breath.'

Dunne stood in silence for a moment.

'I'm sorry I can't help you, Lieutenant,' he said.

'Is your gun loaded?' I asked.

'Yes,' Dunne said. 'And properly registered.'

'And you have some training?' I asked.

'I spent a day at a combat ranch.'

'Shooting steel plates and cardboard bad guys?'

'I scored very well,' he said.

'Good,' I said. 'I ask because I believe the man who killed Earl Moon is now looking for the person he talked to at your firm.'

'Good night, Lieutenant.'

'One last question,' I said and Dunne nodded. 'How did Lawrence Simms come to be on your board?'

He thought about it for a moment. 'Charles met him at a conference in England.'

'Beckwith?'

'Yes.'

'Was it at Oxford?' I asked.

He shrugged. 'It may have been.'

I glanced at Dylan.

'Do you have a cell number for him?' Harrison asked.

Dunne hesitated and then nodded. 'Yes.'

'Call it.'

'Now?'

'Right now,' I said.

We followed Dunne into the house where he retrieved a cell phone from a table and dialed. He waited for a moment and then shook his head.

'It's saying the circuits are jammed and to try again later.'

'Does he live alone?' I asked.

'He's divorced, son lives with his mother.'

'I'll need that number,' I said.

Dunne wrote it down on a notepad and gave it to Harrison.

'If you hear from him, I want you to give him a message,' I said to Dunne.

'What?'

'If he's at home, tell him to get out of the house and drive to police headquarters in Pasadena. If he's not, tell him to go to the nearest police station, they'll know how to get in touch with me.'

'Is this really necessary?' Dunne asked.

'If he wants to see the dawn, it is,' I said and walked out.

'You think he's lying?' Harrison asked as we reached the squad.

Through the glass cubes of the house I could see Dunne's light as he moved through the interior, checking and locking every door and window.

'He could be just trying to protect the firm,' I said.

'But you don't think so?'

I shook my head. 'No, I don't think I do.' I glanced back at the house. 'What did he say? He had heard looting was spreading into the hills? No electricity, no radio, no TV, no phone. How did he hear that? He was afraid of something but it wasn't that someone was going to break in and steal his big-screen TV.'

We crossed over to the valley side of the hills to avoid Hollywood and then drove east back toward Pasadena. We called dispatch to have a black and white sent to

Beckwith's address, though whether it would arrive before we did, given the call levels, was anybody's guess.

Charles Beckwith lived north of Orange in one of the grand old craftsman homes of Pasadena. A black and white was parked outside when we arrived. We pulled up behind it and the uniformed officer got out as we did.

'Nothing going on here, Lieutenant. I just got a break-in call; you want me to stay?' he asked.

'Did you go up to the house?' I asked.

He shook his head. 'Dispatch said just to wait for you.'

The house sat back from the street on a double lot shaded by large magnolia trees. There were no candles flickering in any of the windows.

'You can go,' I said.

The officer took off and Harrison and I started up the path toward the house, stopping at the steps to the porch.

'If Beckwith is as frightened as Dunne,' I said, 'let's do this carefully. I don't want to step on that porch and have bullets flying through the door.'

'I'll see if I can get through.' Harrison took out his phone and dialed. A moment later the faint sound of a phone ringing could be heard from somewhere inside. After half a dozen rings, it stopped. 'The circuit just went down again.'

I turned on my flashlight, stepped up on to the porch and shined it on the front door.

'Whatever happened here already took place,' I said.

In the thick leaded glass of the door's window was a single hole. Harrison slipped his gun out and held it at his side as I stepped to the door and reached up to the bullet hole in the window and ran my finger around the edge of the broken glass.

'Small caliber, the shot came from inside,' I said.

Harrison pointed his light across the landing of the porch.

'Doesn't look like he hit anything, no blood.'

We stepped to either side of the door and Harrison pounded on it with his fist.

'Police, Mr Beckwith,' he shouted.

There was no response from inside. I took hold of the handle and turned it.

'It's open,' I said and pushed the door.

'Mr Beckwith, this is the police,' I yelled into the house and again there was no response.

I slipped my gun out and eased around the door, pointing the light into the interior as Harrison moved in behind me. We walked through the entry and stopped. To the left was a living room and to the right a dining room. A stairway led upstairs.

'I'll go through down here, you check upstairs,' I said.

Dylan climbed the stairs to the second floor and I walked through the dining room and started to push open the swinging door and stopped. There were more bullet holes in the door, five in all. Spread in a wide pattern across the door as if the hand holding the weapon had been wildly shaking as the trigger was pulled.

I stepped to the side of the door and called out again.

'Mr Beckwith, this is Lieutenant Delillo. I'm going to open the door.'

There was no response on the other side. I reached out

and pushed the door so it swung open a few inches, waiting for the sound of a shot. There was nothing.

I pushed the door wider and stepped around, raising my weapon and the light. The revolver that had fired the shots lay on the floor across the kitchen. Beyond that the back door was open. I walked over to the door and pointed my light out into the back yard.

'There's nothing upstairs,' said Harrison, stepping into the kitchen.

'He's out there,' I said.

In the middle of the expansive lawn a figure sat upright, his back to us. I stepped out of the door on to the patio, holding the light on the still figure. He was dressed in a T-shirt and boxer shorts.

'Mr Beckwith?' I said.

The figure didn't move and we stepped across the patio and on to the lawn.

'I don't see any visible wounds,' said Dylan.

We stopped a few feet from the figure.

'Mr Beckwith,' I said again.

Dylan glanced at me and shook his head. I slowly moved around the sitting figure and raised the light to his face. Beckwith's eyes reacted to the light though he made no effort to shield them with his hands. He continued to stare past me as if I wasn't there. There was no sign of an injury, though his shirt was soaked with perspiration.

'Are you injured?' I asked.

Again he didn't react. I holstered my weapon and then reached out and touched the back of his hand in his lap.

'What happened here?' I asked.

His eyes blinked and then he reached out and grabbed my wrist.

'I thought—' he said and stopped.

'You thought what?'

He took a breath. His eyes appeared to jump back into the present, realizing where he was and to whom he was talking. He looked into the light and then held up his hand to shield his eyes.

'I thought he—' He stopped again. 'I thought I heard someone in the house.'

'Who did you think was in the house?' I asked.

He started to answer and then seemed to reconsider what he was about to say.

'A burglar,' he answered.

'You said "he" was in the house. What did you mean?' I asked.

He looked up at me. 'I just assumed it was a man.'

'Did you?' I asked.

He nodded.

'Why are you sitting out here, Mr Beckwith?'

He stood up and looked back at the house.

'It's very hot inside,' Beckwith said.

'Did you talk to Lawrence Simms tonight?' I asked.

The question clearly caught him off guard. He looked at Harrison and then back at me.

'Why would I have done that?' he asked.

'Mr Beckwith, the man you thought was inside your house tonight is going to kill him – he may already have. And if he comes for you, he's going to do the same thing. Now I can help you stay alive, but you have to help me.'

'It was just a burglar,' he repeated.

'Tell me about Simms,' I said.

'I don't know what you're talking about, Lieutenant,' he said.

'No, of course you don't. You've just shot holes in your house and are sitting on your lawn at three thirty in the morning in your underwear because it's hot,' I said.

'Yes, it's very hot,' he said.

'Do you know where Simms is?' I said.

'No.'

'When was the last time you talked to him?'

'I don't remember.'

'When was the last time you talked to Earl Moon?' I said.

The name clearly surprised him, just as it had Dunne.

'I'm sorry, who?'

'The private detective you hired,' I said.

'I have no idea what—'

'He's dead,' I said. 'The man you thought was inside your home put a knife to Earl Moon's throat and cut it in half.'

Beckwith stood in silence, showing no reaction to what I had told him.

'You want to continue this fiction you're clinging to?' I said. 'I know O'Brien was involved with Simms's drug business. Did you hire Moon to find how deeply he was involved, or to cover it up because the involvement went beyond O'Brien?'

'I can't help you,' he said.

'I don't care if you or your firm has broken laws,' I said.

'I do care if I have to walk into another crime scene with a butchered body. Even if it's yours.'

'I am a certified financial advisor,' Beckwith said.

'I wouldn't cling to that as a guarantee of longevity these days,' I said.

'I hold the trust of all my clients,' he said for reasons that weren't entirely clear.

'I'm sure they will all feel a great sense of security knowing you were sitting in the back yard in your underwear after shooting holes through your kitchen door,' I said.

'I think I'll go inside now,' he said and started walking toward the back door.

'When you met Simms in London,' I asked, 'did he introduce you to his business partner?'

Beckwith stopped and turned back to me. 'I'm sorry, I don't know what you're talking about.'

I walked over to him. 'You did meet Simms at a conference in London?'

'I met many people in London,' he replied.

'Including Simms.'

He took a breath. 'Yes, including Simms. Is there a point to this, Lieutenant?'

'His partner would have been a student, in his early twenties, probably quite brilliant.'

'Oxford is full of brilliant people,' he said, his eyes unflinching in their resolve.

'Perhaps you're telling the truth, maybe Simms didn't introduce you to someone.'

'Thank you,' he said.

'But if you see a face walking toward you on the sidewalk or stepping out of a car outside your house, and you remember meeting him in England, take a good deep breath because it will be your last one.'

'Thank you for that helpful advice, Lieutenant. Are you quite finished?'

'It's illegal to fire a weapon within city limits,' I said.

'Are you going to arrest me?' he asked.

I shook my head. 'No. I'm going to wait for the man you thought was here tonight to come back for you, and if I'm lucky, I'll stop him before he carves you into pieces.'

Beckwith took a breath and started to turn away.

'One last thing, Mr Beckwith,' I said.

'What?' he said.

'Do you know how Jim O'Brien met Lawrence Simms? Was it when Simms joined the board?'

Beckwith hesitated. 'O'Brien was a Rhodes Scholar.'

'They met at Oxford?'

'Yes. Are you finished?'

'For now,' I said. 'You might want to change your shorts, they have grass stains on them.'

'I think you should leave,' he said, then turned and walked inside and closed the door.

Harrison and I walked around the side of the house to the squad parked in front.

'You want me to get a unit here to watch him?'

I nodded. 'The same with Dunne.'

Dylan opened the squad's door and made the call on the radio.

I glanced at my watch. It was nearly 4 a.m. I looked back

at Beckwith's house and then down the dark street. There wasn't a sound anywhere. Not the constant background noise of traffic that was usually always present, no birds, no sirens or helicopters. With the night nearly over, it was as if the city had taken a collective breath of relief. Dylan stepped back out of the squad.

'There'll be a squad here in ten minutes,' he said.

I looked at Beckwith's house. Occasionally the closed blinds would open a crack as Beckwith peeked outside.

'It's possible he didn't meet Shelton in London,' I said. 'I don't see how it would have been to Simms's advantage to parade around a young business partner he was breaking the law with.'

'Or he met him, and didn't know who he was,' Harrison said.

I nodded. 'Well, he sure is afraid of someone and I don't imagine it's a professor of experimental finance.'

'What about O'Brien? If his connection to Simms goes back to Oxford, he might have met Shelton.'

I nodded. 'Unfortunately he's no longer able to talk.'

'What should we do?' Harrison asked.

'You mean besides sleep?' I said.

'I'd settle for that,' said Dylan.

'If we're right about Pullian having been set up to be a fall guy,' I said, 'then with him dead, there's no point in Shelton trying to maintain the fiction of the serial killer at work.'

'You think that will alter the way he functions?'

'I doubt that Earl Moon knew Shelton's identity. But Shelton didn't hesitate, why take the risk? He murdered

Moon coldly and efficiently with no attempt to make it appear to be something it wasn't. I'd say that changes the landscape.'

'There's more than that,' Harrison said.

'What?' I asked.

'He knows that Moon wasn't the only one down in that tunnel tonight. You were there.'

I nodded.

'Which means he knows we connect him to Simms,' Harrison said.

'Which connects him to Oxford.'

Dylan worked the details in his head for a moment.

'You think he believes we connect him to a little boy named Richard Shelton?' he asked.

'I don't know. He's got at least two identities between him and Shelton and a justice system that seems intent on protecting that secret.'

'The minute he believes we've connected him to his past, or have found his new identity, he'll either disappear or—'

'Eliminate that threat,' I said.

Dylan nodded. 'Which makes him more dangerous than the fictional killer we thought we were after. And that puts you right back in the cross hairs.'

'Not just me,' I said. 'He'll kill anyone he thinks is a threat.'

I looked back at the house and my heart rate began to jump as I realized we might have missed something.

'Jesus . . .' I ran back up the front steps to Beckwith's door. Dylan caught up with me as I pounded on it.

'What is it?' he asked as the door opened.

Beckwith was now wearing a robe.

'What now?'

'Was Jim O'Brien married to Cathy when he went to Oxford?'

He shook his head. 'He's dead, leave him—'

I grabbed the front of his robe and pushed him against the doorframe.

'I need to know right now,' I said.

Beckwith thought for a second.

'I think so. That's the best I can do,' he said.

I released him and started back to the squad.

'We can't wait for the backup to get here,' I said.

'You think she knows Shelton?' Harrison said as we reached the squad.

'It's possible.'

'She already said she never saw the killer, so how does that change anything?'

I opened the door. 'She's alive because her living helped create the fiction of a serial killer. As long as that story held, she was safe.'

'And now that story's over,' Harrison said.

I nodded. 'She can't identify a killer, but she might remember an old friend from Oxford,' I said.

'And that makes her a threat,' said Dylan.

'Call the hospital and have security at her room,' I said and Harrison made the call.

I took out my phone and dialed Utley who answered on the second ring.

'Don't you ever sleep?' he asked.

'Did you get those composites done of what Shelton may look like now?' I asked.

'I guess you haven't been in the office,' he said.

'We've been out.'

'They were supposed to have been messengered to you last night. Whether they'll be of any use is another question. There are three versions. I personally prefer number two.'

'Any particular reason?'

'It's what I would want to look like if I was trying to escape a past.'

'And how is that?' I asked.

'Nearly invisible,' Utley said.

seventeen

The images of Shelton were waiting at headquarters just as Utley had promised. Three versions of a boy all grown up. He was right about whether they would be useful. Connecting the computer-generated faces to the one photograph we had of a nine-year-old murderer seemed at best an exercise in conjuring more suited to a magic show on the Vegas strip than serious police work.

Utley was right about the second drawing too. There were hints in it of the boy Richard Shelton had been. The way the mouth turned at the edges as he smiled, the shape of the eyes. But what was most striking was what wasn't present in the face. The experiences that form character in an individual – the things that escape definition in a person – weren't there. There was no history in the face, no pain or joy, not a single memory seemed hidden behind the eyes. It was as if a mirror had been held up to a large crowd, yet all that the glass contained was the reflection of a single face cobbled together out of the hundreds that stood before it.

Security was in place watching Cathy O'Brien at the

hospital; when her doctor returned in the morning, we would talk to her. So as we waited for dawn to break I lay on the couch and tried to sleep. The dream that came in its place resembled an amusement park ride more than rest. One moment I was in an examination room, naked, surrounded by doctors, their faces hidden by masks. The next I was moving through the tunnels under Caltech, except I wasn't the pursuer. I was running for my life, the sounds of my chasers right behind me in the dark, their fingers occasionally reaching out and pulling at the fabric of my shirt as I ran deeper into an ever-expanding maze of tunnels.

I felt the light touch of a hand on my shoulder and I quickly opened my eyes. Chief Chavez was sitting in a chair next to me. The sun had risen. The sound of morning traffic drifted up from the streets below. Across the room, Harrison was asleep in a chair.

'What time is it?' I asked.

'Just after eight,' Chavez said.

I started to sit up, but the muscles of my back where I had hit the wall of the tunnel had stiffened as I slept and fought every movement I made.

'Looks like you had a full night,' Chavez said.

He took my hand and helped me to sit up, then reached out and touched the bruise on my cheek.

'I thought I gave you instructions not to be alone.'

'The man who did that apologized. Nothing to worry about,' I said.

'You keep taking physical punishment like this and you'll be old before your time.'

'I'm a mother, I'm already old before my time.'

He sat back and looked at me the way a disapproving parent might.

'What is it?' I asked.

'You've been dreaming,' he said.

He reached over and picked a mug of coffee up off the table and handed it to me. I cupped it in my hands and inhaled its warm vapors then took a sip.

'How long have you been sitting here?' I asked.

'You were talking in your sleep,' he said.

'Nothing incriminating, I hope.'

'You were dreaming about doctors. What's going on, Alex?'

I took another sip of coffee and leaned back into the cushion.

'You know how dreams are,' I said. 'I don't remember.'

Chavez looked at me for a moment, his big brown eyes taking on a wounded quality.

'There's not much we haven't gone through together, so why for the first time are you lying to me?'

I eased myself up off the couch and then leaned in and kissed him on the cheek.

'You mean it's the first time that I lied to you that you know of,' I said.

I stepped over to the window and looked down on to the street. The nearest traffic light was functioning.

'What time did power come back?' I asked.

'About six,' Chavez said. 'The heat is supposed to begin to break by Saturday, until then rolling blackouts will continue. We'll probably start to see some here in the late afternoon.'

'What day of the week is it?' I asked.

'It's Thursday.'

The Chief walked over to the window.

'Tell me about him – are we closer?' he asked.

'Closer?' I shook my head. 'He's a psychopath but he's not a madman. There's a purpose behind all this.'

'Is that good or bad news?' Chavez asked.

'I don't know.'

Harrison sat up.

I looked at him for a moment and then turned back to the Chief.

'I need to get to the hospital,' I said.

Chavez reached into his pocket, removed a note and handed it to me.

'A Doctor Moikenah returned your call while you were asleep. She'll meet you at the nursing station in critical care in twenty minutes.'

The backlog of patients needing treatment from the overnight hours had begun to ease as we walked in through emergency. Staff were busy resupplying the trauma stations with bandages and IVs in anticipation once again of the rise in temperature in the coming hours.

We stepped off the elevator on to the second floor and started walking toward the nursing station in the critical care unit. A single nurse was working the desk, trying to oversee the beeps of the monitors surrounding her; there was no sign of Dr Moikenah.

'I'm meeting a Dr Moikenah here,' I said.

The nurse looked at me and shook her head. 'I haven't seen her.'

'She's attending Cathy O'Brien,' I said.

The nurse looked down at her charts. 'You're sure the name was O'Brien?'

'Yes. There would have been security watching her room,' I said.

The nurse nodded in recognition. 'She was moved this morning after the incident.'

'Incident?'

'She began screaming that a doctor was trying to kill her. Apparently there was an altercation of some kind.'

'What was the name of the doctor?' I asked.

The nurse shook her head. 'I just came on, I don't know.'

'Where did you move her?' I asked.

She searched the desk, trying to find an answer, and then picked up the phone and asked whoever was on the other end and then turned to me.

'She's upstairs on the fourth floor, room four ten.'

'Was she injured?' I asked.

'That's all the information I have.'

We walked to the elevator and took it up to the fourth.

'You think there's a problem?' Harrison said.

'If it were any other patient I'd say she was practicing sound common sense.'

The door opened and we stepped out on to the fourth floor. The nursing station was down the hallway to the right. Harrison checked the room numbers then motioned toward the other end of the hallway.

'She'd be down there, past the nursing station.'

We walked to the nursing station as a series of pages

went out over the PA system. There was no one at the desk.

'They must be doing rounds,' I said.

Harrison was looking down the hallways that spilt off in two directions from the station.

'Her room would be there,' Harrison said, motioning to the right.

I turned and looked.

'There's no security at her room,' I said.

We started to walk when a nurse stepped out of a patient's room and strode toward the desk.

'Can you tell me why there's no security on Cathy O'Brien's room?' I asked and showed the nurse my badge.

'The doctor had them removed,' she said.

'When?' I asked.

'A little while ago. He said it was upsetting her.'

'Did you say he?'

She nodded. 'Yes.'

'Which doctor?'

'The attending, I suppose.'

'You're not familiar with him?' I asked.

She shook her head. 'I'd never seen him before.'

'How long ago was this?'

'Twenty minutes at most.'

'Have you seen the doctor again?'

She thought for a moment and then glanced down the hallway toward O'Brien's room.

'That's him.'

I turned. A doctor wearing a long white jacket was walking toward O'Brien's room from the other end. I stared in silence for an instant. Was it Shelton? Until that moment I wasn't certain that he even existed. I glanced quickly at Dylan as he dropped his hand to the weapon on his belt.

'Did he have a British accent?' I asked the nurse.

'Yes. How did you know that?'

I took a step away from the desk and the doctor looked in our direction and stopped. From this distance I couldn't make out his features beyond dark hair and glasses.

'Call security, have them come up to Cathy O'Brien's room right now,' I said.

I moved my hand casually down to my gun, took a step and the doctor turned and bolted in the other direction.

'He'll try and get out of the building. Get to the nearest exit,' I said as I began to run and Harrison took off for the elevator.

I reached Cathy O'Brien's door just as the doctor disappeared through a stairway door at the end. I quickly pushed open Cathy's door and looked inside. She lay on her back, her head turned away. Under the sheet I could see her chest steadily rise and fall with each breath.

I stepped back and rushed over to the stairwell door, slipped my weapon out and pushed it open. From below I heard the sound of footfalls on the metal stairs and then a door opened and closed and the stairwell fell silent.

I made the third-floor landing taking two steps at a time and continued down without slowing until I reached the second floor and stopped. On the floor lay a white doctor's lab coat and a pair of glasses.

My hand tightened around the handle of my gun and I

pulled the door open and stepped out into the hallway. A nurse was pushing a patient past in a wheelchair. A family stood outside a patient's room holding hands. Down the corridor an orderly pushed a food cart. Beyond that, two doctors leaned against the wall engaged in conversation.

I stepped back into the stairwell and continued down until I reached the first-floor landing where the stairs went down another flight to the parking garage. I opened the first-floor landing door and stepped out into the front reception lobby of the hospital. Dozens of people were moving in every direction. I held my gun close to my hip to keep it as inconspicuous as a weapon could be. The glass doors of the main entrance were to the right. Emergency exit signs pointed down the lobby to the left.

I moved through the crowd towards the doors, my gaze pausing on the back of a head, a passing face, the turn of a shoulder or a body moving through the crowd a little faster than everyone around it.

Someone bumped me from behind and I started to turn as they said, 'Excuse me,' and vanished into the crowd.

As I reached the doors, I saw Harrison standing outside, looking up and down the street. I turned and looked back into the lobby, scanning any face with dark hair. Nothing.

I began to turn toward the doors to step outside when I caught movement – the stairway door I had come out of fell shut. I started rushing back through the crowd to the stairway. As I reached for the door, it flew open. I instinctively raised my gun but stopped as two blond teenagers came bounding out, laughing at each other. I lowered the gun to my side and stepped back into the stairway and rushed down to the garage level and opened the door.

The air was heavy as if I had just stepped into the humid heat of the east coast. The hum of ventilation fans filled the space. A car engine came to life and tires squealed on the polished concrete.

I started walking across the garage, looking up and down the rows of parked cars. Behind me a door opened and closed and I swung round to see a woman step out and start walking toward the elevator next to the stairs.

At the far end of the garage a dark sedan heading round the corner toward the exit ramp stopped. Behind the darkly tinted windows the driver was invisible. I took a step forward and the engine revved. I started running toward the car.

Ten feet from the car, the window began to come down and I stopped and raised the Glock. Halfway down, the window stopped and I saw the glow of a cigarette fly out and skitter across the concrete. A young woman with cropped dark hair was staring at me, her eyes fixed on the gun in my hand.

I lowered the gun and the woman stepped on the gas, sending the car swerving up the exit ramp and out into the bright sun and was gone.

I took a breath and looked back into the garage, slipped the gun into the holster and walked up the ramp to the street. In the bright glare of the sun I looked up and down the block. Nothing was out of place. No car was moving too fast. No pedestrian drew attention by the way they moved.

I walked up to the front entrance where Harrison was still standing.

'If he came this way I didn't see him,' Harrison said.

'He dumped the white jacket and glasses in the stairway,' I said.

'We missed our chance,' Harrison said.

I nodded. 'Yes, but we know more than we did before.'

'Cathy O'Brien knows him?'

'Even if she doesn't realize it.'

I turned and looked into the busy lobby and then back at the pedestrians walking the sidewalk in front of the hospital. 'He's probably watching us right now. He would enjoy that,' I said. 'He could have reached out and touched one of us and we wouldn't have known it.'

'Counting coup,' Harrison said. 'Like a Sioux warrior.'

I nodded and looked back into the lobby.

'Someone did bump into me,' I said, trying to remember a face.

'Did you see him?'

I shook my head. 'No, I turned and they were gone.'

'Which way?'

I walked back into the lobby retracing my steps and Harrison followed. A few feet inside I stopped.

'He could have gone in any direction.' I looked over to the bank of elevators. 'He could even have gone back up.'

We were moving before I had even finished the words. We stepped out on to the fourth floor and started toward the nursing station. A security guard was leaning on the desk, talking to the nurse.

We ran past them on towards O'Brien's room and as we approached, the door opened and we started to reach for our weapons.

'Lieutenant.'

I stopped and moved my hand away from the gun as Dr Moikenah closed the door.

'What's going on here, Lieutenant?' she asked. 'My patient is moved without my permission, then you show up and chase a doctor down a flight of stairs.'

'He wasn't a doctor,' I said.

'What do you mean he wasn't . . .' She stopped herself and looked down at Harrison's hand, which was still touching his gun.

'It was him?' she asked. 'In the hospital?'

'He was posing as a doctor.'

'Did he get inside her room?' she asked.

'If he had I don't think we would be having this conversation,' I said.

'I don't understand. If he had wanted to harm her he could have done that before. Something's changed?'

I nodded. 'She isn't aware of it, but we believe she knows him.'

Moikenah looked back in confusion. 'If she's not aware of it, what possible threat does—' She stopped herself again. 'You're aware of it, that's why you're here.'

'Yes.'

'And that puts her in danger?'

'Very much so. We'll have our officers here to watch over her before we leave. Can she talk to us?' I asked.

'You think she can help you?'

'We're trying to find a face from her past. She's the only one who can do that.'

'She was confused about being moved,' she said. 'I've sedated her, that's helped, but . . .' Moikenah paused, carefully considering her next words. 'She believes you are in part responsible for what happened to her husband. She may react badly to you. You understand that?'

'I often draw that kind of reaction from people,' I said. 'We'll be as brief as possible.'

'I would prefer that she not know he was in the hospital.'

'Of course.'

'I'll need a word with her first,' Moikenah said then turned and entered the room.

She walked back out a moment later and held the door open for us and we walked in. Cathy O'Brien's eyes followed me as I moved across the room. Her face remained expressionless, more like a mask, disconnected from the intense gaze that followed my every step. I went to the left side of the bed, Moikenah went round to the right.

'I have some pictures I need you to look at,' I said.

Her jaw muscles flexed with tension. And she looked away from me over toward the window.

'I never saw him, I told you that,' she said in a flat, emotionless voice.

'I know.'

'Then you must be stupid,' she said.

'We think you've seen him before.'

'Before what? Before killing my husband?'

'When you were at Oxford,' I said.

She slowly turned away from the window and looked at me.

'I don't understand,' she said.

'He would have been a student, like your husband. You may have met him through Professor Simms,' I said. 'These are guesses of what he may look like now, we don't have a name.'

'Guesses . . . you talk like it's a game.'

'Approximations,' I said. 'It's all we have right now.'

She stared at me for a moment. 'You're not very good at what you do, are you?' she said.

'I have many failings,' I said. 'That's why we need your help.'

Harrison handed her the pictures one at a time. She stared at each of them intently, though I couldn't be sure how much she was truly seeing beyond the trauma still inside her. When she had finished looking at them she held them up and looked away.

'These mean nothing to me,' she said.

'Are you certain?' I asked.

'Yes,' she said.

Moikenah glanced at me and shook her head, not wanting me to press her any further but I couldn't stop quite yet.

'I need to ask you one more question,' I said.

If she heard my words she gave no indication of it.

'How much money was in the freezer?'

She turned to me. 'What is it you want?'

'I want to stop him from killing again,' I said.

'By hurting my husband?' she said.

'I can't hurt your husband now,' I said. 'But I may be able to stop another death.'

She looked toward the window and then a tear slid down her cheek.

'How much money was in that freezer?' I asked again.

She took a deep breath as if to brace herself. 'It changed. Sometimes it was full, other times there would be less. He was always moving money.'

'Did you know where it came from?'

She shook her head. 'Trades and commissions was all Jimmy would tell me. He said he didn't want to put it back in the market until it had stabilized.'

'Did you believe that?' I asked.

She closed her eyes. 'I wanted to.' She took a shaky breath and looked back out the window. 'You get used to things, and after a while it becomes easier to say nothing than to ask a question. I never said a word.'

'Do you know where he would move it when he took it out of the freezer?' I asked.

'He would tell me he was investing it in something safe and secure.' She turned and looked at me. 'Safe?'

'He would have kept records of this somewhere,' I asked. 'Do you know where that is?'

'There was nothing in the house or on our computers. I looked once.'

'Could it be at the office?'

She shook her head. 'He was always meeting with Lawrence about it. He called them strategy sessions.'

'Simms?' I asked and she nodded.

'It was the money, wasn't it?' Cathy asked. 'What happened was because of that?'

I nodded. 'Yes, I think so.'

She clenched one of her fists, driving a nail into the palm of her hand.

'Would Jimmy be alive if I had asked him?' she said. 'Could I have stopped all this?'

'I don't know,' I said.

Her eyes remained focused on me for a moment then she sank back into the pillows as if she was falling from a great height. Moikenah looked at me and nodded. Harrison and I turned and walked out of the room.

'Could we be wrong about this? Is there another reason he might have come?' Harrison said as we walked down the hallway.

I stopped and looked back toward the room. 'No, Shelton would not have risked coming here unless she knew him. She clearly doesn't have a clue about the money.'

'Shelton might not know that.'

'Shelton knows how to find the money, and that's through Simms. It's why Earl Moon's dead. What did she call her husband's meetings with him?'

'Strategy sessions.'

I nodded. 'A nice word for money laundering.'

'That doesn't get us any closer to him if she can't recognize him,' Dylan said.

'Maybe she's not the only one who can find that face.'

'What are you getting at?'

'Memories,' I said. 'Everyone has them, they keep them in drawers and closets.'

'You've still lost me,' he said.

'In O'Brien's office at Beckwith, Myers and Dunne, he had snapshots in the bookcase.' I turned and walked back into the room. Cathy appeared to have sunk deeper into the bed, almost as if she was trying to disappear into it.

'Lieutenant,' Moikenah protested.

'Just one question,' I said. 'It's very simple.'

Cathy opened her eyes and looked at me.

'I'll try,' she said.

'Do you have pictures of your time in Oxford?'

She shook her head in confusion. 'Pictures?'

'Snapshots, photo albums. Do you have them somewhere in the house?'

The words began to make sense to her and she nodded. 'Jimmy liked to take pictures . . . I used to kid him about it.'

'Where would I find them?' I asked.

She struggled as if trying to reach back to a life she no longer had. 'Find them?'

'Where in the house would they be?' I asked.

'The closet.'

'Which closet?'

'The office downstairs,' she said.

'Would there be pictures from your time in Oxford?' I asked.

She nodded. 'Everything we did is in them,' she whispered and closed her eyes.

eighteen

When a uniformed officer arrived to watch over Cathy O'Brien, we left the hospital and drove across town to the O'Briens' address on Sequoia. Crime scene tape still surrounded the property, seals forbidding entry covered all the doors.

As we stepped inside, the odor of dried blood filled the interior like air-freshener gone bad. We walked downstairs and stopped outside the office. Re-entering a crime scene with new knowledge is a little like stepping back in time after rewriting history. The evidence you thought you had understood so clearly before now appears entirely different. Knowing that the violence that had taken place inside this house was part of a charade somehow made it even crueler. This wasn't the work of a serial killer. The messages, the peepholes in the bedroom door, the money Shelton left behind; it was stagecraft, sleight of hand by a violent magician trying to conceal his greed.

I stepped into the office and turned on the light. Fingerprint dust covered nearly every surface. There were two closets in the room. I took one, Harrison looked in the other.

'They're in here,' Dylan said.

I went to the other side of the room and looked in the closet.

'She wasn't kidding,' Harrison said. 'He liked to take pictures.'

Several shelves in the middle of the closet were devoted to storing photo albums.

'There are a couple dozen here at least,' Harrison said. 'Where do you want to start?'

'Pick one,' I said.

Harrison slipped one out and opened it up.

'They're indexed by place and date,' he said, scanning the page.

'O'Brien was thirty-two,' I said. 'That would put him in Oxford sometime in the last six to twelve years.'

We started working our way back through a life that now only existed in snapshots – anniversaries, barbecues, Dodger games, birthdays, the Grand Canyon, Baja, dinners, and picture after picture of moments that had no place in history at all other than a smile, the turn of a head or fleeting laugh.

'Here it is,' Harrison said, running his finger down the index page. 'England, London, Oxford. Eight years ago. From the dates here it appears he was there for only one year.'

Dylan carried it over to a desk on the other side of the room, took out the three images we had of a possible Richard Shelton and then began to page through photographs hoping to find even the faintest of connections.

'Buildings,' Harrison said. 'This is all London.'

We skipped ahead until we found the first photographs of Oxford. More pictures of old buildings, dining halls, churches, page after page of it.

'More old stuff.'

'I think I have some of the same travel snapshots at home,' I said.

Harrison closed the album and shook his head. 'This isn't what we're looking for, it's not here.'

I walked back to the closet and began skimming through the rest of them. The third one I opened appeared more promising.

'I think I found it,' I said and brought it over to the desk and opened it.

'England, people, friends,' Harrison said, reading the index page.

'If Shelton's here, this would be it,' I said.

'He would have been in his early twenties.'

We began slowly going through each photograph, looking for the faintest of resemblances to the three possible Sheltons. The way the line of hair fell over a forehead, the shape of the mouth. Jim O'Brien was a social animal. His coverage of old buildings was comprehensive but it didn't hold a candle to the number of pictures he took of people. Dozens of young men in the pictures fitted the age profile, not one seemed to fill in the blanks the computer images had generated.

'I wonder if there was anyone in England he didn't take a picture of?'

Harrison turned the page and his eyes fell on an image on the bottom right page.

'Simms,' he said.

'It's in a pub.'

Simms was holding up a pint of beer toward the picture taker. A man who appeared to be in his early fifties, with slightly graying hair, was sitting to his left, looking away from the camera. To his right, the shoulder of someone sitting next to him was visible – a dark blue shirt and the edge of a collar, but nothing more.

'What does that look like to you?' I said.

'Stout,' Harrison said. 'But it's not Guinness, it's not black enough.'

'Next time we find an Irishman murdered, remind me to put you in charge.'

I reached out and tapped the picture with my finger. 'Look at what he's doing. He's talking and he's holding up a glass.'

'He's toasting something,' Dylan said.

I nodded.

'That could be anything,' Harrison said.

'Look at the person to his right, the angle of the arm.'

'It's raised too.'

'To what, is the question,' I said.

'Even if we knew that was Shelton sitting to the right, it doesn't help us.'

'What about the man to the left?'

'He's looking away and his arm isn't raised. I'd say he's unconnected.'

'Check the next page.'

Harrison turned it and my eyes fell on the very first picture. We stared in silence for a moment. It was the next picture in the sequence from inside the pub. O'Brien had moved the camera to include the man in the blue shirt next to Simms. The man on the left was no longer visible. The blue-shirted man held a glass up toward the camera, obscuring the right side of his face. I reached down and picked up the second computer image of a possible Shelton, and then looked back at the face of the man in the pub.

'What do you think?' I said.

'It's only half a face,' Harrison said.

I quickly looked over the rest of the page in the album. There were more shots from inside the pub.

'Look at this one, it's taken from the other side of the bar, looking back at the table where they were sitting,' I said.

Simms had turned and was looking at the camera. The man in the blue shirt was blurred as if he had turned away just as the picture was snapped. Harrison quickly paged through the rest of the album but the man in the blue shirt didn't make another appearance.

We turned back to the two pub pictures.

'Out of all the photographs in this album he's in only two, and in neither one is his face completely visible,' I said.

'What are the chances of that?'

'Not very good.'

'Doesn't sound like coincidence, does it?' Dylan said.

I reached down and slipped the picture of him holding the beer to the camera from its sleeve and turned it over. Nothing was written on the back of it, no date, no name. I laid it back down.

'What do you see?' I said, staring at it.

'As in?' he asked.

'Every picture has a story. What's this one's?'

Harrison studied it, examining every detail within the frame.

'His expression is different from Simms's,' Dylan said.

'How?'

Harrison's eyes moved back and forth between Simms and the man in the blue shirt.

'His mouth is open but he's not talking like Simms, and the look in his eyes, his focus, is different. It's not the same emotion at all.'

I nodded.

'He's laughing,' Harrison said.

'But not at something funny,' I said.

'You're right. It's like he's laughing to himself,' he said.

'Or at a secret.'

We sat in silence for a moment.

'You think it's Shelton?' Harrison said.

I nodded. 'It will do until the actual Shelton shows up.'

'You want to show this to Cathy O'Brien?'

'Yes.'

'And if she still can't ID him?'

'We'll try Caltech. Perhaps someone there would know him, or if he's a student we can match it to an ID photo.'

'And short of that?'

'We find Simms before he does,' I said.

'If he isn't dead already.'

*

When we walked back into Cathy O'Brien's room, she was out of bed and was staring out the window. She didn't turn when we walked in; I wasn't even certain she had heard us. She was staring at the lock on the window as if trying to understand in her confused mind how to open it. I motioned to Dylan and he stepped back out the door and I walked over to her.

There was a bandage on the palm of her hand where her nails had dug into her skin. Her eyes had more clarity than when we had seen her earlier, though what she saw when she looked at the world I still couldn't imagine.

'The window's sealed,' I said. 'It can't be opened.'

She stared straight ahead without turning to acknowledge me. 'Did you think I wanted to jump, Lieutenant?'

I stood next to her. 'I know something about PTSD.'

'As a policeman?' she said coldly. 'Did you have a training session?'

I shook my head. 'No.'

She turned and looked into my eyes.

'I was raped,' I said.

She stared at me for a moment and then looked back out the window at the people walking below on the street.

'Do they know? How many of them know?' she asked.

'Know what?'

'How dark the night can be?'

'The lucky ones don't,' I said.

'And everyone else?'

'They live their lives, that's all there is.'

'Is it enough?' she asked.

'Some days it is,' I said.

'And the other days?'

'You get through them.'

She lowered her head and shook it. 'How?' she asked.

'Any way you can,' I said.

'And if you don't want to?'

'You wait for the day where you do want to get through.'

She took a breath and then took a half step away from the glass of the window.

'Did you find what you were looking for?' she asked.

'Perhaps. Would you look at it?'

I held it out to her and she took it. As she studied it, her face remained expressionless.

'Do you remember this picture?' I asked.

'It's a pub we'd go to once or twice a week. That's Lawrence on the left.'

'And the other man?'

She stared at it in silence, occasionally moving her head as if she were trying to see around the beer glass that obscured the face.

'You think this is the man who murdered my husband?'

'I don't know,' I said.

'But out of all the pictures my husband took in Oxford, this is the only one you bring me to look at.'

'I need a name,' I said.

She shook her head. 'I wasn't there when this picture was taken. Why don't you ask Lawrence?'

'When I find him I will,' I said.

Cathy looked at me for a moment and then back at the picture. 'There was someone I met once or twice, it could be him.'

'Do you have a name?'

She shook her head. 'I don't think I knew his last name. I think his first name was Peter.'

'You're sure about that name?'

'I think so.'

'Is there anything about him you remember?' I asked.

She stared at the picture and nodded. 'He was different from any of the other students I met.'

'So he was a student, you remember that?'

'Yes.'

'How was he different?'

'He didn't seem to belong there,' she said.

'Like he was out of place?' I asked.

She shook her head. 'No, like he held the other students in contempt.'

'For what?'

'Their stupidity.'

'You got the impression he was quite smart?'

'No, I got the impression he was a genius.'

'Did your husband ever talk about him?' I asked.

'Once. It was after the first time I met him.'

'What did he say?'

'Jimmy said if I was ever out alone somewhere and I ran into him, that I should leave and not talk to him.'

'Did he tell you why?'

'He didn't have to,' she said.

'You thought he was dangerous?'

She nodded. 'You could see it in his eyes.'

'What about them?'

'They were like a cat's.'

'What do you mean?'

'It was the way they looked at you. Like he was hunting, always looking for a weakness.'

'Is there anyone else you can think of who might know him?' I asked.

'No. Like I said, I only met him once or twice.'

She took one more look at the picture and then I thanked her and started for the door.

'Where did the money my husband had come from, Lieutenant?' she asked.

I stopped and turned. 'Maybe this isn't the time.'

'Do you know what it's like to discover that half of your life is a lie? Is there a good time to learn that? Please tell me.'

'The money came from drugs,' I said.

She mouthed the words the way I had whispered cancer to myself after the doctor informed me of the mass in my breast.

'He did this with Lawrence?'

I nodded.

'Can you prove it?' she asked.

I looked at her, reluctant to say any more.

'Can you, Lieutenant?'

'I'm not a narcotics officer, it's not my job.'

Cathy O'Brien played the meaning of my words, or rather the unsaid meaning, over in her head.

'I see. You know it's true because he was murdered.'

'Yes,' I said.

She turned and looked out the window and shook her

head. 'Was what happened to you your worst nightmare, Lieutenant?'

'No, I survived that. The worst is the one that hasn't happened yet,' I said, involuntarily putting my hand up to my chest.

'If you don't catch him, will I always be waiting for him to step out of the darkness?'

'I'll catch him,' I said.

She turned to me. 'Promise me.'

I nodded to her. 'I promise.'

I turned to the door.

'Norton,' she said.

I stopped. 'I'm sorry?'

'If that's a picture of the person I think it is. His last name was Norton.'

'You're certain?'

She hesitated for a moment and then took a breath. 'I'm not certain of anything any more, Lieutenant, but if it's him, that's his name, or was.'

'Thank you,' I said.

I started down the hallway with Harrison. 'We have a name,' I said.

'She's sure?' Harrison asked.

'Not that you'd take to court, but it will have to do. The name's Peter Norton.'

'Since he's changed it, how does that help us?' Harrison said. 'We're not even certain that this is a picture of our suspect. She may have the right name but there's no guarantee that it's Shelton.'

'It's him,' I said. 'It has to be.'

'Why?

'Her husband warned her to stay away from him because he thought he was dangerous. And when she described him, she called him a genius who held the other students in contempt. Sound familiar?' I said.

'It's a start.'

'There's another reason.'

'What?'

'We've wasted far too much time if it isn't him.'

'That still doesn't alter the fact that he came over on a different passport, and the only image we have of him is half a face at best,' Harrison said.

'If she could ID him from it, someone else may be able to. And if Agent Utley can convince his contacts at Scotland Yard that our suspect is this Peter Norton, then perhaps they will confirm that he was Shelton.'

'And we get a complete photo of him,' Harrison said.

'Even without the name he traveled on, at least we would have the photograph.'

We took the elevator down and stepped back into the heat outside. As we reached the squad, I checked my watch and realized I had fifteen minutes to get to my doctor's appointment for the biopsy.

'Can you get back to headquarters on your own?' I said. 'I have to be somewhere.'

Harrison took his hand off the door handle and looked across the car roof at me.

'I'll talk to Utley,' I said. 'I want you to get over to

Caltech and start showing that picture around.'

Harrison shook his head. 'Did I miss something?'

'What?'

'I have specific orders not to leave you alone. I don't think that's changed,' Dylan said.

'Shelton isn't testing himself against anyone, that was all a fiction,' I said. 'I'm no more in danger from him than you are. We don't have the time to waste for you to come and hold my hand at a doctor's appointment that isn't your business.'

I could see in Harrison's eyes that my words stung.

'Are we talking on a personal or professional level?' he said. 'Maybe I'm wrong, but I've always found making love to be of a fairly personal nature.'

'I didn't mean that the way it sounded,' I said.

'How did you mean it then?' he asked.

I shook my head. 'Not that way.'

'You've been avoiding telling me something, but it's there, sitting silently between us. Talk to me, Alex,' he said. 'I don't know what you want, but if it's not me, I'd prefer you just tell me.'

I walked around to his side of the car, the words sticking in my throat. Then I held his hand in mine, took a deep breath, and placed it on my right breast, the words suddenly stumbling from my mouth.

'They found a lump in there. I have trouble finding it myself, but having once been a teenage boy, maybe you've spent more time investigating breasts than I have.'

I took my hand away. Harrison's hand lingered for a moment, then his fingers gently slipped away.

'Kind of takes the fun out of copping a feel, doesn't it?' I said.

'Stop,' he said.

'Stop what? The mass, the growth, the lump?'

'Stop,' he repeated softly, his eyes locking on mine, and as always, from the first time I looked into them with intent, they went through me, taking any sense of self with them.

'As you might guess, Shelton is the last thing I'm frightened of right now,' I said.

'How long have you known this?' Harrison's voice had a remote quality that I didn't know how to take.

I took another deep breath to try and slow down my heart, which was beginning to beat against my chest.

'A few days.'

'Have you told Lacy?'

'Yes . . .' I paused and looked into his eyes. 'You, you're the only other one. It's just a biopsy today.'

'What have they told you?' he asked.

'That I have nothing to worry about.'

Dylan shook his head. 'Those weren't the right words, were they?'

'No, they were just about the worst possible thing to say to a cop.'

I looked at him for a moment, trying to understand what was going on behind those green eyes of his. Was it doubt, fear, was he looking for the exit door?

'So what do we do now?' I asked. 'Shall I run through the possible scenarios of what you have to look forward to with me?'

'Stop,' he said again.

'How?' I asked. 'I'm not in control of this.'

'When will you have the results?' Harrison asked.

'I'm not sure. A few days maybe.'

'I'm sorry.'

'It's not exactly what I imagined for myself.' I paused. 'I suppose you're thinking the same thing.'

Harrison began to say something and then the words slipped away.

'You don't have to say anything, you've had enough tragedy in your life, you don't need another.'

'Is that what this is?' Dylan asked.

'Call it a preview of coming attractions,' I said.

'That's not like you, Alex,' Harrison said.

'What isn't?'

'To make conclusions about evidence that doesn't exist.'

'Well, I've never had a case like this before.'

'What can I do?'

'Talk to the Dean of Students at Caltech. We need that list of students from the UK.'

'That's not what I meant.' He looked at me for a moment, the disappointment evident, and then started to turn.

'I don't know how to deal with this quite yet, it's all rather new,' I said.

Dylan hesitated and then looked back. 'You will,' he said. 'You're the most fearless woman I've ever known.'

I stepped over to him, placed my hand on his chest, started to lean into him, but stopped myself.

'If this is more than you bargained for, don't tell me for

a few days,' I said and then stepped back. 'I'm not quite that fearless.'

Harrison nodded.

'I'll go to my appointment and then meet you at Caltech,' I said.

'When they have the results, I'd like to take you to that appointment,' he said.

I nodded. 'I'll take your offer under serious consideration . . . Thank you,' I said.

'All right,' said Harrison.

'There is one other thing,' I said.

'Name it.'

'I don't know where any of this is going. And when I get there I don't know if I'll have anything to give to you . . . perhaps before then, we should try making love when we haven't found a body,' I said.

Dylan nodded and smiled. 'I thought you were going to ask me something difficult.'

I shook my head. 'I'm saving that one.'

nineteen

The half dozen people inside the elevator in the medical building stood nervously waiting to reach their floor before the power once again shut off and trapped them inside. With each floor that we stopped at I could hear an audible sigh of relief as people stepped out and walked quickly away as if trying to put space between themselves and the elevator.

The receptionist at the doctor's office watched me suspiciously as I signed in then took the sheet in her hand and double-checked my name. I had forgotten that I had slept in the clothes I was wearing. Being knocked about by Earl Moon hadn't done much for my appearance either.

'It's pronounced Delillo,' I said.

I took a seat in reception and waited with the half dozen other women all in various stages of what I assumed was a possible version of my future. Bald wearing a baseball cap, bald wearing a wig, hair coming back, a woman dressed in a business suit trying very hard to remember that she was an executive who commanded respect as she waited to receive the results of her biopsy.

The woman in the baseball cap noticed my badge and the handle of my weapon just visible under my jacket. In most instances the presence of a cop, and if not the cop at least the gun, sends uneasiness through a room, but not in this one. There was no rank, no job, no kids, no history at all when you stepped into this world.

After a moment of watching me, she got up and walked over, taking the seat next to me.

'Are you here for a biopsy?' she asked.

'You should be a detective,' I said.

'I've spent a lot of time in these rooms, you become a student of the genre.'

She appeared to be a few years older than me, though her treatment made determining her age a little difficult. There was something familiar in her face, the way an old faded photograph sometimes is, but I couldn't place her.

'If the gun is bothering you . . .

She shook her head. 'I think you might be on to something. If every doctor knew the patient they were treating had a gun on their hip, the quality of care would skyrocket. Which doctor are you seeing?'

I started to answer and then realized I had no idea what his name was.

'He has a lot of ear hair,' I said.

'That would be Shaw,' she said. 'He's good, I saw him with my first cancer.'

I wasn't used to hearing the word cancer thrown about in casual conversation, or at least not the way she used it. Cancer in most circles was something you talked about in the third person, like a work of fiction. She used the word as if it were a relative that had come to stay for what was a very long visit.

'What procedure are they doing today?' she asked.

Again I was at a loss for what the doctor had told me about it.

'They'll be using a needle,' I answered.

She nodded enthusiastically. 'That's good.'

'It is?' I asked and she nodded again.

'It probably means there's just as much of a chance that it's a cyst as it is a cancer.'

The receptionist called my name and I started to get up and then looked back at her.

'I know you – we've met somewhere?' I asked.

She shook her head. 'You might recognize the old me, I was a lawyer with the DA's office in LA. I interviewed you once for a gang shooting. That was another lifetime ago.'

I recognized her then and realized she wasn't my age at all but at least ten years younger. I reached out and shook her hand. The frailness of her grip betrayed the strength of her spirit.

'If they ask you to take the gun off, Lieutenant,' she said and smiled, 'tell them it's against regulations.'

I thanked her and then was walked by a nurse to the examination room.

'If you would remove everything on top and then slip into the smock on the table,' she said and then her eyes drifted down to the Glock on my waist. 'You can put that on the chair in the corner.'

People who had never spent time around weapons rarely called them what they were, it was always a 'that' or a 'thing'.

'You mean the gun?' I said, already clinging to it as if it were a life preserver.

'Yes,' she said. 'You can put it on the chair.'

'I'll have to keep it,' I said. 'I'm on a case.'

She looked at me nervously then turned and quickly left. I walked over to the examination table and picked up the smock and then looked around the room. It was painted a cheery pale yellow. There was a drawing of a covered bridge over a New England river which was probably an attempt to offer a kind of natural sense of tranquility that the Los Angeles landscape just didn't afford. There was nothing else on the walls, most specifically no mirror.

I removed my blouse, carefully slipping it off my sore shoulder and ribs where Earl had knocked me down, and put on the smock. I realized I had forgotten to call Utley at the FBI so I dialed him.

'Lieutenant,' he answered. 'I've got no more news from London,' he said.

'Would a name help?' I said.

'Do you have one?'

'Cathy O'Brien remembered a man from when they were in Oxford named Peter Norton.'

'You think it's Shelton?'

'It's possible. Perhaps Scotland Yard can match him to that name.'

'You got any more details?' Utley asked.

The door opened and the doctor walked in, followed by a nurse carrying a tray covered with a large syringe and some other items that I didn't bother to look at. I reached down and placed my hand on my hip, pushing back the smock just enough so the doctor could see my weapon.

'He was a student at Oxford who took classes from Simms. The three of them may have been involved together in something, probably drugs, but I have no evidence to back that up,' I said.

'That should be enough,' Utley said.

'I need a current photograph.'

'It's going on ten at night there already. I'll see what I can do,' he said and hung up.

I put the phone away and turned to the doctor.

'All set?' he asked with an edge of impatience in his voice. 'Let's have you up on the end there and lie down on the table. This won't take long.'

I lay on the table. The nurse placed a copy of my mammogram on the light box and the doctor slipped on a pair of surgical gloves.

'What we're doing is called a fine needle aspiration. I'm going to swab the area where the needle will penetrate with a sterile solution, and then anaesthetize the area. The nurse will then apply some gel to assist the ultrasound so I can get a more accurate picture of the mass as I take the samples. To get the best possible results I'll take either two or three samples. The solution and the gel are a little cold,' he said as he studied the mammogram. He then turned and stepped over to the table.

He opened the right side of the smock, pulled it back

and both he and the nurse reacted to what they saw.

'Has anyone looked at these bruises?'

'You're the first,' I said.

'You could have some broken ribs here, and there's some hemorrhaging in your breast. Are you all right?'

'I would describe the man who did this last night as bigger than a small prick but smaller than a Buick.'

'Would you like to wait on the test?'

'No,' I said. 'I wouldn't like to.'

'This may be more uncomfortable than it normally would be.'

'Well, since I normally don't get needles stuck into my breast, I'll just assume you're correct on that.'

He did a quick examination with his hands to locate the mass and then swabbed my breast with the sterile solution.

'You'll feel a small prick now,' he said and began working the needle into my breast. 'Are you all right?'

I nodded rather than say what I actually thought about his understanding of the nature of small pricks.

'Just a little more,' he said and I found myself watching his ears to see if the hair was growing.

'You'll begin to numb up very quickly and then I'll take the tissue sample.'

He waited a moment and then placed his hand back on my breast.

'Can you feel that?' he asked.

The very first boy in high school to ever touch my breast asked exactly the same thing, which didn't infuse me with a great deal of confidence that a medical degree did much for men's understanding of the female anatomy.

'I don't feel anything,' I said, which was exactly the same answer I gave Davy Zurker in eleventh grade.

The nurse then applied the gel and began to move the ultrasound back and forth until they got the picture they wanted of the mass.

'This won't take but a moment,' he said. 'You may feel some pressure but there shouldn't be any discomfort.'

It was over in less than a minute. He handed the two syringes to the nurse who walked out of the room with them as if they were a secret to be hidden from view.

'When will I know something?' I asked.

'It's possible we may have something for you tomorrow, but most likely it will be early next week,' he said. He applied a small bandage to my breast and then slipped off his surgical gloves. 'The nurse will be back in and she'll get you cleaned up. You may have a little discomfort when you move your right arm, so you should limit your activity as much as possible. Though given what you've already been through, you may not notice. It's also not uncommon for a small amount of hemorrhaging to take place after the procedure. As long as it's minimal, it's nothing to worry about.'

'Do I call you or you call me?' I asked.

'The office will call with the results and to set up a follow-up appointment if necessary.'

'The follow-up would be the bad news version?' I asked.

He walked over to the sink and began washing his hands.

'You're a policeman,' he said.

'A detective,' I said.

'Jumping ahead of things isn't terribly useful, I find,' he said. 'I imagine like police work you'll do better if you only deal with the facts as they come.'

'If I limited myself to only dealing in facts, the only murders ever solved would be because of confessions,' I said.

He stepped back over to the table as the door opened and the nurse walked back in.

'A vivid imagination is not your ally at this moment,' he said. 'Try to remember that.'

'What is my ally?' I asked.

'Remembering what you know, not what you think you know.'

My phone rang.

'I'll have to take this,' I said.

'We'll talk as soon as we have some results,' he said and walked out of the room.

I opened up the phone and answered it.

'What do you have?' I said to Harrison.

He hesitated. 'You OK?'

I glanced down at my breast, which I couldn't feel and was covered in antiseptic.

'I suspect I have too much imagination to do this very well,' I said. 'Do you have something?'

'The Dean of Students is putting together a list of present and past students from the UK.'

'When will she have it?' I asked.

'I'm on my way over there now.'

The nurse walked over with a small basin and some sponges to clean me up.

'I'll meet you there.'

twenty

Harrison was waiting outside the Dean of Students' office when I pulled up. As I walked over, Harrison's eyes followed me the way they might if I was a suspect he was trailing: looking for the smallest gesture that might give away the secrets I carried inside. I reached the door to the building and he looked at me for a moment and then started to say something.

'Don't,' I said.

'Don't what?'

'Don't look at me like I'm in a line-up. Aside from my chest being numb, I'm as healthy as you until they tell me otherwise.'

Dylan shook his head. 'That wasn't why I was looking at you.'

He reached out and took hold of the front of my shirt with his thumb and forefinger.

'You missed a button.'

'Thank you,' I said.

He slipped it into place, his hand lingering for a

moment, holding on to the fabric of my shirt.

'The President of the college is going to be at the meeting,' he said.

'Then you should probably let go of my blouse,' I said. 'For the moment anyway.'

His fingers released the fabric of my shirt and he turned and opened the door.

Dean Greer was waiting outside her office with the college President. Keller was a tall, angular man with thick silver hair and pale skin. Greer introduced us and then showed us into her office and we took our seats. On her desk were two manila folders.

'I've put together the list you requested,' she said. 'But there are conditions.'

'And those would be?' I asked.

'You must agree before looking at any of these that all student records are confidential.'

'I'm not interested in anyone's grade point average,' I said.

She shook her head. 'What I mean is that since nine eleven we've had a number of issues with Homeland Security requesting information on students,' she said. 'Foreign students in particular.'

'We're naturally protective of them,' said Keller. 'If our student body were to believe that we were spying on them or helping the government spy on them for political reasons it would damage the trust that must be present in the institution for it to function properly.'

'Two people have been killed on your campus. When your students begin looking at each other wondering if the other is a killer, I'd say trust is the least of your problems,' I said.

Greer cleared her throat and nodded. 'You will only be able to look at these here in this room, and I cannot allow any photocopying.'

'I understand your concerns, we have some of the same problems with HSA ourselves,' I said. 'Perhaps we won't even need to look at them.'

Harrison took out the photograph that Jim O'Brien had taken in Oxford and handed it to the President of the college.

'Can you identify the person on the right?' he asked.

The President shook his head. 'I don't have the kind of contact with the entire student body that Dean Greer has. Is that Professor Simms on the left?'

'Yes,' I said.

He looked at it again. 'Is his presence in the picture related to the break-in at his office last night and the killing in the tunnel?'

'Yes,' I said.

'May I ask how?'

'Beyond saying that Professor Simms is very probably a target of the killer, I'm not able to discuss details of the case.'

'Lawrence Simms a target?' the President asked.

I nodded. 'He's in a great deal of danger.'

'You're serious?'

I nodded.

'Do you really believe one of our students could have done this?' he asked with the kind of ivory tower cluelessness that sometimes develops after years of living in the cloistered world of academia.

'That's what we're trying to determine,' I said.

'I find that difficult to believe,' he said.

It was all I could do to stop myself from telling him that one of his professors was also a drug dealer.

'The world is full of surprises,' I said.

Harrison took the picture from Keller and handed it to Greer. She looked at it for a moment and then shook her head.

'Perhaps if I could see his entire face,' she said. 'This is the only picture?'

'Yes,' Harrison said.

'Is that the person you're looking for?' Keller asked.

'At this point I would say he is a person of interest who we want very much to talk to,' I said.

'Are there any others?' he asked.

'No, he's the only one,' I answered.

'Do you have a name?' Greer asked.

'We have two names,' I said.

'Shelton and Norton, neither of which he is using,' Harrison said.

She stared at the picture. 'I've known every student who's stepped on to campus in the last five years.'

'Is he one of them?' I asked.

Greer shook her head. 'There's something familiar, but I don't believe he's one of our students.'

'You're certain of that?' I asked.

She opened up one of the folders containing the records and began paging through them until she found what she was looking for. She stared at the picture again for a moment and then shook her head.

'No, his eyes are a different color, it's not him.'

'Could I see that?' I asked and she handed it to me. One glance was all I needed to know that this wasn't him. I reached over and picked up the picture of Shelton. 'What is it that's familiar about him?' I asked, holding it up.

'I don't know,' she said.

Harrison took out the computer image that best seemed to match the photograph that Cathy O'Brien had identified as Shelton and handed it to Greer.

'Could it be this person?' he asked.

She studied it for a moment and again shook her head. 'Like the photograph, it seems familiar, but I'm sure it's not a student,' she said.

'Could he have been one that was only here for a short time?' I said.

'I don't think so.'

'Could it have been someone you met or saw with Terry Pullian?' Harrison asked.

She immediately shook her head. 'Terry rarely took part in social functions.'

'So what is it about that person that seems familiar?' I asked again.

'I'm not sure. Maybe I'm wrong.'

'Perhaps you met at a function outside school,' I said.

She looked again and shook her head. 'I don't know.'

'I'd still like to go through the list of other students. It's possible we might see something that you would miss.'

She nodded and we began paging through the student IDs. I paused on several pictures but not long enough to suggest we had a possible suspect. Shelton simply wasn't there.

We walked back outside into the heat and stood by my squad.

'Have we missed something?' Harrison said.

'Just the boat,' I said.

'Perhaps Scotland Yard will come through with an ID.'

'If Cathy O'Brien's right about the name Norton, and Shelton wasn't already using several different aliases, the name Norton may mean nothing to them.'

'Which puts us where?'

I looked across the commons toward the building where Simms's office was.

'I need to look at something,' I said and started walking toward Simms's building.

Dylan quickly caught up.

'And what would that be?' he asked.

'I'll know it when I see it,' I said.

We crossed the commons and entered the same door we had the night before.

'Crime Scene went through Simms's office, they didn't come up with anything other than Moon's prints,' Harrison said.

I looked up the stairs and then down the length of the polished floors of the hallway toward the other end of the building.

'Why were we thinking Shelton was a student here?' I

said and started walking down the hallway.

'Because he's brilliant,' Dylan said. 'It would be the kind of place he could fit in without sticking out.'

I nodded. 'But he didn't come here for a degree.'

'No, he came for money and revenge.'

'But what was it about the deaths that have happened that made us think he was a student?' I said. 'O'Brien wasn't killed here.'

'No, he was killed at home.'

'So what is it about Pullian's murder that connects it to Moon's?'

'They happened on campus.'

'In the middle of a blackout,' I said.

'What is it you're getting at?' Harrison said.

I stopped next to the service closet that I had entered last night while following Earl Moon.

'Two deaths, one at the top of the tallest building on campus, the other in a system of old steam tunnels.'

'And the point is?'

'I was lost in these tunnels last night, so was Moon. And even in the daylight when we went up to the roof of the library, we wouldn't have found our way without the security guard giving us directions, yet Shelton did it in the middle of the blackout.'

'And he found his way out of the tunnels like he knew exactly where he was,' Harrison said.

I nodded. 'Shelton knows his way around this campus like a student would, only he's not a student,' I said and looked over at the service door. 'We're looking at the wrong records. We should be talking to personnel.'

'He could be a security guard?' Harrison said.

I looked down the corridor and then out the window. 'He could be almost anything.'

twenty-one

The Human Resources Director looked at us and shook her head.

'You don't have a name?' she asked.

'No.'

She took a deep breath, which seemed mostly for effect, and leaned forward on her desk. She was in her late thirties. Her eyes seemed to hold a kind of weary knowledge about just how screwed up the human soul could be – not that different from a cop's eyes.

'Are you aware of how many employees you're talking about?' she asked.

'Quite a few, I imagine,' I said.

'Nearly three thousand when you consider all the divisions.'

'We're looking for someone whose job would give them an intimate knowledge of the campus.'

'That could be almost anyone in any position. Our employees have full access to any of the facilities.'

I handed her the picture of Shelton in the bar in Oxford.

She took it in her hand and examined it the way she might if conducting a job interview. Her eyes moved over the picture as if searching out any character flaws that might be present.

'This is the individual?' she said.

I nodded. 'Our guess is he would take a position that would be low profile, something that wouldn't attract much attention to himself. He's probably working with a green card from the UK.'

'It would be more helpful if one could see his entire face,' she said.

'I'm aware of that,' I said.

'That's Professor Simms,' she said.

'Yes,' I answered and she returned her attention to the picture of Shelton.

'He's not with security. I make a special point of interviewing every security officer, given the nature of what they do.'

'A janitor?' Harrison asked.

She stared at the picture. 'He's not British,' she said.

'Excuse me?' I asked.

'He's not British,' she said.

'You know him?' I asked.

She looked at the picture for a moment longer. 'I'm not certain it's him, but it's possible. But we don't have any British employees. The person I'm thinking of is Canadian, and you're right, he was a janitor.'

'Was?'

'Yes. He stopped showing up for work about two weeks ago. He was terminated after not responding to repeated attempts to contact him. That's the only reason I remember him – I never met him.'

She spun around in her chair to face her computer and then worked the keyboard. She tried several different things and then shook her head.

'That's strange.'

'What's strange?'

'His personal file's gone,' she said. 'It should be here, but it's not.'

'Could it have been altered or hacked?' I said.

She stared at the screen and shook her head. 'It can't be accessed without my ID and a password.'

'You're surrounded by some of the smartest people on the planet, that would be a yes,' Harrison said.

'You're saying a janitor did this?'

I nodded. 'He's not your average janitor.'

'Why would he do that?' she asked. 'His work record was excellent until he didn't show up.'

'His picture's on it,' I said. 'How long was he employed?'

'A little over nine months, if I remember.'

She got up and walked over to a filing cabinet.

'I make a hard copy of every termination and keep it for a year in case something is contested.'

'You have his file?' I asked.

She fingered through the files and then pulled one out.

'Yes,' she said and walked over to the desk.

Harrison and I both stepped around the desk to get a closer look.

'James Dixon,' she said. 'That's right, he had the same

name as one of our professors. We have a Professor James Dixon in the engineering department.'

She picked up the picture from Oxford. 'It could be the same person. Curious that a janitor would be in a picture with a professor.'

She handed me the file and we both stared in silence for a moment.

'Is that who you're looking for?' she asked.

I looked into the eyes – were they the same eyes I remembered from the picture of the nine-year-old killer? I couldn't be sure. The rest of the face was different than I had imagined him. The hair was dark, the face obscured by a thick beard.

'Look at the eyes,' I said.

'Shelton?' Harrison said.

I shook my head. 'I don't know. Do you recognize the address?'

Harrison nodded. 'South Pasadena.'

I scanned the rest of the file, looking for anything that stood out. There was one reprimand from his supervisor.

'It says here that last January he was reprimanded for excessive personal use of a computer,' I said.

She took the file and looked at it.

'Is it usual for a janitor to be reprimanded for use of a computer?' I asked.

'It's never happened before,' she said.

'I wonder what else he hacked into,' Harrison said.

'Can you make a copy of this for me?' I asked.

*

It was nearing five o'clock when we stopped at the corner of Mission and Milan ten minutes south of the Caltech campus. It was an old street by Pasadena standards. Post-war bungalows intermixed with pre-war apartment buildings. The numbness in my chest was giving way to the feeling that a nail had been stuck in my breast.

'He had to assume that we would find him,' Harrison said. 'Even with removing his personal file, he had to know we would eventually track him through his Canadian passport.'

I looked at the file in my hand. 'If this is him, he would also have figured that he would be long gone before we did.'

Harrison looked down the street. 'Unless of course us sitting here is something he planned on all along.'

'Nobody's that smart,' I said.

'You sure about that?'

'What do you mean?'

'What if there are two Sheltons?'

I looked at Dylan. 'What are you getting at?'

'One Shelton is after the money and revenge. The other Shelton is a psychopath who killed for the first time when he was nine years old. And everything that Shelton has done and said is also true.'

'Including that I inspire him?' I said.

'What if that Shelton knew we would be sitting here and is waiting in that apartment for you to step inside?'

'I'm not going in first, you are,' I said.

'What I'm saying is that maybe it would be a good idea to have a tactical unit go through that door.'

I shook my head. 'If I'm right, and Shelton doesn't know we're this close to him and we come storming in with a tactical unit and he's not there, every resident on this block is going to have seen what happened. Shelton gets within shouting distance of this building, he'll know something isn't right and we will have lost that chance to catch him.' I held out the personal file. 'If you're absolutely sure that this is Shelton I'll make that call to tactical right now.'

Dylan looked at the picture and shook his head. 'Perhaps we should wait for Utley to produce the ID from Scotland Yard.'

I picked up my phone and called Utley. He answered on the third ring.

'How much longer on that ID?' I asked.

'My contact's talking to his contact, who is . . . it's the middle of the night there, my guess is that we'll have it by mid-morning their time. You have something new?'

'It's possible he's traveling on a Canadian passport under the name James Dixon.'

'I'll talk with HSA and see what I can find. When would he have crossed the border?'

'Nine to twelve months ago.'

'I'll get back to you,' Utley said and hung up.

I turned to Harrison and slipped my phone away.

'Could be another five or six hours before we get the ID from Scotland Yard. You want to wait?'

We drove halfway down the block and pulled to the curb across the street from a large Mediterranean-looking apartment complex with the name Sheltering Palms in large letters next to the entrance. The letters had begun to rust and the sheltering palms had been reduced to large stumps.

Through the central entryway I could see into a courtyard with a small pool. The sound of Mexican and Filipino music drifted out from several of the open windows, along with the drone of electric fans and air conditioners.

'Apartment three eighteen,' I said and stepped out of the squad. Dylan followed.

I looked up and down the street for something that might suggest Harrison was correct and Shelton was waiting for us to step out of the squad. I saw nothing.

'I'm still standing. Perhaps we've surprised him,' I said and smiled to Harrison.

The music and the sound of fans and air conditioners abruptly fell silent as the power failed once again.

'You were saying,' Harrison said and stepped back to the squad and removed two flashlights.

We crossed the street to the building, stepped into the front lobby and looked through into the courtyard. The building was in the shape of a large horseshoe. The residents that were home, mostly mothers with small children, were already beginning to walk down to the courtyard in what by now was a practiced routine to escape the heat of apartments with no fans or air conditioners.

Harrison walked over and checked the schematic of the building's layout on the wall by the entrance as I checked the names on the mailboxes.

'There're two stairways at each end of the horseshoe,' he said. 'Shelton would be at the far end on the left side.'

'The name on the mailbox is Pullian, not Dixon,' I said.

'His fall guy,' Harrison said.

'You take the back, I'll take the front.'

Dylan hesitated.

'Do you really believe Shelton is waiting up there in the dark for me?' I said.

'Define belief,' Harrison said.

'The unshakeable understanding that your Lieutenant's judgement is always correct,' I said.

'That sounds more like adoration,' Harrison said.

'That works too. I'll meet you at the door,' I said, turned on my flashlight and started up the stairway.

The air still contained the scent of sweet perfume from a resident that had passed by minutes before I started up. As I hesitated at the second-floor landing, the light of candles flickering inside an apartment was visible down the hallway through the open door. The soft murmur of a voice in Spanish and the cries of a baby were the only sounds.

From above I heard the sound of a door open and close and then what sounded like footsteps coming down. I raised the light and started up towards the third floor. There was no one there, no sounds. I continued up, stepped into the hallway and looked down its dark length.

There were no doors open here. I shone the light down the corridor toward the far end and Shelton's apartment. A brief shriek of laughter rose from behind one of the closed doors and then just as quickly fell silent.

I started forward and switched the flashlight to my left hand and slipped my gun out of its holster. Even-numbered apartments were on the left, odd on the right. As I passed the middle of the hallway, a door opened on my right and an old Filipino man in a white T-shirt silently watched me pass and then closed the door.

I passed room three-sixteen and stopped a few feet short of Shelton's apartment. Another twenty feet beyond his door were the other stairs. The faint glow of a light illuminated them below. I waited a moment for the sound of Harrison's footsteps to become audible, but nothing moved on the stairs. I took a few steps to Shelton's door, and then eased in and listened for movement inside the apartment. Silence. I leaned back and looked at the faint glow of light coming up from the stairs and resisted the urge to call Dylan's name as my heart rate began to climb. He should be coming up, but wasn't. Why?

I slipped past Shelton's door and over to the landing, expecting to hear him taking the steps. Nothing, no one was coming up. I glanced back to Shelton's door for a moment and then stepped out on to the landing and looked down the stairs. On the second-floor landing I could see the handle of a flashlight lying on the floor.

I glanced back at the apartment door and then rushed down the first flight of stairs and looked toward the second-floor landing. Dylan's light lay next to the entrance to the corridor. He was nowhere to be seen. I raised my gun toward the dark corridor and carefully took one step at a time, listening for movement as I descended.

I reached the landing and stepped over to Dylan's light. A bag of groceries lay scattered on the floor, but there was no blood.

I pointed my light down the length of the second-floor hallway. It was empty.

'Dylan,' I called out but nothing came back.

I stepped over to the stairs and looked down toward the first floor. The sound of squealing tires rose from out on the street and I rushed down until I reached the first-floor landing.

I raised the light into the first-floor corridor and, like the second floor, it was empty. A door to the left led out into the central courtyard of the building. A second door exited the back of the building. I stepped over to it, took hold of the handle and flung it open. The heat from the blacktop surged through the door like an ocean wave. The white light of the sun blinded me until my eyes adjusted.

A small Latino boy was standing in the middle of the alley, looking at me.

I stepped outside and looked left and right. Most of the building's parking spaces were empty.

'Aquí,' the boy said and I turned and looked at him. 'Aquí,' he said again and raised his hand and pointed down the alley.

I rushed over to him and looked down the alley.

'There,' he said in a heavy accent.

Something in the middle of the alley reflected the bright sun. I took a step and then ran until I reached it and stopped. My heart began to pound against my chest. Dylan's cuffs lay on the cement. I reached down and as I picked them up my hand began to tremble.

The boy was still standing there and I rushed back to him and knelt down.

'What did you see?' I asked.

His eyes moved nervously back and forth. 'See?'

'Yes, did you see the policeman?' I asked.

'I saw the man run.'

'Was it the policeman you saw?'

The boy shrugged his shoulders.

I held up Harrison's cuffs. 'The policeman, the man who had this, where did he go? Did you see him?'

'Yes,' he said.

'Where?'

The sound of a siren became audible in the distance and the boy pointed back down the alley.

'He ran there,' he said, pointing toward a small detached garage in back of a house down the alley.

'Did you see another man running?' I asked.

The boy nodded.

'Where was he? Where did he run?'

The boy pointed in the same direction.

I got up and started running toward the garage. As I reached the back corner, I heard movement coming from around the other side. I started to raise my weapon as the figure came into view. The silver flash of a revolver became recognizable as it moved in my direction. I tried to stop my momentum but a hand was already reaching out and taking hold of my shirt. I tried to spin and pull away.

'Police,' I started to yell and then the grip on my shirt relaxed and I pulled free.

'Son of a bitch,' Harrison said, staring into my face. 'I lost him. I thought he had backtracked to go after you.'

There was a cut above his left eye, a thin stream of blood

trickled down over his cheek and spread out across the line of his chin.

'Are you all right?' I asked.

He nodded. 'He surprised me on the stairs.'

'Did you get a look at him?'

Harrison shook his head. 'He was coming down the stairs carrying a bag of groceries. By the time I realized you don't carry groceries out of a building you carry them in, I tried to turn but he was already moving. I should have reacted faster.'

'You're bleeding,' I said and reached out and gently touched his cheek.

'I think he hit me with a can of beans,' he said. 'I'm not sure how long I was lying there, couldn't have been long. He got my badge and cuffs.'

I held the cuffs up to him.

'He left these in the alley,' I said.

Dylan took them and slipped them back on his belt. 'I guess he knows who your partner is now.'

'He probably already knew,' I said.

'He could have taken my gun, but didn't,' he said.

'I don't think Shelton has much use for guns. If you had a knife, he probably would have taken it. Maybe even used it.'

'That should produce some good dreams,' Harrison said.

He reached up and touched the cut and then shook his head.

'I guess that answers the debate as to whether we found Shelton,' he said.

'Did you see what he was driving?' I asked.

'No, I heard some tires squeal and I ran through to the other street, but he was gone. Sorry.'

I shook my head. 'You were right, we should have had a tactical team.'

Harrison looked back toward the apartment building. 'No, I just should be more careful with people packing cans of vegetables.'

We bandaged the small cut back at the squad and then found the building's superintendent, a nervous Iranian man sitting by the pool wearing a Baywatch swimsuit with an enormous set of keys on a ring clipped to the waistband.

He identified himself as Mr Arash and started walking us back to the lobby.

'I'd prefer you wait here,' I said, and then reached out for the key.

'But I'm the building's superintendent,' he said as if back home that title carried the weight of a small-town mayor.

'And I'm the police,' I said. 'I don't want you to get injured.'

'Injured?' he said, staring at the small bandage on Harrison's head. His fingers quickly worked through the keys until he found the one he was looking for. He slid it off the ring and handed it to me.

'I'll be by the pool if you need anything,' he said and rushed away.

We walked back to the rear entrance and retrieved

Harrison's flashlight by the can of beans that Shelton had used on his head.

'Does anything strike you as odd about this bag of groceries?'

'You mean aside from them being used as a weapon?'

I nodded. 'Look at all this crap. Baked beans, SpaghettiOs, cookies.'

'A nutritionist's nightmare.'

'It's more than that,' I said.

'What?'

'I'm not sure,' I said and we ascended the stairs to the apartment.

I slid the key into the door and hesitated for a moment, the way one might when stepping up to the edge of a cliff.

'What exactly are we expecting to find in here?' Harrison said.

'The dark side of the moon,' I said and turned the key.

I pushed the door open. It was dark inside, the shades being drawn on all the windows.

'You don't suppose he left behind any surprises for us?' Harrison said.

'Like a booby-trapped can of beans?' I said.

Harrison nodded.

'Just be glad it wasn't a canned ham,' I said and stepped inside.

'What's that smell?' Harrison said.

'It's as if you threw bags of popcorn, chips and a few burgers into a blender and turned it on.'

'I'll open the shades,' Harrison said.

He walked over to the windows on the other side of the

room and began to open them. What was revealed as the light illuminated the room was not what I was expecting.

'What does it look like to you?' I said as I looked around the room.

'A frat house?' Harrison said.

'Not exactly,' I said. 'It's more like a child has been living here.'

The floor in front of the TV was full of stacks of video games. The walls of the room were covered in drawings of bodies all suffering from violence in one form or another. The detail was precise but executed with little polish.

'A disturbed child,' he said.

I stepped over to one of the walls and the drawing of a man whose head had been cut off.

'That looks familiar,' Harrison said.

I reached out and ran my fingers over the surface of the wall.

'He's been throwing knives at this,' I said.

Harrison stepped over to another wall. 'Look at this one.'

I walked over.

'A body falling off a building,' Dylan said.

'Terry Pullian.'

'Video games, drawing like a kid would do in a scrapbook. Could this really be a man who made Pullian feel intellectually inadequate?' Harrison said.

I picked up an 8x10 photograph lying on the floor. 'Orson Welles, the picture removed from the taco stand.'

'Perhaps as you said before, there's more than one Shelton.'

I turned around and looked at the rest of the room. The

kitchen was to the left, a hallway led to the right. Harrison stepped into the hallway as I walked over to the kitchen. There were no pots and pans or cooking utensils of any kind. The cabinets were empty of any food. The oven appeared to have never been used. The countertops were covered with bags and boxes of fried chicken and opened cans of baked beans and SpaghettiOs that had been either warmed in the cans or eaten cold.

'This looks familiar,' I said, picking up an empty box of chicken. 'He puts Pullian's name on the apartment, eats what Pullian ate.'

'Terry the killer,' Harrison said.

'Shelton is very thorough in his fiction.'

'I'll look at the other rooms,' Dylan said.

I opened the refrigerator. It was filled with soda and beer. I opened the freezer and it was empty. Harrison stepped back into the living room.

'I think you better see this.' Dylan said nothing else. He knew that I preferred to create my own first impressions when walking through a crime scene.

I went out of the kitchen and started across the living room toward the hallway.

'The first door on the left,' Harrison said.

I went to the door and stopped.

'What was that you were saying about more than one Shelton?' I said.

'They each have their own room,' Harrison answered. 'This one apparently got the brains in the family.'

'Books,' I said as I stared across the room.

The floor was covered with stacks of them four feet

high; against the walls they were even higher. A path had been left through the center of the room.

'There must be hundreds of them,' I said and started walking down the path to the center of the room.

'Probably well over a thousand,' Harrison said.

In the middle of the room I picked up a book at random. 'I don't remember having this on my nightstand.'

Harrison walked over.

'*The Selected Essays of Montaigne*,' I said and handed him the book.

'French Renaissance,' said Dylan.

'You've read this?' I asked.

He shook his head. 'An essay or two in college. This must be the philosophy section,' he said and handed it back to me.

I opened it.

'He's written something here.' I slipped out a small note card. ' "Man cannot make a worm, yet he makes gods by the dozens",' I read and handed it to Harrison.

' "Obsession is the wellspring of genius and madness",' he said, reading the next line.

'Well, he found his muse, didn't he?'

Dylan nodded.

'I didn't realize I had missed out on so much fun by not taking any philosophy classes.' I picked another book. 'Nietzsche.'

'Another guy who knew how to have a good time,' Harrison said.

'This is from the library,' I said.

Harrison looked through a couple others.

'They all are,' he said.

I glanced once more around the room and then stepped back into the hallway and looked toward the last room.

'I can't wait to see what's in his bedroom,' I said. 'Have you looked in there?'

Dylan shook his head.

'Perhaps there's another Shelton waiting.' I walked up to the room and pushed the door open.

The blinds were drawn as in the other rooms. Dylan walked over to the window and opened them. The room was sparsely furnished like the rest of the apartment. There was a folding card table and chair next to the window. A mattress was against the opposite wall, but none of the furnishings were what we were looking at.

On the wall above the mattress a grid-like structure resembling more than anything else a family tree had been drawn. Photographs were attached to it in places. In other places names were written. In the center of it all was the image of the eye that we had seen before. Among the photographs were two he had taken of me.

'He's full of surprises,' I said.

Harrison stepped up and looked at the first picture.

'He must have been following me,' I said.

'Where is that?' Harrison asked.

'I was walking out of the doctor's office after they had told me that a mass had been found. Do you suppose he knows my diagnosis?'

'I guess we know where this one was taken,' he said, looking at the second picture.

'He was outside,' I said.

The picture had been taken through a window in my house. Harrison was removing my shirt.

'If there's any doubt that this man's a threat to you, I think that's over,' Harrison said and then reached up and removed the picture of the two of us, folded it in half and placed it in his pocket.

'That's evidence,' I said.

Dylan shook his head. 'No it isn't.' He motioned toward the other picture. 'That's evidence. The one in my pocket was never here.'

I didn't argue. The photograph of the two of us together wouldn't get us any closer to an arrest and wouldn't do either of us any good within the department.

'If someone is going to tamper with evidence, I'd prefer it to be me,' I said and reached out for the picture.

Harrison slipped it out of his pocket and then tore it into several pieces.

'What picture?'

'Whoever said chivalry is dead?'

Harrison shook his head. 'I don't know, but he was an idiot.'

Harrison put the pieces into his pocket; one of them fell to the floor in the process. I reached down and picked it up and stared at it for a moment.

'What are you thinking?' Dylan said.

'This could be the reason he took your badge,' I said.

'He could have taken my badge for any reason.'

'Including wanting to know the name of my lover.'

Harrison looked over at the drawing on the wall and the other pictures.

'After what we've seen inside this apartment, I suspect there's little Shelton doesn't know,' he said.

I stepped back and looked at the rest of the wall.

'Victims, before and after pictures.'

'A trophy wall?'

I shook my head. 'This is something else.'

I stepped over and looked at the picture of Jim O'Brien's slaughtered corpse lying on bloodstained sheets and the homeless man who had died first.

'There's no photographs of Moon or Pullian,' Harrison said.

'There wouldn't be,' I said. 'Once Pullian was dead, there was no point in continuing the fiction he had created that Terry was a killer.'

I looked at the wall for a moment.

'This is like a prop in a stage play. Just like everything we found in O'Brien's house. The eye is here, darkness; he did this for us, to help convict Terry once Shelton had gotten what he wanted and vanished. There's no point in having pictures of Moon, or any of his future victims. There is no fall guy any longer, no fictional killer, only Shelton.' I stepped up closer. 'So how does this help us? Do you see any order to it?'

'Some,' he said. 'If you follow the branches, they all seem to connect back to Pullian and the eye. The problem is it's unfinished.'

'The moment Terry went off that roof, this was obsolete.'

Dylan nodded in agreement.

'Which still leaves us trying to understand what it would have looked like completed.'

Harrison looked at it for a moment. 'It's simpler than it appears at first.'

'All the better to frame Pullian with,' I said.

Harrison began to trace with his finger out from the center of the tree.

'If you connect theses lines here, it would give the impression that the murders of the homeless man and O'Brien grow directly out of Pullian. From there the lines seem to connect to the picture of you and two other empty spaces with no pictures. That's where it ends.'

'There're two other victims he has plans for,' I said.

'Three if we include you in this,' Harrison said.

'That gives me a real sense of belonging,' I said. 'What about the other two? Who are they?'

'Simms would be one,' Harrison said.

I nodded in agreement. 'And the other?'

'We know it's not Moon.'

'So who are we missing?'

Harrison shook his head. 'It's either someone we haven't identified yet, or perhaps Shelton left it purposely ambiguous.'

'No, Shelton is far too thorough for that.' I stepped back and then looked at Dylan. 'Your badge, it could be you.'

He looked at me and smiled. 'Now you're just being protective. That was a chance encounter. If he took my badge for a reason, it was for something else.'

I had to agree.

'I'd like to know what that reason is,' Harrison said.

'So would I.'

I looked one more time at the picture of me and then walked over to the card table by the window. There was a computer on it, and what appeared to be some dried blood along the bottom.

'The computer that Earl Moon lifted from Simms's office,' I said.

Harrison stepped over, knelt down and looked at it closely. 'From the denting on the bottom here it looks like it was dropped.'

'That happens when you have your throat cut,' I said. 'See if it still works.'

Dylan sat down at the table, opened it up and pressed the power button. The computer powered up and the screen came on. Harrison began working the keypad, but nothing happened.

'There's nothing here, or else that bump in the tunnels knocked it senseless.'

'Or Shelton found what he was looking for,' I said.

'A money trail.'

'And then he emptied everything.'

'That's what it looks like.'

'Can anything be retrieved from the hard disk?' I asked.

'Things can always be retrieved to some degree, there are no absolute secrets in the chip world.' Harrison picked up the computer and flipped it over. 'Unless of course you remove the hard disk and take it with you.'

He opened the back of the laptop and took a quick look inside.

'Whatever was in this is gone, it's just a useless bit of plastic now.'

I turned and looked around the room. There was something I hadn't noticed before.

'What don't you see in this room?' I asked.

Harrison shrugged.

I walked over to the closet and opened the door. There was a small chest of drawers inside and a few wire hangers on a rail above it. I went through the chest, opening the drawers.

'They're all empty.'

Harrison looked at the chest and then around the rest of the room. 'No clothes.'

I nodded. 'For the same reason there's no food in the other room.' I walked out of the room into the bathroom down the hall and Harrison followed.

'What are you looking for?' he asked.

'When Shelton ran out, you didn't see his face, right?'

'The bag of groceries was in front of it.'

'Look at the sink,' I said.

Dylan stepped over to it.

'He tried to clean up but missed a few,' I said.

'He shaved off the beard,' Harrison said.

'He wasn't just walking out because we showed up, he wasn't coming back. He was even taking some food with him,' I said.

'Which means he's on the move.'

'The question is why? Was he leaving here because it no longer served a purpose, because he knew we would find it, or because he's gotten what he came for and is leaving?'

'It could be any of those reasons,' Harrison said.

I walked back down the hallway into the bedroom and stared at the wall again.

'At some level Shelton is in here too,' I said. 'The only piece of this that is fiction is who the killer is supposed to be.'

Harrison stood next to me.

I turned and looked out the window. 'It's starting to get dark. We need to figure out who that second victim he's after is.'

'You mean if it's not you?'

I shook my head. 'It's not me, I'm on that wall for show. Shelton didn't come here to kill a cop. He's after money and because he likes inflicting pain on people who annoy him.'

'Which gets us back to Simms.'

'And that second blank space on the wall,' I said.

'Could be Beckwith. The man was more than frightened.'

'If he wanted Charles Beckwith dead he could have done that easily. Same with Dunne.'

'Maybe Shelton doesn't know who that other person is.'

I thought about it for a moment.

'That might explain the way O'Brien died,' I said.

'You mean Shelton tied him to the bed and tortured him to get that second name out of him.'

'Which means O'Brien would have told him.'

'How can we be certain of that?' Harrison said.

'When was the last time you ever heard of a broker keeping a secret?'

Harrison turned and looked at me. 'Unless . . .'

'Unless what?'

'Unless O'Brien didn't know the name of the second person,' Harrison said.

'Play that out,' I said.

'Let's say O'Brien was a junior player in the enterprise,' Harrison said. 'A bagman shuttling cash through his freezer.'

'If the second person worked within the firm, it would be in his best interests to keep O'Brien in the dark.'

'Which gets us back to Simms,' Harrison said.

'He knows whose face is supposed to fill that empty space.' I glanced once more at the grid on the wall. 'Myers was the partner at the firm who died in France, right?'

'Yes. He died of a heart attack while waterskiing.'

I looked at Harrison. 'What if it wasn't a heart attack?'

'Shelton?'

I stared at the wall for another moment and then shook my head.

'What's bothering you?' Harrison asked.

'Unless there's something or some other person we don't know about, we're saying one of the partners at Beckwith, Myers and Dunne was going to have his picture in that empty space.'

Harrison nodded. 'Seems likely.'

'Why?'

'What do you mean, why?'

'O'Brien working with Simms has a certain sense to it. For Simms it probably began as an intellectual exercise. He leads O'Brien into it. But accusing a partner in a large firm of the same crime is a different ball game.'

'How different?'

'Consider the amount of money to be made in the market by a partner in a large firm,' I said.

'A lot barely begins to describe it.'

'Why risk getting involved with drugs?' I said.

'Greed and a sense of scale rarely go together.'

'Perhaps.' I walked over to the window. 'None of which really changes anything for Shelton.'

'He's going to try and kill two more people,' Harrison said.

'And anyone else who gets in his way,' I added.

Dylan looked at me. 'Including you.'

'It's starting to get dark,' I said. 'If a piece of Shelton is on that wall, it's the part of him that comes out at night. That's not fiction.'

I looked down at the bloodstained computer.

'If he found what he was looking for in that, then tonight he's going to finish it.'

'You think he found out where Simms is?'

'He must have found something in there,' I said.

twenty-two

We waited for Crime Scene to show up at the apartment and then made our way back to headquarters in the failing light. Traffic was better than it had been the previous rush hours during the blackouts. Whether Angelenos were learning how to cope or had just given up on trying to live normally and had retreated to homes at the first flicker of lights was anyone's guess.

Agent Utley walked into my office shortly after eight with Chief Chavez and produced the photograph of Shelton we had been waiting for all day. A wall in my office had been covered with images from the case. We tacked it next to the ID photo we had from Caltech and stood back and looked at it.

'There's a difference in age,' Utley said.

'When was it taken?' I asked.

'The year he was released from juvenile authorities.'

'He's little more than a boy in it,' I said.

Chavez looked at it for a moment and then shook his head. If there had been any doubt that the picture we had from Caltech was Shelton it was gone.

'Some boy,' Chavez said.

'He was never a boy, not as we understand it, anyway,' Utley said. 'One look into his eyes and that becomes clear. They're not a child's eyes, they're barely human at all.'

'He's human, it's the part that is never going to fully grow up,' I said. 'It's why we'll catch him. He'll make a child's mistake.'

'He already has,' Harrison said.

I nodded.

'What mistake?' Utley asked.

'He thought he had buried the past,' I said.

'Has anything changed from this picture?' Utley asked, motioning toward the Caltech ID.

'He's cut the beard off, and I wouldn't be surprised if he's altered the color of his hair also.'

'You think he's getting ready to run?' Utley asked.

'If he gets what he's after, yes. Unless I'm wrong, he already has a new identity, new passport, probably had it before he entered the country.'

'He could also have a new identity that allows him to stay right here,' Harrison said.

'So how do we find him?' Chavez said.

I looked over the evidence tacked to the wall and pointed at the picture of the Aston Martin.

'We either find Simms, or . . .'

'Or what?' Chavez asked.

'Something you said to me,' I said, looking at him.

'What would that be?'

'The money,' I said. 'What's the easiest way to move large amounts of cash?'

'Move in what sense?' Chavez said.

'From a place it can be found to somewhere it can't. Once Shelton gets what he's after, he's going to have to move it.'

'How much money are we talking about?'

I shrugged. 'Enough to kill for. I'm guessing it's enough for him to disappear for the rest of his life.'

'Thousands,' Chavez said.

'Many thousands,' I said. 'Perhaps a lot more than that.'

'You don't move it, not in the physical sense,' Utley said.

'Exactly,' I said.

'What do you mean?' Chavez asked.

'The easiest way to move money is with a touch of a button,' I said.

'That leaves a trail,' Chavez said.

'Does it?' I said. 'How many investors have lost everything because they thought they had a paper trail of statements only to find out they were fiction?'

'What are you getting at?' Utley asked.

'Beckwith, Myers and Dunne,' I said.

'The firm where the first victim worked.'

'Second victim if you count a homeless man who was in the wrong place at the wrong time,' I said.

'You're suggesting that Beckwith, Myers and Dunne is involved?' Chavez asked.

'There are two people Shelton wants to kill. Simms is one, the other one is connected in some way to Beckwith, Myers and Dunne.'

'Why?' asked Chavez.

I tried to put the pieces together. 'An associate there is

dead. A former member of their board is running for his life, and a private investigator they hired to break into his office and steal a computer is dead.'

'A computer that Shelton killed him for,' Harrison said.

'That makes them involved,' I said.

'Beckwith, Myers and Dunne involved in drugs,' Chavez said.

I stared at the pictures of the room inside Simms's house that had been turned into a packaging facility for dope.

'How much dope could you move through this room and not have it noticed by someone?' I said.

'A few hundred pounds at a time at most,' Harrison said.

'What are you thinking?' Utley said.

'At best, Simms could have been producing hundreds of thousands of dollars, no more.'

'That's no small amount of money,' Chavez said.

'It is in some worlds,' I said.

'Which world?' Utley said.

'Beckwith, Myers and Dunne's world.'

'The market,' Utley said.

I nodded.

'I think I see what you're getting at.'

'I don't,' Chavez said.

'Why would a respected brokerage firm risk being involved in drugs for the amount of money an operation of this size could generate?'

'You're assuming they're respectable,' Utley said.

'Exactly,' I said.

'What are we talking about here?' Chavez said.

I looked at Dylan. 'What was it Simms did at Caltech?'

'He ran the Laboratory of Experimental Finance.'

'Experimental finance?' I said. 'What does that mean?'

'I can barely balance my checkbook, don't ask me,' Chavez said.

'What if drugs were only a small piece of what he was doing with Beckwith, Myers and Dunne?' I said.

'And the other part is what?' Utley said.

I looked at the evidence photograph of Shelton's apartment wall.

'Fiction,' I said.

'What do you mean?' he asked.

'Creating millions of dollars in profits where there is none.'

'Of which you have no proof,' Chavez said.

'None.'

'Which gets us where?' Utley said.

'What if drugs were being used to produce short-term cash while the real money was being stolen from investors?'

'A Ponzi scheme,' Utley said.

'Or something like it,' I said.

'I reiterate, you have no proof of any of this?' Chavez asked.

I nodded. 'All I have is dead bodies.'

'You better have more than that before making that kind of accusation about Beckwith, Myers and Dunne in public; they have a lot of powerful friends in this city.'

'I'm trying to catch a killer, not thieves.'

'Which leaves us where?' Utley said.

'Shelton is after two people, Simms and another individual we haven't identified.'

'Beckwith or Dunne would be likely candidates,' Utley said.

'It would seem so,' I said.

'There is another possibility,' Utley said and walked up to one of the evidence pictures from Shelton's apartment. 'There's a photograph of you on that wall,' he said.

'My picture is a relic of him trying to set Terry Pullian up as a killer. I'm in no danger.'

Harrison shifted uneasily in his chair.

'You disagree,' Chavez said.

Harrison looked at me for a moment and then shook his head.

'No, I think Alex is right,' he said.

'So what do you need?' Utley asked.

'Short of finding Simms alive?' Chavez said.

Utley nodded.

'What can you find out about Beckwith, Myers and Dunne?' I asked him.

'Such as are they defrauding investors of millions of dollars?'

'All I need is something that connects Simms to the name of that last victim.'

'I know some people at the SEC, but that feels like a shot in the dark.'

'There was a third partner in the firm,' I said.

'Derrick Myers,' Harrison said.

'What about him?' Utley asked.

'According to his partners, he died while waterskiing in France nine to twelve months ago.'

'You think there may be more to it?' Chavez said.

'If I have the timing right, that would have been just after Shelton vanished in England,' I said.

'I'll make some inquiries with the French National Police,' Utley said.

'What about Beckwith and Dunne?' Chavez asked. 'Are you watching them?'

I walked over to the window and looked across at the dark offices of the brokerage firm.

'We had units outside each of their homes last night. Neither of them went into work this morning, they're both still inside.'

'Why don't we just bring them in?' Chavez said.

'We do that we could lose our chance at Shelton,' I answered.

'Unless Utley's right about that picture of you, and you're the last target.'

'She won't be alone,' Harrison said.

'Make sure of it,' he said.

The door opened and Traver walked in.

'You got something?' I asked.

'A man registered under the name of Long at a thirty-five dollar a night motel near Santa Anita racetrack.'

'Is there something interesting about that?' Chavez said.

Traver nodded. 'He was driving a car worth a quarter million dollars.'

'The Aston Martin,' I said.

Traver grinned. 'That would be Bond, James Bond . . . I always wanted to say that.'

'How old is this information?' I asked.

'A few hours,' he said. 'It came to me second-hand through a guy in narcotics in Arcadia.'

'Have you checked with the motel office?'

Traver nodded. 'Phone's not working.'

twenty-three

The Sunshine Motel on East Colorado was the kind of motor coach motel built in the late thirties to accommodate the growing number of travelers on route 66 – a dozen rooms built around a central parking lot that you entered by driving under an arch decorated with a series of neon suns.

If it had once had an air of romance and adventure, it was long gone. The arch was overgrown with ivy. The neon tubes on the suns had been stolen. The only people who stayed now were illegals working at the racetrack, or a down-on-his-luck handicapper who had placed everything he had left on a horse named Lucky Legs that got one furlong out of the gate and broke down.

If Simms had thought he was going to disappear in a place like this, he could have chosen better. Parking a quarter-million-dollar car outside a room with plastic on the mattresses wouldn't remain a secret for very long. Even if the knock that came on his door wasn't Shelton, it would no doubt be someone a professor of economics wouldn't want to spend much time with.

It was nearing nine o'clock when we stopped across the street and turned out our lights. The faint shape of Simms's car was visible in the motel's parking lot. According to Traver's information, Mr Long was registered in room six.

'He picked the one room where he could see the street,' Harrison said. 'It's also where anyone driving past would see his car.'

'He would have done better to have stayed at a four hundred dollar a night room at the Hyatt,' I said.

'What do you want to do?' Harrison asked. 'Wait and see if Shelton shows up?'

I glanced up and down the street at the handful of parked cars.

'That would be fine unless he's already been here.'

'Shall we check with the office, see if he's had any visitors?'

I looked through the arch into the parking lot of the motel.

'Your eyes are better than mine. How many cars do you see in there?' I said.

'Three. There could be one or two more parked where we can't see them.'

I nodded toward the office. 'Look at the sign in the window.'

'No vacancy,' Harrison said.

'Does this place look full to you?'

'This place looks like it hasn't been full in twenty years.'

'I think we better go knock on the office door.'

Harrison pulled the squad around to the other side of the street and stopped in front of the office, out of sight of the rooms. We stepped out into the darkness. The night wasn't as hot as the previous few, though the temperature still must have been in the mid-eighties. The first hint of a breeze had risen from the west, carrying the scent of the horse stables from the racetrack.

I went over to the office door. The bright yellow paint that once colored it like the noonday sun was now cracked and covered in a thick layer of grime and soot. A screen door with bars on it covered the entrance. From inside the sound of salsa music from a transistor radio or tape deck drifted out.

'Music,' Harrison said and knocked on the door.

No one responded. Harrison knocked again with the same result.

'Police,' he said loud enough to be heard inside, but still no one answered.

Dylan turned to me. 'What do you think?'

I reached out and took hold of the door handle and it swung open. A few feet inside the dark room, a cherry popsicle lay melting on the carpet where it had been dropped.

'How long would a popsicle last in this heat?' I said.

'Half an hour, forty-five minutes, maybe.'

I slipped my gun out of its holster and stepped inside. The room smelled of forty years of aftershave and perfume. A counter faced the room where an easy chair, its fabric cracked open like a wound, sat. Beyond the counter a narrow hallway led into darkness. I eased over to the door to the right of the counter, pushed it open and walked in.

The salsa music was coming from down the hallway. I slipped my flashlight out and went over to the desk behind the counter where the motel register lay open. The office phone was on the floor, its line ripped out of the wall.

'How did Traver get this tip?' I asked.

'A narc officer.'

'The manager must be a snitch,' I said.

Harrison reached down and picked up the phone line.

'Looks like a call got interrupted,' he said.

I checked the register.

'There're only a few names to a page in this,' I said. 'Look at these.' I handed the book to Harrison. He began reading through it.

'The Smiths and Joneses seem to vacation here at the Sunshine Motel every few days,' he said. 'It appears they get an hourly rate. The rest of the names I can't make out, except for one.'

'Long?' I said and Harrison nodded.

'When did he check in?'

'Two days ago,' Harrison said and showed me the line in the book. The writing had a kind of flourish you might see on a blackboard in front of a large classroom.

'Only a college professor would have handwriting like that,' Harrison said.

I turned and pointed the light down the short hallway. At the end there appeared to be a small living room where the music was coming from. There was one door on the right. A woman's gold-colored flat shoe was on the floor just past the door.

I pushed the door open. It was a small bathroom with a

shower stall. Some underwear and nylons were strung on the shower curtain line. The odor of skin cream filled the air. In the hallway next to the door a piece of the wallpaper had been torn off where the shoe lay.

I raised my weapon and walked to the room at the end and stepped in. The smell of body fluids filled the air and I swung the light across the room. A small table had been knocked over. The transistor radio sat on the nightstand next to a roll-out bed. The legs of the victim were visible sticking out behind the bed. There were two windows in the room. One had an air conditioner in it. The other was closed and covered on the outside by heavy iron bars.

'There was no way out of this room,' Harrison said.

'Just death,' I said.

I stepped around the bed over to the body. She was face up, staring lifelessly at the ceiling, wearing a floral pattern nightgown that concealed her thin frame. Her brightly dyed blonde hair spread out across the floor. Her face was heavily made up in an attempt to conceal her age, which I guessed was mid-sixties. Her lipstick was bright red. I imagined she once had dreams of becoming the next Marilyn, and when that dream died she had spent the rest of her life trying to look like her.

'Why would Shelton kill her? What's the sense in that?' Harrison said. 'He knows we know who he is.'

I looked back down the hallway. 'Maybe she tried to call her narc.'

'You think she was the contact who told him about the Aston Martin?'

I nodded. 'Then again maybe she just annoyed Shelton.'

I slipped my gun back into the holster and then knelt down next to her. The fingers that had choked the life out of her were faintly outlined by hemorrhages in her pale papery skin. Clutched in her right hand was a piece of faded wallpaper she had ripped from the hallway as she struggled to stay alive. I reached down and pressed my fingers against her neck. There was no pulse.

'There's still warmth in her skin,' I said and stood up. 'She hasn't been dead long.'

I glanced at the window and then rushed down the hallway to the office.

'Where're the keys kept?' I said.

'Here.' Harrison stepped over to the back of the office door.

'Is Simms's room there?'

'No.'

'Shelton could still be in there,' I said and ran out past Harrison and back into the night.

For the first time in days the air felt nearly cool in comparison to inside where the night manager lay in that closed little room. I took several deep breaths, trying to get rid of the taste of death that lingered on my lips. I stopped at the corner of the building and looked into the parking lot and the dozen rooms that lined it.

'How about I get some backup this time?'

I stared at the dark window of the room where Simms was supposed to be. In the blackness I couldn't tell if the shades were drawn or open.

'If you see a can of beans coming at you, you have my permission to shoot it,' I said.

'We could at least get Traver here,' Harrison said.

'That will take time. Simms could be dying in there. And if he's already dead and we call this in, Arcadia PD will be here,' I said. 'These will be their murders. I want to be able to get a complete look inside Simms's room before we lose control of the scene.'

I slipped my gun out, stepped around the corner of the ivy and started along the semicircle of rooms that lined the parking lot. Two Latino men sitting on folding chairs in front of one room took notice of our movement and immediately got up and went inside and closed the door.

One room from where Simms had checked in we stopped. From there we could see the curtain covering Simms's window, but it didn't quite cover the far side next to the door. We crept along under the window and then took positions on either side of the door.

'You want to knock or just go in?' Harrison whispered.

The door appeared to be light, the lock cheap. On the concrete next to the door's threshold were several dark drops of thick liquid that I assumed were blood.

'Take the door,' I said.

Harrison stepped out and with one kick just below the handle the rotting frame around it snapped and the door flung open.

'Police,' I yelled, raising my weapon into the room.

Nothing responded from inside, there was no movement.

'Police,' I started to yell again, then stopped. 'Did you hear that?' I asked Harrison.

He shook his head. It sounded like a breath taken through a thin layer of water, like someone trying not to drown in a lake. I listened for a moment but the sound didn't repeat.

'Nothing,' Harrison said.

I flipped on my flashlight and raised it into the room. We both stared in silence for a moment.

'Lord,' Harrison said softly.

The room had been torn apart, in what must have been a desperate fight for life. In places bloody handprints streaked the walls and in others a trail was on the carpet where someone had crawled. I moved the light across the room and saw a body lying motionless in front of the bathroom.

'We're too late,' Harrison said.

I stepped into the room and cleared behind the door and the closet, then turned to the body. He was lying on his back, one arm along his side, and the other bent underneath him. His face, arm and much of his shirt were stained with blood.

'I'll check the bathroom,' Harrison said and stepped around the body.

I knelt down and looked at the motionless figure.

'There're bullet holes in here,' Harrison said.

I started to look up toward the bath when the faint sound of a breath came from the figure I was kneeling next to. Before I could react, the hand that had been tucked underneath him rose up, the chrome of a pistol briefly reflected the beam of the flashlight before it was pressed against my throat just under my chin.

'Who are you?' he said, his words garbled by the blood in his throat.

I looked down at his face.

'I'm a policeman,' I said to Simms.

Harrison stepped to the door of the bathroom with his gun pointed down at Simms's head. I glanced at him and ever so slowly shook my head.

'You don't want to hurt anyone, Professor,' I said.

His eyes seemed to struggle with the meaning of my words.

'You're a teacher,' I said. 'You don't want to do that.'

'A teacher?' he whispered through gritted teeth.

'That's right,' I said.

What came out of his mouth was a laugh like I had never heard before. A kind of self-mocking cry that came from some place inside him he had long ago lost touch with.

'Put the gun down,' I said.

'Gun?' he said as if surprised by the word.

He tried to press it harder against my neck but his hand began to tremble. Harrison took a step closer, zeroing his weapon in on Simms's head.

'Tell me about experimental finance,' I said.

I saw a tear well up in the corner of his eye and his bloodstained teeth became visible as he tried smiling through a spasm of pain.

'Theory,' he said.

'That got out of control,' I said.

'A volatile market,' he said.

'Put the gun down and I'll get you to a doctor.'

'No,' he whispered.

The sound of air escaping from a wound in his chest sounded like a kid blowing bubbles.

'What happened here, Professor?' I asked.

He opened his mouth several times as if he was trying to gulp air.

'Bad planning,' he said, his voice barely above a whisper, then his hand began to tremble and the gun slipped from his fingers.

Harrison stepped over, kicked it away and then took out his phone.

'I'll get paramedics going,' he said and walked over to the door.

'Who did this to you?' I asked.

'I did this to myself,' he said.

'Was Richard Shelton here?' I asked.

'Who's Richard Shelton?'

I realized he didn't know Shelton's real name.

'You met at Oxford,' I said.

His eyes flashed recognition. 'Prince of darkness,' he said.

'Yes, that's him, was he here tonight?'

He tried to laugh through gritted teeth.

'Was it Shelton who did this?' I asked again.

The air escaping from his chest grew louder.

'Cold,' he said.

He then shook his head as if angry at his failing body.

'Who are you?' he said.

'Lieutenant Delillo,' I said.

Blood bubbled out through the corners of his mouth as he tried to laugh.

'No tenure now,' he said.

'Who was in this room, who shot you?' I repeated.

'Do me a favor,' he said.

I looked at him for a moment and then shook my head.

'I don't do favors,' I said as Harrison stepped back in the room.

'Paramedics are on the way,' he said.

I looked down at Simms. His eyes were wandering around the room, unfocused.

'Professor, can you hear me?' I asked.

His eyes found me.

'Tell me about the money and Beckwith, Myers and Dunne,' I said.

He stared at me for a moment and then his eyes began to move around the room again.

'Whom were you working with, other than O'Brien?' I asked.

His eyes stopped on me and for a moment appeared to focus.

'Cold,' he said again.

His hands shook as if jolted with a shock and he let out a whimper.

'What happened?' he whispered.

His body tensed and then his breathing began to slow, one breath after another, the time between them getting longer until it was nearly a minute until his last taste of this world. His body relaxed into the floor like a rag doll. We both stared at him in silence for a moment.

'I'll cancel the paramedic,' Harrison said.

I stood and reached up to where the barrel of the gun had been placed against my neck.

'You OK?' Harrison asked.

I looked down at Simms.

'Yeah, I'm fine,' I said.

'Did he tell you anything?' Dylan asked.

'Nothing that would help us.'

Dylan looked around the room. 'What happened here?'

'Reality collided with theory,' I said.

'This is not what we were expecting,' Harrison said.

'Or what Simms was expecting,' I answered and then knelt down and examined the body. 'No knife wounds,' I said. 'From what I can see there appear to be two wounds in the chest.'

'Why would Shelton use a gun?' Harrison said.

'I don't think he would.'

'Which means what?' Harrison said.

'Either he killed in an entirely new way, or someone else did this,' I said.

We looked at each other for a moment.

'The second man on Shelton's wall,' I said.

'The one without the picture.'

'Could be.' I stepped over to the bathroom door and shined my light around the interior.

'I count three different shots fired in here,' I said and went over to the bullet hole in the glass shower door.

'How big a round do you think it is?' Harrison asked, stepping in.

'No larger than a thirty-eight,' I said.

'The toilet seat's up,' Harrison said.

I pointed the light into the bowl. The water appeared colored with urine.

'Simms was taking a piss and he's shot from behind,' Harrison said and then looked over the bathroom and the placement of the bullet holes. 'Two rounds in the wall above the toilet, the third in the shower glass. Either the first two rounds missed and hit the wall or they passed through him. Simms then turns and the next round misses and hits the shower door.'

'And then?' I asked.

'The professor comes charging out of the bathroom and puts up a fight.'

'Which explains the blood all over the room,' I said.

'But not who he was fighting.'

'Other than it wasn't Shelton.'

Harrison nodded. 'No, if it had been Shelton, I doubt the professor would have made it out of the bathroom.'

'Which means it was another amateur like the late Professor Simms,' I said. 'Someone who knew what they were doing would have put that first bullet in the back of Simms's head.'

I looked down at Simms. And then turned and looked around the room.

'Simms spends two days hiding out in this flea trap, and then turns his back on the man who kills him to take a piss,' I said. 'What does that tell you?'

'He wasn't afraid of the person who killed him,' Dylan said.

'Exactly what I was thinking.'

'He could have been surprised and didn't hear him enter the room.'

I shook my head. 'I don't think so. The door would have been locked.'

'He could have opened it because of the heat,' Harrison said.

'If you were hiding from shadows like him, would you have opened that door?' I said, looking down at Simms.

Harrison shook his head. 'No, I think I would sit in here and sweat.'

'Which leaves the first option,' I said.

'He wasn't afraid of the man who killed him.'

'Which rules out Shelton.'

'And leaves us with the second man on that wall in Shelton's room,' Harrison said.

'The one we have no picture of,' I said. 'The rats are turning on each other as the ship goes down.'

'Which takes us right back to the same rabbit hole we were going down before,' Harrison said.

I looked down at Simms's bloody body.

'Not quite, there's one less character in the story,' I said and then walked over to Simms's gun.

I hadn't looked at it closely before. It was a small caliber, probably a twenty-two revolver. The kind of cheap gun people who have no business having one keep in the nightstand drawer next to the bed, thinking it will protect them.

'The professor didn't know much about self-defense.' I picked it up carefully by the barrel and opened the cylinder. 'He got off one shot.'

'He could have emptied every chamber and still not have done enough damage to stop the attack without a perfectly placed shot,' Harrison said.

I set the gun back down, walked over to the door and moved the light over the pavement outside the room.

'He hit something,' I said.

Drops of blood led off into the darkness.

'That would explain why his attacker left him alive in there,' Harrison said.

'Panic,' I said.

'So where's Shelton through all of this?' Harrison said.

I looked out into the darkness. 'Waiting his turn.'

'I'll get on the phone to all the hospitals, see if we get a bullet wound that might match what happened in here.'

I turned and looked back into the room.

'How was he found?' I said.

'What do you mean?'

'I understand how Shelton would have been able to find Simms here, he knows the streets, but if it wasn't him, then how was Simms found?'

'Simms called his killer,' Harrison said. 'It was a planned meeting.'

'Exactly,' I said and stepped back into the room. An old rotary phone lay on the floor next to the bed where it had been knocked over during the fight. 'You see a cell phone anywhere?'

Harrison started looking around the room while I stepped over to Simms and searched the body.

'It's not on him,' I said.

Dylan checked under the bed and then stood up. 'Nothing. I'll get a trace started on the room phone.'

'We need it done quickly,' I said. 'And then check with the officers watching Beckwith and Dunne, see if they've left their houses.'

I pulled some car keys out of Simms's pants pocket and walked out to the Aston Martin. I went to the trunk and opened it up. There were a couple of grocery bags inside. I opened one and it was full of clothes. The second one contained money, the bills all bound with rubber bands. Harrison came out to the car.

'Bad planning, that's what Simms said in there,' I said. 'This is apparently what it looks like. Stick underwear, socks and a few thousand in slightly used twenties in paper bags and run. Not the picture of a former Oxford don that comes immediately to mind.'

'Things are in motion to trace the calls,' Harrison said. 'Shouldn't take long.'

'Anything on Dunne and Beckwith?'

'Nothing new, haven't stepped a foot outside their houses.'

I walked around to the driver's door and unlocked the car. The inside didn't seem to belong to the events that had taken place around it. It was like looking at a piece of history that had been frozen in time. Even the leather smelled as if it had just rolled out of the tannery.

'The rich are different from us,' I said. 'Shelton got that part right.'

'In this case they're also dead,' Dylan added.

I opened the glove box and then searched under the seat.

'Nothing,' I said. 'Whoever killed him probably took it.'

My phone rang and I picked up. It was Agent Utley.

'Simms is dead,' I said. 'Along with the night manager of the Sunshine Motel.'

'Shelton?' he asked.

'No, I don't think so.'

Utley was silent for a moment.

'The second man on Shelton's wall.'

'If you've got a better idea, I'm willing to listen,' I said.

'You asked about the third partner in the firm.'

'The one who died of a heart attack waterskiing.'

'Derrick Myers,' Utley said.

'You find something?'

'There are some issues surrounding his death that are still unresolved.'

'Such as?'

'Cause of death is preliminarily listed as drowning. The heart attack part of it only shows up in the Swiss report. According to them he was seen clutching his chest before crashing. The French report makes no mention of it.'

'Two reports?'

'It happened on Lake Geneva. There are some jurisdictional issues. It's unclear whether he was skiing in Swiss or French water. Hence, the conflicting reports.'

'The cause of death wasn't determined in the autopsy?' I asked.

'You need a body for an autopsy.'

'It was never recovered?'

'No. The water at the time of death was rough, according to the Swiss police. The French have made no determination as to lake conditions where he was supposed to be skiing.'

'You said he was seen clutching his chest. Who witnessed it?' I asked.

'This is where it gets interesting. According to the Swiss authorities, there was one person on the boat when it came ashore.'

'And the French?'

'They cite an eye witness in another boat as saying he saw two people in it when it returned to shore.'

'Did they interview the driver of the boat?'

'He told the French there was only him on the boat when he returned to shore. According to his account, Myers was moving very fast when he fell, his life jacket came off and he disappeared in the waves before he could turn the boat around. By the time he came back to the marina, it was dark.'

'People often report seeing things that on closer examination are wrong,' I said. 'Particularly in the dark.'

'I would agree except for one thing.'

'And that is?'

'A week after Myers drowned, the driver of the boat was killed in a traffic accident,' Utley said.

'Bad luck.'

'Bad something.'

'Any description of the second man claimed to have been seen in the boat?'

'Well, like you said, it was dark.'

'What do you think happened?' I asked.

'Think? Or believe happened?' Utley said.

'That depends on whether you favor the heart or the mind,' I said. Without realizing it, I placed my hand over my chest. The small wound where the needle had entered my breast now ached like a bee sting. 'I go either way depending on the day,' I said. 'At the moment I think the mind is winning, but I'm hopeful for a turnaround.'

'Well, I'm a Fed,' Utley said. 'You don't last long here if you put too much importance on the heart.'

'You don't buy it?' I said.

'Call me old-fashioned but I like to have a body, and I like my witnesses to not die in accidents,' he said.

'You think Myers could have faked his death?'

'I think I don't know enough to answer that.'

I turned and looked towards the dingy little room where a college professor lay on the shag orange carpet stained with blood.

'The Swiss,' I said, thinking out loud.

'What about them?' Utley asked.

'What are the Swiss known for?' I said.

'Money.'

'More specifically, keeping secrets about it.'

'It always seems to get back to that, doesn't it?' Utley said.

'Would you check and see if Simms made any trips to Switzerland since Myers' death?' I asked.

'You think it could be connected?'

'Someone put some holes in him and it wasn't Shelton.'

'I'll let you know.'

I hung up and walked over to the door of the motel room and looked in at Simms.

'What is it?' Harrison asked, stepping up behind me.

'Derrick Myers reportedly drowned in Lake Geneva, only there's a problem,' I said.

'What?'

'They never found a body.'

'You don't think it was an accident?'

'I'm full of doubt about most things at the moment,' I said.

'Lake Geneva? Cold fresh water, low oxygen levels, that wouldn't be unusual for a body to sink. Are there witnesses?'

'The French believe there were two, the Swiss one. The only witness that is certain is the driver of the boat and he died in a traffic accident a week later.'

Harrison looked at me for a moment. 'Myers faked his death?' He stared into the room.

'What?' I asked him.

'I'm thinking about cuckoo clocks,' he said.

'I could ask why, but I don't want to embarrass myself.'

'I think Shelton figured it out,' Harrison said.

'Why do you say that?'

'The movie Shelton turned Terry Pullian on to.'

'*The Third Man*.'

'Yeah. Orson Welles plays a crook named Harry Lime who's selling tainted penicillin on the black market. To get away from the Allied authorities he—'

'Fakes his death,' I said.

'Myers isn't dead, he's the other person on Shelton's wall,' he said.

I turned and looked into the room.

'You think Myers did this?' Harrison said.

'Let's say for argument's sake that about the time of Myers' death, all the money from their little scheme disappeared.'

'Myers ran off with the church's funds, and then faked his own death.'

I nodded.

'So how do we get from there to here?' he said.

'Simms figures it out, manages to get in contact with Myers and threatens to expose him if he doesn't come up with some money,' I said.

'Myers comes to meet Simms and things get ugly.'

'Killing isn't as easy as it's made out to be, particularly for someone who doesn't know what they're doing,' I said.

'Why would he kill the night manager?' Harrison said.

'She must have seen him. He's already killed, or thinks he's killed, Simms. He's got nothing to lose.'

'So he strangles her to protect the fiction that he's a corpse.' Harrison paused. 'So how did Simms figure it out?'

'Walking completely away from a life and becoming someone else isn't easy either. Perhaps Myers didn't walk away as cleanly as he thought,' I said.

'Someone knew he was alive and talked to Simms.'

'Utley is checking to see if Simms made any trips to Switzerland after Myers' death.'

'Then Shelton shows up to collect his piece of the prize

and discovers most of the cash has disappeared with Myers,' Harrison said.

'The third man,' I said.

'So he begins to extract his pound of flesh.'

'And they have no idea who they pissed off,' I said.

'They had a better idea after O'Brien had his head hung from a door,' Harrison said.

A gust of wind began sending leaves swirling across the parking lot.

'We need to find out how Simms learned Myers wasn't dead,' I said.

I looked around the parking lot and then back into the room.

'Call Arcadia PD, this is theirs now,' I said. 'Then talk to Traver and have him start collecting everything we can about Myers. I want to know who he left behind.'

twenty-four

It took a little over two minutes for the first patrol unit from Arcadia PD to arrive. The single officer who stepped out of the cruiser appeared to be sixteen and was the size of a large double refrigerator. If he had ever been the first unit on the scene of a killing, he did a good job of hiding the experience. We walked him through both killings, giving just enough information so he wouldn't blunder about and mess anything up for either Arcadia's detectives or ourselves and then we walked away from the Sunshine Motel.

As we drove back to Pasadena, the moon began to rise for the first time since power had begun to fail – a sliver of a crescent rising out of the shadow landscape to the south where twelve million people waited anxiously for dawn or the Department of Water and Power to bring back the light.

Traver and Chief Chavez were waiting in my office when we walked in. There were two messages from a Detective Munson in Arcadia who wanted, as he put it, to know what the hell was going on and why we hadn't waited for his arrival.

'What about Myers?' I asked.

'He was in the process of getting a divorce when he died, so technically that makes him still married before he died – if he's dead. His wife or widow lives in Pasadena on Laguna on the west side of the arroyo. I don't know about girlfriends,' Traver said.

'Kids?'

'One, born six weeks ago.'

I looked at Harrison.

'He could have come back to see his child,' Harrison said.

'A real family man,' I said.

'You want to fill in the blanks for me or just let me twist in the breeze?' Chavez said.

'A dead man's come back to life,' I said. 'The third partner at Beckwith, Myers and Dunne faked his death, and probably killed Professor Simms earlier this evening and then the night manager of the motel.'

'I'm assuming this has to do with the money,' Chavez said.

'He was the third man in their scheme.'

'And now Shelton is after him?'

I nodded. 'Myers is the last man standing, and probably the one who knows where the money is, most likely in some Swiss or offshore account,' I said.

'Professor Simms apparently wounded him with a twenty-two when they had their meeting in the motel,' Harrison said. 'We're hoping he'll walk into an emergency room.'

'If he's wounded severely enough,' Chavez said.

'This is what greed looks like,' Traver said and handed me a photograph from the DMV.

'Myers?' I asked and Traver nodded.

Derrick Myers was fifty-three years old with slightly graying hair. He had the kind of hard look that comes from either too much stress or a lot of money, or perhaps both. His skin was tanned, he had a strong neck and shoulders, and he was wearing a suit and tie that appeared tailored and expensive.

'A master of the universe,' I said.

'One of the guys who drove the economy off the cliff, if you ask me,' Traver said.

A uniformed officer stepped in the door and motioned to Harrison.

'You wanted information on any gunshot wounds walking into an emergency room,' the officer said.

Harrison nodded and the officer handed Harrison a sheet of paper.

'Be careful what you wish for, Detective,' the officer said.

Harrison looked down at the sheet. 'It's been a busy night. There're a dozen so far and the night is young.' He scanned the list. 'Not a white male in the bunch.'

Harrison's phone rang. He picked up and listened for several moments and then hung up.

'Simms made four calls from the room, two to a residence in Pasadena, one to a pizza takeout, and the other to a prepaid cell phone. No name attached to the cell, but it's a local number.'

'And the residence?'

'The widow Myers,' Harrison said.

'Which call was made first?' I asked.

'Myers' wife.'

'She knew her husband was alive,' I said.

Harrison nodded. 'It would seem so.'

'And gave him up.'

'Nothing like love,' Harrison said.

I looked at the Chief. 'You think you could talk with Utley and see if the FBI can give us a location on the cell phone?'

Chavez nodded. 'I'll see what I can do, but you know the Feds, that could take a while.'

'Keep trying.'

'What are you going to do in the meantime?' Chavez asked.

'Have a chat with Mrs Derrick Myers,' I said.

It was a little over ten minutes to Myers' neighborhood on the west side of the arroyo. Most of the houses on Laguna had a few candles flickering inside or the odd lantern. Halfway down the block one house had lights – it looked like a Christmas tree lit up in dark woods. We pulled to a stop outside and checked the address.

'Why am I not surprised?' Harrison said.

'An entire city in darkness and one of the few people to have lights is a man who faked his own death,' I said.

'Solar panels,' Harrison said, motioning up toward the roof. 'He's a man who knows how to plan ahead.'

'Shelton must have come as a great shock to him,' I said.

We got out of the squad and started up the fieldstone walk to the house. The home was large and spread out on a single level like a Wright prairie-style home. Everything about the exterior that I could see was immaculate and in the yard not a leaf or a blade of grass appeared out of place.

'You think she knew he faked his death?' Harrison said.

'At some point she must have.'

I stepped up to the front door and reached for the intercom.

'May I help you?' asked a voice before I could push the button.

'Pasadena Police,' I said.

'Is there a problem?' the woman asked.

'Mrs Myers, I'd like to talk to you. We have a few questions.'

There was silence for a moment.

'Is this necessary?'

'I'd prefer to have this conversation inside rather than out here,' I said. 'My name is Lieutenant Delillo.'

'It's a little late, Lieutenant,' she said. 'Would you hold your IDs up to the camera so I could see them.'

We held our IDs up and a moment later the door swung open. Mrs Myers appeared to be in her late thirties, was dressed in running tights and shoes and a USC T-shirt. If she wore any make-up I didn't see it, and given her looks I doubted she needed any. A Hispanic nanny stood in the entrance to a hallway twenty feet away.

'Thank you, Marta, you can go back to the baby,' she said to the nanny.

We stepped in and she closed the door. In the cuticles of several of her fingernails I noticed dark stains.

'What would you like to ask me?' she said.

'I'd like to talk to you about your husband.'

'I've already talked to the police about this. I don't understand why you want to talk again.'

'Would you mind if I use a bathroom?' Harrison asked.

She started to point down the hallway and then stopped.

'Why don't you come and sit in the kitchen,' she said and walked us through the living room and into the kitchen. 'There's a bathroom through that door,' she said.

Harrison walked out and I took a seat at the kitchen table.

'What would you like to ask?' she said. 'There's not much I can tell you, I only know what the Swiss police have told me.'

'I'm not here to talk about what happened in Switzerland,' I said.

'I'm afraid I don't understand.'

'Lawrence Simms made two calls to this house today,' I said.

She nodded. 'Larry's a good friend.'

'He's dead,' I said.

Her face flushed. 'Dead?'

'He was shot to death in a thirty-five dollar a night motel.'

She began to shake her head as if trying to dislodge the thought.

'It's our belief that your husband fired the gun.'

She tensed in the chair the way a kid would that had just been caught in a lie.

'My husband is dead,' she said.

'That's a fiction, Mrs Myers,' I said. 'And if you are party to it, you could be in a great deal of trouble.'

She glanced over her shoulder toward the door.

'You should consider your next words very carefully,' I said. 'You have a child to take care of.'

She looked at me and then seemed to sink in the chair as if the air had been taken out of her.

'I don't understand any of this,' she said. 'Why would this happen?'

'Money, that's why it happened, a great deal of money, and people are dying because of it. And your husband will be the next one if I don't find him.'

She shook her head, still trying to push back against the reality that was facing her.

'Mrs Myers, I'm a homicide detective, I'm not interested in the money or who stole what. Your husband got caught up in something and made some terrible mistakes, but you have to understand one thing. He's not going to just slip away into another life now. Things have gone too far. If I find him, he'll live. If I don't, the other person looking for him won't be as understanding.'

'This isn't possible,' she said, still fighting it.

'The man who is looking for your husband found Jim O'Brien. After torturing him, he cut off his head and hung it from a door.'

She began to tremble and put her hand over her mouth.

'Oh my God,' she said, barely able to speak.

'When did you find out your husband was alive?' I asked.

I went over to the kitchen counter and poured a glass of water from the tap and brought it to her.

'Drink this,' I said.

She clasped the drink in both hands and shakily drank from it.

'We were getting divorced,' she said.

'I know,' I said.

'He had changed in the last year,' she said.

'Did he tell you anything about what he was involved in with Simms and O'Brien?'

She shook her head. 'No, he never talked about work with me. I come from money, Lieutenant, Derrick didn't. It was always there between us, like a faceless third person standing in the room.'

'Did you know he was alive before he came here tonight?'

She looked at me, trying to form a response.

'It can be tricky to get blood out from under fingernails,' I said, reaching out and taking hold of her fingers. 'I've had the same problem myself before.'

She pulled her hand from mine and closed it into a fist.

'How badly is he hurt?' I asked.

She took a breath and touched her upper arm. 'He said he was attacked by a mugger getting into his car. There were some cuts on his hands and scrapes on his face and he was bleeding from his arm.'

'Did you believe him?'

She bit her lower lip and shook her head. 'I didn't

know what to do, he wanted to see his daughter. He was agitated, I don't think he had slept in a long time.'

'He wasn't attacked by a mugger, he was shot by Lawrence Simms.'

Harrison stepped back into the kitchen from the living room through which we had entered. In his hand he held a small towel with bloodstains on it.

'I really believed he was dead,' she said.

'When did you find out he wasn't?' I asked.

'A few weeks ago. I was getting out of my car at the mall and he pulled up in another one and opened the door.'

'Tell me about the wound. Did you stop the bleeding?'

She shook her head. 'No, it was still bleeding. I put some bandages on it and wrapped it with tape.'

'How much did he tell you about what he had done?'

'He said he had done it to start over, that's all.'

'You knew there was more to it than that,' I said.

'I suspected he had broken the law, but I thought it had something to do with the market, that's all.'

'When was he here tonight?' I asked.

'He left a little over an hour ago.'

'Was he going to a hospital?' I asked.

'I told him to go to one. I let him see the baby and then he left.'

'When Lawrence Simms called, he knew your husband was alive, didn't he?' I asked.

Mrs Myers nodded.

'Did he say how he knew?' I asked.

'He said something about some Swiss accounts, and

then said Derrick needed to know what else he knew or he could be in a lot of trouble.'

'You told him how to get in touch with your husband?'

'When Larry called a second time, I told him.'

'Did your husband tell you what name he was using?'

'No.'

I wrote down the number we had traced from the motel and showed it to her.

'Is that your husband's phone?'

She looked at it and nodded.

'I need you to call him for me,' I said.

She began to shake her head.

'It may be the only chance I have to keep him alive,' I said.

She took a deep, nervous breath. 'What do I tell him?'

'Tell him you have a picture of the baby you want him to have,' I said. 'See if he'll agree to meet you somewhere.'

'I can't—'

'You're not going to meet him, we will.'

'What if he doesn't believe me?'

'Make him believe you.'

She thought for a moment and then reluctantly nodded.

'Which phone would he recognize?' I asked.

'He knows my cell number,' she said. 'It's in the other room.'

'Go get it,' I said and she got up and walked out of the kitchen.

'You think he'll buy this?' Harrison asked.

'We don't have a lot of other options,' I said.

Mrs Myers walked back into the kitchen, sat down and nervously moved the phone in her hands.

'Can you put it on speaker?' I asked and she nodded.

'What do I say?'

'Just talk to him.'

'Trust wasn't the strongest part of our marriage at the end,' she said.

'What's your daughter's name?' I asked.

'Lindsay,' she said.

'Tell him you want your daughter to know her father.'

She tried to smile. 'Have you ever been divorced, Lieutenant?'

I nodded.

'So I should lie is what you're saying,' she said.

'You may be saving his life.'

Myers shook her head. 'He doesn't have a life any more.'

She opened the phone, took a deep breath to steady herself and then dialed the number. The phone rang once and then again and continued to ring unanswered, nine, ten, eleven times.

'This isn't—' she started to say and the ringing stopped.

She looked at me, her eyes on the verge of panic and I nodded to her.

'Talk to him,' I whispered.

'Derrick?' she said. 'It's me.'

There were voices on the other end, like the low murmur of a crowd.

'There are things I want to say. Something I want you to have,' she said.

It sounded like a breath on the other end. Mrs Myers

started to shake her head and I whispered, 'You're doing fine.'

She took another breath and started again.

'Derrick, talk to me. I want the father of our daughter to know what she looks like, to not forget her.'

'You shouldn't have called,' he said.

'Why?' she asked.

'Phone calls can be tracked, you shouldn't be connected to this,' he said.

'There's nothing so bad that can't be fixed,' she said.

There was a long silence on the other end.

'Yes there is,' he said. 'I've done them.'

'I want to see you,' she said.

'No you don't,' he said.

'I have a picture I want you to have, it's of Lindsay.'

He was silent again.

'She's your daughter too,' she said.

'I'm no father,' he said. 'A father wouldn't have done the things that I have.'

Mrs Myers' eyes became moist with tears. 'Let me help you.'

Again silence.

'Derrick?' she said.

'No one can help me. If you call again, I won't answer,' he said and then the line went dead.

Mrs Myers stared at the phone in her hand.

'Try calling him again,' I said.

She redialed and the ringing went on and on with no end until I slipped the phone from her hand and closed it.

'I'm sorry,' she said.

'Did you see what he was driving?' I asked and she shook her head.

'No, but knowing Derrick I'm sure it's expensive.'

'What was he wearing?' I asked.

'Blood,' she said without thinking and then thought the answer through. 'Dark pants, light shirt, pale blue, I think.'

'Do you know where he was staying?'

She shook her head. I took out a business card and placed it on the table in front of her.

'I'll have a squad watching the house, so you have nothing to worry about. If he calls back, I want you to call me immediately.'

'Lieutenant, are you sure he killed Larry?' she asked.

I nodded and she wiped a tear from her eye.

'I don't even love him any more, the things he's done . . . why am I crying?'

'You're crying because someday your daughter is going to ask you about her father, and you'll have to tell her.'

We walked back out to the squad, back into the darkness and the still hot air that carried the scent of a eucalyptus tree from somewhere close by. We got inside, but I made no attempt to drive away.

'I'll get a squad to watch the house,' Harrison said.

I nodded and he made the call to dispatch and then turned to me.

'You think he might come back here?' he said.

I shook my head. 'No, staying away from this house and his child may be the only decent thing he will do in the rest of his potentially short life.'

I looked back at the house.

'What did you hear in the background of the call she made to him?' I asked.

Dylan thought it through for a moment.

'You're talking about the voices.'

I nodded. 'What did they sound like? Were they close, distant?'

'It was indoors,' Dylan said.

'A large building.'

'Most of them were close, but not so close that you could pick out individuals.'

'Except for one,' I said. 'It was louder than the others, seemed to echo.'

'A PA system,' he said.

'He's in a hospital waiting room or an emergency room,' I said.

'I think you're right.'

I picked up my phone and dialed Traver who answered on the second ring.

'Myers is in a hospital right now, I need to know which one and quickly,' I said.

'I'll call you right back,' he said and hung up.

I set the phone down in my lap and looked across the expanse of lawn at Myers' home – a single place of light in a city of darkness. Where had it gone so wrong that the life being lived inside those walls wasn't good enough? How much more money would it take to fill the empty spaces that existed in his world? How could so many smart people collectively make such terrible choices? A certified financial planner had killed two people, one was a friend, the other an old woman just counting the days, trying to get through without the wrong guest checking into a rundown motel. Why? How much more money would it take to buy the dream he hadn't found or couldn't purchase with what he already had?

I understood why the Richard Sheltons of the world make the choices and take the actions they do, even if how we had created them would continue to be a mystery. There will always be destructive rogue waves that move through this world, not subject to the rules that the rest must follow. But why do the Myers of the world drive so frequently into the ditch with what seems to be so much ease? If you were to create a poster for the path to success, you might place O'Brien, Simms, and Myers front and center as examples of what we are capable of. Now one was a murderer and two were dead. And when the grim tally becomes final, and the last body is pulled from the wreckage, what will the answer be when someone asks why?

My phone rang and I picked up to hear Traver's voice.

'Three male Caucasians have been admitted to emergency rooms in the last hour,' he said.

'The bullet wound would be in the arm,' I said.

'There's nothing here about the nature of the wounds other than that one was admitted in critical condition.'

'Which eliminates that one. What about the other two?' I asked.

'One is at USC, the other is in Glendale.'

'Which hospital in Glendale?'

'Methodist, just off Brand.'

USC had one of the largest hospital emergency rooms in the nation. Army surgeons had trained there in preparation for the carnage they would see on the streets of Baghdad. Glendale was small in comparison.

'Which one would you go to?' I said to Harrison.

'A wound to the arm, Myers might sit for hours before being treated at USC,' Dylan said. 'The longer he remains in any one place, the greater the danger he's placing himself in. We're only ten minutes from Glendale, he would be seen there much quicker.'

'But at USC he would more easily be able to slip through the cracks without being noticed. Be in and out before any serious questions were asked,' I said.

'What do you want to do?' Traver asked.

'We pick the wrong one, we may lose our chance,' I said.

'Your call,' Harrison said.

'Call USC and give them Myers' description and the nature of the wound. It would be a small caliber in the arm, and some cuts on the hands and face. Tell them he could be armed. We're closer to Glendale, we'll take that,' I said and we pulled away.

twenty-five

Glendale Methodist was a level-one trauma center, though they saw far more heart attacks and car wreck victims than those suffering from gunshots. We took the freeway to Brand and then headed south past the empty shopping malls and dark car lots waiting for the return of power and the making of deals.

At the south end of Brand the hospital stood like the Myers' home, the only building with lights. Two blocks to the east, the ornate gates and the dark expanse of Forest Lawn Cemetery stood.

We circled the building, scanning the various parking lots for cars that might fit Myers' sense of self, though making those kinds of judgements in LA wouldn't get you very far on a normal night.

At the entrance to emergency, we pulled in. A Glendale black and white squad had stopped near the doors to the hospital. We pulled up behind it and got out. Three ambulances stood by the trauma entrance, and next to them a line-up of BMWs, Mercedes and a few older sedans were parked in the rest of the available spaces.

We walked over to the parked cars and quickly shined our lights into their interiors, looking for any signs that a wounded person had been inside.

Harrison shook his head. 'He would have parked on the street and walked in, he wouldn't want his car noticed.'

The flashing lights of another ambulance rounded the corner to the west and pulled up at the entrance. The back doors of the ambulance opened and two paramedics began wheeling out a victim on a gurney and headed in through the automatic doors to emergency.

We followed them inside and stopped. The corridor was full of people in various forms of distress, most appearing to be heat related. The occasional cry of pain stood out from the white noise of the voices that filled the space.

'Myers could have been right here when he answered the phone,' I said.

'The sound seems right,' Dylan said.

I nodded and dropped my hand to my weapon and began slowly walking toward the admitting desk, my eyes scanning each face as we passed. Over a hundred languages are spoken in the LA public schools. In the thirty feet it took to pass through the sick and injured, I think I heard half of those languages, all saying more or less the same thing. Help me.

'He's not here,' I said to Dylan.

He looked around once more and nodded. 'He could have been admitted already.'

'Or we just went to the wrong hospital, if he even stepped foot in one.'

I walked over to the admitting desk where an exhausted nurse looked up.

'You look like cops, and you don't look sick,' she said. 'Is that good or bad news for me?'

'We're looking for a gunshot victim,' I said.

'You have a name?' she asked.

I shook my head. 'No name, just the wound. It would be in the arm.' A metal tray fell to the floor in one of the treatment stalls, briefly silencing the voices waiting their turn to see a doctor.

'Hang on and I'll check for you,' the nurse said. She walked over and took a look at a chart and then walked back.

'White male wounded in the upper arm.'

'That could be it,' I said. 'Is he still in the hospital?'

She nodded. 'He should be being prepped for surgery.' She looked down at the chart. 'A vascular surgeon is doing the procedure, there must have been some arterial damage.'

'Is there an officer present?'

'They interviewed him in emergency, I don't know if they went up to surgery.'

'Do you have a name and age?' I asked.

She scanned the chart. 'Listed as late forties, name John Smith.'

'Smith?' I said.

The nurse nodded. 'Is there a problem I need to know about?'

'Has anyone else asked about him?'

She nodded.

'Male or female?'

'Male, his son.'

'In his twenties?'

She nodded.

'How do we get to surgery?' I asked.

'One flight up, elevator's down the hallway over there past the man holding the ice bag on his head.'

We rushed down the corridor and reached the elevator as the doors opened. It was filled with doctors and nurses attending a patient on a ventilator.

'The stairs are right there,' one of them said and we rushed over to the door and started up to the second floor.

On the second floor, we stepped out into the corridor. Post-op was to the left, surgery to the right. A central nursing station was straight ahead. We rushed over to it where two male nurses sat staring at some monitors.

'I'm looking for a patient named Smith,' I said.

One of the nurses looked up. 'Gunshot?'

I nodded.

'He'll be in surgery any minute, you'll have to wait.'

'This can't wait,' I said.

He looked at the other nurse who shrugged and the nurse pointed down the hallway to the right.

'Number three operating room, they may still be in prep. Knock on the door, don't go in.'

'There was a son of the victim,' I said.

The nurse nodded. 'The waiting rooms at the end of the hallway, straight down there.'

We moved down the hallway, passing the first two operating rooms and stopped at number three and knocked. A moment later the door swung open and a masked and gowned nurse stood there. I showed her my badge.

'We need to take a look at the patient,' I said.

'He's been intubated and is going to sleep right now, you'll have to wait.'

I slipped out the DMV photograph and held it up to the nurse.

'Is this the patient?' I asked.

'I didn't prep him, I couldn't tell you. He'll be in post-op in about forty minutes, you can wait there, he's not going anywhere.'

'Did you see his son?' I asked.

She shook her head and stepped back in, closing the door behind her.

'He could be in the waiting room, he's got no reason to think we're here,' Harrison said.

'You mean other than the fact that he's a genius and has figured everything else out,' I said.

We ran down to the far end of the corridor and stopped a few feet from the door to the waiting room.

I slipped my weapon from the holster and held it close to my side. Curtains had been drawn shut over the window into the waiting room. Harrison stepped over to the other side of the door and drew his Beretta.

'You open it, I'll go in,' I said.

Harrison nodded.

'Now,' I said and he took hold of the handle and pushed it open.

I swung around the corner of the door and into the

waiting room, keeping my weapon down. A woman was asleep in a chair, a book clutched to her chest. The rest of the room was empty. On the screen of a silent TV in the corner a rerun of a sixties game show was on. I held my weapon for another moment then placed it back into the holster.

'It wouldn't be like Shelton just to sit and wait,' I said. 'He would be planning something.'

'But what?'

'Where would you be if you were him?' I said.

Harrison looked back into the hallway. 'Figuring out a way to kill inside a hospital and not get caught.'

'He already did that when he tried to kill Cathy O'Brien,' I said.

'He dressed as a doctor,' Harrison said.

We stepped back into the hallway and I looked down toward the nursing station and my hand fell back to my gun. A young man was standing at the station, leaning over, talking to one of the nurses.

'Or he's just playing the dutiful son. Is that him?' I said to Harrison.

The nurse behind the desk raised his arm and pointed in our direction. The young man at the desk took a step away from the station, stared at us, and then turned and ran the other way.

'That would be a yes,' Harrison said. 'I'll take the stairs at this end and try to cut him off on the first floor.' He rushed across the hallway and into the emergency stairway.

I ran down to the nursing station and stopped.

'Where did he go?' I asked.

'The stairs,' the nurse said and I headed off down the hallway.

I reached the door to the stairs, pulled it open and raised my Glock as I stepped inside. The sound of footsteps moving up abruptly fell silent. I waited a moment, then let the door fall shut behind me and the footfalls immediately began again and then I heard the sound of a door open as he exited the stairwell.

I stepped back into the hallway and over to the elevator, hitting the up button. The elevator began to descend, stopped two floors above, and then began to descend again. My hand tightened around the handle of my weapon and I took a step back. It passed the floor above and then a bell rang and the light lit up.

The doors began to open and I raised my weapon as a figure inside rushed toward me.

'Freeze!' I yelled.

He jumped back inside and hit the door close button. I stepped forward and blocked the doors, and trained my weapon on the figure.

'Get down on the floor,' I yelled.

The figure dropped to the floor at my feet and I reached around and pulled the stop button on the control panel.

'If you move even an inch, I'll put a bullet in your head,' I said.

I stepped around him, keeping my gun trained on the back of his head.

'Put your right arm behind your back,' I said.

He silently did as I had told him. I knelt down, putting

a knee in the small of his back, and began to slip a cuff on his wrist.

'You got me, dude,' he said in a voice straight out of the San Fernando Valley.

'What did you say?' I said.

'I ain't resisting,' he said.

I stared at the back of his head for a moment and then stood up over him.

'Roll over,' I said.

The kid rolled over and I looked into his face and slipped my gun back in the holster.

'Who the hell are you?' I asked.

'Josh Smith,' he said.

'And that's your dad in surgery?' I said.

He nodded.

'Why did you run, Josh Smith?' I said.

He looked at me for a moment, surprise in his eyes.

'The parking tickets,' he said.

'Tickets?'

'Yeah, sixty of them. I thought you were here because of that,' he said.

I stepped back and shook my head.

'No, I'm not here for your tickets,' I said. 'Go wait for your father.'

'Really?'

'Go before I change my mind and turn you in.'

He quickly got to his feet and rushed out of the elevator. I released the stop button and went down to the first floor. Harrison was standing there, about to raise his weapon.

'We picked the wrong hospital,' I said and started out through emergency, with Harrison quickly following.

'You found him?' he asked.

I nodded.

'Who was it?' he asked.

'That was Josh, a serial parker.'

We reached the squad and started east on San Fernando as I dialed Traver.

'He wasn't at Glendale,' I said as he picked up. 'What have you heard from County?' I asked.

'Nothing, I haven't been able to get through.'

'You can't get through?'

'From what I've heard on the scanners, there's some incident or power issue there, they're sending incoming patients to other hospitals.'

I looked over to Harrison.

'Incident?' he said.

I looked around at the dark streets.

'I think you better drive faster,' I said and he hit the flashers and pressed his foot on the accelerator.

twenty-six

LA County USC medical center rose out of the southern skyline, its white stone visible in the surrounding darkness. In a city that on its best days barely manages to function, the hospital was there to pick up the pieces, even if it could not always put them back together as they once had been.

Ten thousand babies are born there each year. The number of gunshot wounds, knife wounds, car wrecks, psychic meltdowns and any other trauma imaginable dwarfs that number by a factor of ten. If you're poor it's where you go to see a doctor for a sore throat, sprained ankle, or a heart attack. It has its own jail, pharmacy and college classrooms. If you're dying in the city of angels, your last breath will more than likely be inside one of its rooms.

It took us fifteen minutes to make the drive from Glendale. We stopped outside the entrance to emergency and looked across the street at the hospital's main building. There was no obvious evidence of a breakdown in its ability to function, except for the lack of traffic both coming and going. Nothing appeared different from the other times I had been here to question a suspect or interview a witness.

'If Myers is still here, finding him will take a little bit of luck,' Harrison said, looking at the huge complex of buildings.

'Perhaps that's why he chose this hospital,' I said.

High up on the main hospital tower, several floors of lights flickered on and off. We both stared at it for a moment, silently wondering the same thing – Shelton. Paranoia does not skip those wearing badges, particularly in the darkness.

'You don't suppose among Shelton's many skills he's also an electrician?' Harrison said.

I glanced around at the surrounding darkness.

'He giveth and taketh away?' I said.

'I was thinking more along the lines of the four horsemen of the apocalypse with an electrician's union card.'

I motioned forward and Harrison drove down the entrance ramp to the trauma centers located under the main building. Half a dozen ambulances were lined up in a row. We rolled to a stop behind them and got out. On the back step of the first ambulance I noticed fresh bloodstains. We both stared at it for a moment.

'If anyone's interested, I have a bad feeling about this,' Harrison said.

'Everyone has a bad feeling when they step into a hospital,' I said and walked over to the glass doors leading to the admissions area.

What I had witnessed in the other hospitals the last few

days didn't prepare me for the scene in front of me. Harrison looked inside and shook his head.

'Something's happened,' he said and we started forward.

The sound of chaos greeted us as the doors opened. Bloodstained stretchers were spread across the floor. Some still contained victims. I passed a young Hispanic who looked to be little more than thirteen or fourteen. Some party ribbon was wrapped around his wrist just below where the IV needle was stuck in his arm. No one was attending him any longer. A small neat hole in his cheek marked the spot where the bullet had ended his life.

'This is why they weren't answering Traver's calls,' I said.

We walked past another half dozen shooting victims being treated by young interns wearing face shields to protect them from blood splatter and over to the admitting desk. An Indian attendant wearing the turban of a Sikh looked up and I showed him my badge.

'We're looking for a gunshot victim,' I said.

He looked at the victims filling every available space. 'Take your pick, we have all shapes and sizes,' he said with a heavy Indian accent.

'It would be a white male, early fifties, with a wound to the arm.'

The attendant shook his head. 'Apparently no such guest was present at the barbecue that someone used as target practice.'

'There are no other patients other than from this incident?' I asked.

He looked up and sighed. 'We haven't admitted a new patient for over an hour, we're out of beds, doctors, we're short on blood and if this keeps up I suspect faith is in deep trouble. Are you sure he was admitted here?'

'Yes,' I said.

He motioned down the hallway with a pencil. 'Try the other clinic, they handle minor trauma, he's probably there.'

Behind the curtains of a trauma bed a high-pitched squeal of pain silenced the rest of the room. The attendant looked at us for a moment, his eyes no longer able to mask the toll the night had taken. He looked over toward the source of the sound and then at the doors leaving the building.

'Tomorrow is a new day,' he said and turned to me. 'At least for some of us.'

We walked away down the hallway, following the signs to the minor trauma unit.

'Jesus,' Harrison said as we stepped to the doors.

The room was filled not only with those who would normally be seen here, but also those who would have been treated in the other unit. Young, old, injured, sick, they were all here; their faces and skin color could fill in a good portion of the map of the world.

We slowly walked through the crowd, checking each face for Myers. He didn't appear to be present. I walked over to the admitting desk. The attendant was trying to communicate with a young Filipino woman whose English skills were failing her. He would ask a question and each time she would respond with the same exasperated answer. 'Sick, sick.'

He nodded and then handed her a clipboard and pencil as a child began to wail somewhere in the room.

'Name, put down your name,' he said and then pointed toward a group of other Filipinos. 'Have them help you.'

She walked away and we approached the desk.

'I don't suppose you speak Filipino, our translator is sick,' he said to me.

I shook my head and then held out my badge. 'I'm looking for a gunshot victim.'

He pointed back toward the other clinic. 'They would be over there.'

'They sent us here. The victim is a white male, wound in the arm.'

'I just got on,' the attendant said and turned to a nurse further down the desk. 'Roberta.'

Roberta didn't look up.

'Go talk to her, she's been on longer,' he said. 'Next in line, step up,' he said.

We worked our way through the crowd to the other end of the admitting desk. Roberta had the arms of a weight-lifter and the face of a mother superior. I imagined no one messed with Roberta.

'You're looking for someone?' she said.

I showed her my badge. 'Gunshot victim, white male, wound in the arm.'

She reached around behind her and picked a chart off the wall.

'James Long?' she asked.

'I don't have a name, he would be in his early fifties.'

She nodded. 'He's here, bullet was lodged next to the bone. Surgeons had to remove it. He may be in a recovery room by now.'

'Where?' I asked.

She pointed through the crowd. 'Down that hallway, take a left at the security desk and then go upstairs to three and follow the signs.'

We started to turn.

'You're with Pasadena?' she asked.

I stopped. 'Yes.'

'Don't you talk to each other?' she said.

The lights began to flicker and the room fell silent as everyone looked up at the ceiling, waiting to see if we would be plunged into darkness. The lights settled and Roberta sighed in relief and the voices of the sick and injured began to rise again.

'When it rains, it pours,' she said.

'What is causing that?' I asked.

'Age,' she said. 'The emergency generating system is old and overtaxed.'

'Who did you say we should talk to?' I asked.

'Each other,' Roberta said.

'What do you mean?' I asked.

'One of your people is already here questioning him.'

I glanced at Harrison and my heart rate began to jump.

'When?'

'Half an hour ago, maybe a little more.'

'What was the officer's name?' I asked.

She thought for a moment and then shook her head. 'Honey, it's been a long night already, I don't remember.'

'Uniformed officer or detective?'

'Detective.'

A young Salvadorian woman holding a baby stepped up next to us.

'I'll be with you in a moment, darling,' Roberta said.

'Was his name Harrison?' Dylan asked.

Roberta turned back to us. 'I'm sorry?'

'The officer, was his name Harrison?' Dylan repeated.

'Yeah, that's it, very polite, sounded English. What you doing with an English cop in Pasadena?'

'What was he wearing?' I asked.

Roberta chuckled. 'He's a cop, a cheap suit.'

We turned and started working our way through the crowd, moving toward the corridor.

'Shelton's using my badge,' Harrison said.

We stepped through the doors and into the hallway, heading in the direction Roberta had pointed us. The corridor was a good fifty feet long and we ran down to the end where it split in three directions. Surgery was to the right, security to the left. Where the middle corridor went was anyone's guess.

We started down the corridor toward the security office. The door was cracked open when we reached it. I pushed it open the rest of the way and glanced inside. No one was there.

'I suppose this is normal on a busy night,' Dylan said.

A cup of coffee lay overturned on a desk.

'Sure, they probably went looking for a mop,' I said.

We glanced at each other, not believing the words for a second.

'Probably,' Dylan said and we rushed out of the office and took the elevator up to three, stepped out and began following the signs to post-op.

We reached the end of the hallway and rounded the corner. The entrance to post-op recovery was through two glass doors. Inside, two nurses sat at a counter. We stepped through the doors and they both looked up. The quiet in the room seemed unnatural after being in the emergency room. The walls were painted a pale yellow, I suppose to simulate the rising sun. Behind the counter and to the right a door led to the actual recovery rooms.

'Can I help you?' asked one of the nurses.

I showed her my badge. 'A patient, James Long, is he inside?' I asked.

She checked her chart. 'Yes, bed eight.'

'Was there another policemen here?' I asked.

'Yes.'

'How long ago?'

'Twenty minutes, maybe half an hour. I think he's still in there,' she said and then looked at the other nurse. 'Did you see that cop come out?'

The other nurse looked up and shook her head. I slipped my gun out and started for the door. The nurse stared at my weapon for a moment and then stood up.

'What the hell's going on here?' she said.

I stepped around the counter and over to the side of the door, avoiding the window in it.

'Which is bed eight?' I asked.

'Fourth from the end on the right side,' she said.

'How many other patients in there?' I asked.

'Six,' she answered.

The lights began to flicker again and we all stopped and looked at them.

'I wish they wouldn't do that,' said the second nurse.

The lights settled and the nurse took a deep breath.

'You didn't answer my question,' she said to me. 'I've got patients in there, what's going on?'

'That wasn't a policeman,' I said. 'Stay here until we come back out.'

'And if you don't come back out?'

'Is there another exit in there?' I asked.

She nodded. 'Emergency stairwell at the far corner.'

'Where does it lead?'

'It goes down to the ground floor or up to the top.'

I looked over at Harrison and nodded and he pushed the door open and I stepped through. The lights were kept low in the room to ease patients' transition back to consciousness. I stood with my weapon up for a moment and then let it down to my side. It was a large room, a dozen beds lining each side. It was like stepping back in time when there was no such thing as private rooms in hospitals. IVs hung from stands next to several of the beds where patients lay.

I walked over to bed eight.

A few of the patients stirred as we walked by, but most were still held in the deep grip of a narcotic sleep. I stopped at the fourth bed from the end. An IV bottle hung from the stand next to the bed. Its line connected to a needle that lay on the empty bed; a small stain of blood on the white sheet surrounded the needle.

'It's possible he got up and walked out before Shelton came in here,' Harrison said.

I nodded and looked over to the emergency door in the corner.

'Yes, it's possible,' I said.

'But you don't think so.'

I walked a few steps toward the door to the emergency exit and knelt down. A tiny trail of blood drops led straight to the door.

'No, I don't think I do,' I said and looked across the rest of the room. 'Tell the nurses they're missing a patient, I'll check the other beds to make sure Shelton isn't playing with us.'

I walked up the row of beds on the other side, glancing at the faces. A child, an old man, a woman whose features looked Egyptian. Myers wasn't among them.

The door opened and the lead nurse came rushing in, with Harrison right behind her. She walked over to the bed and stared at it for a moment.

'Dammit,' she said to herself.

'How long was it between the last time you saw him and when the policeman walked in?' I asked.

'Just a few minutes, perhaps a little more.'

'Could he have walked out of here on his own?'

She reached down and picked up the IV needle and looked at it. 'If he did, he wouldn't have walked very fast.'

'Where are his personal effects kept?'

She motioned toward the door and some lockers lining the wall. 'Right there. Most of these patients will go home after surgery.'

We moved to the lockers.

'Numbers match the beds?' Harrison asked and the nurse nodded.

He opened number eight. A shirt with bloodstains on the arm, a pair of pants, shoes, that was it. Harrison patted down the pants and checked the shoes.

'No wallet, no passport,' he said.

'Would valuables be kept somewhere else?' I asked.

The nurse shook her head. 'No, it would all be in there.'

We walked over to the exit door. A drop of blood stained the handle.

'What's on the ground floor where this comes out?' I asked.

The nurse thought for a moment. 'I think it comes out in the lobby, I've never walked it.'

'How many floors above?'

'We're in the old section, there're twelve above us.'

'Are they all full?' I asked.

She shook her head. 'Some of the critical care and surgery units have moved all their patients to the new building. Those floors are empty at the moment.'

Harrison reached out and opened the door.

'I don't hear anything,' he said.

'Did you get a good look at the policeman who came in here?' I asked.

She shrugged. 'I looked at him, but not closely.'

'Call security and give them a description of both him and the patient you're missing,' I said. 'Tell them he's posing as a cop and that he is probably armed with at least a knife.'

She heard my words but hesitated.

'Go on,' I said.

The nurse turned away and we stepped out into the stairwell and let the door close behind us.

'Go down and see if they came out below. I'll go up and see if there's any blood above,' I said.

'Wait for me,' Harrison said.

I nodded. 'Now go on,' I told him.

Harrison hesitated and then started down and I began climbing. A door opened and closed somewhere above but there was no other sound to follow. I stepped up to the fourth floor. There was no blood on the landing, none on the door. I continued up, winding my way up floor after floor, with no sign of blood. On the ninth floor I stopped. A single drop of blood had fallen on to the floor in front of the door.

Below I heard the sound of a door open and shut and then footsteps moving back up. I reached out and took hold of the door handle, pulled it open and stepped through into a large ward with half a dozen beds. An old woman sitting in a wheelchair spun it around and looked at me. I realized she wasn't old at all, just ill. She wore a baseball cap on her bald head. I glanced quickly around at the other beds. They were all filled with women, all of them bald.

'Can I help you?' the woman in the chair asked.

Under her gown I could see the shape of bandages covering her chest where her breasts had been removed to stop the spread of cancer. Around her wrist was a bright pink bracelet. I started to ask her a question, but the words seemed to slip away.

'Are you all right?' she asked. Her voice sounded like something coming out of a hollow reed.

A few of the other patients looked in my direction, their eyes sunken in their faces, their thin frames barely visible under the sheets of the bed.

'Did someone come through this door?' I asked.

She shook her head. 'It opened and someone looked in, but then it closed.'

'Did you see more than one person?' I asked.

She shook her head, her thin neck seemingly barely able to support the movement.

'How long ago?' I asked.

She smiled and shook her head. 'We don't keep time here, no watches, no clocks.'

I looked at her, wondering if I was looking at a reflection of my future.

'It wasn't long, twenty minutes, but that's a guess,' she said.

I started to turn back into the stairway.

'Are you a survivor?' she asked.

The words startled me and I stopped and looked back at her, her eyes finding mine.

'You have the look,' she said. 'When you've done this as long as I have, you can tell,' she said.

'Can you?' I said and she nodded.

My heart began to race.

'I don't know,' I said.

'I'd say you're a survivor.'

I looked at her for a moment longer and then pushed the door open and stepped back into the stairway and let it close behind me. I started to take a step but my legs balked at the notion and I leaned against the door, trying to slow my breathing down. Gradually the air returned to my lungs and I stepped away and started up the next set of stairs. As I took the first one, there was movement behind me and I spun around, slipping my weapon from the holster.

'It's me,' Harrison said.

My hand holding the Glock was trembling and I placed it back into the holster.

'Are you all right?' he asked.

I nodded. 'I've just had my fortune told.'

Dylan looked over to the door, not understanding.

'Did you find anything below?' I asked.

'There was blood on the first-floor landing. There's a security station right outside the door in the lobby. I think he took a look and came back up.'

'They passed here, and kept going up,' I said. 'I think Shelton's looking for someplace to take Myers to get what he wants out of him.'

'The empty floors the nurse talked about,' Harrison said.

'Seems like a good bet,' I said and started up the next flight.

We opened the doors on to the next two floors and both were in full use. On the twelfth-floor landing, we stopped. A small smear of blood painted the wall next to the door.

'Fingers marks,' Harrison said.

'Like Myers tried to hold on as he was pulled through.'

I took hold of the handle and opened the door. There was no movement, no sound, only a few dim lights lit the length of the corridor. Scraps of paper and pieces of tape and used latex gloves littered the floor as if it had been evacuated in a hurry.

'The empty wards,' I said.

We stepped out on to the floor and let the door close silently behind us.

'There,' Harrison said, motioning toward several drops of blood leading down the empty corridor.

'Shelton found what he was looking for,' I said.

Dylan nodded. 'A nice quiet place to do his work.'

I slipped my gun out and Harrison did the same. We followed the drops of blood down the hallway to a junction with another corridor. There was no more blood visible, the trail vanished. Old signs pointed to a critical care unit to the right, surgery to the left, radiology straight ahead.

'We guess wrong and Myers is dead, if he isn't already,' Harrison said.

I stepped over to a phone on the wall and picked it up. No dial tone.

'You check critical care, I check surgery,' I said.

Harrison started to shake his head.

'You said it yourself. We guess wrong, Myers is dead,' I said.

The lights began flickering on and off again.

'A bad idea just got worse,' Harrison said.

The lights settled, leaving behind the hum of a faltering fluorescent tube somewhere ahead.

'When you've cleared it, come back here,' I said and started down the corridor following the signs to surgery. Harrison went in the opposite direction.

Offices lined the corridor on either side. There were still pieces of furniture in some of them. It felt like coming across one of those old abandoned farmhouses in the Midwest. Pieces of lives left behind in the race to leave quickly. If you paused long enough, I began to imagine you could hear the echoes of conversations that had taken place inside the walls. It didn't take much imagination to hear the words. *We have some good news . . . the results are not what we were hoping for . . . we found a mass.*

I glanced quickly in each one that I passed until I reached a double set of doors that led into surgery. I pushed one of the doors open and then stopped as I heard what sounded like a muffled cry of pain. I glanced back in the direction I had come. Harrison was out of sight.

I slowly stepped up to the abandoned counter; a few empty patient charts lay about, along with the kind of everyday things that get left behind during a move. The odor of disinfectant hung in the air. A wing of operating rooms led off to the right, more were down a hallway to the left. I listened for a moment, trying to hear the sound I had heard before but there was only silence.

I stepped around the counter and into the left hallway of operating rooms. I eased up to the first room, took hold of the door and pushed it open. There was nothing inside except for some discarded surgical gowns hanging on a hook against the wall.

On the far side of the room another door led to the operating room. I walked over to the door and looked through the window. A bare metal table lay in the middle of the room, a smashed light bulb littered the floor; there was nothing else there. I moved back to the corridor and started toward the next surgery when I heard the sound of something metallic hit the tile of the floor and echo down the corridor behind me.

I spun around and raised my weapon. The sound had come from the other bay of surgical rooms beyond the counter. I moved back down the hallway to the counter. What sounded like a series of quick breaths – like a mother in labor would produce – came from beyond the swinging doors that led to the operating rooms.

I eased around the counter to the swinging doors, pushed them open and stepped through. At the far end of the hallway a bright light spilled out of the last surgery and into the hallway. The sound had silenced. I stopped and listened for a moment but it didn't resume.

Slowly I began moving down the hallway toward the light at the end, pausing at each door just long enough to glance inside and then move on. A few feet from the last door I stopped, took hold of my weapon with both hands and pressed myself against the wall and steadied myself.

'That may sound bad, but I wouldn't worry about it,' I said silently, repeating the words my doctor had said to me.

The lights began to flicker again and I spun around and opened the door into the outer room of the surgery. The bright light that was now flickering like a strobe was coming from the operating room. I moved across to the door and listened for movement on the other side and then eased up to the window and looked through.

My heart began to pound against my chest as I stared through the glass at what was inside the next room.

'No,' slipped softly over my lips, the way a muscle might involuntarily twitch.

I tried to take a breath but the air in the room seemed to have vanished. I let go of the Glock with my left hand, pushed the door open and stepped inside, raising the gun into the room as the lights began to flicker again.

I moved to the side, pressed myself against the wall and swung the gun across the room. Shelton was already gone, but I continued to hold the weapon as if he was still in the room.

In the center of the room a figure lay stretched out on a stainless steel operating table. His wrists had been tied down but now hung free from the restraints that dangled from the table. His head tilted back. In the flickering light the scene appeared more like something from an amusement park ride through a haunted house, but this wasn't make-believe, no matter how much I wanted it to be.

I held my weapon on the figure and moved slowly forward to the side of the table. I held the gun for a moment longer, gripping it like you would a lifeline thrown from a boat.

The lights began to settle again and the hum of fluorescents filled the room. I stared for a moment and then looked away. Myers' patient gown had been pulled down to his waist. Where his chest had been, all that was visible was a dark pool of blood. The white edge of his sternum where the ribs had been cut away to open his chest shined like polished stones.

I lowered the gun and began to walk around the table to the other side when I saw a faint ripple of movement in the pool of blood filling his chest cavity. I stopped and stared at it for a moment, wondering if I had really seen what I thought I had. It happened again, like a pebble dropped in a pond sending ripples across the surface. Myers' heart was still beating. He was alive.

I turned and stepped closer to him. If there was life behind the blank eyes that stared up at the ceiling, I couldn't detect it.

'Can you hear me?' I said.

There was no response.

'Myers, can you hear me?' I asked again.

His eyes blinked, but they continued to just stare straight up. I leaned closer to get in his line of sight.

'Can you—'

His hand reached up, grabbed my shirt and began to pull me toward him. I took hold of his wrist and began to push against his grip but he still pulled me closer.

'No,' I said, struggling against his strength.

He inched me closer to his face. I released his wrist and pressed my hand against his neck and tried to pull away. A faint breath slipped through his teeth and the muscles in his arm began to tremble and then his fingers relaxed. I pulled free and his arm fell limply away.

I took a breath and then another, trying to gather

myself. Another ripple of movement spread across the surface of blood in his chest.

'Can you hear me?' I said, trying again.

His eyes blinked and his mouth moved but no sound came forth. I braced myself, leaned in, placing myself into his line of sight. The vacant stare in his eyes was now replaced by a faint sense that something was behind the surface of the eyes.

'Can you understand me?'

He blinked and then silently mouthed *yes*.

'I'm a policeman, I'm going to get you some help.'

His eyes closed and the muscles in his neck tensed and he whispered, 'No.'

'What did you tell Shelton?' I asked.

He took a shallow breath and mouthed something unintelligible. I leaned in closer.

'Try again,' I said.

His entire body seemed to tense and then, 'Everything,' slipped out of his mouth, sounding like a voice calling from a distant room.

He looked at me, and for a split second his eyes reflected the horror of what had happened to him and then just as quickly they began to lose focus.

'I'll come back,' I said but the light of recognition that had been in his eyes began to fade like night falling on an empty landscape.

One last ripple spread out across the pool of blood in his chest and then all movement stopped as death silenced his heart.

I stared at him for a moment, trying with all my will not

to imagine what he had just been through and then turned and pushed open the door and stepped into the corridor. I took a few steps and quickly ran out of breath. I reached out and braced myself against the wall and tried to get air back into my lungs.

'Everything,' I whispered to myself.

What was everything? Would that be enough for Shelton? Would he slip quietly away into the darkness now that he had what he wanted? Or was he so broken that nothing would ever fill that void inside him?

A door opened somewhere beyond the surgery. I turned and took a few steps, stopped and listened for more movement. Had a door closed, or did I imagine it?

I stared at the exit to surgery and then rushed forward through the double doors and into the waiting area. There was nothing there. Somewhere from deep under the floor, the sound started again – or did it? I waited and it seemed to be there for a second and then it wasn't, like holding a seashell up to your ear.

I crossed over to the door into the corridor and tried to understand the direction the sound was coming from. As I turned the corner, the sound took on a form – footsteps, echoing across polished floors. They moved and then stopped, moved again and then just as quickly fell silent.

I took a step and then a few more and the footsteps began to move again in the distance. I sprinted down the corridor not bothering to glance at the doors. I passed the first junction of corridors, pausing just long enough to hear the movement straight ahead and then ran to the next junction and stopped.

I was standing in what had been a central nursing station. Hallways spread out in four directions. There was nothing there, not a sound, no movement coming from any direction. I spun left and then right, pointing my gun into the dimly lit corridors, and then saw the blood on the floor. I took a quiet step forward and then another.

A piece of glass cracked under my foot. I froze and waited for a reaction. The lights began to flicker again. Then a squeak of a door hinge came through the silence – or did I imagine it? Was it the spark of a faltering light? I looked left, then heard the soft sound of a door opening, coming from the opposite direction. I spun to my right as the footsteps moved quickly away and I followed all the way to the end of the corridor and another nursing station. Like the other station, four more corridors led in more directions.

I slowly walked around the counter of the nursing station and then stopped at the far end. There was blood on the floor. A thin line and then a few drops moving down the corridor to the south. I took a few more steps, following the blood trail, but there was no more, it ended as abruptly as it had begun. I took a few more steps to be certain and then heard a footstep and then another from behind me and I spun around.

'Dylan,' I whispered to myself, looking up and down the different corridors for the source of the sound.

Something moved, or took a breath, down the corridor leading away from the station and I ran forward until the hallway turned. I rushed down its length and found myself standing in the first nursing station I had already been in.

The broken glass I had stepped on was there, but there was blood now, just a few drops, that hadn't been there before.

A sound came from beyond a door down the hallway to my left, as if someone was struggling to open it. I took a step, and then another, and realized I was wrong about the direction and what the sound was. I knew this sound. I felt the rush of adrenalin that comes with fear. The voice in my head began yelling *no, no, no* as the glass cracked behind me. I spun and raised my weapon but Shelton was too fast. It was just a blur of movement, like the wings of a bird sweeping past my head, and I felt the blow glance the side of my face and I fell backward against the counter to the floor.

I heard my gun hit the floor as it fell from my hand but I didn't know where. I tried to spin away and get to my knees but Shelton was already back on me. His kick struck the side of my chest and I hit the edge of the counter, knocking the air from my lungs.

The voice in my head was panicked now as he came toward me again. *Move, move, move*, it was screaming. Shelton swung his leg again and I turned away just enough so the kick glanced off my shoulder, knocking me backwards on to my knees.

My eyes focused and I saw the dark shape of my gun lying on the ground several feet away. *Reach for it*, the voice inside my head was saying, *move, now, right now*, but my arms wouldn't react.

Shelton took a step toward me and then another and the voice in my head began pleading with me. *Move now, get up, don't look back, just move, move, move, move.* I started to look back.

No, the voice screamed. *Don't look, just move.*

I heard another step, saw the faint shape of his shadow on the tiles of the floor, moving toward me. My hand closed around a piece of broken glass and I spun around and threw it. Shelton hesitated, turned his head and raised an arm to block it.

Now, said the voice in my head, *do it now.*

My hand slipped and then I lifted my foot and pushed forward, crawling across the floor until my hand found the grip of the weapon. I rolled on to my back and raised it.

'Don't fucking move,' I said.

Shelton stopped and stared at me as if not entirely believing what lay before him. He took half a step.

'The next step will be your last,' I said.

I sat up and clutched the gun with both hands, holding it on the center of his chest. Shelton held out his hands to show they were empty.

'You move, I'll kill you,' I said.

He looked at me and took an exasperated breath.

'Will you really?' said Shelton. The first words that I had exchanged with him since that initial phone call. His English accent wasn't as pronounced as it had been on the phone.

'Yes,' I answered and I slowly got to my feet.

Shelton's face appeared younger than in the computer-generated picture Utley had had made up. It was as if his features were still being formed. His eyes, though, were just as I imagined, black like pools of ink, cold and empty. He wore the long white lab coat of a doctor.

'Get down on your knees,' I ordered.

'And if I don't?' he said.

'I'll put a bullet in you.'

'As you wish, Lieutenant.'

'Keep your hands out to your side,' I said.

Shelton slowly lowered himself on to his knees.

'You're under arrest,' I said.

He chuckled. 'It's a long way from here to the squad car.'

'It will just fly by, I promise you,' I said.

He looked at me for a moment.

'Did you know Myers killed his best friend?' he said. 'Shot him in the back.'

'Yes, I know.'

He shook his head. 'They all would have killed each other eventually, I just accelerated the process.'

'Is that what happened to Terry Pullian and Jim O'Brien?' I said.

'Well,' he said, barely containing a chuckle. 'It's not as if their lives mattered. The rest of them, I showed them a way to destroy each other, and they did it. And all for the money.'

'And now the money will be yours.'

'Is that really why you think we're standing here?'

'No,' I said.

Shelton looked at me for a moment and then the corner of his mouth curved into what appeared to be a smile, but one that held no sense of joy.

'Do you understand the nature of justice, Lieutenant?'

'I understand it.'

'My entire life has been shaped by it. It's what I am; it's all I've ever known. Every breath, every thought, every memory. It's not blind like they say, it sees everything, it just doesn't care.'

'You're insane, Richard.'

The smile disappeared.

'Did you enjoy the little charade I created with the all-seeing eye and the darkness? It was why I picked you.'

'Picked me?'

'A lesser detective might have failed to appreciate what I created. I wish I could take credit for the blackouts. It was nice of the power companies to melt the grid down. Added a nice bit of atmosphere.'

'I'm afraid the ending you planned will be a little different,' I said.

'Will it?'

'Yes.'

'So what do we do now? Wait for your partner – excuse me, your lover – to show up.'

'Something like that,' I said.

'What if he doesn't come, what if he can't come?'

'He'll be here.'

'How do you know? What if I visited him, and he's lying somewhere out there bleeding to death?'

I looked past him down the long corridor.

'I don't believe you,' I said.

'Yes you do, you're already starting to doubt everything.'

A sound came from down the corridor.

'Call him if you like, I'm sure he'd love to hear from you,' he said.

The sound was there again but I couldn't tell if it was from the right or the left corridor. I stepped carefully around Shelton, trying to work out where the sound was coming from, but couldn't.

'Do you know how much blood a body can lose and still live? Quarts of it, it's really amazing.'

'Harrison,' I yelled.

There was no response.

'Dylan,' I shouted again, my voice echoing down the empty hallways.

'Now don't you feel better?' Shelton said.

I turned and pressed the gun to the back of his head.

'Where is he?'

He shook his head and I pressed harder.

'You kill me, I won't be able to tell you where he is. So many rooms to search, so little time.'

'Harrison!' I yelled.

'Would you really let him bleed to death just so you can hold me? Is success that important to you?' He shook his head. 'How will you look at yourself in the mirror?'

'Harrison!' I yelled again, my mind racing, but there was only silence.

I reached into my pocket and slipped out my phone and hit his number. After four rings his message picked up.

'I guess he can't answer,' Shelton said.

'Put your hands behind your back,' I said and began to reach for my cuffs.

The hum of electricity seemed to surge, almost as if the

building was trying to breathe. The lights briefly dimmed and then went out with a soft click – like fingers being snapped.

The darkness was complete. I couldn't see my hand holding the gun.

'If you move, I will hear you and I'll drop you,' I said.

Nothing came out of the darkness. Not a breath, no movement. I took a step forward and stopped, holding the gun on the spot where Shelton had been. A faint breath of air seemed to touch the left side of my face and I spun around, holding the gun and fired into the darkness. The muzzle flash briefly lit the room like a strobe and I saw Shelton's face to my right. I swung the weapon and held on the spot I had seen him and fired.

Again the flash lit the room, but he had slipped into the blackness, which appeared to swirl like a pool of water.

I stepped to the right and swung the gun back and forth searching for a target. Ten seconds passed, then another and then the hum of electricity rose like a murmur and the lights began to flicker again and came on.

Shelton was gone. I walked over to where he had been standing when I fired the shot. If I had hit him there was no evidence of it, no blood, just a small hole where my round had struck the wall. I stood still for a moment, listening for movement, and then I heard the distinct sound of a door latch falling shut down the hallway to my left.

I started moving, checking the doors I passed, faster and faster until I was running and yelling Harrison's name, my heart threatening to jump out of my body. I reached the end and stopped.

A breath. Nearly silent, but it was there. Then another. It was behind me. I spun around. It was a door to a stairway.

'Harrison?'

I walked over to it. There was a smear of blood on the handle.

'Dylan?' I said.

The handle turned ever so slightly. I raised my weapon and then reached out as the handle continued to turn. I heard the bolt slip past the jamb and I pushed it open and raised my weapon.

Dylan tried to get up off his knees but couldn't make it.

'Dylan,' I said and rushed to him, the tears welling up in my eyes. There was so much blood.

I reached out and he leaned into my arms. His back was stained with blood from where the knife had entered.

'How bad are you hurt?'

He looked into my eyes.

'Bad,' he said.

'Can you get up?'

'Not comfortably,' he said, his voice weak and thready.

I slipped my gun into the holster and reached around him and helped him to his feet.

'I think I may pass out,' he said faintly.

'There's an elevator down the hallway,' I said.

He shook his head. 'I tried it, it's turned off to this floor. The stairs would be better. If I pass out, you can slide me down them.'

I eased him over to the railing and we started down.

'Where's Shelton?'

'I don't know.'

His knees buckled and he started falling forward. I caught him and tried to stop his fall but we both tipped over and rolled down the flight of stairs to the next landing.

The breath was knocked out of my lungs and I lay there for a moment, gasping for air.

'That wasn't a very good slide,' Harrison said.

He was lying on his back staring up at the ceiling. I got up on my knees and crawled over to him.

'I'll get you up again,' I said.

He shook his head. 'I don't think so.'

I took a deep breath, trying to get enough air into my lungs to get moving.

'Yes you can,' I said.

'No,' he answered. 'Go get Shelton.'

'Fuck Shelton. Get up.'

He took a weak breath. 'I can't,' he said.

'I'll pull you.'

I crawled around him and put my hands under his arms to drag him over to the next flight.

'This isn't going to work.'

I began pulling him over to the edge of the stairs. Pain shot through the bruised muscles of my chest from Moon's attack and where the biopsy had been taken. He slipped from my grasp and then again.

'You've got to help me,' I said.

He started to shake his head.

'Yes you can!' I yelled at him. 'Push with your feet.'

Dylan weakly raised his right leg.

'Now push when I pull you.'

All he could manage was a nod as he tried to focus his strength.

'Now,' I yelled and strained to move his weight and he began to move across the floor. 'Now again . . . and again.'

We reached the edge of the stairs and I dropped to my knees to catch my breath.

'Are you sure your doctors would approve of this?'

'Shut up,' I said and looked down the stairs. 'This is going to hurt,' I said.

'As opposed to being stabbed,' he said.

I put my arms around him and slowly pulled him over the edge and began sliding him down one step at a time. My side where Shelton had kicked me was going numb. Halfway down the flight, my left hand slipped out from underneath Dylan and he began to slide. I caught him with my other arm and pulled him toward me as we bounced down the rest of the stairs to the landing.

We both lay there for a moment, stunned.

'You were right, that hurt,' said Harrison.

I pulled myself out from under him and leaned over him. His green eyes found mine.

'I'll get a doctor,' I said. 'Get you down to trauma.'

'Hurry,' he said faintly.

I got to my feet and rushed over to the door and opened it. The corridor was busy with activity. To the right was a nursing station. I stepped out into the hallway and ran to it. It was decorated with balloons. A child in a wheelchair was being pushed along by a young mother; in fact, all the patients I saw being moved about were children. I was in a pediatric unit. The nurses working the phones seemed frantic.

'I need a doctor,' I said.

'Admitting is downstairs,' she said without looking up. She then yelled into the phone.

'He's somewhere, find him,' she said.

'I have an injured police officer in the stairwell. He's been stabbed,' I said.

The nurse turned and looked at me for the first time.

'I need a gurney and I need a trauma team and I need it now.'

'Are you injured?' the nurse said.

I realized my shirt was stained with Harrison's blood.

'It's not mine, he's bleeding to death, he needs help now.'

She punched another line on the phone and called for a trauma team and then hung up. I started running back to the stairwell and she followed. I pushed the door open and she rushed in past me. She took one look at Harrison and then yelled back toward the nursing station.

'I need bandages and some help here now!' she yelled.

She rushed over to Harrison and knelt down. His eyes were closed and his breathing had gotten even slower.

'Where was he stabbed?'

'Lower back,' I said. 'Help him please.'

Harrison's eyes opened and locked on mine.

'I'm sorry,' he said weakly.

'You're going to be all right,' I said, taking hold of his hand and gripping it.

A spasm of pain hit him and he flinched. His eyes began to drift as he fought to remain conscious.

'Look at me,' I said.

He tried but failed.

'Dylan, stay with me, look at me now.'

He struggled for a moment and then he found me. Tears began to well up in my eyes and slip down my cheeks.

'Don't cry,' he whispered.

'You're not going to die,' I said. 'You're not going to leave me, do you understand?'

He tried to say something but couldn't manage it and I leaned in closer.

'Get him,' he whispered.

His eyes held mine for a moment and then they slipped away.

'I'm not leaving you,' I said.

His eyes reacted to another spasm of pain and then through gritted teeth he forced a slight smile.

'Yes you are,' he said and then his hand began to lose its grip on mine and my heart began to race.

'Dylan,' I said but he drifted away into unconsciousness.

Another nurse entered the stairs carrying some bandages.

'Do something,' I said.

'Help us roll him over,' said the first nurse.

We rolled Harrison over and she began to pack bandages on to the wound and apply pressure to it. Another nurse arrived and began to assist, followed by another who moved me out of the way.

'We'll take care of him. The best thing you can do is stay out of our way and let us do our job,' she said and I stepped back as more help arrived.

I watched them as they stripped him of his shirt, exposing the dark slit of a wound in his lower back. A nurse covered it with more bandages and applied pressure with both her hands.

'Please,' I whispered silently to myself as a doctor rushed in and I stepped into the hallway. I took one more look at Dylan and then turned and looked down the hallway. It was abuzz with activity, but not for Dylan, something else had taken place. I tried to focus on what was going on around me, but it was all little more than a blur.

'Shelton,' I whispered to myself, trying to step back into the moment.

A nurse came rushing by and I stopped her.

'What's happened?' I asked.

'A patient's missing, someone saw him with a doctor but we can't find him.'

'A doctor?' I asked and she nodded.

'How long ago?'

'Just a few minutes. He was being taken to prep for surgery.'

'The patient's a child?' I asked.

'Yes, a little boy, two years old, dark short hair. He was in that chair by the elevator.'

I looked over at the empty wheelchair by the elevator

and my heart began to pound against my chest and adrenalin surged through me once again.

'That wasn't a doctor,' I said as a trauma team rushed out of the elevator and past me into the stairwell.

They began to take Harrison's vitals and prepare his arm for an IV. I stared at Dylan for a moment and looked over to the empty wheelchair.

One of the nurses on the stairway came over to me.

'We'll need some information on him before we take him to surgery,' she said. 'Is he allergic to any drugs?' she asked. 'Does he have medical conditions, heart, respiratory, that we need to be aware of?'

I shook my head. 'No.'

'Is there anything else you can think of?' she asked.

I nodded. 'I love him,' I said softly.

The nurse hesitated and then started to turn away and I glanced back at the empty wheelchair.

'What's the fastest way out of the building?' I asked.

The nurse looked at me but didn't understand the question.

'What floor do I get off at?'

'The lobby,' the nurse said.

I rushed over into the elevator and pressed the button for the lobby. As the door closed, the paramedics and nurses lifted Dylan's limp body on to the stretcher, and then I started down. The elevator seemed to move in slow motion, the passing floors marked with electronic tones.

As the elevator passed the second floor, I reached down and pulled my weapon. The elevator slowed and then settled with a jarring stop and the doors opened. I stepped out into the lobby. It was crowded with people; some had blood on their shirts or pants. I imagined they were witnesses and family members from the shooting that had filled the emergency room with victims.

I started walking through the crowd, looking for the white coat of a doctor. The lobby was full of them, some coming and going through the doors, others attending to the minor cuts and bruises some of the partygoers had suffered trying to flee the gunfire.

I rushed over to the exit door and looked outside into the darkness. If I had missed him, there would be no finding Shelton. He would slip away and it would be over. I turned back and scanned the lobby. A woman started screaming and I began working my way toward the sound as the crowd parted around her. A heavyset woman in her forties was on her knees, shaking her head. Two people were on either side of her, trying to hold her up. A uniformed security guard was kneeling in front of her.

I turned and scanned the lobby, looking left and right, and then I saw a door open and a flash of white coming out of it. I stepped around a group of people and lost sight of it, and then started rushing across the room in a straight line toward the exit.

The figure in the white coat stopped. I stepped up behind him and started to raise my weapon when he turned. His Asian eyes moved past me and he raised his hand and waved to someone behind me. I lowered the weapon and stepped past him, moving again toward the door, when I stopped. A child was crying. I spun around looking for the source of the sound. I took a few steps back toward the center of the lobby and I saw the child across the room, moving through the crowd, weaving in and out, heading toward the front doors in the arms of a doctor.

I pushed past several people and then another, trying to keep visual contact with him. He was thirty feet from the door and then twenty. I couldn't tell if it was Shelton. I caught glimpses as he moved in and out of people, the child held tightly to his chest, his face obscured by the child's head.

'Get out of my way,' I said to a large group of people. They quickly parted and let me pass.

Fifteen feet.

I cut to the left and began to move parallel to the doctor's steps as he closed in on the door.

Ten feet.

The doctor moved his hand across the child's back. A small stain of blood was visible on the cuff of his jacket from where I must have grazed him with my shot. Something shiny was cupped in the hand that supported the boy's back.

Five feet.

Two teenagers stepped in front of me, bouncing a miniature soccer ball, and I pushed one of them aside and yelled.

'Shelton.'

There was no reaction, he continued straight for the door. I raised my weapon and shouted again.

'Don't move, Shelton.'

Several people saw the weapon in my hand and backed away. Another woman began to scream and more people hurried away. Shelton slowly turned his head and looked at me and then tightened his grip on the boy.

'You're not leaving,' I said. 'Put the child down.'

The lobby fell silent and Shelton looked at the doors a few feet away, smiled and turned back to me.

'I need security here, right now,' he yelled.

A guard was already moving toward us, his weapon drawn.

'The woman has a gun,' yelled Shelton. 'Everyone step away, you won't be hurt.'

The guard stopped a few feet away and raised his weapon toward me.

'Put the gun down!' he yelled.

'I'm a police officer,' I said.

'I'm a doctor,' said Shelton. 'She's not a policeman. She's trying to kidnap this child, she already injured it.'

'He's not a doctor,' I said.

'Put the weapon down!' the guard yelled at me.

'She's an imposter,' Shelton said, taking another step toward the exit. 'Look at her, look at the blood, she's not a policeman.'

'He's armed with a knife, he killed one man upstairs and wounded an officer.'

'For God's sake, do not let her touch this child,' Shelton said. 'She's insane, she believes the child is hers.'

'Put your weapon down,' the guard yelled.

'I have to get this child out of here, do you understand?

She intends to harm him, she's already wounded a policeman upstairs,' Shelton said.

'You're not leaving, Shelton,' I said.

'Drop the weapon,' the guard yelled.

'You are not going to hurt this child,' Shelton said.

'Put the boy down,' I said.

'Shoot her,' he said and stepped toward the door.

I started to move and the officer yelled.

'Don't move another step.'

'Shoot her,' Shelton yelled.

'Put the gun down now or I will shoot you,' the guard yelled. 'Do it now! You will not get another warning.'

'He cannot go out that door,' I said.

'Drop the gun and get down,' the guard repeated. 'I will not give you another warning.'

I held my weapon on Shelton for a moment and then lowered it.

'On the floor,' the guard yelled. 'Drop your weapon and get on the floor.'

Shelton looked at me and began to smile as I got down on to the floor and set the gun aside.

'Thank you, officer,' Shelton said.

The guard walked over to me.

'Keep your hands out to your side and your mouth shut,' he said and picked up my gun. Shelton took a step toward the door.

'Look at my badge,' I said.

'I said, keep your mouth shut.'

'You're making a mistake, look at the badge, do it now,' I yelled.

The guard hesitated.

'She's very dangerous, officer,' Shelton said. 'Do not listen to her.'

The guard cautiously reached down and removed my badge from my waistband.

'Pasadena. We had a report of someone posing as a Pasadena cop.'

'Named Harrison,' I said. 'Look at my name.'

'I didn't hear about any name,' the guard said.

'Don't listen to her. She's not really with the police,' Shelton said. 'Use your head, man.'

The officer looked at the badge as Shelton again started moving toward the door.

'Don't let him walk out,' I said.

The officer turned to Shelton.

'Wait,' he said and began moving toward him.

Shelton stopped and turned.

'I'll need to see some ID,' the officer said.

'His parents are waiting, and they're very frightened.'

'This won't take a second to sort out,' the guard said.

'Don't,' I said.

'Certainly, officer,' said Shelton. 'Would you hold the baby?'

He held the child out to the officer, who reached out to take the boy.

'No,' I yelled, getting to my knees.

As the officer's hands closed around the child, I saw the quick thrust of Shelton's arm strike the officer's side. The officer stiffened and then crumbled like a doll to the floor, with the boy on top of him. His blood began to spread out across the white of his shirt. People began screaming and Shelton turned and started moving again toward the exit. I rushed over to the guard whose panicked eyes looked at me. I slipped my gun out from his belt where he had tucked it and swung on Shelton as he reached the automatic doors, which opened.

'Shelton!' I yelled.

He looked back over his shoulder and I got a glimpse of the corner of his mouth as he smiled and began to step out into the darkness.

'Freeze,' I yelled again but he kept moving. The doors began to close behind him.

My hand tightened around the handle of the gun and I fired. The round hit the safety glass, fracturing it into thousands of pieces. I held on the same spot for a moment but the shattered glass obscured the view outside.

The concussion of the shot reverberated through the lobby with a deafening crack. A few bystanders had their hands over their ears. Others just stood or crouched for cover, their eyes staring at the gun in my hand. I turned and looked back at the child resting on the chest of the motionless guard. I slipped my gun into the holster and rushed over and picked the boy up. The guard looked at me; his mouth moved, silently trying to form words.

'He's all right,' I said. 'You saved him.'

The blood from his wound was now beginning to spread out on the floor beneath him.

'Get a doctor over here,' I yelled.

A nurse ran over and I handed the child to her.

'They're looking for this boy upstairs in surgery,' I said.

She nodded and I slipped my gun out of the holster and ran to the shattered door. I could see nothing through the broken glass except for the bit of darkness that was visible through the bullet hole. I raised the gun and stepped into the motion sensor and the door opened.

Shelton wasn't on the pavement outside the door. I held still for a moment, expecting a response from him, then cautiously moved outside, swinging the gun back and forth across the darkness. Nothing. He was nowhere to be seen. I took a few more steps and stopped. There was blood on the pavement.

I slipped my light out of my pocket and turned it on. The beam flickered for a moment and then stayed on. I began to follow the blood trail. It was only a few drops at first, moving toward the darkness, but with each step I took, the amount of blood increased.

I reached the bottom of the steps and followed the trail to the sidewalk where it abruptly stopped. I swung round, looking for more signs, but none were visible. Nothing was moving in the dark, there wasn't a sound. I took a step and then another and was about to run when I stopped and raised the light. There was blood on a car where he had tried to open the door. I shined the light inside – it was empty. On the next parked car, blood stained the handle in the same way.

In the distance I could hear the sound of sirens. I glanced back toward the entrance to the hospital, but no help was coming from there. I moved to the next car and then the next and the next. All were stained with his blood.

I started toward the next car and stopped as I raised my light. The dark shape of a figure was visible sitting in the driver's seat, the head leaning against the glass of the window.

My heart began to pound and I raised my weapon. Slowly I moved around the car to the driver's side and stopped by the back door.

'Open the door and step out!' I yelled.

The figure didn't move.

'Get out of the car now!' I yelled again.

The head of the figure slowly began to turn.

'Open the door and step out with your hands to your side where I can see them. Do it now.'

The door opened a few inches and stopped.

'Get out now,' I said. 'I won't tell you again.'

The door opened the rest of the way and he stepped out. I raised my light into the face of a middle-aged man with graying hair.

'My wife's a patient,' he said, his voice trembling with fear. 'I was just getting some rest. Did I do something?'

I lowered my gun.

'No,' I said. 'My mistake.'

He took a relieved breath as his eyes focused on something behind me and I saw the reflection of movement in the glass of the window. I spun around, raising my weapon. The blade moving through the darkness reflected the beam of the flashlight as I fired.

I saw Shelton's face contort in pain. The knife landed on the pavement in front of my feet as Shelton collapsed to his knees. I kicked the knife away and held my weapon on

Shelton, waiting for him to make another move. His arms hung motionless at his sides. He took a shallow breath and then another. I turned to the man holding on to the door of his car.

'Go tell them we need an ambulance here.'

He hesitated.

'Go on,' I said.

He took a step and then rushed off toward the entrance of the hospital. I moved forward, keeping my gun pointed at Shelton's head. His right arm was soaked in blood from the first shot at the hospital entrance. More blood began to stain his shirt just under the right collarbone where I had wounded him.

I watched his chest rise and fall with a breath, and then another.

'It's over, Richard,' I said.

Down the street a squad car came speeding around the corner, its lights flashing and siren wailing.

Shelton raised his head, looked at me.

'Over?' he said weakly. 'Is it, Lieutenant? If you want it to be over, pull the trigger again. You don't have much time, you know you want to.'

I stepped toward him, my hand tightening around the handle of the gun.

'What will you dream about tonight, Lieutenant? Shall I tell you about how I slid the knife into your lover?'

I stepped forward and leveled the barrel of the gun at his face.

'Dreams,' I said, inching the gun closer to him. 'What would you know about dreams?'

The corners of his mouth turned into a smile and he began to laugh – a wild mad hatter kind of laugh that began to mingle with the singsong of the approaching siren.

I held my weapon on him for a moment longer, then my hand began to shake and I lowered it to my side and stepped back. I looked down at his face, trying to picture the boy he once was and find a clue to the violence that had ruled his life, but if it was there, it eluded me. Did Richard Shelton ever truly exist? Was there ever an innocent little boy inside the man in front of me?

More sirens began to fill the night as other LAPD units responded. The first squad pulled up and an officer stepped out with his gun drawn and pointing at Shelton.

'Are you all right?' he asked, staring in wonder at the figure laughing before him.

'Yes, I'm fine,' I said, turning and looking back at the lights of the hospital. 'I need to get back inside, he wounded my . . . partner.'

Another squad arrived and two more officers jumped out and hesitated as the sound of Shelton's mad laughter pulled them into his world. As they cuffed him, his eyes found mine for a moment, and then I turned away and rushed back toward the hospital and Dylan.

As I approached the doors, a sound I hadn't noticed in days caught my attention. I stopped and looked back as an ambulance pulled up to where Shelton lay on the street. There was no laughter, or if it was there it had blended into the other sounds that fill a city. Traffic, a radio, birdsong, the squeal of brakes, the drone of a fan blowing air through a hot apartment, a lovers' argument, a newborn baby crying, a mother and father weeping in joy, the soft murmur of prayers. It was all there if you listened close enough.

'Yes, it's over,' I said softly.

For the first time since the heat wave had begun, I could smell the crisp scent of the ocean in the air. In the distance a grid of lights came back online, and then another and another as the power began to return. With each returning light, the stars overhead began to fade, and then slip away into the dull grey night as darkness lost its grip on the City of Angels.

epilogue

Harrison was in surgery for two hours as the surgeons repaired the damage the knife had inflicted as it tore into his back. Twice on the operating table he lost all vital signs as his heart stopped beating and each time the doctors coaxed him back to this world. What I felt in those moments I have no words to describe, except to say that whatever I may have believed I understood about loss in no way prepared me for the silence of those missing heartbeats.

In an operating room only a few feet away, another team of doctors repaired the damage my gunshots had inflicted on Shelton. With no real understanding of what resided in the dark recesses of Shelton's mind, a doctor reported when he stepped out of surgery that the patient would live a normal life.

For the rest of that night I sat in recovery, watching the steady rise and fall of Harrison's breaths, each one a step back toward the light of the coming dawn. If it had taken the act of a madman to show me that I was in love or, more accurately, ready to love, then I would bear that burden and keep it hidden in a place that Harrison would never discover.

In the days that followed I observed as a steady stream of detectives from LAPD and the FBI interviewed Shelton in his secure hospital room, searching and probing for a crack that would allow them to see inside his twisted mind.

They found no such fissure. He lay in his bed, not moving or responding to their questions; only his eyes flickered as they took the measure of each of his interrogators as if he was cataloging information for another dark night yet to come.

Some of the money that had ravaged so many lives was recovered, though some remains hidden in unknown accounts, awaiting the touch of a keypad and a six-letter password spun from Shelton's nightmare. On several occasions he asked to see me, but each time I declined. He had nearly taken the life of the man I loved, and I had no intention of giving him the opportunity to ever snatch so much as a second from my life again.

The only piece of the mystery that remains unanswered for me is the one Shelton probably has no answer for anyway. What makes a nine-year-old boy become a killer? What happened on that cold spring morning when he put his arm around his friend and stepped out of the light and into the darkness?

Of all the questions surrounding the damage inflicted by Shelton, that would be the one that I would never let go of. Not because I don't believe that an answer couldn't be found if one looked deep enough, but rather because of what one might discover about ourselves hidden inside that answer.

If we are to believe that a child like Shelton is an aberration that will never repeat itself, then lock your doors against the night and don't venture out because another Shelton will step out of the shadows if we look away from our children long enough. In fact he's probably there already, walking to school, playing ball, looking out from a bus window as it drives past on its way to the next stop.

On a bright clear morning that seemed an attempt by nature to make up for the days of heat, I waited outside the hospital for Cathy O'Brien to take her first steps back into the world, if not entirely back into the light. Why she had asked me to drive her back to the house where her husband was murdered I wasn't certain. Perhaps it was because what we shared, no one else in this world would understand, or perhaps she was just trying to shield the terrible truth of what had happened from the people left in her life that she loved. She said nothing on the drive, and when we arrived, instead of entering the house, we sat in silence for nearly an hour and then she thanked me and got in her own car and drove away in search of sanctuary in some far-off place, where the nights are cool and never quite as dark, never to return.

As I watched her leave, my phone rang and I looked down at the number. It was the doctor's office with the results of my biopsy. On a quiet street where a nightmare had come to life, under a sky as perfect as I had ever seen, I let it ring half a dozen times, and when I couldn't not answer any longer, I looked back at the house that held a darkness so deep no light would ever again fully illuminate its walls or the people unfortunate enough to have stepped inside, and then I too turned away, opened the phone and took my first step toward the future.

Acknowledgements

I would like to thank Vicki Mellor for her keen insights and sound judgement. They have made this a better book.

Don't Look Back

Scott Frost

Staring at a frozen body isn't how Lieutenant Alex Delillo planned to start her day.

Alex's only clue to the girl's death: her pose echoes a Goya sketch that's left at the scene. But why was she chosen to die?

Then another tortured body is found. Alex is certain that the two victims are connected, but how, and could the answer lie in the past?

It's dangerous to look back, but when a killer is seeking revenge you have no choice. Alex is about to learn the devastating truth that for some the past is always there waiting . . .

Acclaim for Scott Frost:

'Take a deep breath. Things move so fast you won't have a chance to catch it later' Linwood Barclay

'Exhilarating' *Guardian*

'Not to be missed' *West Australian*

978 0 7553 7001 6

headline

Point of No Return

Scott Frost

ONE DECISION AND YOUR WORLD CHANGES, SPIRALS OUT OF CONTROL. YOU ARE ALONE. YOU CAN TRUST NO ONE.

Lieutenant Alex Delillo's decision to help a wife find her husband will change her life for ever. When Jack Salem, an ex-LAPD cop, fails to return home from a placement with a private security firm training policemen in war-ravaged Iraq, his wife believes he's in hiding. Afraid for his life, she turns to Alex for help.

Why did Salem go to Iraq – for financial gain? Was he working undercover? As Alex searches for Salem, a conspiracy with terrifying implications unfolds. Alex will be forced to challenge her belief in herself, her job and her government. She will be pushed to the edge.

Scott Frost's stunning new novel will make you question everything you thought you knew. Are you ready?

Acclaim for Scott Frost:

'NEVER FEAR is as tough a crime novel as I have ever read, with a plot that twists and turns like a snake on crack' *Independent on Sunday*

'Scott Frost's blend of action and psychological intrigue is here to stay' *Daily Mirror*

978 0 7553 3395 0

headline

Run the Risk

Scott Frost

A MURDER; A BOMB EXPLOSION; A PARTNER LYING IN INTENSIVE CARE

When Lieutenant Alex Delillo's partner almost dies in a bomb explosion, Alex is catapulted into the middle of an incendiary and deadly game being played with ever-increasing stakes.

The annual, televised Rose Bowl parade is two days away and all indications suggest the bomber is intent on making the parade his final target. As the clock ticks down, Alex is closing in on her prey when the unthinkable happens and the bomber takes the most important person in Alex's life hostage as collateral.

Almost paralysed by fear, Alex will have to use all her skill if she is to find the bomber, before he forces her to make a choice that will change her life forever . . .

Acclaim for Scott Frost's NEVER FEAR

'*Never Fear* is as tough a crime novel as I have ever read, with a plot that twists and turns like a snake on crack. A classic crime novel' *Independent on Sunday*

'Frost's combination of psychological depth, complex plotting and an evocative Los Angeles setting will have fans of intelligent suspense counting the days until his next book' *Publishers Weekly*

'A fast read . . . Frost has definitely set himself up to become the next big thing in action thrillers' *Shotsmag*

978 0 7553 3392 9

headline